KIM BOCK

THE LAST MAGE

BOOK I

The Chronicles of Erenor

The Series: The Chronicles of Erenor

AN OVERVIEW

In *The Chronicles of Erenor*, readers are pulled into a capti-vating world of magic, adventure, and destiny. From the first introduction of Lysandra in *The Last Mage* to the cosmic rift that distorts reality in *Erenor's Dawn* and the climactic battle against the evil sorcerer Malachor in *Erenor's Destiny*, this epic fantasy series weaves a compelling tale of intricate characters, rich world-building, and thrilling action.

Every page is filled with tension and wonder, inviting readers to embark on a journey where ancient prophecies, untamed magic, and the power of courage and friendship hold the keys to survival and victory. *The Chronicles of Erenor* is a must-read series that guarantees an unforgettable adventure, seamlessly blending romance, profound themes, and the eternal struggle between light and darkness.

Contents

ELARION AND WHAT CAME BEFORE

Lysandra wielded her blade in the ancient forest, each strike revealing the whispered secrets of the woods. Her face glistened with sweat, and her eyes shone with determination. The runes etched on her sword glowed faintly, a testament to the magic pulsing beneath her skin.

She reminded herself to prioritize precision over power, transitioning smoothly from a thrust to a parry. Beside her, Shadow, her fierce companion, mirrored her movements with a playful growl, its shadow dancing amidst the dappled light.

Lysandra was startled when she heard a voice from the edge of the clearing. She spun around, her sword raised defensively. Master Elarion stepped into view, his presence commanding yet calm. His gaze held hers, not just observing but seeming to see beyond her facade.

"Master Elarion," she acknowledged with a nod, lowering her weapon but maintaining her guard. "To what do I owe this intrusion?"

"An intrusion implies unwanted company," he replied, his eyes fixed on hers. "But perhaps it is destiny that has led me here."

Lysandra let out a short, humorless laugh. "Destiny? I have little use for such notions."

"Even if it is your own?" Elarion advanced a step closer, the air thrumming with unspoken energy. "Lysandra, there is more to you than skill with a blade or fledgling sorcery."

"Is that so?" she challenged, though her pulse quickened. Despite her bravado, curiosity sparked within her, mingling with an innate sense of importance that had always simmered just out of reach.

"Indeed." Elarion's tone softened, and he spoke solemnly. You are the direct descendant of the First Mage—the last hope for restoring magic to Erenor."

Her grip tightened around the hilt of her sword, and somewhere deep inside, a door creaked open, letting in the truth she had long denied. She remained silent, wrestling with the implications.

"Your lineage is no mere chance," he continued, undeterred by her silence. "It is a calling. The blood of the First Mage flows through you, granting you a connection to the arcane that none can rival."

"Connection?" Lysandra echoed her voice, a mixture of awe and skepticism. "Or a burden?"

"Both," he admitted, "and neither. It is a path only you can choose to walk."

"Choose?" Her laugh was sharper this time. "It seems like my birthright is the only thing determining my choices."

Elarion looked at Lysandra and spoke with conviction: "Birthright guides us, Lysandra, but it does not bind us. True power lies in your actions and will."

Lysandra stroked the wolf at her side and asked Elarion, "What would restoring magic to Erenor mean?"

Elarion's expression turned grave as he responded, "It could mean revival or ruin. Magic is the lifeblood of Erenor, and without it, darkness encroaches. You've seen the signs yourself."

Lysandra had indeed noticed the ominous signs of a world on the brink of destruction. The forests were rotting from within, shadows lingered too long after dusk, and whispers of despair echoed in the daylight.

Lysandra asked Elarion, "Are you saying that restoring magic to Erenor would come with its own set of dangers?"

Elarion nodded. "Some forces would prefer to see Erenor remain trapped in its current state or worse."

Lysandra's anxiety grew as she asked, "Am I meant to face these dangers because of who I am?"

Elarion corrected her gently, "Because of who you can become. You have immense potential, child of the First Mage."

The idea of having such power overwhelmed Lysandra. However, fear clung to it like a shroud. She wondered if she could genuinely be the one to usher in a new era for Erenor or become another casualty in a war she had never asked to fight.

Elarion advised patience, "Destiny may call, but it is patience that often leads us to answer."

Lysandra repeated the word as she contemplated the forest that was her sanctuary—a solitude that may very well be ending.

Lysandra took a deep breath and asked Elarion, "What can I

do?"

Elarion replied, "Continue to learn and grow. When the time comes, you will know what to do."

Lysandra felt a glimmer of hope. "And what if I fail?"

Elarion smiled warmly at Lysandra, encouraging her: "Don't worry about failing. It's a natural part of the journey. Just keep moving forward, and you'll find the way to succeed."

Lysandra looked at him incredulously and asked, "Descendant of the First Mage? You talk as if legends walk among us. If I had such power, wouldn't I know about it?"

Elarion explained, "Knowing oneself is not always easy. Sometimes, it's like finding a gem buried deep within the earth; it takes time and effort. But I believe you have the potential to discover your true power."

Lysandra was skeptical and asked, "How do you know all this? You're just a traveler passing through these parts."

Elarion smiled and replied, "I'm more than just a traveler. I'm a keeper of history—our history. And I believe I can help you understand your heritage."

Lysandra was intrigued and asked, "Tell me more about my heritage. What do you mean by the First Mage?"

Elarion began to tell her the story of Erenor, a land of magic and wonder ruled by the First Mage. He explained how the people of Erenor abused their power over time and how greed led to the rise of a tyrannical king named Draven, who used magic to subjugate his people.

Lysandra was horrified by the tale and asked, "Was magic used to oppress people? How is that possible?"

Elarion explained, "Those who resisted Draven's rule had their magic sealed away, or worse, turned against them. The land became sick, and nature itself rebelled against the people. The forests grew darker, and the winds carried the cries of the helpless."

Lysandra listened intently to the story, and Elarion gestured towards the gloomy forest. "Look around you, Lysandra. The trees whisper of suffering, and the winds carry the cries of the helpless. But your heritage and power could free them from this tyranny."

Lysandra hesitantly replied, "I don't know how to control my power or even if I have any. How can I face a king and restore broken things when I can't master the simplest spells?"

Elarion reassured her, "Control can be learned, Lysandra. Your swordsmanship is proof of your discipline. Magic is just another tool for you to master. I believe you can do it, and I'll help you every step of the way."

She paused, considering the weight of his words. Her hands, calloused from years of training, suddenly felt alien, clutching the familiar hilt. Could they wield magic as deftly as steel?

"Even if I believed you," she said slowly, her eyes clouded with uncertainty, "how would I confront such corruption? How does one fight a shadow that strangles an entire kingdom?"

"I'm not sure I'm the right person for this," Lysandra said, her voice shaking.

Elarion cryptically stated, "Light casts shadows." "And you, Lysandra, might just be the dawn Erenor awaits."

Lysandra didn't understand what he meant. She had always just tried to survive. Was she meant to be a savior?

"Is it destiny or folly that you're talking about?" Lysandra asked, feeling a mix of defiance and awe. "Because the line between them is thin."

"You must discover that for yourself," Elarion said, "and we don't have much time."

Lysandra's heart raced as she looked at the castle in the distance. She had seen enough blood spill already.

"Accepting this destiny could mean my end," she said, barely above a whisper. "And what about the people I care about?"

"You must have the courage to face your fears," Elarion said.

"Courage?" Lysandra whirled around to face him. "Or is it recklessness? To invite death upon myself and those who are important to me."

"We all face death," Elarion said solemnly. But how we face it and what we leave behind matters."

"Is it worth the sacrifice?" Lysandra tightened her grip on her sword's hilt.

"You come from a powerful lineage," Elarion said.

"Lineage doesn't matter," Lysandra said, her wolf growling beside her.

"You are the heir of magic itself," Elarion said. "You can harness and wield the elements like you do your blade."

"Is that even possible?" Lysandra asked, doubt creeping into her voice.

"I've seen sparks of your magic," Elarion said. "With guidance, you could turn the tide against the darkness that engulfs Erenor."

Lysandra wondered if she could do it. The fate of kingdoms rested on her decision.

"Believe," he urged, reaching out to place a hand over hers on the sword's hilt. The runes flared to life under his touch, casting an ethereal glow.

"Belief won't shield me from shadow hounds or a tyrant's wrath." She pulled away, but the light did not fade.

"Perhaps not," Elarion conceded. "But belief will ignite the spark within you, and once kindled, no shadow can withstand its blaze."

"Easy for you to say," Lysandra muttered, but her gaze lingered on the glowing runes, a silent confession of her intrigue.

"Nothing worthy is ever easy," he said. "But you, Lysandra, were born for this. To be Erenor's beacon in the encroaching night."

"Born to fight or die?" she asked, lacing her tone.

"Born to change the world," Elarion countered with unwavering conviction.

Lysandra gazed into the darkening woods, the wolf pressing close to her leg and offering silent support. Should she change the world or let it perish? The sword in her hand suddenly felt heavy, not just with metal but with fate.

"Normal," she whispered between breaths. "I just wanted normal."

"Normal is a prelude to complacency," Master Elarion said, emerging from the shadows of ancient oaks. His robes whispered secrets against the fallen leaves, the air thrumming with unspoken power around him.

She halted mid-swing, her chest heaving. The wolf at her side tensed, its ears flicking back, before recognizing the old mage. "And what is my life now? A prelude to war?"

"Your life is a melody yet to find its chorus," he replied, stepping closer. "You hold the harmony Erenor needs in your very blood."

Lysandra dropped the sword's tip to the ground, the runes dimming like stars at dawn. "Show me, then. Show me this power I'm supposed to command."

Elarion extended his hand, his palm upturned. "Close your eyes. Feel the pulse of the world, the ebb and flow of magic that courses unseen."

Reluctantly, she obeyed, her eyelids falling shut as she sought the rhythm he spoke of—the invisible dance of energy. Her brows furrowed with concentration, a silent struggle against the skepticism that clawed at her resolve.

"Focus," he urged. "Not with your mind, but with your essence."

A whisper of wind caressed her skin, sparking something deep within. It was faint, a flicker of warmth against the chill of doubt.

"Can you feel it, Lysandra?" Elarion's voice wrapped around her like a mantle. "I... There's a tingling," she admitted, her surprise coloring the words.

"Good. Now, harness it. Imagine the light of your soul reaching out to touch the magic."

As if compelled by forces beyond her comprehension, Lysandra pictured a silvery flame igniting within her core, reaching out tendrils towards the elusive magic. The tingling grew, intensifying until it filled her veins with liquid stars.

"Open your eyes."

She did, and she gasped. Around her, the forest seemed to lean in, the trees bending towards the light she had conjured.

"See what you are capable of?" Elarion's tone held a reverence that bordered on awe.

"Is this... me?" Lysandra's question was barely above a whisper, fear and wonder warring within her gaze.

"Only a glimpse," he confirmed, pride swelling in his chest. "There is so much more waiting for you."

"More..." She repeated the word, tasting its possibilities and its dangers. The blade in her hand no longer felt foreign; it was part of her, an extension of the burgeoning power she could no longer deny.

"Embrace it, Lysandra. Embrace your heritage, your fate."

The wolf nuzzled her hand, its golden eyes glowing fiercely. Even the beast sensed the change within her—the Birthright that pulsed, eager to be unleashed. She looked down at her companion, seeking courage in its unwavering loyalty.

"Embrace it," she echoed, not as confirmation but as a whisper to herself. Could she dare to step into the unknown, to become the beacon Elarion believed her to be?

"Embrace it," the forest seemed to echo, a chorus of whispers urging her onward.

"Embrace it," the runes sang, their light a testament to the legacy coursing through her veins.

"Embrace it," the world demanded—a symphony of magic that might await the conductor of its revival.

Lysandra looked around her. The forest around her held its breath, the ancient trees standing sentinel to her burgeoning power. She turned to Elarion, the question spilling from her lips like a cup too full.

"Master Elarion," she began, her voice a blade cutting through silence, "why now? Why have these powers chosen this moment to awaken within me?"

Elarion's gaze was solemn as he spoke to Lysandra. "Your abilities are surging forth now for a reason, Lysandra. Erenor is suffering from the celestial fracture."

Lysandra looked at him with confusion. "What's the celestial fracture?" she asked.

Elarion explained, "It's a cosmic tear from the last great Mage War." "It's draining magic from our world."

Lysandra's eyes widened in understanding. "Draining... but then what?" she asked.

Elarion nodded gravely. "Without magic, King Draven's rule will become absolute. Your awakening is timed with the prophecy. You are the only one who can save Erenor from falling into darkness."

Lysandra's heart raced with fear. "What prophecy?" she asked.

Elarion explained, "You are descended from the First Mage. Your bloodline has been dormant for centuries, waiting for this moment. You are the only one who can stop King Draven's tyranny from becoming absolute."

Lysandra felt the weight of her responsibility. "What if I can't do it?" she asked.

Elarion's eyes were grave. "If you fail, Erenor will fall into darkness. You are the fulcrum upon which Erenor's fate teeters."

Lysandra's mind raced with doubt and fear. Could she be the savior that Erenor needed?

"Fail," Elarion continued, his voice dropping to a calm tone and clawing at her resolve's edges. Eternal darkness reigns. Our mission—your mission—is paramount."

"Darkness eternal..." The possibility loomed—a specter over

her future, over all of Erenor. Her hands were clenched, her knuckles white, as if holding on to the last vestiges of light.

"Indeed," Elarion confirmed, the set of his jaw resolute. "The time for doubts has passed, Lysandra. Destiny waits for no one, and least of all for us."

The wind whispered through the leaves, a susurrus of unseen forces. Lysandra's gaze fell upon her sword, the runes aglow with a promise of might and magic, a silent call to arms for the battle ahead.

Silver strands of Lysandra's hair danced in the cool, dusk air as she stood amidst the ruins of an ancient watchtower. The weight of her lineage bore down upon her like the very stone blocks that lay strewn about—relics of a bygone era. She felt the suffering of her people twined around her heart, a noose tightening with every shallow breath.

"Master Elarion," she said, her voice barely above a whisper, "how can I turn away from this?" Her eyes, fierce as the ocean during a storm, met his.

The old mage, cloaked in wisdom and sorrow, stepped forward. "You can't," he replied firmly. "And you mustn't."

Lysandra gripped the hilt of her sword tightly. She knew what lay ahead, and the thought made her uneasy.

"Embracing this means forsaking everything else," she said to Elarion.

He nodded gravely. "Yes, it does. But what you gain will be

worth the sacrifice. You will help restore magic to the world."

Lysandra hesitated. She knew she was meant for something more significant than the mundane tasks that filled her days. But the idea of giving up everything she had ever known was daunting. Her wolf companion lay nearby, watching keenly as Lysandra struggled to decide.

"Guide me," she said, turning to Elarion. "I cannot face this darkness alone."

Elarion smiled. "Never alone, child of Erenor. Together, we shall turn the tide. And you will have some very unusual but trustworthy companions."

Lysandra swallowed hard. She knew she had to do this. "Teach me," she said, her grip on the sword firming. "Show me the extent of my powers."

"Patience, Lysandra," Elarion cautioned. "You must not rush into the weave of magic—it is delicate and intricate."

"Time is a luxury we don't have!" she shot back, her words slicing through the twilight silence.

Elarion nodded. "True. But recklessness invites disaster. We will hone your martial and arcane skills until you are ready to confront Draven."

Lysandra's thoughts whirled. She knew she couldn't let fear dictate her path. "Ready or not," she said. "I must face him."

Elarion's eyes gleamed with pride. "Good. Fear is but a shadow. And shadows yield to light."

"Then let us bring forth that light," Lysandra declared, her determination echoing through the grove.

"Indeed. We start at dawn," Elarion said, turning to leave her to her contemplations. "Prepare yourself, Lysandra. Tomorrow, you begin anew."

As the last light of day yielded to the encroaching night, Lysandra felt the stirrings of her latent powers, like an ember waiting to be fanned into flame. With Master Elarion's guidance, she would rise to meet her destiny head-on.

The night she had fallen over the secluded grove, a velvet tapestry pierced by the cold light of countless stars. Lysandra stood amidst the ancient oaks like a pale ghost in the moonlight.

She knew what lay ahead would be challenging but was determined to face it head-on. She had always known she was meant for something more significant, and with Elarion's help, she could finally fulfill her destiny.

"Isn't fear rational here?" Her hand trembled upon the hilt of her sword, betraying her inner conflict. "Every step toward this fate feels like a march into oblivion, where sacrifice seems the only end."

"Even the First Mage faced such fears," Elarion replied, stepping closer, the lines of age and wisdom etched deeper into his face by the moon's glow. "Yet she too found the courage to wield her power for Erenor."

Lysandra shook her head, the motion sharp, a cut through the ties that bound her to prophecy. "But at what cost, Master? The life I knew was already slipping through my fingers like grains of sand. And for what? A chance to battle a tyranny that has crushed far greater than me?"

"Your heart is strong, Lysandra. Stronger than you know," he insisted, his tone earnest, almost pleading.

"Strength does not quench the fire of loss," she countered, her words slicing through his hope. "Nor does it shield those I love from the dark tide of war."

The wolf nudged her hand, a silent ally amidst her struggle. Its presence reminded her of the shadowhounds they had both escaped. Its loyalty was unwavering, but even that bond could not anchor her to a destiny she feared would sever all others.

"Then you choose to turn away?" Master Elarion asked. His question was devoid of judgment, yet it hung heavy in the charged air.

"Choosing implies desire, and there is none in this refusal," she said, meeting his gaze with a turbulent storm in her own. "Yes, duty binds me, but love also does. I will not willingly cast aside the latter for the former."

"You know, Master Elarion, love is supposed to be a guiding light in times of darkness," Lysandra said, her voice tinged with frustration. "But what if the darkness calls you to forsake everything else?"

"I understand your concern, Lysandra," replied Elarion, his expression calm and understanding. "But you must remember that your journey is your own. You have to make your own choices in your own time."

Lysandra felt a sense of acceptance settles within her. "I know, Master Elarion. I'm just scared of what the future holds."

"I know. It's not easy to face the unknown," Elarion said, his voice gentle. "But you have to reach for your destiny. You can't let it drag you down."

Lysandra nodded, determination flashing in her eyes. "I'll keep my hand at my side until I'm ready."

"May that time come swiftly," whispered Elarion, turning away.

The silence between them was heavy as if the weight of their words had settled like a fog around them. Lysandra's breath formed a mist in the chill air as she considered the choice.

"Well, this is where we part," said Elarion, his voice low.

Lysandra nodded, her tone betraying the turmoil within her. "For now."

Elarion stepped back, creating distance between them. "Your destiny is not a straight or safe path to walk, Lysandra. But it's yours to walk—or not."

Lysandra felt her fingers twitch at her side, longing for the comfort of her sword. "And if I choose 'not'?"

"Then Erenor will continue to bleed under Draven's rule," said Elarion, his gaze unwavering.

Lysandra felt fear wash over her, but she stood her ground. "I can't be what you want me to be."

"I don't want you to be anyone other than who you are," Elarion said softly. "You have to be true to yourself, Lysandra, no matter what that means."

Her wolf, shadow-sleek and silent, brushed against her leg, a comforting presence amid the disquiet. It whined lowly, sensing the shift in the air and the parting of ways.

"Will you be there?" She asked, suddenly vulnerable,

"When—if—I call?"

"Always." The assurance was as solid as the ancient oaks that stood sentinel around them.

"Then I'll keep my sword sheathed... for now." Lysandra squared her shoulders, watching Elarion's form become one with the encroaching dark, a part of the night itself.

"Be watchful," he intoned, the words almost lost to the wind. "Darkness grows bolder by the hour."

"I will be ready," she answered, more to convince herself than him.

"May the stars guide you until we meet again." With those final words, Master Elarion turned and strode away, his figure dissolving into the shadows that stretched across the land, leaving Lysandra alone with the weight of an unclaimed future.

She watched him go, the cold bite of the air a sharp contrast to the heat of the turmoil within. The wolf nudged her hand, its golden eyes holding an understanding beyond words. Lysandra released a breath she hadn't realized she'd been holding and turned away from the space where Elarion had been. The night felt deeper now, fraught with unseen dangers and whispered secrets.

"Come," she commanded her four-legged companion, her voice barely above a whisper. "We have much to prepare for."

As they walked away, Lysandra couldn't shake the sensation of being watched, of eyes that lingered just beyond sight, waiting for her to embrace her Birthright—or to falter. The choice hung over her like the sword of Damocles, a constant reminder of the power she held at bay. For now, she would keep her own counsel, but the future was a vortex, and in its depths, the siren song of destiny called ever louder.

Master Elarion echoed in her heart, "May that time come swiftly."

Chapter 1

LYSANDRA

Lysandra's boots glided against the smooth cobblestone as she walked through the maze-like streets of Tyrannis. The city was a vibrant hub of activity, pulsing with life and energy. Every corner was filled with the sounds of merchants hawking their wares, the clattering of horse hooves, and the chatter of people going about their business. The air was thick with the smell of spices and fresh bread, and the colorful storefronts and bustling markets almost made it seem like a happy city.

"Fresh bread, warm from the oven!" a voice bellowed to her left. "Silks from the Eastern Lands!" hawked another to her right.

Lysandra slipped past a raucous crowd of sailors without making contact with anyone, and her hair flowed lightly in the breeze. She moved with the grace of a natural predator who had learned to conceal her true nature beneath a veneer of normalcy.

"Watch where you're going, girl!" A burly man snarled as she sidestepped his lumbering gait at the last moment.

She could feel the familiar weight of her sword against her thigh, a comforting reminder of her strength in a land that had all but forgotten the song of magic. With each step, she felt the pull of her destiny, "The pull towards a future full of both uncertainty and hope."

Lysandra and her wolf companion, Shadow, approached an inn. Its wooden frame leaned slightly, weary from shouldering the weight of countless secrets. They entered the dimly lit common room and scanned the sparse surroundings.

"Quiet here, good," she noted, scanning the room. "Too quiet?" Shadow's whine scratched at the silence.

"Stay sharp," she advised. "But for tonight, this is home."

"Home..." Shadow seemed to agree with a soft yip, his tail a cautious pendulum behind him.

"Tomorrow, we move again," Lysandra vowed. "But tonight, we rest, sharpening both blades and wits."

"Rest," Shadow seemed to agree, settling by her feet, a sentinel even in repose.

"Rest and be ready for what real shadows may come," she concluded, her thoughts a swirling tempest as relentless as the sea in her eyes.

Her hand rested lightly on the pommel of her sword. The runes were etched into its hilt, hidden beneath her cloak—a secret symphony of power in a land that had all but forgotten the song of magic.

She could feel its familiar weight against her thigh, a comforting reminder of her strength, even as the rest of Erenor lay cloaked in enforced mundanity.

"Hey! You there, with the hair like starlight!" A grizzled fruit vendor waved a wrinkled apple at her. "Care for a taste of summer's kiss?"

"Maybe another time," Lysandra replied, her words as soft as a shadow's caress, slipping by before he could press further.

In the sun-dappled streets, her hair betrayed her, catching stray beams and setting them ablaze with incandescent defiance. With each twist and turn, she felt the pull of her destiny—the inevitable tug toward a future filled with uncertainty and the faintest whisper of hope.

"Coins for your fortune, Miss?" asked the old woman. Lysandra ignored her, walking away and dodging her outstretched hand.

She measured the street's rhythm and the crowd's ebb and flow with every step. She moved with the precision of a chess piece, advancing across a board of human obstacles—calculating and deliberate.

"Silver threads among the brown and black!" a child's voice

piped up, clear and tinged with innocent wonder. "You shine like Lady Luna!"

"Shh, child," a mother's calm tone followed, heavy with caution. "It is not our place to comment."

But Lysandra was already gone—a whisper of silver in a world growing ever darker.

"Easy, Shadow," Lysandra whispered as the wolf nipped at her heels. The creature's dark fur was a muted echo, and its bright, vigilant eyes mirrored her tireless watchfulness.

"Where to now?" Shadow tilted his head, and his ears perked as if he understood her every word.

"Somewhere we can disappear," she murmured back, her gaze catching the outline of an inn ahead. It stood like a forgotten relic, its wooden frame leaning slightly, weary from the weight of countless secrets.

"Keep close." She patted Shadow's head, connecting deeper than any spell could forge. They approached the inn's weathered door, scarred with the stories of all who had passed through it.

"Remember, we're just travelers looking for rest," she coached herself more than the pup.

"Another night, another shadow," she mused, her hand resting on the hilt of her rune-etched sword. "We'll be ghosts before dawn."

"Best kind," Shadow seemed to agree with a soft yip, his tail a cautious pendulum behind him.

"Let's hope the walls are thick and that there are not many

patrons tonight," Lysandra said, pushing the door relentlessly. The hinges groaned in protest, a sound that echoed her reluctance. Inside, the inn's dim light embraced them, starkly contrasting the glaring sun outside.

"Quiet here, good," she noted, scanning the sparse standard room. "Too quiet?" Shadow's whine scratched at the silence.

"Stay sharp," she advised. "But for tonight, this is home."

"Home..." Shadow's tongue lolled out, a momentary lapse into carefree innocence.

"Tomorrow, we move again," Lysandra vowed, the weight of their purpose heavy on her shoulders. "But tonight, we rest and sharpen not only our blades but also our wits."

"Rest," Shadow seemed to agree as he settled by Lysandra's feet. He was a constant presence, even while at rest.

"We'll take a break tonight and stay alert for whatever challenges may come," she added, her mind swirling with thoughts.

As Lysandra entered the cozy inn, her eyes scanned the room like a sentinel, taking in every detail.

The inn was a peaceful sanctuary amidst the chaos of Tyrannis, telling tales of weary travelers looking for a dry and warm place to sleep.

Lysandra moved gracefully, ready for any unexpected turn of events. "Easy, boy," she whispered to Shadow, who was equally vigilant, listening carefully to the sounds of the patrons and the creaking of the floorboards.

"Ah, the wanderer returns!" Silas, the innkeeper, emerged from behind the bar, his face weathered by age and experience.

"And this time, with a companion!"

"Silas," Lysandra acknowledged with a nod, her tensed muscles relaxing slightly while still maintaining her watchfulness. "The roads are dangerous."

"More so for some than others," Silas replied, eyeing the sword at Lysandra's side. His smile was a ray of warmth in the dimly lit tavern, genuine amidst the false pleasantries of his profession.

"Trouble finds us all eventually," she said, her hand brushing against the pommel of her sword, feeling the runes etched into it—a reminder of her burden, her cause.

"Yet here you are, defying it again." Silas gestured towards an empty table near the hearth. "Will it be as usual?"

"Something warm. Quiet," Lysandra said, guiding Shadow with a gentle press of her leg toward the sanctuary offered.

"Right away," Silas said, his gaze lingering on Lysandra for a moment longer before returning to his duties.

Lysandra took a moment to assess the room again and whispered to Shadow, her companion, whose amber eyes reflected wisdom beyond its years, to stay watchful. "Always," came the unspoken reply, a shared bond of survival between woman and beast.

"Tomorrow, we face the unknown," Lysandra thought, her gaze never still. "But tonight, we find strength in the familiar." She hoped for a moment's peace and a transient respite in the eye of the storm that was her life.

"Your usual room, Lysandra?" Silas inquired, his voice a low rumble as he reached for the iron key behind the counter.

"Higher ground tonight," she replied curtly, her eyes tracing shadows that clung to the tavern's corners.

"Top floor it is," he acknowledged, understanding the unspoken need for a strategic vantage point. As Silas handed over the key, Shadow circled once before settling at Lysandra's feet. The warmth from the hearth drew a contented sigh from the creature. It was a small comfort, this semblance of home amidst their relentless pursuit.

As Silas handed over the key, Shadow circled once before settling at her feet. The warmth from the hearth drew a contented sigh from the creature. It was a small comfort, this semblance of home amidst their relentless pursuit.

"Keep the door bolted," Silas advised, his words weighted with concern.

"Always do," she returned, her voice steady as she pocketed the key and ascended the creaking stairs, Shadow trailing silently behind.

Once inside the sparse chamber, she secured the lock and surveyed the room through Shadow's keen senses. The air was stagnant but held no scent of malice. With a nod, she allowed herself a measured breath, her armor momentarily shed.

"Rest, Shadow," she murmured, watching the wolf curled up on the threadbare rug, its amber gaze never leaving her.

She unsheathed her sword, the metal whispering promises of battles yet to come. Candlelight danced across the runes etched into the blade, the secrets of an ancient craft few now remembered. Each rune hummed with potential, awaiting her command and will to bend the arcane.

"Sharp enough to cleave shadow from the flesh," she mused, running a whetstone along the edge with practiced ease. Her movements were rhythmic—a warrior's lullaby, honing her weapon and resolve.

"Tomorrow, we confront destiny," she thought, the stone grating against the blade steadily. "Magic's last dance with darkness."

"Or its first steps toward dawn," her heart countered, daring to embrace the hope that had become her silent companion.

She drew out her sword, and the metal made a sound that hinted at the battles yet to come. The candlelight created a beautiful dance across the runes carved into the blade, revealing the secrets of an ancient craft that only a few people remembered. Each rune on the sword hummed with potential, waiting for her command and her will to bend the arcane to her will.

"This sword is sharp enough to cut through anything," she thought, running a sharpening stone along the blade with practiced ease. Her movements were rhythmic, like a warrior's lullaby, honing her weapon and resolve.

"Tomorrow, we confront destiny," she thought as the stone grated against the blade steadily. "Magic's last dance with darkness."

"Or its first steps towards dawn," her heart countered, daring to embrace the hope that had become her silent companion.

With each stroke, she reaffirmed her oath and her duty to Erenor. The weight of her quest to bring magic back to Erenor and save it from dying a slow, dark death pressed down on her, a familiar burden she bore with pride. And even though shadows gathered beyond the inn's walls, she created a sanctuary within this room, where only the sound of steel singing and loyalty rested at her feet.

The peace within the inn's walls shattered as loud laughter and clinking tankards bled into Lysandra's sanctuary. She stopped, the sharpening stone poised mid-stroke above the runes that thirsted for battle. Her eyes narrowed, and she tried to figure out what was causing the disturbance.

"More ale, you crusty barnacle! Or do you fancy I take it myself?" bellowed a husky voice, thick with the brine of drink and arrogance.

Shadow's ears twitched, amber eyes flaring beneath a furrowed brow. The wolf's instincts mirrored Lysandra's—a tempest rising against the din. She rose, sword sheathed yet her hand resting upon the hilt, a silent promise to those who dared threaten her reprieve.

"Keep your gold pouches tight, gents!" another voice jeered. "It looks like we've got ourselves a lively crowd tonight."

Booted feet trampled the tranquility beneath their soles, dancing in discord among the wooden tables. Lysandra's gaze swept across the tavern's standard room, descending on the group of rowdy patrons—men bloated with bravado and ale, their presence spreading like a stain over the timeworn floorboards.

"Silence would suit you better," Lysandra said, her tone steel wrapped in velvet, cutting through the din.

"Who's this, then? Alass thinking herself a knight?" taunted the ringleader, giving her that look that she knew only too well.

"Don't worry about who I am," she replied confidently, stepping forward. "You should worry about the chaos you're about to cause with all this noise."

Everyone in the tavern went quiet, watching with bated breath as the tension in the air grew thick with the possibility of violence. Her trusty companion, Shadow, stood by her side, his dark form blending in with the shadows.

The ringleader spat on the floor, clearly unimpressed. "We're just having some fun," he sneered.

"But that fun could turn ugly," Lysandra warned, her words tightening around the room like a noose. And I don't like disturbances when it's time to rest."

"Look at her, boys!" The ringleader burst out laughing. "She thinks she can control the tides!"

Lysandra's hand hovered over her sword, the runes beneath it itching to be unleashed. But she knew that she would win this fight without a blade.

"Can I control them? No," she replied softly as if sharing a secret with her fellow warriors. But I can calm them."

The ringleader raised an eyebrow, his mockery turning to doubt as he sensed the power in her stance.

"Really?" he asked, his forehead creased with confusion.

"Really," Lysandra replied, relaxing her posture. "Words can do more than weapons sometimes. Leave now and keep your dignity intact."

The ringleader considered it momentarily, weighing his pride against the warning in her eyes. The tavern was silent, and the tension was palpable. Finally, a subtle nod from the innkeeper sealed their fate.

"Fine," the ringleader growled, swallowing his anger. "This place is not any fun tonight anyway."

With that, they all shuffled out, grumbling and cursing under their breath. Lysandra stood there, watching them go until the door thudded shut, sealing out the cold night air and the promise of a fight.

"Come, Shadow," she whispered, the pup's eyes gleaming with loyalty and understanding. Together, they returned to their haven, the sense of foreboding ebbing away, leaving only the echo of magic's call and the sharpening of blades.

The room's atmosphere shifted from one of the brewing storms to a grateful reprieve as the rabble exited, their threats dissipating into the night. The innkeeper, a tapestry of wrinkles etched by years of toil, approached Lysandra with an appreciative nod. "Bless you, lass," he uttered, his voice gravelly but sincere. "Tyrannis could use more like you."

"I only did what anyone should." Her response was terse, clipped by the knowledge that every interaction weaved a tighter web around her secrets.

"Still," another patron said, an older woman whose eyes twinkled with a knowing light, "takes guts to stand up like that. Not many are willing to step into the fire."

"Fire can be quelled," Lysandra murmured, glancing toward Shadow, the wolf pup at her heel. His ears twitched, sensing the shift in his companion's mood.

"Your room is ready, the same as always," said the innkeeper, leading the way through a maze of tables. The patrons watched her, curiosity and respect mingling in their silent stares.

"Thank you," she offered with a small, guarded smile, ushering Shadow ahead. With each step, she felt the weight of watchful eyes like the pressure of an unsheathed blade against her neck.

Once inside the sanctity of her chamber, Lysandra let out a breath she hadn't realized she'd been holding. Shadow circled twice before settling at her feet, his amber gaze locked onto hers, mirroring a vigilance born not of training but of survival.

"Today was too close, old friend." She whispered to the wolf. "We walk a knife's edge, you and I."

Shadow whined softly, pressing his nose against her hand. His presence reminded her of the sacrifices made and the path they still needed to travel. She leaned back against the headboard, closing her eyes momentarily, allowing herself the luxury of stillness.

"I can't stay long in Tyrannis," she mused aloud. "Eyes are prying; whispers are growing louder." The need to remain invisible warred with the burning desire to reclaim what had been lost and ignite the dormant magic within her veins.

"Tomorrow," she promised, her eyes opening, stormy and relentless, "we move before dawn."

"Rest now, Shadow." As the candle flickered, casting shadows that danced eerily along the walls, Lysandra's hand rested on the pommel of her sword, the only sentinel against the darkness that pursued them.

The chamber held a hush of secrets, the walls seeming to lean in with anticipation. Lysandra's fingers danced across the whetstone, sharpening her blade in swift, decisive strokes.

"Rest won't come easy," she muttered to Shadow, whose ears twitched at the sound of her voice. "Not with the weight of Erenor on our shoulders. We must try to bring magic back to Erenor. That's the only way we can save it. If only King Draven hadn't been so scared that he would lose all his power if it came back, we could have had some help, but he and his hunters only wanted to kill us." She sighed.

Shadow let out a low growl. His instincts tuned to the unease in her tone. The wolf's eyes, reflective pools of liquid gold, followed her every movement.

"Tomorrow, we seek the crystals of Tandar," she continued, her words a quiet vow slicing through the silence. "With them, the magic..."

"Magic that can burn," Shadow seemed to say with a whine, shifting closer.

"Or heal," Lysandra countered, her gaze hardening. She sheathed her sword and rose, pacing the room. Her steps were silent and practiced—the prowl of a predator made for these times of shadow and blood.

"Power will be ours again," she said, more to herself than to the wolf. "To mend this fractured land."

Shadow's head cocked to the side as if considering her words.

His tail thumped once against the wooden floor, echoing hope among the gathering darkness.

"First light, then," she announced, her voice edged with steel. "We breach the Veilwood, where spirits linger and the dead whisper."

"Whispers that guide or deceive," Shadow's eyes seemed to warn.

"Both, likely." Lysandra's laugh was short and without any warmth. She kneeled beside him, her hand resting atop his warm fur. "But we're no strangers to deception, are we?"

"Nor to danger." Shadow's posture spoke of readiness despite the encroaching weariness.

"Then it's settled." Her resolve wrapped around them like a cloak. She glanced at the window, where the moon cast its pale judgment upon the world.

"Sleep now, guardian of my soul." Lysandra's command was gentle yet firm. She curled beside Shadow, the wolf warming her side, his breaths in steady syncopation with her own.

"Tomorrow," she whispered into the encroaching dreams, "we chase destiny."

Outside, the wind carried the promise of storms and the scent of adventure, untold dangers, and magic waiting to be awakened. In the heart of Tyrannis, Lysandra and her faithful companion stood on the threshold of legend.

Chapter 2

FEYLA

Lysandra woke up and followed her usual routine in her dimly lit chamber at dawn. She wore her mercenary attire—a leather cuirass reinforced with iron and gauntlets marked with scars from countless battles. Her companion, a wolf with fur as dark as a moonless night, stirred from his place by the cold hearth, his amber eyes tracking her every move.

"Another day, another coin to be earned, eh, Shadow?" She muttered, fastening her scabbard around her waist. The wolf huffed in response. The sound was almost like agreement.

Her sea-green eyes, stormy and untamed, scanned the postings on the tavern's job board. Each parchment told a tale of desperation or greed. "Escort here, bounty there... Ah, what's this?" Her finger stopped at a notice inked in bold letters:

"RETRIEVE STOLEN ARTIFACT. GENEROUS REWARD."

"Looks promising," she said, snatching the paper.

"Oi, Lysandra!" the barkeep, a portly man wiping down the counter, called out. That one's trouble. A band of thieves—virtual ones."

"Trouble is my trade, Bram." She cast him a wry smile, her voice steady and calm. "Besides, I've got Shadow and my sword."

"Your sword won't save you if magic's involved," Bram warned, but she was already heading for the door.

"Magic hasn't fazed me yet," she tossed over her shoulder.

The thieves' camp was rumored to nestle in the heart of the Darkwood, where twisted trees clawed at the sky. Shadow padded alongside Lysandra, silent as the grave, as they approached the thicket. The air grew heavy, charged with tension that had nothing to do with the coming storm.

"Stay alert," she commanded in a low voice, her hand resting on the pommel of her sword. The blade hummed softly, sensing the latent danger.

"Who goes there?" challenged a voice from the shadows.

"Mercenary for hire," Lysandra replied, stepping into the clearing with feigned nonchalance. "I heard you might have work."

"Or perhaps she's come for the artifact?" sneered another figure, emerging with a knife gleaming in his hand.

"Perhaps," Lysandra conceded, undaunted. "But let's not be hasty. What do you say we talk terms?"

"Cut her down!" ordered the first thief.

Lysandra's sword sang free from its sheath as the bandits

lunged, a flash of silver against the brooding forest backdrop. She dodged, spun, and struck with lethal precision, embodying grace and fury. Shadow leaped, too, a phantom delivering swift justice.

"Come then!" she taunted, driving them back. "Let's see if you're as good as your word!"

Blades clashed, metal rang, and shouts filled the air, mingling with her companion's growls. Lysandra fought with a relentless pace, each movement honed by years of mercenary life. The dance of combat was second nature, a deadly rhythm she followed without thought.

"Enough!" she barked after disarming the last of her assailants. "The artifact. Now."

"Take it," gasped the thief leader, throwing a cloth-wrapped object at her feet. "It's cursed anyway."

"Everything has its price," she said, picking up the bundle and unwrapping it just enough to glimpse the artifact's ancient craftsmanship. A surge of power coursed through her, a whisper of magic that caressed her senses.

"Let's go, Shadow." She tucked the item away securely. "We have what we came for."

As they vanished into the trees, the rain began to fall, washing away the traces of their presence, leaving only the legend of a mercenary who could stand against darkness itself.

Lysandra's boots crunched on brittle leaves, her breath steady as she scanned the treeline. Shadow trailed her; his ears perked, and her nose twitched for danger.

"Circle left," she whispered to the wolf, who obeyed without sound, a dark ghost flitting through the underbrush.

"Show yourself!" a gruff voice called out from ahead. Unknown men came forward, ragged cloaks clinging to their frames like shadows made flesh.

"Four against one," Lysandra murmured, her hand resting on the hilt of her rune-etched sword. "Odds I can work with."

"Hand over the artifact!" demanded the largest of the thieves, a brute with a scarred face.

"Make me," she taunted, drawing her blade in a swift arc that caught the dim light filtering through the canopy.

The first lunged, steel meeting steel. Parry. Thrust. She danced back, her movements precise and deliberate. The second thief joined, swinging wide. A feint—she ducked low and rolled, coming up behind him, her sword kissing his hamstring. He crumpled, cursing.

"Devil's spit," spat the third, cautiously advancing.

"Come closer, and you'll taste more than spit," Lysandra retorted, eyes locked onto his, her grip on her sword unyielding.

"Enough of this!" The scarred leader charged, greatsword raised.

She sidestepped, using his momentum against him, guiding his swing wide. With a quick twist, her blade found the gap in his armor—a gasp and a thud as he fell.

"Yield!" she commanded, pointing her sword at the last standing foe. "Damn you," he breathed, dropping his weapon.

"Smart choice," she acknowledged, binding his hands with a

length of rope. "Who are you?" came a soft voice from the trees.

Lysandra stiffened, her eyes searching the greenery. A figure appeared: a young woman dressed in leather, carrying a satchel brimming with odd contraptions. Her curious gaze held Lysandra's own eyes.

"Someone who doesn't like to be followed," Lysandra said, wary.

"Your skills... they are remarkable," the stranger said, stepping closer. "I'm Feyla." "Watching was a risk," Lysandra replied, her tone guarded but intrigued.

"Risk seems to be your trade," Feyla observed, a faint smile on her lips. "Mine too, in a way."

"Shadow, keep an eye on our new friend here," Lysandra instructed. The wolf growled softly, never taking its gaze off Feyla.

"Is it true what they say? That you're not just a mercenary, but something... more?" Feyla asked, inching closer, her interest peaking with each step.

"Rumors are like wildfire," Lysandra said, tucking her sword away and securing the artifact in her belt. They're unpredictable and dangerous."

"Something tells me you're no stranger to either," Feyla noted, her eyes glinting with respect and curiosity.

"Nor you," Lysandra said, her instincts telling her there was much she didn't know about this Feyla. "Why were you following me?"

"Perhaps I'm seeking something more than the mundane,"

Feyla admitted, her hands resting on her hips near her satchel. "And perhaps I've found it."

"Let's hope for your sake; it's not more trouble than you bargained for," Lysandra warned, a hint of a smile playing at the edge of her lips.

"Trouble," Feyla echoed, "has a way of finding us all, doesn't it?"

"Indeed, it does," Lysandra conceded, her mind already racing with the possibilities this chance encounter could bring.

The evening air clung to Lysandra's skin with a chill that whispered of coming storms. Her braided hair caught the glint of the fading sun like the sheen of a sword unsheathed in twilight.

"Your blade works," Feyla started, stepping closer, her voice low and steady. "It's not just training; it's instinctual."

Lysandra halted, assessing. Shadow, her ever-watchful companion, mirrored her tension, his ears pricking forward. She scanned their surroundings, the alley's mouth gaping behind them, a maw of secrets and shadows.

"Admiration feels like a thin veil for curiosity," Lysandra said, her voice betraying none of the wariness that knotted her stomach.

"Perhaps," Feyla conceded, her hands never straying far from her satchel, her stance open yet ready. "But skill like yours draws eyes. It speaks of tales untold."

"Most tales are better left unspoken," Lysandra replied, her thoughts whirling with suspicion and the tempting whisper of trust. Could Feyla be another threat or an unlikely ally in this world bent on unmaking her kind?

"Yet how dull would our existence be without stories?" Feyla pressed, inching into the space Lysandra kept carefully between them. The setting sun cast elongated shadows, intertwining theirs on the cobblestones.

"Stories can kill as swiftly as steel," Lysandra countered, her fingers twitching toward the runes etched upon her sword's hilt—hidden knowledge, concealed power.

"True." Feyla nodded, her eyes alight with a spark that belied her non-magical nature. "But so can silence. It festers and grows heavy."

"Weight is something I've learned to bear," Lysandra said, her gaze flickering to the artifact at her belt. Its presence constantly reminded her of her burdens: mercenary, mage, and fugitive.

"And yet," Feyla persisted, "even the mightiest warriors need to rest sometimes. Need... companionship."

"Companionship invites betrayal," Lysandra shot back, her past a tapestry of betrayal and loss. Shadow growled softly, a rumble of agreement from her only true confidant.

"Or salvation," Feyla countered; the word hangs between them, a promise or danger.

Lysandra's mind raced; each thought was a dagger thrown in the dark—trust was a luxury she could not afford. Yet, there was something about Feyla—a resonance that beckoned like a beacon in the fog.

"Perhaps," Lysandra finally allowed her voice to murmur to

the encroaching night. "But some doors, once opened, cannot be closed."

"Ah," Feyla said, a knowing look in her eyes. "But imagine the wonders they might reveal." "Imagine the horrors," Lysandra added, her inner voice a tempest of warnings.

"Life is a balance of both, isn't it?" Feyla proposed a rhetorical question wrapped in an enigma.

"Balance," Lysandra echoed, the concept foreign yet enticing—a dance of light and shadow, a path she had yet to tread thoroughly.

"Walk with me," Feyla invited, gesturing down the cobbled lane where the first stars dared to pierce the dusk. "Share the road, if not the burden."

Lysandra hesitated, her instincts warring with the faintest hope of camaraderie. Shadow nudged her hand, silently counseling caution and companionship. With a final glance at the horizon, where day bled into night, Lysandra took a step forward, her choice made, her fate entwined with the enigmatic figure beside her.

The narrow alleyway echoed with the soft patter of their footsteps, and the walls steeped in the scent of damp stone and forgotten tales. Moonlight filtered through the haphazardly stacked buildings, casting a silvery glow that danced upon Lysandra's blade, the runes shimmering like captured stars.

"King Draven fears what he cannot control," Lysandra confessed, her voice barely above a whisper as if the very stones might betray her secrets. "And I... I am his greatest fear made flesh."

Feyla's eyes held a depth of empathy that felt almost tangible. "Fear can be a prison, Lysandra. But you wield your sword with a grace that speaks of freedom."

"Freedom?" Lysandra scoffed, her laugh hollow. Shadow growled softly at her feet, sensing the turmoil within. "My powers are shackles. One slip, one display of magic, and Draven's hounds will be upon me."

"Yet here you stand," Feyla countered, her tone steady. "Defiant. Alive."

"Because I hide!" Lysandra's outburst was a crack of thunder in the quiet night. She turned away, clenching her fists, feeling the weight of her revelation like chains around her heart.

"Everyone has something they hide," Feyla said gently, stepping closer. Her hand reached out, not touching but offering, "Even those without magic."

Lysandra faced her, her eyes uncertain. "You speak as though you know this well."

"Because I do." Feyla's smile was a flicker of light in the darkness, her secrets shadowed but present. "Our non-magical abilities have worth too. They've kept us alive, haven't they?"

"Perhaps." Lysandra's gaze drifted to her sword, the runes winking as clouds veiled the moon. "But can they change our fates?"

"Alone? Maybe not." Feyla's words were a lifeline thrown across the chasm of doubt. "Together? There's nothing we can't face."

"Even a king?" The question hung heavy in the air, challenging both the universe and them.

"Especially a king." Feyla's resolve was as fierce as the edge of Lysandra's sword. "Trust is rare, but I offer mine to you."

Lysandra searched Feyla's face, seeking the lie and the hidden agenda. Finding none, she let out a breath she didn't realize she'd been holding. "And I accept it," she said, her decision a leap into the unknown.

"Good." Feyla's grin was infectious—a spark of camaraderie in the gloom. "Because I have a feeling our journey has only just begun."

"Journey..." Lysandra mused, the word holding more promise than peril now. "Yes, I suppose it has."

They walked ahead, leaving the dark alley behind them. Their growing trust lit the path against King Draven's oppression.

The scent of damp earth clung to the air, heavy with the promise of a storm. Lysandra's hair lay plastered against her forehead as she walked beside Feyla through the dense forest that bordered the Kingdom of Erenor. The wolf, a shadow among shadows, trailed silently alongside them.

"I never thought I'd find companionship in these woods," Lysandra said, her eyes scanning the thicket for unseen threats.

"Outcasts tend to flock together," Feyla replied, her steps light and soundless, her dark eyes reflecting an inner strength. "You wield your sword like it's a part of you."

"It feels like it is sometimes." She flexed her hand, feeling the familiar grooves. "It's one of the few things that doesn't betray me."

"Betrayal…" Feyla mused, trailing off. A pause hung between them before she added, "You're not the only one hiding from something, Lysandra."

"Your inventions," Lysandra ventured, a spark of curiosity in her gaze. "They are unique."

"Unique enough to evade King Draven's ever-watchful eye." Feyla reached into her coat, withdrawing a small metallic object that gleamed with intricate gears. "And useful. This little gadget can pick any lock in Erenor."

"Useful indeed," Lysandra conceded, watching as Feyla's fingers deftly manipulated the device.

"Let me help you," Feyla offered earnestly, with a flicker of excitement. "My gadgets could be just what we need to stay one step ahead."

Lysandra hesitated, her instincts warring with the burgeoning trust she felt for Feyla. "It's dangerous," she admitted, her thoughts clouded by past alliances that had turned sour.

"Life's dangerous," Feyla shot back with a grin that didn't quite reach her eyes. "But I'm tired of running alone. Aren't you?"

"More than you know." Lysandra's voice was a whisper, carried away by the wind that rustled the leaves.

"Then let's run together," Feyla said, extending her hand with her invention and the partnership offer.

"Alright." Lysandra clasped Feyla's hand in agreement, their pact sealed with the weight of their combined resolve. "But remember, we're playing with fire."

"Fire has a way of purifying," Feyla replied, her tone laced with a hint of mystery. "I say it's about time we cleanse Erenor of its corruption."

A distant thunderclap punctuated her words, and Lysandra couldn't help but feel the shiver of destiny coursing through her veins. They were two outsiders against the world—a mercenary with a magic sword and an inventor with a penchant for creation. Together, they would forge a new path that twisted through the darkness toward a shimmering, uncertain future.

Lysandra studied the horizon, where dusk flirted with the edges of Erenor. The sky bled crimson and gold. She turned toward Feyla, feeling the weight of a decision that could bind or sever their fates.

"Your inventions, while ingenious, haven't been tested in the maelstrom I dance with daily," Lysandra stated flatly, her voice betraying the trepidation that coiled tight in her chest.

"Neither have you until you were forced to," Feyla retorted, her gaze unwavering. "I can handle it."

"Can you?" The question hung between them like a challenge. Lysandra's fingers twitched at her side, itching for the familiar hilt of her sword. It was a craving for comfort and control.

"Look, I've survived on my own thus far." Feyla's hands delved into her leather satchel, drawing out a small device that gleamed under the waning light. "With this, we can survive together."

"Survival isn't enough," Lysandra said, stepping forward, the twilight shadows creeping around her. Her wolf, a silent sentinel, mirrored her movement, its amber eyes fixed on Feyla. "We'd be inviting death every step of the way."

"Then we invite it to dance." Feyla clicked a button on the device, and it whirred to life, tiny cogs spinning with whispered promises of untapped potential.

A sudden rustle nearby had them both on edge, muscles tensed, but it was only the wind playing games with the trees. Lysandra exhaled slowly, allowing uncertainty to seep through her hardened exterior. "If we do this—if I say yes—it means there's no turning back. For either of us."

"Good." Feyla's response was instant and fierce. "Because I don't plan on going back."

"Nor do I," Lysandra murmured, her resolve hardening like steel tempered in fire. She extended her hand, not just as a mercenary but as a comrade. "Partners then?"

"Partners." Feyla clasped her hand firmly, her smile ablaze with rebellious hope.

They turned in unison to face the darkening landscape, each lost in thought. Lysandra's mind raced with strategies, routes, and contingencies—each more dangerous than the last. Yet, amidst the turmoil, a sense of anticipation stirred—an eagerness she hadn't felt in ages.

"North lies the Crypts of Sorrow. People are talking about a relic," Feyla began, tracing a map in the dirt with the toe of her boot.

"Rumors tend to speak truth in Erenor," Lysandra interjected, her eyes narrowing as she envisioned their next quest.

"Then it's settled." Feyla wiped her hands on her tunic, the gears of her device still humming softly. "We set out at dawn."

"Agreed." Lysandra nodded, the pact sealed beneath the watchful eyes of the stars. "Rest well, Feyla. Tomorrow, our journey begins anew."

"And so we chase destiny," Feyla whispered, her words carried away by the night as they retreated to their camp. Each step was a silent promise for the path ahead—the forging of a legend that would ripple through the ages.

Chapter 3

FORBIDDEN MAGIC

The air was thick with acrid smoke, and the wails of timber surrendered to the inferno.

Lysandra's hair clung to her face in sooty strands. Her eyes darted frantically across the crumbling structure.

"Anyone!" she cried out, her voice barely piercing the roar of the flames. "Is anyone there?"

A whimper answered through the crackling destruction—a child, somewhere beneath the charred remnants of the ceiling. Lysandra moved swiftly as a shadow, each step an assertion against the conflagration's rage.

"Keep calling out!" Lysandra shouted, closing in on the sound.

"Here! I'm here!"

Lysandra cautiously approached the fire's source, her heart pounding with anticipation and fear. The area was dimly lit, and she strained to make out a faint glow from the center. She took a deep breath to steady her nerves and extended her arm, revealing the ornate runes etched into her skin. The ancient markings glowed faintly, lending her a sense of otherworldly power.

As she moved closer, she heard a low groan from above, and the ceiling threatened to collapse. Lysandra braced herself, ready for anything.

Despite the danger, Lysandra remained calm and composed, relying on her training and skills to face any challenge that came her way.

"Come to me, quickly!"

The child emerged, smeared with soot and tears, and lunged towards Lysandra's arms. As the timbers rose above them, a dome of translucent energy materialized, encasing them in a protective bubble. As debris hammered against the shield, its force dissipated, falling harmlessly to their sides.

"By the gods," the child gasped, eyes wide with fear and wonder.

"Stay close," Lysandra instructed, her voice steady despite her racing heart. "I've got you."

She could feel the strain of magic coursing through her veins, an explosive power she had long feared unleashing.

"Who are you?" the child asked, clinging to her.

"Just a friend," she replied. "Now, let's get out of here."

They moved together, Lysandra keeping one arm firmly around the child, the other guiding the shield before them, 7refused to be tamed. But Lysandra would not yield; she couldn't—not when innocent lives hung in the balance, not when her destiny beckoned her onward.

Lysandra emerged from the fire's smoke and noise, coughing and holding the child tightly. Her shield flickered weakly, but she felt hope as they saw daylight ahead, a glimmer of light in the encroaching darkness.

"We're safe now," she gasped, her heart pounding like war drums. The child's grip loosened, but before she could feel relieved, a man appeared from the shadows, his dark eyes piercing through the smoke.

"Who goes there?" Aerin demanded, his voice slicing through the chaos. He stood tall and courageous, a hunter poised at the edge of certainty and doubt.

"Stand back!" Lysandra's words came like a whip crack, her sword drawn in a flash. "I mean no harm!"

Aerin firmly gripped the hilt of his sword. He looked intently at Lysandra, ready to strike at a moment's notice. "Put down your weapon," he ordered in a firm voice.

Lysandra looked at him pleadingly, saying, "Please, listen to me! I only fought to protect this child."

"King Draven has ordered all magic users to be detained," Aerin replied, stepping closer, his sword glinting menacingly in the light. "Your powers make you a threat."

Lysandra looked at him with fear and defiance, saying, "I only use my powers to protect the innocent. I'm not a threat."

"Look around you!" Lysandra exclaimed, gesturing towards the destruction around them. Her frustration was evident in her tone. "I use my magic to protect us, not to cause harm."

"Actions speak louder than words," he replied, moving closer calmly and measuredly. "Surrender, and let the King decide your fate."

"I will not be judged unfairly!" Lysandra's voice thundered with defiance and determination. She knew that she couldn't let fear dictate her path. Not when freedom was within reach, not when Erenor needed her.

Aerin hesitated, his conflicted expression revealing his inner turmoil. "You may be telling the truth," he admitted, his voice softening slightly. "But can you blame me for being cautious? Darkness is spreading, and people are afraid of what they can't control."

"Then witness control!" Lysandra's cry cut through the air as she channeled her dwindling strength. Her shield expanded in a brilliant display of light and force. Debris deflected off the magical barrier, a testament to her command.

"Magic..." Aerin murmured, her awe mingling with uncertainty. His sword lowered an inch, intrigue warring with duty.

"See? I am not your enemy." She locked eyes with him, her plea laced with urgent sincerity. "Will you let fear rule you, Hunter?"

"Perhaps..." Aerin trailed off, his resolve wavering like a flame in a storm. But the moment passed, and his expression hardened once more. "No. The risk is too great."

"Then you leave me no choice." Lysandra's grip tightened on her sword, her mind racing with escape plans. She would not bow to tyranny—she would forge her destiny with fire and steel if necessary.

"Neither do I." Aerin's stance mirrored hers, a mirror of determination and regret.

"Ready yourself," she whispered to the child, her voice filled with determination and reassurance. "Stay behind me."

"Always the protector…" Aerin remarked, his tone begrudgingly respectful.

"Always," she affirmed, awaiting the opportune moment to act. Due to the magic flowing through her veins, her resolve was unwavering.

Their standoff hung precariously like a suspended sword, each waiting for the other to make the first move. In the heart of destruction, amidst the cries of the wounded and the crackle of devouring flames, Lysandra knew that whatever happened next would determine the fate of Erenor and her own.

"Give it up, Mage!" Aerin's voice cut through the smoke and ash; his words were a death knell.

Lysandra's heart hammered against her ribcage. She could see it in his eyes—no plea would sway him. He was a hunter, and she was prey destined for King Draven's merciless hands. A shiver of dread snaked down her spine, but she masked it with a defiant glare.

"Never," she spat back, clutching her sword with white-knuckled resolve. Her mind whirred, plotting as she edged backward, putting space between her and the encroaching hunter.

"Stop this madness!" His command boomed over the crackling flames. "Yield now, and your life may yet be spared."

"Spared? For what?" Lysandra scoffed, her voice barely a whisper. Chains? A cell?" She couldn't let that happen—not here, not now.

"King Draven will decide your fate."

"Damn, King Draven." With a swift incantation, she conjured a blinding flash, the light erupting like a starburst. Aerin recoiled, shielded eyes betraying a flicker of surprise.

"Go!" She didn't think twice, grabbing the child and darting into the inferno's angry dance.

"Curse you, witch!" Aerin's curse chased her as she wove through alleys choked with debris and despair. She heard the hunter's footsteps pounding after her, relentless as the beating of war drums.

"Stay close!" she urged the child, leaping over the smoldering rubble, the heat searing her lungs. She called upon her power again, drawing protective runes in the air, their glow warding off falling embers.

"Where do you think you're going?" His voice grew closer, too close.

"Anywhere but here!" Lysandra shot back, her words fueled by a wild cocktail of fear and adrenaline. Ducking under a collapsed beam, she emerged onto a street lit by the eerie orange of destruction.

"Give up, Lysandra! You cannot outrun me!"

"Watch me!" she retorted, feeling the pulse of magic within her veins. It was a wild thing, untamed and hungry for release.

"Look out!" the child screamed, breaking Lysandra's concentration. A shadow loomed overhead, and she instinctively spun around, thrusting her palm outward. A force surge erupted from her hand, blasting the falling timber aside in a shower of sparks and cinders.

"By the gods," Aerin muttered, his shock and awe apparent.

Lysandra turned to face him, her eyes cold and determined. She was ready for whatever he had planned next. Aerin couldn't help but feel a grudging respect for her. "Impressive," he grunted, still in disbelief.

"Keep moving!" Lysandra didn't have time to celebrate her achievement. Every second counted, so she turned down another alleyway.

"End this foolishness!" Aerin's voice was now a distant thunder, but Lysandra knew better than to underestimate him. He was a hunter, hunting her, and would not give up.

"Never!" she screamed into the night. She would fight, she would run, and she would survive. For herself, for the child, for Erenor.

"Your wolf won't save you this time!" Aerin's taunt reached her ears, a reminder of the companion who had been her shadow since the darkest times.

"Maybe not," Lysandra whispered, her breath ragged, "but I can save myself."

With a final burst of speed, she vanished into the smoke, her heart pounding a fierce escape rhythm.

Lysandra's lungs screamed as much as the city around her. The acrid smoke filled the air, stinging her eyes and clawing at her throat. She dove into a narrow passageway she knew well, its cobblestones slick with water from buckets thrown haphazardly to fight the fire.

"Stop, mage!" Aerin's voice roared from behind, relentless as the flames.

She glanced back, seeing his silhouette framed by a firelight. With a start, she vaulted over a fallen beam, her runic sword bouncing against her hip.

"Never," she spat out between breaths, focusing on the path ahead.

A firewall loomed before her, its timbers groaning and threatening to collapse. Without hesitation, Lysandra summoned her magic, a shield shimmering into existence around her. She charged through the inferno, the flames licking hungrily at her protective bubble.

"By Draven's crown, you will surrender!" Aerin was closer now; she could hear the determination in his stride.

"Surrender to tyranny? I'd rather die free!" Lysandra retorted, her voice laced with defiance.

Once vibrant and bustling, the market square opened before her, now a war zone of sparks and ruin. She darted left, then right, her knowledge of the city a tapestry she wove herself through, always one step ahead.

"Your tricks won't work forever!" Aerin bellowed, the crackle of fire punctuating his threat. "Neither will your threats!" she shot back.

An explosion rocked the ground, sending shards of stone skyward. Lysandra rolled away just in time, feeling the heat graze her skin. Her heart raced, but she couldn't afford to slow down or be caught.

"Come out, witch! Face me!"

"Face a hunter? You wish to cage me like some animal?" Lysandra's laugh was bitter as she dodged another collapsing facade—the once majestic inn is now a deathtrap.

"Better caged than dead!"

"Are we not both in this hell?" Lysandra shouted as she hurried through the shortcuts she knew so well. Her mind was racing with thoughts of survival. "Survive," they kept echoing, "survive and fight another day."

"Death would be a mercy compared to King Draven's dungeons!" she exclaimed in frustration.

"Then let's see if mercy finds you today!" Aerin's presence sent a shiver down her spine, even though the heat around them was unbearable.

"Mercy is for the weak!" She didn't believe it, but fear had sharpened her tongue. She bound up a series of crates to a rooftop, her agility her savior as tiles slid into the abyss below.

"Careful, mate! Even cats fall from roofs!" Aerin taunted, but she could sense his frustration.

"Then hope I land on my feet," Lysandra quipped, leaping across to an adjacent building, the gap a chasm of uncertainty that she crossed with desperate grace.

"Your nine lives are running out!" His voice was closer now, too close.

"Then I'll make this one count." She slid down a drainpipe, landing in a sprint. Every moment was a choice, and every turn was a chance.

"Enough games!" Aerin's growl was lost in a cacophony of destruction.

"Games?" Lysandra's thought twisted with irony. 'This is survival.' She spared a fleeting thought for her wolf companion, hoping he was safe, far from this madness.

"King Draven will hear of this defiance!"

"Let him hear! Let all of Erenor hear!" Lysandra called out, her voice carrying over the roaring flames.

"Your pride will be the cause of your downfall!"

"Perhaps," she conceded inwardly, "but not today."

Today, she would run, evade, and live to fight another daybreak.

Lysandra's breath came in ragged bursts, her boots pounding against the cobblestones as she wove through an alley choked with smoke and embers. A wall of flame reared up before her, a menacing barrier, but she could not—would not—allow it to end her flight.

"Yield, Lysandra!" Aerin's voice cut through the crackling fire. "No more running!"

"Yielding is surrendering," she shot back, her words laced with grit. With a surge of will, her outstretched hand summoned a gust of wind, parting the flames like a curtain. She dashed through, feeling the heat lick at her skin, singeing her silver hair.

"Stubborn witch!" he cursed from behind.

Her heart hammered against her ribs, echoing the chaos around them. The city was a labyrinth, one she knew by rote, yet now it felt foreign and hostile. Each turn was a gamble, and each decision was a potential trap.

"Close calls are still missed!" she retorted, ducking a falling timber, its end ablaze. Her eyes mirrored the fury of the inferno surrounding her.

"Misses that get narrower every time!" Aerin's silhouette loomed behind her, a relentless hunter among the shadows, and she was the prey.

She skidded around a corner, barely avoiding a collapsed balcony. Her sword, etched with runes, rattled against the stone walls, a reminder of battles past and the steel within her. 'Fight,' her mind urged. 'Survive.'

"Courage alone won't save you!" he bellowed as a thunderous crash sounded to her left. She leaped away instinctively, debris raining down where she had stood moments before.

"Neither will threats!" she called over her shoulder, her pulse racing.

A sudden gap yawned between two buildings—too broad, too treacherous. But hesitation spelled capture.

With a burst of adrenaline, she launched forward, fingers grazing rough brick as she cleared the expanse. Her landing was a jarring thud that stole the breath from her lungs.

"I almost had you!" Aerin's voice was laced with grudging respect.

"Almost isn't enough!" she gasped, pushing through the pain. Magic simmered beneath her skin, a storm waiting to be unleashed. But not yet. Not until she had no other choice.

"Your defiance fuels my resolve!" His footsteps drew nearer, a relentless drumming that echoed her heartbeat.

"Good," she spat, rounding another bend. "You'll need it!"

The chase was like a deadly dance, with each step taken out of necessity and each move a close call to death. However, Lysandra was not defeated yet.

Her will was as strong as iron, and her spirit was unbreakable. She resisted giving in to fear or fate.

"Where is your wolf now?" Aerin mocked, his words full of malice. There is no wild animal to protect you this time."

"Be silent, hunter!" Lysandra growled, even though she thought of her missing companion. Inside, she hoped he was safe.

"If you give up, your punishment will be quick!" Aerin was getting closer now; his determination was almost palpable.

"Never," whispered Lysandra, making a vow. She summoned all her cunning and courage, determined not to accept defeat.

She was the last mage of Erenor, and she would not go down without a fight.

Lysandra's lungs burned from the acrid smoke that filled the alley. Aerin's boots against the cobblestones echoed through the alley as he turned the corner, his golden eyes ablaze with excitement.

"End of the line, mage!" Aerin barked, his words cutting through the haze.

The alley seemed to betray her, as there was no way out. It was a dead end; the walls were too slick and tall to scale. Lysandra's back pressed against the cold stone as she searched for a way to escape. Her heart raced with fear and desperation.

"Trapped like a doe," she muttered, her voice a mix of scorn and desperation.

"Surrender, Lysandra." Aerin's stance was unyielding, his broadsword gleaming sinisterly in the firelight. "Your tricks won't save you now."

Her fingers twitched toward her sword, but magic pulsed eagerly and insistently beneath her skin. 'Not yet,' she warned herself. She needed a clear head, not a vortex.

"Never to the likes of you," she retorted, defiance lacing every syllable. King Draven will hear of your sorcery. You can't escape justice."

"Justice?" a bitter laugh escaped her. "Your king knows nothing of it," Lysandra said.

Aerin advanced towards her.

Lysandra's mind raced; there had to be a way out.

Suddenly, a familiar and unexpected shape flickered at the mouth of the alley—a shadow.

"Shadow!" Relief surged within her, but she quickly masked it and feigned despair. The wolf locked eyes with her, and a silent conversation passed between them.

"Even your beast knows it's over," Aerin sneered, misunderstanding the exchange.

Lysandra's gaze remained fixed on Shadow.

The wolf leaped into the fray in one fluid motion, snarling and a whirlwind of fur and fangs. Aerin spun around, caught off guard, his sword meeting only air as Shadow darted away, drawing him to follow.

"Go now!" Lysandra whispered to herself. She grabbed the opportunity amidst the chaos and ran despite her protesting muscles.

With each desperate footfall, the noise of Aerin's battle cries faded.

"Curse you, Lysandra!" Aerin's fury echoed off the walls, but Lysandra was already gone, slipping again into the maze-like city. Her heart pounded with a wild rhythm of survival.

"Thank you, my friend," she breathed into the night, knowing the wolf would hear her gratitude on the wind.

Chapter 4

AERIN

The forest of Tyrannis loomed around Aerin, a labyrinth of ancient trees shrouded in secrets as old as time itself. His boots sank into the mossy earth, tracking almost invisible footsteps, save for his trained eyes. Leaves rustled under his weight, betraying the silence of the hunt.

He whispered, "Come out, Lysandra." His voice was both threatening and pleading as it echoed through the trees. "This chase is pointless. You can't hide forever." But there was no response from the wilderness, only the mocking caw of a distant raven.

The delicate silver strands of hair he found caught on a thorn bush taunted him with their fragility, like moonlight threads. He knew she was close; he could smell her presence in the air—a mix of wildflowers and rebellion.

Aerin stopped to rest, leaning against a large oak tree, feeling the rough bark against his palm. He allowed himself a moment of rest and closed his eyes. Doubt crept into his thoughts as he muttered, "King Draven's iron fist crushes everything it touches. Is he doing justice, or is it just tyranny?"

He couldn't escape the image of King Draven's icy gaze, which seemed to pierce through one's soul, leaving nothing but dread behind. Yet loyalty bound him tighter than chains, gnawing at his conscience with sharp teeth.

"Should I be the sword or the shield?" he asked the wind. "When does the hunter spare the prey?"

His golden eyes snapped open, catching a flutter of movement—a shadow dancing beyond his sight. It could have been her, the last mage of Erenor, the woman who reared a wolf from a pup and wielded a rune-etched sword.

"Your tricks won't save you," Aerin called into the thickening gloom, his voice rising above the forest's whispers.

He sprinted forward, branches clawing at his face, leaving thin trails of blood that mingled with sweat. Each drop felt like a question, a challenge to his chosen path. Was he the hunter or the haunted?

His heart hammered against his chest with every stride, a drumbeat of conflict. For all his strength and skill, Aerin was a man torn between duty and doubt—a servant to a king whose crusade against magic seemed more like a personal vendetta than a noble cause.

"Is it honor that drives me? Or fear?" The words escaped him in ragged breaths, each heavier than the last.

Off in the distance, a wolf howled, a sound that spoke of freedom and wild, untamed power. Could it be Lysandra's companion? Was it a sign of her bond with nature and her defiance of the king's decrees?

"Why can't I catch her?" He growled, his frustration building like a storm.

Aerin was chasing her relentlessly, but Lysandra was quick and elusive. She moved through the trees like a ghost, always one step ahead, leaving behind only echoes of her presence. With each fleeting sign of her passage, Aerin's confidence faltered, unraveling like a cloak that had seen too many winters.

"Answer me, Lysandra! Are we pawns or players in this game?" he shouted, knowing full well the forest kept its secrets.

No answer came, just the fading light filtering through the canopy, casting long shadows that seemed to reach for him as if the very earth whispered of paths untraveled, choices unmade.

"Where does your loyalty lie, Hunter?" a voice asked, though whether it was his own or an apparition of the dusk, Aerin could not tell.

"Where indeed?"

Aerin's boots crunched through the underbrush, a staccato rhythm against the hush of the wild. The odor of damp earth rose in the air, mingling with the sharp tang of pine. He sharpened his every sense, becoming attuned to the whispers of the forest and the quarry he sought.

"Tracks here," he muttered, his eyes narrowing at the fresh disturbance in the loam—a delicate imprint half-hidden by a splay of ferns. You're close."

His fingers traced the outline, reading the story written in the dirt. Lysandra's steps were light but spoke volumes to a hunter's trained gaze. A snapped twig here, a displaced stone there—she was moving, yet her path was deliberate, almost mocking in its clarity.

"Always a step ahead," he grunted, wiping his brow. The weight of his sword at his side was a constant reminder of duty, its blade catching the dying light in a promise of cold steel.

He heard the faint rustle of leaves and spun, hand going for the hilt. But it was just a shadow dancing on the edge of his vision, a trick of the fading day. Lysandra was adept at bending nature to her will, her presence as elusive as the wind that now whispered through the branches.

"Come out and face me!" Aerin called out, his voice carrying further than he intended, laced with an edge of desperation he despised.

"Would you have me surrender to your king's justice?" Her voice floated back, ethereal and laced with irony. It was only a wisp of sound, yet it wrapped around him tighter than any shackle.

"Justice? Is that what we're calling it now?" he shot back, scanning the woods, trying to pinpoint her location. He pushed forward, every fiber straining to glimpse silver-blond hair or the gleam of her runic sword.

"Your words betray your doubts, Hunter," came her taunting reply, drifting from somewhere to his left, or was it his right?

"Cease this game!" he shouted, frustration boiling over.

"Perhaps when the game ceases to be deadly," she retorted, the air around him vibrating with the unspoken power of her words.

Aerin's stride quickened, his mind racing as fast as his feet. He ducked under a low branch, noticing the scratch it left across his cheek. His golden eyes scanned the twilight, seeking any hint of movement, any flicker of magic.

"Are you so certain of your cause, Aerin? Or does doubt gnaw at your heart?" Lysandra's voice teased, closer now, a phantom weaving between reality and illusion.

"Certainty is a luxury I cannot afford," he growled, leaping over a fallen log. "My cause is not my own."

"Then whose is it?" she challenged. A flutter of movement caught his attention—a scrap of cloth snagged on a thorn bush. It bore the same hue as the skies before a storm, the color of her eyes.

"Damn you, Lysandra," he breathed, snatching the fabric. It was part of her cloak, torn, a breadcrumb on a trail that led ever onward. His heart hammered against his ribs. Each beat a drum of war between duty and doubt.

"Will you chase shadows all your life, Aerin?" Her voice was almost tender now, a caress against the raw edges of his conscience.

"Better than living one," he spat, pushing through the undergrowth. His resolve hardened like the earth beneath the frost. The hunt was all he knew, the chase in a rhythm as old as time itself. Yet with each step and breath, the certainty of his purpose slipped like sand through his fingers.

"Seek, and you shall find," Lysandra murmured, her words a spell that seemed to hold the stars in thrall.

"Find, and you shall question," Aerin replied, his voice a whisper lost in the gathering darkness.

Aerin stood alone amidst gargantuan whispering pines. They stretched towards the sky like green fires at midday, providing a roost for invisible crows whose distant caws disturbed the eerie silence. He had become its lone sentinel in this mind-bending world where things were twisting out of sense.

His grip grew tighter around a fabric relic clenched within his fist - a shred torn from his cloak. The coarse weave made comforting impressions on his palm, while its dank scent conjured memories of rain-soaked nights under these trees. Its familiar taste lingered at the back of his tongue as if etched into existence by forgotten spells, a strange flavor that was earthy and raw.

This tangible remnant brought him closer to an elusive truth that gripped him just as tightly. It was elusive but authentic enough for him to feel its weight in every fiber of that decaying cloth, no less present than the cold, harsh reality of abandonment in this splintering world.

Aerin's boots sank into the soft loam, his breath ragged in the chill air. He scanned the silent forest, seeking any sign of Lysandra—a flicker of silver hair, a rustle in the underbrush—anything.

"Always one step ahead," he muttered, eyes catching on a fresh set of prints. Wolf tracks alongside humans, their path winding through the trees. Lysandra's wolf companion, no doubt. They were close now, closer than ever before.

The rustling of leaves to his left had him spinning, sword drawn. But it was only a bird, taking flight with a startled flap. His grip on the hilt tightened, frustration simmering beneath his skin. Lysandra was near a whisper in the wind, a ghost he couldn't grasp.

"Come out, Lysandra!" His voice broke the silence like a crack of thunder, and the forest held its breath. "This ends now!"

"Does it, Aerin?" her voice sang back, ethereal. "Or does it merely begin?"

He lunged toward the sound, but she was not there. Only shadows danced in mockery where he expected her to be. Her laughter echoed, a sound both haunting and beautiful.

"Your conviction, it falters," she called from somewhere unseen. "Can you not feel it?"

"Silence!" he shouted, chasing the echo. Branches snagged at his cloak, and thorns bit his flesh, but he pressed on. His heart raced, not just with the hunt but with doubt. Why did her words ring with such unsettling truth?

"Admit it, hunter," Lysandra taunted, her tone laced with challenge. "You fear what you might find."

"Never!" Aerin's reply was instant, a reflex born of stubborn pride.

Yet as he paused, chest heaving, he could not ignore the seed of uncertainty sprouting within. Her determination, her unwavering belief in her cause – it was something he couldn't dismiss. It gnawed at him, a persistent ache that begged attention.

"Face me!" he called into the gloom.

"You're not ready to see," she responded, almost gently.

Aerin charged through a thicket, emerging into a clearing. There, poised with her rune-etched sword, the wolf at her side, her stormy eyes met his golden gaze, fierce and unyielding.

"Ready or not, here I am," he growled, advancing.

"Look at you, so certain, so blind," she said, backing away with a grace that matched the wind.

Their swords clashed, creating the sound of a bright, metallic cry in the quiet woods. Sparks flew, reflecting in their eyes. She moved like water, flowing around his every strike, out of reach.

"Open your eyes, hunter," Lysandra breathed, ducking beneath his swing. "See the world for what it is."

"Enough of this!" He snarled, feinting left and striking right. But she was gone again, a wisp of smoke carried off by the breeze.

"Your king fears what he doesn't understand," she stated, her voice coming from everywhere and nowhere.

Aerin spun, searching, his sword a useless weight in his hand. "I serve the crown!"

"Serve or enslave yourself?" The question lingered, hanging between the trunks like a morning mist.

"Where are you?!" His roar was that of a wounded beast torn between rage and despair.

"Close," she whispered, so near he felt her breath in his ear. He whirled, but once more, she slipped from his clutches, leaving him grasping at empty air.

"Damn it!" Frustration boiled over. This game of cat and mouse wore thin the fabric of his resolve. Each narrow escape chipped away at the foundation of his beliefs. What was this elusive quarry that refused to be caught?

"Question everything, Aerin," Lysandra's voice floated back to him. "Even your loyalty." "Never." Yet even as he spoke, his conviction wavered like a flame in the wind.

"Until we meet again, hunter," she promised, her presence fading like the last star at dawn.

"Wait!" But it was too late. She vanished into the embrace of the forest, leaving Aerin alone with his swirling thoughts and the echoing doubt that maybe, just maybe, she was right.

Aerin's breath became ragged as he stumbled through the underbrush, the scent of damp earth and sweat mingling in his nostrils. He had lost sight of Lysandra moments ago, her trail a vanishing whisper among twisted tree roots and shadowed hollows.

"Confound it," he cursed under his breath, his fingers curling tighter around the hilt of his sword. The once-proud weapon felt cumbersome, an anchor dragging him deeper into confusion.

"King Draven speaks of purity, of cleansing Erenor from

corruption," Aerin muttered, words slicing through the quiet like his blade through the air. "Yet here I am, hunting one who may be the purest soul I've ever encountered."

The forest seemed to listen, ancient trees standing sentinel to his inner tumult. He paused at a brook, its waters babbling over stones, indifferent to the tempest brewing within him.

"Is it purity? Or fear?" His reflection stared back at him, his eyes the color of a lion's mane— predatory yet filled with an unspoken plea for understanding. "What do we become when we fear what we don't comprehend?"

"Speak your mind, hunter," a voice coaxed from the foliage, Lysandra's tone laced with a challenge that prickled his skin.

"Silence!" he shouted, swinging his gaze toward the sound. "You'll not turn my thoughts against me!"

"Your thoughts, or your king's?" Her question was a whisper, yet it roared louder than any battle cry in his ears.

"Draven seeks to protect us!" Aerin shot back, though the conviction waned, a dying echo in his ears.

"From what? Our true selves?" Another rustle, a flutter of leaves, and she might have been a ghost for all the presence she held.

"Enough! Come out and face me!" His command fell flat, merging with the forest's cadences.

"Face you, or face yourself? You hunt me, but it is your doubt that pursues you," she retorted, the truth of her words coiling around him like vines.

"Damn you, Lysandra," he seethed, slamming his fist against

a tree trunk. The bark bit into his skin, a tangible pain easier to confront than the mire in his heart.

"Your loyalty has blinded you, Aerin. King Draven drowns in paranoia, and you are with him. Magic is not our enemy; ignorance is." Her voice was a caress, both soothing and scorching.

"Magic killed my parents!" Aerin's shout tore through the woods, a raw wound exposed to the elements.

"And yet here you stand, a magic-bearer himself. What does that make you in the eyes of your beloved king?" The silence that followed was pregnant with unvoiced fears.

"An aberration? A mistake?" His questions bore down on him, heavier than any armor.

"Or perhaps, a savior waiting to awaken," she offered, her voice now so distant it could have been a dream.

"Stop playing games!" he demanded, tension knotting every muscle.

"Life is no game, hunter. We play for keeps. And sometimes, we must decide which side we're truly on."

"Where are you?" he growled, desperation bleeding into his words.

"Everywhere you are not," she replied, the sound retreating until they left him with nothing but the echo of his conflicted soul.

Aerin's breath misted in the chill morning air, a spectral dance of heat and life in the cold. He crouched low, his golden eyes scanning the dew-kissed underbrush for signs of her passage.

Lysandra was out there, always just out of reach. The memory of her voice lingered, a haunting melody that clashed against the ironclad oaths he'd sworn to King Draven.

"Confound it," he muttered, touching a blond hair caught on a bramble—a deliberate sign from Lysandra. His hand recoiled as if stung; doubts crept in like serpents through the cracks of his resolve.

"Your father would've never wavered," a gruff voice shattered his solitude. Commander Verek emerged from the shadows, armored in the regime's dogma. "Time is short, Aerin. We can't afford your sentimentality."

"Sentimentality?" Aerin echoed, rising to face Verek. "Is it sentimentality to question what we hunt? To wonder if we're hounds or wolves?"

"Questions are luxuries, boy. The King wants results, not philosophy." Verek's gaze fixed on him, a vice tightening around Aerin's chest.

"Her conviction... It's unshakable," Aerin confessed. His voice was just above a whisper, each word a stone in his belly. "She fights for something greater than survival."

"Survival is all there is," Verek snapped. "Catch her, or I will find someone who can."

"Understood." Aerin's response was automatic, honed by years of obedience. Yet, as he turned away, his heart rebelled, a drumbeat of defiance growing louder within.

Every step was a battle. With Lysandra's subtle taunts leading him ever onward, memories ambushed him. He recalled the smoldering remains of the mage guilds, the screams still echoing in his ears. He had been too late then, just as he was now—always chasing, never catching.

"Who am I hunting for, Verek?" Aerin's thoughts were knives, cutting into the fabric of his beliefs. "For the King? Or for peace of mind?"

"Peace is a lie, Aerin. It's the control that keeps the realm together," Verek called out, following him with the persistence of a shadow.

"Control..." Aerin tasted the word, bitter and metallic, on his tongue. "Or fear?"

"Enough!" Verek's patience frayed. "The mage must be stopped. You know the chaos magic bringers wrought upon our world."

"Stopped, yes. But at what cost?" Aerin's gaze traced the horizon, where the wilderness of Tyrannis whispered secrets he was only beginning to understand.

"Whatever cost is necessary," Verek declared, steel in his voice. "You are the hunter, Aerin. Now hunt!"

"Or be hunted," Aerin murmured, more to himself than Verek. The commander's words fanned the flames of urgency, yet Aerin felt the weight of his conscience, heavy as the sword at his side.

"If you Fail, it won't be just her blood staining your hands," Verek warned before disappearing into the thicket.

Alone once more, Aerin pressed on, tracking Lysandra through the dense wilderness. Each clue she left was a breadcrumb leading him further into a labyrinth of moral ambiguity. His superiors demanded victory, but the price of such victory gnawed at his soul.

"Magic killed my parents," he repeated the mantra, trying to stoke the embers of hatred he once held. But the fire wouldn't catch; an icy dread settled over him, chilling him.

"Yet, here I am," Aerin conceded, his powers slumbering within, a dragon awaiting the kiss of consciousness. "What does that make me? A traitor to my king? Or a traitor to myself?"

With every step, the hunter felt more hunted, pursued by the specter of truth he was not yet ready to face.

Aerin's breath misted in the cold air as he crouched, fingers brushing over the disturbed earth. The imprint of a boot, not yet filled by the falling ash, pointed northward. A smirk touched his lips; Lysandra was close. Too close for comfort.

"Running won't save you," he whispered to the silent forest, his voice a blend of threat and grudging respect.

The wolf that shadowed Lysandra had been clever, erasing much of her trail, but the snap of a twig underfoot betrayed her presence. Aerin surged forward, muscles coiling and uncoiling like a spring, his golden eyes scanning for the fleeting silver flash of her hair.

"Come out, Lysandra!" he called out, his voice echoing through the barren trees.

There was a rustle to his left—a whisper of movement—and then he saw her. Silver hair cascaded down her back, stormy eyes glaring at him from behind a thicket. She brandished her sword, runes glowing along the blade. Her wolf growled a low, threatening sound that raised the hairs on Aerin's nape.

"Yield," Aerin demanded, drawing his weapon. "Never." Her voice was ice, her stance unyielding.

They circled each other, two predators locked in a dance as old as time. His heart hammered against his chest—not with fear, but with the thrill of the hunt and an emotion he couldn't quite name.

"Join me," he yelled, "end this madness."

"Madness?" she spat, lunging forward. Their swords clashed, sparks flying. "Your king's crusade is the madness!"

He dodged, but she was quick, slipping away like water between his fingers. As she retreated, a lock of her hair brushed against his cheek, leaving a scent that stirred memories he struggled to suppress.

"Draven's reign is just," he countered, though his voice lacked conviction.

"Justice?" Lysandra laughed, her voice bitter. Where's justice for those with magic in their blood?"

Aerin hesitated, her words slicing through him more effectively than any blade. He thought he saw a flicker of sympathy in her gaze, but it vanished as quickly as it appeared. She feinted left, then pivoted right, forcing him to stumble backward.

"Blind loyalty will be your downfall," she taunted, her confidence fueling his frustration.

"Perhaps," Aerin grunted, narrowing his eyes. "But it's not today."

Their blades met again, a symphony of metal and might. Yet, with each exchange, Aerin found his admiration for Lysandra growing. She fought with conviction, with a fire that seemed to burn away the lies they had fed him.

"Is it worth it, Aerin?" she pressed, her words punctuated by the clash of steel. "Hunting your kind?"

"Silence!" he barked, unwilling to entertain the doubts clawing at his mind.

But the silence did not follow. Instead, a thunderous rumble shook the ground beneath their feet. They paused, weapons still crossed, as a flock of blackbirds erupted from the canopy above, fleeing into the gray sky.

In that moment of distraction, Lysandra's eyes met his, and he saw not a fugitive but a warrior—undaunted and unwavering. Before he could react, she slipped away once more, vanishing into the woods with her loyal wolf at her heels.

"Damn you," Aerin cursed, his admiration tinged with ire. She was more than just a quarry; she was his equal or better.

"Next time," he promised the empty air, knowing their game of cat and mouse was far from over.

Aerin's boots sank into the soft earth as he trudged through the dense underbrush, each step a silent oath to his duty. The scent of pine and wet moss clung to the air, thick as the fog that shrouded the forest of Tyrannis. His breath formed white clouds in the chilling night, and his eyes scanned the shadows for any sign of Lysandra.

"Where are you?" he muttered, more to himself than to the

elusive mage he pursued.

The forest replied with a mocking whisper, carried by the wind rustling through the leaves—a symphony of nature that cloaked her movements. He pushed forward, his hand tight on the hilt of his sword, the weight of his superiors' expectations pressing down like the overbearing canopy above.

"Running won't save you," Aerin called out, his voice edged with a blend of threat and plea.

"Neither will blind loyalty," came the retort from somewhere within the scrub, Lysandra's voice dancing just out of reach.

"Show yourself!" He swung his blade, severing a branch that dared to impede his path.

"Are you afraid to face the truth?" Her taunt was a specter, haunting the spaces between the trees.

Aerin halted, weighing her words against the pounding of his heart. He clenched his fists, anger, and uncertainty warring beneath his skin. His belief in King Draven's regime had once been unshakable, but now, cracks formed with every step he took after the defiant mage.

"Truth is a matter of perspective," he growled, slicing through another web of undergrowth. "And mine is clear."

"Is it?" The question lingered, echoing off the ancient trunks surrounding him.

He paused at a small clearing, the moon breaking through the treetops to cast silver light upon the dew-laden grass. The sight of a single crimson petal—a subtle clue left behind by Lysandra—caught his eye. Picking it up, Aerin felt its velvet surface, a stark contrast to the callouses of war etched into his hands.

"Enough games, Lysandra!" His shout pierced the nighttime stillness, demanding an end to the chase.

"Perhaps the game is not ours to end," she whispered, so close he could almost feel the warmth of her breath.

Aerin spun, sword ready, but found only emptiness where she should have been. A cold laugh lingered where warmth had been promised, and his breath hitched in his chest. With each encounter, Lysandra seemed less like prey and more like a mirror, reflecting his deep doubts.

"Join me, Aerin," her voice beckoned a Siren's call amidst the crashing waves of his resolve. "See what lies beyond Draven's deceit."

"Silence!" he commanded the darkness, his voice betraying the turmoil inside. "I swore an oath!" "Oaths can be prisons," she replied, her words an essential turning in the lock of his convictions.

"Or they can be salvation," he insisted, though his heart no longer echoed the certainty. "Look around you, hunter! Who needs saving?"

The question hung heavy in the air, and Aerin felt its weight settle on his shoulders. His orders were clear: capture Lysandra and return her to face the king's justice. But justice, he realized, was another word twisted by perspective.

"Choose wisely," she urged, sensing his inner struggle. "Your future depends on it."

A distant howl sliced through the tension, a primal sound of freedom and wild things unchained. And with it, the world seemed to hold its breath, waiting for Aerin's decision.

His gaze fell upon the trail ahead, the path well-traveled by duty and loyalty. Yet beside it lay another route, obscured by shadows and uncertainty—the path Lysandra walked.

"Damn you, Lysandra," he whispered, his voice only just audible above the heartbeat of the forest.

Aerin realized he had reached a crossroads, his hand loosening on the grip of his sword. The way forward was shrouded in mist and mystery, and his choice now would set the course of his journey.

Aerin's boots sank into the damp undergrowth, each step a silent vow of pursuit. The moon's glow filtered through the canopy, casting a lattice of shadows across his path. Ahead, the trail beckoned, winding ever deeper into the woods that cloaked Tyrannis.

"I can't shake you that easily," he muttered, his eyes scanning for any sign of her passage. His breath fogged in the chilly air, mingling with the earthy scents of moss and decay.

"Where are you?" The words were a peaceful challenge to the night, half expecting a whisper of response from the darkness.

The forest offered no answer, only the rustle of leaves and the distant call of nocturnal beasts. Aerin pressed on; her senses heightened to every shift in the wind and every snap of a twig underfoot.

"Left a mark here," he observed, crouching to inspect a broken branch. "Clever, but not clever enough." His fingers traced the jagged edge, feeling the raw energy humming within the splintered wood.

"Are you still playing games, Lysandra?" His voice was grudgingly respectful—she was skilled, no doubt, but he was relentless.

"Games? No, hunter." Her voice floated out from the shadows, a taunting specter. "I'm fighting for my life."

He spun, hand on the hilt of his sword, seeking the source. "Show yourself!" "Wouldn't be wise." A soft laugh echoed around him. "Not for either of us."

"Defying the king is already unwise," he shot back, squinting into the thicket where he thought she might be hiding.

"Perhaps. But what if the king is wrong?" "Wrong?" Aerin's grip tightened. "He is justice."

"Is he?" The question hung in the air like a spell, potent and provoking.

"Enough of this," Aerin growled, moving forward with renewed determination. He could feel her nearness—a magnetic pull towards an uncertain truth.

"Can you not feel it, hunter?" She was moving now, her presence a fleeting shadow against the moonlit ground. "The magic in your veins, the power you deny?"

"Magic is forbidden!" Aerin's protest was vehement, yet a sliver of doubt wormed its way into his heart.

"By a king who fears it," she countered, unseen.

"Stop!" he bellowed, lunging toward where her voice had last sounded, only to grasp at empty air.

"Make your choice, Aerin," she urged, her tone almost pleading.

His pulse thundered in his ears, the weight of his decision anchoring him to the spot. King Draven's orders screamed in his mind, but so did the echo of Lysandra's conviction.

"Choose." The word was a whisper, a summoning of destiny or damnation.

Aerin's breath came in ragged heaves as the moment's urgency clawed at his resolve. He could almost touch the tendrils of magic that danced just beyond perception, calling him toward a different path—one shrouded in secrecy and sorcery.

"Which way?" he demanded, his voice cracking with the strain of his internal battle.

"Only you can decide that," she replied, her silhouette finally materializing from the gloom.

"Damn it all." Aerin's hand fell away from his weapon, his body teetering on the brink of action and indecision.

"Time waits for no man," Lysandra whispered, and then she was gone once more, leaving Aerin alone with the ghosts of his thoughts and the whisper of possibility that flickered through the forest, as elusive and compelling as the woman he hunted.

Chapter 5

TRAVELERS

A sliver of the moon visible through the window provided dimmer lighting for the space. Piles of belongings were scattered haphazardly across the cold stone floor. Lysandra quickly gathered her things, putting only the essentials into her worn leather satchel.

"We have to travel light," Feyla said urgently, scanning the room with practiced eyes.

Lysandra nodded in agreement, a sense of unease creeping over her. She stopped to pat down her cloak, ensuring the hidden pockets held the artifacts that hummed with magic against her skin. She felt for the talisman of warding, the vial of starlight essence, and the shard of crystal from the shattered spire of Andora.

"Are they safe?" Feyla asked, breaking Lysandra's concentration.

"They're always safe," Lysandra whispered, reassuring herself as much as her friend. The artifacts were her lifeline—the few remnants of a world where magic was alive in every corner.

"Good, because without them..." Feyla didn't finish her sentence, but the implication hung between them like a guillotine's blade.

"Without them, we're as good as dead," Lysandra said, holding her suitcase tightly. Her determination grew stronger with every passing moment. "But we won't fail. Not now."

Feyla nodded in agreement as she slung her bag over her shoulder. Its contents were unknown but undoubtedly deadly. The sound of clinking vials and rustling parchment hinted at hidden secrets—tools of both knowledge and war.

"Shadow!" Lysandra called out softly. The wolf, a silent guardian with fur as dark as night, padded to her side, his amber eyes shining with loyalty and understanding. She placed a hand on his head, finding comfort in his presence.

"Let's go," Feyla urged, peering out the window at the desolate alleyway below. "We have a long road ahead."

"Indeed," Lysandra agreed, slipping her sword belt around her waist. The metal was cool against her fingertips, and there was no turning back.

The two women looked at each other with fear and bravery. They left behind their old lives and the crumbling walls of Tyrannis as they ventured into the unknown darkness of the night.

Feyla clutched a small leather device, and before leaving, she stopped and said, "Wait, we need to take this with us."

Lysandra looked at the device and asked, "What's the use of that thing now?"

"More than you know." Feyla's voice was a whisper, but it carried the weight of stone. She unwrapped the device slowly, revealing a semblance of gears and a vial of murky liquid nestled within. "One twist, a cloud thick enough to blind fate herself."

Despite the gnawing anxiety, Lysandra carved a smile onto her lips. "Clever girl," she murmured.

"Always." Feyla pocketed the invention before they stepped into Tyrannis' labyrinthine alleys.

The city was like a serpent, coiling and twisting with its scales made up of dark buildings.

The two companions silently moved through its streets, their feet touching the cobblestone. Lysandra led the way, her senses alert to every possible danger and threat. Every Shadow and echo was a potential doom to her.

"Take a left here," whispered Feyla from behind. Her words were almost inaudible in the night.

"Are you sure?" Lysandra asked, not looking back.

"Trust me, I've memorized these streets," Feyla replied.

Lysandra thought "memorized" wasn't the correct word. Feyla had devoured Tyrannis's layout, memorizing every alley and byway like a mapmaker's dream.

They dove under low archways and skirted around refuse, the stench a foul reminder of the city's decay. They were phantoms flitting from one pool of darkness to another, each step dancing with danger, each breath a silent plea to remain unseen.

"Almost through," Feyla whispered, eyes scanning the narrow passage ahead.

"Good," Lysandra replied, her thoughts a stormy sea within. The weight of responsibility pressed against her chest, heavier with each step. "We're not safe yet," she reminded herself. "Not until we breach the city's edge."

"Here." Feyla gestured to a door half-concealed by shadows. "Shortcut."

"Or a trap," Lysandra countered, but she followed Feyla's lead, her trust in her friend as unwavering as the steel at her side.

The door creaked open, protesting the intrusion, but they slipped through, the gap swallowing them whole. Inside, the air was musty, the remnants of abandonment clinging to the walls.

"Through here, then right," Feyla directed, her hand steady on the device she had yet to unleash. "Keep it ready," Lysandra said, her heart thrumming fiercely. "Just in case."

"I always am," Feyla assured, a grin slicing through the tension.

They emerged again into the night, the cityscape a tapestry

of shadows and half-lights. Their eyes met—two sparks in the dark, resilience reflected in their gaze.

"Nearly there," Lysandra promised, the taste of freedom bitter on her tongue. "Stay close."

"Where else would I be?" Feyla returned, her loyalty as tangible as the magic pulsing through Lysandra's veins.

Together, they moved, bound by purpose and driven by need. Silence was their ally, and the night was their shroud. And as Tyrannis's walled embrace loomed ever closer, so too did the promise of perilous freedom.

Shadow's hackles rose, a silent alarm in the chill of the night. Lysandra's hand went to the hilt of her sword, its familiar contours grounding her as she pressed against the crumbling wall. The wolf's low growl was almost invisible but spoke volumes to Lysandra's trained senses.

"Shh," she whispered, reassuringly touching Shadow's coarse fur. "Stay quiet, my friend."

Feyla crouched beside her, her breath shallow, her eyes wide with the knowledge of what prowled nearby. The compact device—a lifeline in her grip—seemed to pulse anxiously.

"Patrol," Feyla breathed, barely audible.

"Draven's hunters," Lysandra confirmed, her eyes scanning the darkness. She could feel the pulse of magic within her, an undercurrent to the danger that stalked them.

They heard the clink of armor, the muffled conversation carrying through the still air. The words were indistinguishable, yet the two women did not lose sight of their intent: Capture, conquer, kill.

"Stay down," Lysandra instructed a commander even now. It wasn't just her life at stake; Feyla and Shadow were bound to her fate. Her responsibility.

"Always with the orders," Feyla quipped, a feeble attempt to lighten the heaviness that threatened to suffocate them.

"Would you prefer 'please'?" Lysandra countered, but her smirk was short-lived. They both knew that pleasantries had no place here.

"Save it for when we're clear," Feyla returned, her fingers twitching around her invention. She was ready to unleash chaos if need be, her mind already calculating trajectories and escape routes.

"Can't afford mistakes," Lysandra mused inwardly, her thoughts whirling like a storm. She envisioned the open plains beyond Tyrannis, freedom a mere whisper away.

"Keep it together," Feyla muttered, her gaze never leaving the patrolling figures that lurked dangerously close.

"Of course I will," Lysandra replied, her voice a blade, sharp and sure. Yet doubt gnawed at her—about the journey, the dangers they would face, and the weight of destiny that clung to her like a shroud.

The hunters' voices faded, and tension coiled within Lysandra, springing tight. Shadow's ears twitched, angling toward safety, toward silence. The wolf's instincts mirrored her own: Wait. Watch. Move.

"Go," Lysandra finally said, the word slicing through the

hesitation.

They moved as one, a trio of shadows slipping through the city's embrace, each step a silent vow. With Shadow at her side, his presence a living compass, and Feyla's unwavering courage flanking her, Lysandra found strength in their unity.

"Almost out," she murmured, more to herself than Feyla or Shadow. The words were a mantra, a beacon.

"Then let's not dawdle," Feyla replied, her determination a match for the magic that surged beneath Lysandra's skin.

"Lead on," Lysandra responded, her resolve a fortress against the encroaching darkness.

Together, they vanished into the labyrinth of Tyrannis, the city's secrets cloaking their flight while the thrill of the chase pulsed hotly in their veins.

The city was eerily quiet as Lysandra and Feyla stepped into the open square. The moon cast a pale light on the cobblestones, turning each step into a potential hazard.

Lysandra gripped her sword tightly, ready to defend them from any danger. "Let's move quickly and quietly," she whispered, scanning the area for any signs of trouble.

"Like ghosts," Feyla agreed, clutching her smoke device like a lifeline.

They moved carefully, trying not to make a sound as they ran across the square.

Lysandra led the way, with Shadow, her loyal companion, beside her. Feyla followed closely, breathing steadily to keep her nerves under control. Suddenly, they spotted the patrol, a group of shadowy figures loyal to a king they no longer served.

"We need to avoid them," Lysandra said softly, her voice tense.

Feyla nodded in agreement, and they changed their route, moving quickly and quietly in the opposite direction.

"Get down," Lysandra hissed, and they dropped to the ground, blending in with the shadows as the patrol strolled past, completely unaware of their presence. The air was thick with the scent of iron and oil, and Shadow's growl threatened to escape but remained locked behind bare teeth.

"Let's go," Lysandra commanded, and they rushed towards a decrepit building that looked like it had been abandoned for years, its walls covered in scars of time.

Feyla guided Lysandra towards the entrance, and they slipped inside, the building swallowing them whole.

"Safe...for now," Feyla panted, collapsing against the wall.

Lysandra nodded, catching her breath against the cold stone, allowing herself a moment of weakness. Her hand still clung to her sword, a reminder of the power she held within her.

"We can't stay here for long," Lysandra breathed out, her heart racing with every beat.

"Long enough to plan our next steps," Feyla countered, her

eyes gleaming with a mix of mischief and intellect.

"North," Lysandra decided. "Through the Ashen Woods." " Brilliant and mad," Feyla chuckled. "Just how I like it."

A fleeting smile came and went around Lysandra's lips. "You're the brilliant one. I'm just the mad."

"Without a doubt," Feyla agreed, her wit a brief respite from the weight of their plight.

"Rest. Then we move," Lysandra ordered, though her body screamed for reprieve. She dared not close her eyes, fearing the visions of pursuit that would haunt her sleep.

"Rest," Feyla echoed, though neither moved just yet. They were warriors in a lull between breaths, between battles. The silence of the forsaken room settled around them, a temporary ally in a world brimming with foes.

Feyla whispered, "Whatever happens next, we'll face it together," firmly grasping Lysandra's hand.

"Always," Lysandra replied, returning the grip. They both knew their bond was unbreakable and that they would brave whatever was to come together.

Shadow's growl broke the silence —a low rumble in the dark corner of the old, dilapidated building. The wolf's amber eyes peered through the darkness, sensing the danger that was unseen but deeply felt.

Lysandra's hand rested on Shadow's head, her fingers running through its coarse fur.

"Shadow senses it too," Lysandra murmured, her voice barely audible over the wolf's vigilance. "The danger that's lurking nearby."

"Well, at least he's with us," Feyla replied, crouching beside a contraption of gears and tubes - her latest invention designed to create confusion.

Lysandra looked through the cracked walls into the darkness beyond, her expression filled with worry. "Feyla... this journey is dangerous. I dragged you into this."

"I chose to come," Feyla said, abandoning her device to look Lysandra in the eye. "I stand by you because I want to, not because I was forced to."

"But what if something happens to you?" Lysandra asked, her grip on her sword tightening.

"Stop," Feyla said firmly. "Your path is one of destiny. Mine is one of loyalty. We're intertwined, Lysandra."

"Is it destiny or a curse?" Lysandra muttered, her mind racing as she considered what would happen next.

"Perhaps both," Feyla allowed, standing up. Her hand reached out, clasping Lysandra's shoulder. "But we face it as we always have – together."

"Even against Draven's hunters? Against the whole of Tyrannis?" Lysandra's voice cracked like a whip, her tension palpable.

"Especially then," Feyla affirmed, her resolve steeling. "I'd face down shadow hounds again before I let you do this alone."

"Friends to the end," Lysandra said, a wry smile flickering across her lips.

"Beyond it," Feyla returned, matching the smile with hers. "Now, let's move. Every moment here is a shadow's breadth from death."

"Agreed." Lysandra rose, Shadow at her side, his muscles taut as coiled springs. They stepped out from their makeshift haven, the night air cool against their skin, the promise of sorcery and swordplay written in the stars above.

Lysandra's eyes, stormy as the sea, caught the gleam of starlight on Feyla's compact device. It was a small thing, but in it lay a hope as vast as the night sky above them. Her fingers brushed the runes etched into her sword, feeling their promises of protection and power hum beneath her touch.

"Are you sure about this?" Lysandra's voice was quiet but firm, her gaze locked on Feyla's determined face.

"More than I've ever been," Feyla replied, her hands deftly checking over the straps of her satchel, ensuring everything was secure. "We're not just fleeing. We're advancing towards our fate."

Lysandra allowed herself a nod, the knot of worry in her stomach unwinding ever so slightly. She couldn't deny the truth that resonated in those words. Alone, she was formidable; with Feyla, they were indomitable.

"Then we advance together," Lysandra said, her voice gaining strength. Shadow nudged her hand with his nose, a silent vow to guard and guide.

"Without hesitation," Feyla added, flipping the hood of her cloak over her head, shrouding her features in mystery.

They slipped from the safety of the dilapidated building, the darkness enveloping them like a second skin.

The streets of Tyrannis were a labyrinth, but each twist and turn brought them closer to freedom.

Lysandra felt the weight of her sword at her hip, an old friend whispering reassurances. With every step, her resolve was cemented further.

"Remember, if we're spotted—" Lysandra began, her senses alert for any sign of danger.

"Smoke and confusion," Feyla finished, patting the device. "I remember. But let's hope it doesn't come to that."

"Let's, indeed." Lysandra tightened her grip on her sword handle.

Their path wound through narrow alleys, over crumbling walls, a dance of shadows and silence. They moved as one, a symphony of stealth and determination. Each breath and heartbeat was a step away from tyranny, a step towards destiny.

"Draven can send all his hunters," Feyla whispered fiercely as they paused in the Shadow of a towering oak.

"Let him." Lysandra's smile was a blade in the dark. "We're more than he bargains for."

"Always have been." Feyla's eyes sparkled with a mix of mischief and courage.

With a sharp gesture from Lysandra, they broke into a run, crossing the open square under the cloak of night. Their feet barely whispered against the cobblestones, but her heart roared like thunder inside Lysandra's chest.

They didn't look back when the stakes were life and liberty—or death and chains. The city limits loomed ahead, a line on a map and their lives. Crossing it meant no turning back.

"Ready?" Lysandra asked though she knew the answer.

"Since the day we met," Feyla responded, her grin invisible but palpable.

Together, they stepped over the threshold away from Tyrannis's oppression. Ahead of them stretched the unknown, a realm of magic and mayhem. Lysandra's destiny called to her, a siren song weaving through the fabric of the night.

"Let's find your destiny," Feyla said, her voice low but unshakeable.

"Let's make it ours," Lysandra corrected. And with that, they vanished into the night, two souls intertwined by fate, bound for legend.

The outskirts of Tyrannis were still a labyrinth, a tangle of shadows and whispers where Lysandra and Feyla trod lightly. Overgrown vines clutched at their clothes like grasping fingers, and the ruins of old walls loomed as silent sentinels to the passages they once guarded.

"Through here," Lysandra murmured, pointing to a crevice veiled by the drooping branches of a weeping willow.

"Looks tight," Feyla whispered back, but she didn't hesitate, her figure slipping through the gap with the ease of water flowing around stones. The clinking of her tools was muffled, each one a secret kept closed.

"Trust the paths," Lysandra thought, her mind reaching the city's pulse. "They know our steps."

The passage wound beneath the earth, cool and damp against

their skin. Their breaths came in short, controlled bursts, mingling with the scent of moss and ancient stone. Here, away from prying eyes, magic hummed—a low, vibrant thrum that teased at Lysandra's senses.

"Almost there." Lysandra's voice ricocheted softly off the tunnel walls.

Feyla whispered, "Quick and quiet," her hand resting on the smokescreen device at her belt—her last unused move.

Suddenly, a low growl rumbled through the silence, jolting their nerves. Shadow had stopped in his tracks, on high alert, ears pricked.

Lysandra sensed something was off. "What's wrong?"

"Shadow smells them," Feyla said, her voice tense.

"Stay down," Lysandra ordered, her hand moving to Shadow's fur. The wolf's muscles were taut, ready for action.

Feyla's voice quivered. "Can we sneak around them?"

Lysandra shook her head. "Too dangerous. They're too close."

"We can't stay here in the open," Feyla protested.

Lysandra's gaze fixed on Shadow. "We have no other choice.

Shadow won't lead us astray."

They fell silent, every second ticking by with agonizing slowness. Lysandra's hand rested on her sword hilt, ready to strike if necessary.

The silence was suffocating. Feyla's affirmation broke it. "Right."

A few moments they were passed before the danger seemed to pass. They breathed a sigh of relief and rose.

The sound of faraway footsteps from the hunters above and the steady breathing of two fugitives and their guardian wolf below only broke the monotony of the minutes that passed. As if mocking their situation, shadows danced over the walls, the specters of a fate they hoped to avoid.

"Patience," Lysandra reminded herself. The word was a mantra, a spell woven from the strands of hope and necessity.

"Always," Feyla answered, though no words had been spoken aloud. It was the bond between them—a connection deeper than blood.

Lysandra's fingers tightened on Shadow's fur, and the wolf responded with a nuzzle, his presence a silent vow. They would not be found tonight or when destiny beckoned with such enthusiasm.

"Ready to move?" Lysandra asked when the footsteps faded—more felt than heard.

"Lead the way." Feyla's reply was swift, and her resolve was unbreakable.

They emerged from the Shadow of the tunnel, the city's oppressive weight a receding memory. Ahead lay the freedom of the wilds and the dangerous embrace of an untamed world. Lysandra glanced at Feyla and then at Shadow, the trio united by something more significant than circumstance.

"Let's go," she said, and together, they stepped forward, melding with the night as if they were born from its very essence.

A shadow crept across the cobblestones, elongating like a dark stain as the moon peeked from behind scudding clouds. Lysandra's sea-green eyes flicked to Feyla, a silent command passing between them. They shrank back into the gloom of an alcove, their bodies pressed against the excellent, rough stone.

"Boots approaching," Feyla whispered, her voice barely audible over the thump of her own heart.

"Too many to be casual passersby," Lysandra replied, her hand instinctively reaching for the hilt of her rune-etched sword, though she dared not draw it yet.

The clatter of armored feet grew louder, and Shadow's ears twitched. His body tensed like a spring coiled to release. Lysandra felt each beat of her pulse as if it were a drum of war calling her to action, but she held still, knowing the value of silence over steel.

"Think they know?" Feyla's question hung in the air, ripe with unspoken fears.

"Only if we let them." The confidence in Lysandra's whisper

belied the cold sweat on her brow.

Two hunters emerged, their cloaks billowing and their eyes scanning the darkness with predatory focus. Lysandra recognized the symbol on their breastplates—King Draven's mark—and suppressed a shiver.

"Nothing here," one grunted, his voice gruff and dismissive. "Keep moving," ordered the other. "They can't have gone far."

Shadow's growl was a soft rumble, a warning that death would be promised should they be discovered. Lysandra's grip tightened on Shadow's fur, urging him to be patient.

"Stay down, boy," she breathed, and the wolf obeyed his loyalty ironclad.

The hunters' footsteps receded, their presence diminishing every second until only the night's chorus filled the void they left behind.

"Clear." Feyla finally exhaled her relief, a tangible thing in the cramped space.

"Stay alert," Lysandra cautioned as she led the way forward, her movements dancing light and Shadow. "We're not out of the woods yet."

"Never are," Feyla muttered, checking over her shoulder one last time before following.

They slipped through the city's labyrinthine streets, a maze to trap the unwary. But they were no ordinary prey. With every step, they wove themselves deeper into the fabric of the night, becoming whispers in the wind.

Lysandra said, her voice honed to a razor's edge by urgency,

"Remember the plan."

"Stick to the shadows, avoid open spaces, and keep moving." Feyla's response came as rote; her invention—a compact device ready to spew smokescreen—clutched like a talisman in her hand.

"Exactly." Lysandra's thoughts raced ahead, plotting courses and anticipating challenges. The weight of her destiny bore down on her, but she would not falter—not with Feyla at her side or Shadow as their guardian.

"I thought I'd be sleeping in my bed tonight," Feyla mused, a touch of wry humor in her tone.

"Sleep is a luxury we can't afford," Lysandra countered, but her lips twitched in the ghost of a smile.

"Right. Who needs sleep when you've got adrenaline?" Feyla's chuckle was a muted spark in the darkness.

"Adrenaline, magic, and swords," Lysandra added, her stormy gaze piercing the night. "That's all we need."

And with that, they continued onward, two figures bound by fate, cutting through the dark tapestry of Tyrannis with threads of their own making.

The city's silhouette, a jagged crown against the starless sky, shrank behind them. With each hurried step, Lysandra felt Tyrannis's chains loosen, their escape almost tangible in the cool night air.

"Freedom has a strange scent," Feyla whispered, her breath misting. "Like damp earth after rain."

"Or blood on steel," Lysandra replied.

"Always with the drama," Feyla teased, but her gaze lingered on the walls they'd left behind. "You think we made it? Truly?"

Lysandra's eyes flickered. "We're out, but not safe. Not yet."

"Never simple with you, is it?" Feyla observed, her fingers nervously adjusting the straps of her invention: a click, a buzz, readiness for the smoke that could save or doom them.

"Simple died with my mother," Lysandra snapped, instantly regretting her sharpness. "Forgive me."

"Nothing to forgive." Feyla's soft voice was a balm to Lysandra's fraying nerves. We share this road wherever it leads."

"Even to the end?" Lysandra asked, her gaze fixed on the path unfolding before them—unknown and frightening.

"Especially to the end." Feyla's resolve was ironclad, her loyalty unshaken. "Together."

Shadow padded silently beside them, its fur a ripple of darkness against darkness. The wolf's ears twitched, tuned to threats lurking beyond sight.

"Quiet now," Lysandra cautioned as they neared the crumbling remains of an old watchtower—their final landmark before true wilderness.

"Feels like stepping off a map," Feyla muttered, peering into the abyss where the future lay shrouded.

"Maps can be redrawn," Lysandra said, her tone fierce with conviction.

There was a pause, a collective inhale. They stood on the precipice of their new reality. Every sense was heightened, and every muscle was coiled for action.

"Look back if you must," Feyla said quietly, sensing Lysandra's reluctance to sever the last thread, tying her to Tyrannis.

"Only to burn it into memory," Lysandra resolved, turning for a fleeting glimpse of the city that had birthed and betrayed her. The image seared into her mind—Tyrannis, once home, now a land of ghosts and broken oaths.

"Let's go," Lysandra commanded, squaring her shoulders against the weight of her fate.

"Let's do this," said Feyla, her device held tightly, symbolizing hope amidst the unknown. They took a step forward, and darkness enveloped them. Every move they made challenged the dangers ahead, and they were ready to face them together. They were not just companions but warriors prepared to fight for their cause.

"No matter what comes our way," Lysandra declared, "we will face it together as one."

"We will stick together until the end of the world," Feyla promised, and the vow was sealed in the silence of the void.

Beyond the grasp of Tyrannis' shadows, Lysandra and Feyla disappeared into the unknown, ready to face the trials that awaited them.

They were prepared to fight with everything they had and knew the journey ahead would test them in ways they had never imagined. But they also knew they were strong enough to overcome any obstacle and emerge victorious.

Chapter 6

HOPE AND HEALING

Lysandra watched from a shadowy alley as clanging armor echoed through the dusty streets. The people in the town looked hungry and desperate. A woman approached a soldier, asking for water for her child, but the soldier shoved her away without a word. An older man nearby cursed the king, saying he did nothing to help them. Lysandra couldn't stand idle while the people suffered.

She looked at the sad state of the once-fertile fields, now cracked and barren. The crops were withered and brown, offering no hope for harvest. The older man commented that even the gods had abandoned them, and Lysandra pointed out a dead sparrow lying on the ground as evidence that nature was giving up.

"What hope do we have?" the old man asked, kicking at the dirt.

"Hope is something you make from despair," Lysandra replied, her voice strong and determined. "We cannot allow darkness to consume our land, even though kings and gods may have abandoned us."

As Lysandra spoke, her wolf companion grew restless. She stroked his fur, calming him. "We need to find a way to help these people," she said, eyes scanning the area. "We can't just stand here and watch them suffer."

"Maybe we can gather some supplies and distribute them among the people," the old man suggested.

Lysandra nodded. "That's a good start, but we need to do more than that. We must find a way to bring hope back to this town."

The older man gazed at Lysandra with hopeful eyes. "I believe in you, girl," he said.

Lysandra smiled in response. "Then let's get to work."

The man's eyes narrowed as he asked, "But what can one person do against King Draven?"

Lysandra touched the amulet hidden beneath her tunic. A crystal shard glowed with an inner light, a remnant of magic in a world where magic was dying. "One person can become many," she replied. "And many can change the course of history."

The older man sighed and disappeared into the alleys. Lysandra looked up at the dark clouds gathering in the sky, knowing that her journey ahead would be dangerous. She was determined to heal Erenor and knew her journey was beginning.

She commanded her wolf companion, Shadow, to follow her, and they set out on their journey. Lysandra felt the weight of destiny on her shoulders, knowing that she had an essential role in Draven's war against the Arcane. Shadow turned to her, and she knew he understood her burden.

Suddenly, a voice interrupted her thoughts. She recognized it as a specter from her past. The voice taunted her about questioning destiny and reminded her of the villages that were razed and the screams of innocent people. Lysandra didn't appreciate the intrusion and asked the voice to be silent.

The voice continued, "But can you make a difference, Lysandra? You're just one person against the might of Draven's army. What hope do you have?"

Lysandra gritted her teeth. "I have hope, and that's all I need."

The voice chuckled. "Hope won't protect you from the mage chains or the pyres that consumed innocence. You've seen the horrors that Draven's regime has inflicted. Do you think you can stop it?"

Lysandra's resolve hardened like steel. "I know it won't be

easy, but I must try. I won't let Draven's shadow choke life from this land anymore."

The voice grew quieter. "You've seen and felt the pain of this world. But do you have the strength to carry the burden of its salvation?"

Lysandra's voice was unwavering. "I'll find the strength. I have to."

The voice faded, leaving Lysandra alone with her thoughts. She knew that Erenor needed its last mage and was determined to mend the world with Shadow by her side.

The wolf stepped beside her, a guardian born from shadows, as they moved forward together into an uncertain future.

Lysandra's boots crushed the frostbitten grass beneath her feet as she moved like a specter among the withering fields. The village was a carcass of its former self; the people now gaunt phantoms haunting the edges of their decaying homes.

"Be swift, Shadow," she murmured to the wolf, padding silently at her side, eyes alert for any sign of King Draven's men. She sensed their hatred permeating the air like a heavy burden on the terrain.

A harsh voice shattered the eerie stillness. "Pay up, you wretch! King's tax!"

Lysandra edged closer, behind the skeletal remains of a barn. Two of Draven's soldiers stood over a cowering farmer, his hands trembling as he offered a meager grain sack.

"Please, sirs," the farmer pleaded, "it's all I have left."

One soldier snatched the bag, upending it. Pitiful grains scattered, lost amidst the dirt. "This? This is nothing!"

"Mercy!" The man's plea was cut short by a gauntleted fist that sent him sprawling into the mud.

"Mercy?" the other soldier mocked, kicking the fallen farmer. "King Draven shows no mercy to worms."

"Nor shall he receive any," Lysandra whispered, her grip tightening on her rune-etched sword.

"Stay, Shadow," she commanded quietly, stepping from the shadows. Her silver hair glinted like a blade in the sun, her presence commanding.

"Leave him be," she called out, voice laced with cold authority.

The soldiers turned, sneers twisting their faces. "Look here, a stray wants to play the hero. Run along, girl, 'fore you regret it."

"Regret is your master's domain," Lysandra retorted, drawing her sword with a sound like a wind sigh. Release the man."

"Feisty one," one soldier chuckled, drawing his blade. "I'll enjoy this."

Steel met steel in a dance of death, Lysandra's blade a flickering serpent against their brutish swings. She moved precisely; every strike was a testament to her skill and resolve.

"Stop!" she demanded, twisting her blade to disarm one of them.

"Never," he spat, reaching for a hidden dagger.

Lysandra knocked him unconscious with a swift, non-lethal

blow. His companion fled, stumbling over the rough terrain.

"Thank you," the farmer stammered, his eyes wide with awe and fear.

"Get up," she instructed softly, helping him to his feet. "Not all power is wielded with cruelty."

Lysandra retreated from the village, seeking solace in the nearby woods. Shadow, her wolf, followed silently.

"Draven will answer for his crimes," she vowed, feeling a knot in her chest.

She found a secluded glen bathed in dappled light. Here, she discovered her center amongst the whispers of leaves and the soft murmur of a brook.

"Magic flows through my veins," she confided to the listening forest, touching a nearby oak. "Through my will."

"Balance will be restored," she pledged, reflecting the hues of the wilderness. "By blood or by bond, I swear it."

Lysandra sheathed her sword, glowing faintly in response to her unspoken oath. "Come, Shadow," she said, determination etched in every line of her body.

They crept forward, veils of moss parting before them, revealing a fawn with an arrow in its flank.

"Shh," Lysandra soothed, dropping to her knees. "I won't hurt you."

"King Draven's mark," she spat; the animal's pain mirrored Erenor's agony—once-vibrant magic, now bleeding out into the soil.

"Magic... can you still hear me?" She reached within, beseeching the flickering wisp of power that responded.

"Please," she urged, invoking the ancient words taught by Master Elarion.

"*Vires unum,*" she intoned, the air humming with latent energy.

"Trust the magic," Shadow nudged.

"Heal," Lysandra commanded, the glow enveloping the fawn, seeping into wounds, knitting flesh and bone.

"Rise," she whispered, and it did. The fawn staggered to its feet, strength returning. It darted away, symbolizing renewed life.

"Did you see that?" she asked Shadow.

"Draven's reign… it's a poison," she said, each word a stone laid on the path of her destiny. "An end comes for him. For his cruelty."

"An end… and a beginning," she corrected, rising to her feet as conviction settled in her bones like the roots of the ancient oak.

"By sword and by spell," she vowed, her blade catching the light, "I will end this blight."

"Lead the way," Shadow gazed at her.

"Then we move at dawn," Lysandra decided. "Draven will know justice. By my blood, my bond, Erenor shall be healed."

"Balance will return," she promised to the trees, the fawn, and the essence of magic itself. "Balance will return," echoed Shadow, his yellow eyes fierce with shared purpose.

"Balance will return," pledged Lysandra, the last mage of Erenor, as dusk fell upon a world waiting to be reborn. "Come, Shadow, Feyla must be worried sick."

The embers of their campfire crackled, casting fleeting shadows on the faces of the two women seated opposite each other.

Lysandra's gaze flickered from the dancing flames to Feyla's concerned expression, her face a mask of resolve chiseled with lines of doubt.

"Sometimes," Lysandra began, her voice barely above a whisper, "I wonder if I'm chasing phantoms. The magic... it's so elusive now."

Feyla reached out, her hand steady on Lysandra's quivering shoulder. "Your power is no phantom. It's as real as the bond between us."

Lysandra met her friend's gaze. "But is it enough? Can I mend what's been shattered?"

"Look at you," Feyla said, her tone firm, "reared by wolves and gifted with a blade that sings with runes. If not you, then who?"

"Every step I take feels like a march into oblivion," Lysandra confessed, watching a spark ascend into the night sky.

"Then let it be a beautiful oblivion," Feyla shot back, "one where our final act is defiance against the dark."

Standing abruptly, Lysandra paced to the edge of the clearing. "Spoken like a true warrior," she murmured. Her wolf, Shadow, rose, padding silently to her side.

"Let Draven's minions come," Lysandra declared, the weight of her destiny solidifying into an armor around her heart. "We shall meet them with fire and fang."

"By your side always," Feyla affirmed, standing to join her.

"Then it's settled." Lysandra's declaration cut through the night, as sharp as the blade in her grasp. "I will embrace this heritage, my birthright. I will channel every last ember of magic coursing through my veins."

"Draven has torn the very fabric of Erenor," she continued, her determination rising like a phoenix from ashes of doubt. "But I am the needle. I am the thread. And I will stitch the skies back together."

Feyla supported Lysandra, saying, "Make him fear the day he crossed the last mage of Erenor."

Lysandra vowed, "Let the Celestial Fracture quake. I will heal its wounds, restore balance, and let magic thrive again."

She swore, "Upon my life, upon my soul," holding her sword as a testament to her unyielding spirit.

Feyla echoed, "Upon our lives, upon our souls," mirroring Lysandra's oath.

In unison, they pledged, "Balance will return," creating a binding spell woven from courage and conviction.

The moon was low, casting a silver glow on the ancient grove where destiny beckoned. Lysandra stood before the stone altar, her eyes reflecting the celestial light.

"Here, at the heart of Eleanor's oldest magic," she said, "I claim my birthright."

Feyla watched in silence, her presence a quiet strength beside her friend.

Lysandra extended her hand over the altar, where a circlet of intertwined vines and gems lay—a relic of the First Mages, dormant for centuries. Its emerald centerpiece pulsed faintly, resonating with the latent power coursing through her veins.

"By blood and spirit," she whispered, her fingers brushing against the cool metal, "I awaken thee."

As if responding to her call, the circlet stirred, the emerald glowing brighter, casting verdant shadows on her face.

"Feel its weight, Lysandra," Feyla urged softly. "Let it anchor you to all that has been and must be."

"I will bear the weight," Lysandra vowed, lifting the circle and placing it upon her head. A surge of warmth enveloped her, the magic within bonding to her essence.

"See how it accepts you," Feyla said, a note of awe threading her words. "As we all do, as Erenor itself will."

"I will end Draven's terror," Lysandra declared, the power of the circle now reflected on her sword.

Feyla observed, "Your power grows, but so will his fear, his wrath."

"Let him come," Lysandra responded, her grip on her sword tightening. "I stand ready."

"Magic binds us," she continued, "we rise through shadow and flame, blood and pain."

"United," Feyla affirmed, stepping forward to grasp Lysandra's shoulder.

Lysandra promised, "Balance will be our legacy." The circle upon her brow is now a beacon of hope, symbolizing the restoration to come.

"Tomorrow, we journey forth," Lysandra stated, her gaze fixed on the horizon where dawn would soon break. "To fractured lands, to broken skies."

"To the end of Draven's reign," Feyla finished, her voice barely above a whisper yet carrying the weight of an oath.

"By dawn, by dusk," Lysandra swore, her silhouette melding with the darkness.

"By stars reborn," Feyla echoed, the final word hanging between them like a promise, like a spell cast into the night.

Together, they turned from the grove. The path ahead was difficult, but their steps were sure, their spirits unyielding. The Celestial Fracture loomed, but so too did the promise of magic's return, of balance restored—by the last mage of Erenor.

Chapter 7

A REUNION

The ancient boughs of the oak trees of Silfren Deor loomed over Lysandra as she made her way to the heart of the forest. The whispered secrets of leaves rustling under the breath of a wind that appeared to know her name guided each step that crunched dry leaves and undergrowth underfoot.

The wolf at her side, a silent sentinel with eyes glinting like moonlit steel, moved with a ghostly grace.

"Are you certain he lives here, Shadow?" She murmured to the wolf, studying the trees that seemed to contort in reverence for something unseen. Her breath made the cold air smoke and curl around her face. Her chest suddenly felt constricted.

Shadow's ears twitched, his amber gaze fixed ahead, where Elarion's home lay hidden as if grown from the earth it rested upon. There was no response save for a low growl that vibrated through the ethereal mist shrouding their destination.

"Elarion's home must be close," she said, more to herself than to Shadow. She felt the thrum of magic pulsating in the air—a gentle hum that caressed her senses and quickened the beat of her heart. It was as if the atmosphere teemed with an arcane energy that beckoned her forward and urged her on.

Lysandra and Shadow emerged from the forest into a clearing, and a quaint cottage appeared in the distance. The towering trees around it stood guard, ancient protectors of this sanctum. Vines crept up the stone walls, and wildflowers bowed their heads in quiet homage.

Lysandra felt her heart skip a beat as she gazed at the cottage. "Wow, Master Elarion has chosen a beautiful place to live," she said to Shadow, who padded silently beside her.

A deep and resonant voice echoed through the forest, beckoning them forward. The mist swirled, and the hum of magic grew louder. Then, almost as suddenly as it had appeared, the veil lifted, and Master Elarion stood before them.

"Welcome, young one," Master Elarion said with a kind smile. "I have been expecting you."

Lysandra felt a mix of wonder and trepidation as she looked upon Master Elarion. "Thank you for having us," she said, trying to hide her nervousness.

Master Elarion's eyes twinkled with amusement. "Do not be

afraid, my dear," he said reassuringly. "You are stronger than you realize, and I am here to help you."

Lysandra felt a wave of relief wash over her. "Thank you," she said with a smile. "I am ready to begin my training."

Master Elarion nodded. "Good," he said. "Your training will be challenging, but I believe in your ability to succeed."

Lysandra felt a surge of determination. "I am ready," she said, her voice filled with conviction.

Master Elarion smiled. "Then let us begin," he said, leading them into the cottage.

As they walked, Lysandra gazed around the cottage in awe. The walls were lined with ancient tomes, and the air was thick with the scent of magic. She felt a thrill of excitement run through her.

"This is incredible," she said to Master Elarion. "I can't believe I am here."

Master Elarion chuckled. "Believe it, my dear," he said. "You are here for a reason. You are the Last Mage of Erenor, and your training begins now."

Lysandra felt a sense of pride wash over her. "I will do my best," she said, her voice filled with determination.

Master Elarion nodded. "I know you will," he said. "And together, we will save Erenor."

Around them, the air thrummed with an invisible energy that beckoned her closer, whispering of power waiting to be unleashed.

"Your education begins with understanding," he said, moving towards a collection of parchment cluttering a sturdy oak table. Magic is not just spells and incantations—it is knowing oneself."

"Knowing oneself..." Lysandra echoed, the words sinking in as she watched him prepare the space for their work. He moved with deliberate grace, and every action was measured and confident.

"Indeed," Master Elarion affirmed. "Now, let us start. We have much to do, and time waits for no one, last or first."

"Then teach me," said Lysandra, her resolve hardening like steel tempered in fire. "Teach me so I may heal our world."

"Very well," he replied, a smile gracing his features. "We begin at dawn. Rest now, for tomorrow we unearth the depths of your gift."

"Rest." She scoffed lightly, though weariness tugged at her bones. "I've had little use for it lately."

"Yet it remains essential," he scolded kindly. "Even the mightiest sword needs its sheath."

"Then I'll sheath my worries for the night," she conceded, watching the dancing flames in the hearth cast a luminous spell over the room. "Until dawn, Master Elarion."

"Until dawn," he echoed, the promise of revelation hanging heavy in the air.

Lysandra was standing in Master Elarion's dimly lit cottage. The ancient timbers creaked softly in the stillness of Silfren Deor's night song, like whispers that only magic could decipher. Her hands trembled as she confessed to Master Elarion that she feared she might be the last of the First Mage's lineage. She could feel the power within her, but it was untested, and she doubted that she could use it when it mattered the most.

Master Elarion looked at her with kind, understanding eyes that reflected the flickering light of the hearth. He stepped closer to her, and his presence felt like a lighthouse in the storm of her uncertainty. "To doubt is to be human, Lysandra," he said gently. "But you are more than your fears. You hold a legacy no one else can claim."

Lysandra whispered the word "legacy" under her breath, feeling the weight of untold generations pressing upon her shoulders. The wolf at her side sensed her unease and brushed against her leg in solidarity.

Master Elarion urged Lysandra to listen and reminded her that the Celestial Fracture wept for healing, and Erenor cried out in its suffering.

"Listen to me," he said. "The Celestial Fracture needs healing, and Erenor cries out in pain. We need to restore magic, not just for tradition's sake, but for our survival."

Lysandra was momentarily stilled and echoed the word "survival" upon hearing the gravity of his words, which reminded her of their shared purpose.

"Survival," she said, nodding slowly. "That's what it's all about."

She looked into Master Elarion's eyes and saw belief—belief in her and their cause.

"I believe in you," he said. "We can do this together."

Lysandra drew strength from his conviction and tightened her grip on her sword, feeling the weight of his words settling upon her like a mantle.

"Even the First Mage?" she asked, now with a newfound sense of purpose.

"Especially the First Mage," Master Elarion confirmed with a nod. "Greatness is often born from the crucible of self-doubt."

Lysandra declared that she would face this crucible, and her resolve crystallized like frost upon the windowpanes. The wolf lifted its head, sensing the shift in her tone.

Master Elarion promised to help her bridge the chasm within her and awaken the echoes of her ancient bloodline.

"Until dawn," he said, offering a final smile before retreating to the shadows of his book-laden chambers.

In the pre-dawn murk of SilfrenDeor, surrounded by dew-laden moss in the forest, Lysandra stood, feeling the chill in the air. Her breath misted in the darkness. Master Elarion's silhouette cut a stoic figure against the awakening light, his gaze intent upon her.

"Feel the energy, Lysandra," he instructed, his voice quiet yet precise. "The pulse of the forest, the life within you—bind them."

She closed her eyes and reached out with newly awakened senses, feeling the world thrum with a silent song, an aria of ancient magic that hummed through her veins. The forest pulsed with a life force that she had never experienced before. The power within her surged, and she felt like she was a part of something greater than herself.

Together, Lysandra and Master Elarion stood there, waiting for the dawn to break.

"Focus," Elarion urged. "Channel it."

"Like this?" Her palms faced upward, flickers of verdant light dancing between her outstretched fingers.

"Steady," he said. "Control is critical—not too loose, not too rigid."

"Control..." She repeated the word like a mantra, envisioning a stream of water flowing steadily from a wellspring.

"Good!" Elarion nodded, observing as the light solidified into a radiant orb above her hands. "Now, shape it."

"Shape it," she echoed, furrowing her brow in concentration. The orb split into tendrils, weaving through the air like threads of fate.

"Excellent." A hint of pride shone in Elarion's eyes. "You're learning to weave your will into the fabric of magic."

"Is it supposed to feel like... breathing?" she asked her voice a mix of wonder and exertion.

"Exactly," he replied. "Magic is life's exhalation. Now, cast a spell. Simple. Light."

"Light," she whispered, and with a flick of her wrist, a beam shot forth, piercing the morning fog.

"More!" Elarion's command was sharp, pushing her further.

"More," she gasped, sweat beading on her brow. A second beam joined the first, then a third, until the forest glade shimmered like a starlit sky.

"Enough!" He raised his hand, and the beams winked out, leaving shadows blinking back into existence.

"Did I do it right?" Her chest heaved, and uncertainty crept back into her heart.

"Better than right." Elarion's approval washed over her like a warming tide. "Your control is improving. Your swordplay has honed your discipline. Now, elemental forces. Begin with fire."

"Fire!" she acknowledged, rolling her shoulders to loosen the tension. She pictured the flames of a blacksmith's forge—the heat that shaped destinies in steel and iron.

"Summon it," he coaxed.

"From within?" she questioned, the wolf at her side sensing the shift, its hackles rising slightly. "From all around. Fire is both creation and destruction. Harness both."

Her hand moved with purpose, and a spark ignited before her. It swirled, growing into a small inferno that danced upon her palm.

"Control it," Elarion reminded her. "Do not let it consume. Command it."

"Command," she breathed, feeling the power surge and ebb under her will. The flame condensed, becoming a glowing ember floating before her—a testament to her burgeoning mastery.

"See? You are more than your fears," Elarion said, stepping closer. You are a descendant of the First Mage, indeed."

"More," she vowed, her voice now steadier and imbued with a hard-earned confidence. I will master wind next."

"Then proceed," he conceded, a challenge in his tone. "Wind is elusive. Grasp it."

"Elusive," she acknowledged, extending her arms. A breeze stirred, whispering the secrets of Silfren Deor Forest. She snatched at them, twining them into a gust that circled the clearing, rustling leaves, and sending her silver hair into a wild dance.

"Focus, Lysandra. Bind it to your will."

"Binding," she muttered, the gust sharpening into a vortex that responded to the subtlest motions of her fingers.

"Enough." His voice cut through the whirlwind, dissipating as quickly as it had formed, leaving only the ghost of movement in its wake.

"Am I ready?" Lysandra asked, the weight of her destiny pressing down upon her, even as her powers unfurled.

"Ready?" Elarion repeated, a soft chuckle vibrating in his chest. "You've only just begun. But fear not—the path is long, and you are no longer walking it alone."

"Then we walk together," she proclaimed, her sea-green eyes reflecting the dawn's first light, fierce and clear. "Until Erenor is whole once more."

"Until Erenor is whole," Elarion echoed, his kind eyes meeting hers in silent promise.

The shadows of SilfrenDeor Forest crept closer as dusk approached, the ancient trees whispering secrets of a time before the Celestial Fracture. Lysandra stood before Master Elarion, eyes reflecting the fading light and the flicker of uncertainty that danced within.

"Tell me again," she implored, "about the Fracture."

Elarion gestured to the sky where the first stars dared to blink into existence. "Once, the ethereal wells flowed with pure magic, uniting the realms of Erenor. But greed and war shattered the harmony."

"Shattered..." Lysandra echoed, her fingers tracing the runes on her sword—a blade as much a part of her as her burgeoning magic.

"Indeed," Elarion continued, his voice rustling like leaves. Magic bled out into the void when the Celestial Fracture sundered the wells. If we do not heal it..."

"Darkness prevails," she finished for him, a shiver running down her spine despite the warmth of her wolf companion nuzzling at her side.

"More than darkness," he warned. "Chaos will consume all life, and Erenor will be no more than a myth whispered by the winds of a dead world."

Lysandra clenched her jaw, the weight of her lineage—an anchor tethering her to this dire destiny—threatening to crush her spirit. Yet, amidst the turmoil, a resolve kindled within her chest.

"Then we must begin," she said, her voice steady as stone.

"Begin we shall." Elarion's eyes glinted with a mix of pride and sorrow. "But know this, Lysandra, the path is fraught with peril greater than any beast or blade."

"I understand," she replied, though her hands trembled slightly. Her wolf let out a soft growl, sensing the tension in the air like a storm waiting to break.

"Understanding is but the first step." Elarion stepped forward, placing a hand on her shoulder. "Trust in your bloodline, in the power that flows through your veins as fiercely as the old rivers."

"Trust," she murmured, closing her eyes and inhaling the scent of earth and magic that permeated the clearing. The hum of energy tingled at her fingertips, a reminder of the force she wielded—a force that could mend or destroy.

"Open your senses, Lysandra," Elarion instructed. "Feel the fracture, the jagged wound in the fabric of our world."

She did as she was told, reaching out with her mind. The fracture was a cold void, an absence where the vibrant thrum of life should have been. Her heart raced; panic licked at the edges of her courage.

"Steady," Elarion's voice anchored her. "Do not let fear take hold. You are the descendant of the First Mage. You alone can navigate the chasm between what is and what must be."

"Alone," she repeated, a solitary word heavy with implication. Opening her eyes, they blazed with a fire of determination. "But not unaided."

"Never unaided," he agreed, returning to give her space. "Drawing upon the elements, you've shown aptitude. Now, you must reach deeper, beyond mere control."

"Deeper," Lysandra breathed out, her focus narrowing as she extended her awareness toward the raw essence of magic. It pulsed around her, within her—a symphony of power awaiting her command.

"Good," Elarion nodded. "Let that power become an extension of yourself. Only then can you hope to stand against the tide of encroaching night."

"An extension," she affirmed, her eyes once again locking with his. "I will not fail, Master Elarion. I cannot."

"Nor shall you," he said with a conviction that bolstered her spirit. "We begin at dawn. Rest now, for tomorrow you walk the path set forth by destiny."

As night claimed the SilfrenDeor Forest, Lysandra gazed up at the fractured sky, her thoughts swirling like the leaves in her wind spell. The path ahead loomed daunting but within her chest

beat the heart of a warrior, the soul of a mage, and the unwavering resolve to heal Erenor or die trying.

Moonlight streamed through the dense canopy of the Oak trees of SilfrenDeor, casting a silver glow upon Lysandra's face as she sat on the rough-hewn bench outside Master Elarion's cottage. Her sword lay across her knees. Runes etched along the blade, glinting softly. She traced them with her finger, each line a testament to her lineage and its burdens.

"Are you ready to discuss what lies ahead?" Elarion's voice broke the silence, his form emerging from the shadows of the ancient trees.

Lysandra glanced up, sea-green eyes reflecting the turmoil within. "I am haunted by what must be sacrificed," she confessed. "To walk this path, I abandon much more than mere safety."

"Indeed," he acknowledged, settling beside her. "But remember, sacrifice is not loss—it is the currency of change."

"Change." She turned the word over in her mind, feeling its weight. "And if the price is my life?" "Then Erenor shall remember your bravery always." His voice was gentle but firm.

"Forever is a cold comfort," she said sharply. The wolf at her side shifted, sensing her unrest. She laid a hand on its head, drawing solace from its warmth.

"Yet not all sacrifices are final," Elarion rose to join her. "Many are the steps before fate demands such a toll."

"Steps shrouded in shadow," Lysandra murmured, her gaze locked on the fractured sky.

"Shadows that we will illuminate with knowledge and resolve," Elarion countered, reassuringly touching her shoulder. "Come, let us prepare for what comes with the dawn."

She nodded, steeling herself. They walked back into the cottage, its walls adorned with ancient tomes and artifacts that whispered of old magics.

"Tomorrow, we focus on conjuring fire," Elarion began, flicking a candle with his fingers. Its essence is both creation and destruction—apt for what awaits."

"Fire consumes," she said, watching the flame dance. "It also illuminates."

"True. You must learn to harness its dual nature." He gestured towards the candle. "Try."

Lysandra extended her hand, her brows furrowed in concentration. Slowly, the flame grew, crackling with newfound vigor.

"Control," he advised as she fought to steady the fire. "Harmony between force and finesse."

Her heart raced, but she breathed deeply, finding balance. The flame settled, obedient to her command.

"Good. That control will be crucial when confronting the ethereal wells," Elarion stated, extinguishing the fire with a clap.

"Confronting... or reigniting?" she asked, the challenge clear in her tone.

"Both," he affirmed. "The fracture has weakened them; you must be their strength." "Strength I will find," she vowed, her voice hard with determination.

"Rest now," Elarion urged. "With morning's light, your genuine test begins." "Rest, but not peace," she said quietly, turning to leave.

"Peace is earned, Lysandra," he called after her. "Earn it for us all."

As the door closed behind her, Lysandra stood alone in the stillness of the night, the weight of her destiny pressing down upon her like the stones of an unseen cairn. Tomorrow beckoned, fraught with peril and promise, and she would meet it head-on.

The first light of dawn broke through the dense canopy of the SilfrenDeor Forest, casting

dappled patterns on the forest floor. Lysandra stood at the threshold of Master Elarion's cottage, her silver-blond hair catching the new light, a stark contrast against the dark leather of her traveling cloak.

"Remember," Elarion's voice was steady, "the balance of Erenor rests upon your shoulders."

She glanced back at him, sea-green eyes alight with resolve. "I won't fail," she said, gripping the hilt of her rune-etched sword.

"That, I know." He handed her a small, leather-bound tome. "This will guide you when my words cannot."

"Thank you," she whispered, clutching the book to her chest for a moment before sliding it into her pack.

"Let your instincts lead as much as your magic," he continued. Your swordsmanship and wit are just as vital as the spells you cast."

"Spells I've only just begun to master," Lysandra admitted, shifting her weight.

"Trust in your learning, but more importantly, trust your-self."

Sensing the shift in her aura, her wolf companion nuzzled its snout against her hand. She scratched behind its ears, grounding herself in the familiar.

"Magic is fickle," she muttered, looking down at the beast, "but he isn't."

"Neither is the strength you inherit," Elarion pointed out. The lineage of the First Mage is not just about power. It's about the heart."

"Is my heart strong enough?" The question escaped her lips like a shiver.

"Stronger than you know." Elarion stepped forward, placing a reassuring hand on her shoulder. "You are ready, Lysandra."

"Then I'll find a way," she said, steel threading her tone. "For Erenor." "Go now," he urged, "with the blessings of the ancients upon you."

Lysandra took a deep breath, feeling the hum of magic and the pulse of her life intertwine. She turned from Elarion, stepping into the cool morning air that whispered of adventures yet to come.

"Wait," he called out, and she paused. "Never forget who you are—the last mage, yes, but also Lysandra, the woman who braved shadow hounds to save a helpless creature. Compassion is your truest power."

A small, warm smile tugged at her lips. "I'll hold onto that."

With a last nod, she set off, her boots firm against the earthen path. Each step away from the safety of the cottage steeled her resolve, and with her wolf by her side, she walked towards destiny, the promise of the unknown fueling her heart with a fire no spell could match.

Chapter 8

HARMONY AND BALANCE

Silver tendrils of magic writhed from Lysandra's outstretched fingers, coiling like serpents into the chill air of Elarion's cottage. Her brow furrowed in concentration as she struggled to weave the spell, her eyes reflecting a storm of frustration.

"Confound it!" she spat, the words slicing through the silence as the arcane energy dissipated into useless sparks that danced away like mocking fireflies.

"Easy, Lysandra," she murmured, gripping the hilt of her sword for a moment's solace. The steel felt cold and reassuring against her palm, a reminder of a more straightforward kind of power.

"Focus," she whispered, trying again. She envisioned the spell's intricate pattern, but her efforts crumbled again, leaving her shoulders slumped in defeat.

"Shadow," she breathed, the word a sigh. Her wolf companion, ever her Shadow since she'd rescued him from those vile shadow hounds, pushed his snout into her hand. His warm breath puffed against her skin, a silent reassurance.

"I could use a bit of your instinct right about now," she said, scratching behind his ears with a half-hearted smile.

Beyond the cottage's rustic walls, Feyla was waiting for Lysandra to master the powers that seemed out of reach. Lysandra knew her friend understood the necessity of solitude in these moments, yet she longed for just a glimpse of Feyla's supportive gaze.

"It shouldn't be this difficult," Lysandra muttered, glancing around for Elarion. The tall figure loomed near the hearth, an unreadable silhouette against the flickering flames.

"Shadow, find him," Lysandra commanded softly. Obedient and attuned to her moods, the wolf padded across the room, his nose twitching as he searched for their elusive mentor.

"I can't keep failing like this," she said, more to herself than to Shadow or the absent Elarion. "I need to get this right."

A rustle of movement caught her attention, and she turned, expecting to see Elarion emerging from the shadows with some cryptic advice. But the room remained silent except for the crackle of the fire and Shadow's soft whine as he continued his search.

"Where are you when I need you?" she asked in the empty air, her voice laced with a weariness that betrayed the depth of her struggle.

"I have to do better." Clenching her jaw, Lysandra raised

her hands again, feeling the wellspring of magic within her stir. "This time," she vowed, the words a silent prayer to the ancestors who had wielded this power before her. "This time, I'll succeed."

The air crackled with latent energy, the scent of roasted herbs lingering like a taunting ghost. Lysandra's breath came in sharp gasps as she steadied her trembling hands, but the spell still eluded her grasp. Shadow's concerned whine broke the silence, his warm breath against her palm a fleeting comfort.

"Magic is not just about force," a deep and resonant voice from the doorway said. Master Elarion stepped into the room, his presence commanding yet imbued with a calm that felt alien to Lysandra's stormy frustration.

"Master," she acknowledged with a nod, her eyes reflecting the firelight and her determination.

"Show me," he said, crossing his arms while his piercing gaze settled on her. "Again?" She asked, her question tinged with both hope and dread.

"Again."

She positioned herself in anticipation. She recited the incantation, her voice gaining strength with each syllable, but the magic fizzled like a damp tinder failing to ignite.

"Patience, Lysandra," Elarion chided. "You rush the river's flow. It must find its course."

"How can I guide what I cannot grasp?" Her frustration spilled over, coloring her words with the hue of defeat.

"Watch." Elarion extended his hand, palm upward. He whispered words older than the stones beneath their feet, and the air shimmered around him. Power coalesced above his palm, swirling into a radiant orb of light that bathed the cottage in a tranquil glow.

"See? The balance is delicate. You command the storm, but you must also embrace the whisper of the breeze."

Lysandra watched, feeling a mix of awe and envy. His mastery seemed so far out of reach, like a distant star she might never touch.

"Try once more. Feel the world breathe with you."

She bit her lip, closed her eyes, and reached out with senses honed by desperation. She imagined the gentle ebb and flow of the tide, the soft rustle of leaves in the wind, and the steady heartbeat of the earth itself.

"Control is an illusion," she murmured, echoing Elarion's past lessons. "Indeed," he agreed, the corner of his mouth lifting in approval.

Her hands moved through the motions again, this time slower and more deliberate. Shadows danced at the edge of her vision as she called upon the latent power within her, willing it to obey.

Silver moonlight streamed through the narrow window of Elarion's cottage, casting wavering shadows over the wooden floor where Lysandra stood. She squared her shoulders, focusing on the orb of light she needed to conjure.

"Again," urged Master Elarion, his deep voice resonant in the room's stillness.

Lysandra's now reflected the calm she sought within herself.

Her fingers trembled as she traced the arcane sigil in the air, her breath steady and controlled.

"Feel the energy; don't force it," Elarion instructed from behind her, close enough for her to sense his presence but too far to offer any physical support.

She nodded, drawing in a slow breath. The runes on her sword glinted, reflecting her inner turmoil. Power surged within her, a wild torrent eager to escape. But when she pushed it outward, nothing happened. There was no glow, no magic, just the palpable disappointment hanging heavy in the room.

"Balance, Lysandra!" Elarion's voice cut through her frustration. "Magic is not a blade to be wielded with brute strength."

She let out a ragged breath, feeling the weight of failure. "I can't. It's not working," she admitted, her words laced with defeat.

"Observe." Elarion stepped into the moonlight, his tall figure outlined by the luminescence. He picked up a leaf from a potted plant, holding it up for her to see. "The leaf does not strain to grow; it allows the world's life force to fill it."

Lysandra watched the leaf quiver in his grasp, the veiny patterns like intricate pathways of nature's design. "But how does that help me?" she asked, her voice raw with the need to understand.

"Magic, like this leaf, exists in harmony with nature. It would be best if you became the conduit, not the creator. Feel the pulse of the earth, the river's flow, the whisper of the wind," he explained, his voice imbued with reverence for the world around them.

"I feel it, but..." Her protest waned as she closed her eyes, trying to tune into the rhythm Elarion described.

"Listen to its song, Lysandra. Let it guide you," Elarion coaxed, an undercurrent of urgency in his tone hinting at the importance of her success.

She extended her hands again, touching the invisible threads of energy that weaved through all living things. This time, she didn't pull or twist. She danced with it, moved with it, and became a part of it.

"Embrace it," Elarion prompted, watching her.

A spark ignited within her, a flicker of something potent and ancient. Her heart raced as the spell took shape, guided not by force but by a newfound understanding of balance.

"See? Trust in yourself, in the natural order. Magic is the language of creation, whispered since the dawn of time," Elarion said, his voice just above a whisper, yet it filled the space with warmth.

Lysandra's eyes snapped open, and there, between her palms, a small orb of light flickered into existence. It wasn't the radiant glow Elarion had produced, but it was hers—imperfect and trembling yet natural.

"By the gods," she breathed, her gaze fixed on the shimmering sphere. "I did it."

"Indeed," Elarion confirmed, a rare smile touching his lips. "And so your journey continues."

The orb of light flickered and died between Lysandra's hands, leaving a ghostly afterglow that etched itself into her vision.

"Again," she murmured, more to herself than to Elarion, as she gathered her focus. The echo of his wisdom about balance lingered in her mind, but it warred with the thrumming frustration in her veins.

"Your heart races with the storm, not with the calm sea from whence you draw your name," Master Elarion observed, standing beside her with his hands clasped behind his back. His steady voice countered Lysandra's inner turmoil.

Lysandra exhaled sharply, her sea-green eyes reflecting the storm within. "I know. I'm trying."

"Trying implies struggle. To master magic, you must let go of the struggle." Elarion's dark and fathomless eyes held hers.

"Let go?" She shook her head, tendrils sticking to her damp forehead. "How can I let go when every fiber of my being screams to hold on?"

"Through understanding." Stepping closer, he gestured to the ground. "Sit."

She complied, arranging herself cross-legged, the runes on her sword catching the meager light as it lay beside her.

"Close your eyes," instructed Elarion. "Breathe with the world, not against it."

She obeyed, her breaths deepening, seeking synchronization with the rustle of leaves and the distant murmur of the brook.

"Envision the roots of an ancient tree," he said, his tone coaxing her deeper into the exercise. "They reach the earth, drawing life, yet force nothing."

"Roots..." she whispered, picturing them spreading through the damp soil, dark and robust.

"Good. Now, see yourself as both the tree and the earth. You give and take in equal measure. Do you understand?"

"I... I think so," Lysandra replied, her mind's eye weaving images of giving and receiving. "Balance is not taken; it is granted," Elarion continued. "Your power will flow, not flood." "Granted," she echoed, a sense of peace beginning to seep into her bones.

"Feel the energy around you," he guided. "Do not command it. Invite it."

"Invite..." The word felt alien on her tongue, but she extended her senses outward, caressing the magical currents with a gentleness she hadn't known she possessed.

"Embrace the stillness," Elarion urged. "In stillness, there is clarity."

Her body relaxed further, the tension unwinding like a thread from a spool. The frantic dance of her thoughts slowed until each one glided into place.

"Magic is not a shout," Elarion's voice was now almost a chant, "it is a whisper. Listen."

She did. And in the hush, Lysandra heard the softest susurration—the heartbeat of the world, pulse by pulse, aligning with her own.

"Open your eyes," said Elarion. "But hold onto the quietude within."

Her eyelids lifted, revealing a world that seemed brighter and sharper. She reached for the energy again, this time not as a warrior grasping her sword but as a friend extending a hand.

"Try the spell again," Elarion instructed. "Gently."

With a calmness that belied the intensity of her focus, Lysandra formed the incantation, her words laced with the serenity of her meditation.

The air before she shimmered, and then, as if answering a polite request, the orb of light reappeared—stable, serene, and radiant.

"Master Elarion..." she began, awe coloring her tone.

"See what you can accomplish when you release the tempest within?" he said, the pride in his eyes speaking volumes. "This is but the first step, Lysandra. There are many more to climb."

"Thank you," she said, the light in her palms a testament to her growth. "I won't forget this lesson."

"Nor should you," he responded, turning away to give her a moment alone with her triumph. "Remember, the greatest strength often lies in the gentlest touch."

As Elarion left her side, Lysandra gazed at the glowing orb, her thoughts clear and her resolve unshakeable. She had found a new way to wield her power—not with the storm's might but with the grace of the calm seas.

Lysandra exhaled, a mist curling from her lips into the cottage's chill. Shadows danced as she concentrated, the light orb—now a familiar friend—pulsating in harmony with her breathing.

"Control," she whispered, focusing on the energy vibration

between her palms. The orb expanded, contracting like the heartbeat of some ethereal creature.

"Feel the surge," Elarion's voice resonated across the room, "but do not let it consume."

"Like holding a bird," she muttered, mindful not to grasp too tight yet not too loose. Her gaze was fixed on the radiant sphere. She sensed its power thrumming, responding to her will more readily than ever.

"Good, Lysandra. Now, release it." Elarion's command was soft but firm.

With a flutter of her hand, the light soared upwards, illuminating the rafters before dissipating into the air, leaving behind a trail of sparkling motes.

"Better," she said, satisfaction lacing her tone and her sea-green eyes reflecting newfound confidence.

"Indeed. You are ready for the next challenge." Elarion stepped forward, his robes whispering against the stone floor.

"Another spell?" she asked, brushing a silver lock behind her ear, Shadow watching from the corner.

"Something... deeper. We will draw from the ley lines themselves from the earth's very essence," he explained, his eyes alight with an ancient fire.

"Draw from the earth?" She furrowed her brow. "How does one even begin?"

"Begin by listening," Elarion gestured toward the door. "Outside, where the world breathes."

They stepped into the twilight, the world's edges blurring as night took hold. Lysandra closed her eyes, inhaling the odor of wet soil and pine.

"Extend your senses. Feel the pulse beneath your feet," Elarion instructed.

She reached out, not with her hands but with her mind. A network of throbbing energy revealed itself—a map of living currents coursing through the ground.

"Can you feel it?" he prompted.

"I... I think so," Lysandra replied, uncertainty creeping into her voice. "It's vast." "Focus on a single thread. Draw it up, just as you would draw water from a well."

"Like this?" Lysandra's voice quivered as she visualized grasping the invisible strand. The earth hummed a deep resonance that beckoned her to connect.

"Easy," Elarion cautioned. "Let it come willingly."

A warmth spread through her soles, inching up her legs, filling her with an ancient strength. The natural energy was raw and untamed, yet it yielded to her silent call.

"By the gods..." she gasped, her eyes flying open, aglow with an inner light.

"Channel it, shape it!" Elarion's words snapped her focus back. "Do not let it overwhelm you."

Her concentration honed, and Lysandra shaped the energy into a shimmering barrier that rose around them, the air crackling with power.

"Remarkable," Elarion breathed, studying the barrier. "You've tapped into the heart of Erenor itself."

"Is this what you meant by balance?" she asked, maintaining the spell, her pulse racing with the thrill of success.

"Exactly. Magic is not about dominance; it's about unity," he nodded approvingly. "You must be one with the world around you."

The barrier wavered, then solidified under her steadfast gaze. Lysandra felt the sword at her side, its runes pulsing in symphony with the magic she wielded. For a fleeting moment, she understood—the sword, the spells, her destiny—all were intertwined with the rhythm of Erenor.

"Master," she began, her voice steady as the earth itself. "I am ready."

"Indeed," Elarion replied, a hint of a smile gracing his stern features. "The journey continues, and you, Lysandra, are its herald."

Lysandra stood amidst the tangled roots of ancient oaks, the cool dawn mist weaving through her hair. She exhaled, trying to mimic the ebb and flow of the forest's breath to draw upon the pulse of natural energy that thrummed beneath her feet. But where power surged, there was only silence, an emptiness that gnawed at her resolve.

"Confound it!" Her voice shattered the morning calm, and frustration was boiling over. She thrust her palm outward, willing the energies to obey. A feeble spark flickered and died before it could ignite into flame.

"Easy, Lysandra." Elarion's tone was a balm, soothing yet insistent. "The world does not yield to force."

"Nor does it seem to yield to me at all," she snapped, fingers curling into fists. Her loyal wolf companion, Shadow, crept closer, nuzzling against her leg in silent solidarity.

"Remember the barrier you created?" Elarion stepped forward, his robe whispering against the dew-laden grass. "You must extend your senses. The energy is there, waiting."

"Waiting for what? I'm reaching out as you taught me!" She spun, her sea-green eyes flashing with stormy desperation.

"Reaching is not enough." He placed a hand on her shoulder, grounding her. "You must listen. What does the earth tell you?"

She closed her eyes, took a deep breath, and tried to push away the crushing weight of expectation. The runes on her sword hummed, a reminder of past triumphs and potential within her grasp.

"Listen," she murmured, straining to hear the world's whisper. Soft rustlings spoke of scurrying creatures in the undergrowth; the gentle creak of boughs told of the wind's passage. Yet, the vital undercurrent eluded her.

"Trust," Elarion urged, his voice a lighthouse in the fog of her doubt. "Trust in yourself, in the balance. You are part of this world, Lysandra. Let it embrace you as its own."

"Part of the world..." The words were a mantra that she repeated: trusting and belonging. With a shuddering breath, she released her clenched fists and spread her hands wide.

"Feel," Elarion whispered. "Not with your hands, but with your heart."

Heart. The word resonated, and with it came warmth, a faint

pulsing akin to a heartbeat from the depths of the earth. Her lips parted in awe; the sensation was fragile, like a spider's web thread. It was a connection, tenuous but real.

"Good," Elarion encouraged. "Now, nurture it. Grow it."

Grow it. She focused on the warmth, willing it to expand and fill her with the power she knew it promised. Yet, as she did, it flickered and retreated, leaving her empty-handed again.

"Ah!" Frustration clawed back, fierce and bitter. "Why won't it stay?"

"Because you grasp at it." Elarion's reprimand was gentle but firm. "Do not chase the wind, Lysandra. Be the place where it rests."

"Be the place..." she repeated, her internal turmoil subsiding, replaced by a new determination. She took another breath, deeper this time, and let it out.

"Let go," he advised, stepping back to give her space.

"Let go," she echoed, relaxing her body, mind, and essence. As she did, something shifted—a subtle change in the air, a realignment of herself with her surroundings.

"Again," Elarion prompted.

"Again," she agreed, a renewed sense of purpose steadying her nerves.

And so she reached out again, not with the force of will but with an open heart, ready to be the haven for the elusive energy she desperately sought to wield.

Lysandra's heart hammered against her ribcage, a drumbeat syncing with the world's pulse. She extended her hands, open palms facing the sky, her fingers trembling slightly. Her eyes mirrored the determination that had carried her through countless battles, though none quite like this.

"Concentrate," Elarion's voice drifted on the wind. "Feel the earth's heartbeat."

She nodded, a cascade of silver-blond hair falling across her shoulders. Closing her eyes, she inhaled, the scent of damp soil and ancient magic filling her senses. She exhaled, a whispered incantation dancing on her lips, runes on her sword glowing faintly.

"Thrum... thrum..." The rhythm was there, beneath her skin and around her.

"Let it in." Elarion stood close but hidden, a sentinel in his own right.

"Come on," she urged herself silently, envisioning roots sprouting from her feet and delving into the depths below. The energy teased her, a flicker of warmth inviting her to delve deeper.

"Embrace it; don't force it." Elarion's soft reminder cut through her tension.

"Embrace..." Lysandra's internal mantra shifted her approach. She softened her grip on the power, cradling it instead of clenching.

"Good," he said, as if sensing the change.

"Here goes nothing..." Lysandra channeled the spell with a steadying breath, her voice rising in an ancient chant. She envisioned the energy swirling, responding, forming...

"By Erenor's grace!" A surge rushed through her, a torrent of natural force meeting her call. Her eyes snapped open, a brilliant luminosity reflecting their depths as the spell burst forth, a radiant orb of light hovering above her outstretched hands.

"Did I...?" she gasped, disbelief mingling with triumph.

"You did," Elarion confirmed, stepping forward, his eyes gleaming with approval. "You've found harmony."

"Harmony," she echoed, watching the orb pulsate, a living testament to her breakthrough. "It's so... balanced."

"Balance is key," he said, a smile touching his weathered face. "But remember, Lysandra, the path of magic is fraught with peaks and valleys."

"Peaks and valleys," she repeated, lowering her hands as the orb dissipated into a shower of ethereal sparks.

"Indeed," Elarion nodded. "Today, you stand at the top of a mountain, but be prepared for the days when the valleys beckon."

"I will be prepared," Lysandra vowed, sheathing her rune-etched sword. Shadow padded closer, a silent witness to her success.

"Good," Elarion said, clasping her shoulder. "For now, you can revel in your victory. Tomorrow, we climb higher."

"Higher," she mused, a glint of steel in her gaze. "I'm ready."

Shadow's breath misted in the twilight as Lysandra stood at the edge of Elarion's clearing, her gaze fixed on the horizon, where the last embers of daylight fought against the encroaching night.

The air was thick with the musk of damp earth and pine, and the forest was alive with the whispers of nocturnal creatures.

"Night falls," Elarion intoned from behind her, his voice a low rumble like distant thunder. "And with it, the true test begins."

Lysandra turned to face him, the silver strands of her hair catching the dying light. "The darkness is nothing to fear," she said, her eyes hardening with resolve.

"Ah, but it's what lurks within the darkness that will challenge you, Mage of Erenor," he replied, stepping beside her.

"Then let it come," Lysandra retorted, her hand reaching for the hilt of her sword.

Elarion regarded her with a nod. "Your courage is commendable. But remember, brute force will not always sway your enemies."

"Magic then," she murmured, closing her eyes to recall the sensation of the natural energy flowing through her. A ripple of power teased her senses, an unseen current eager to be harnessed.

"Both," Elarion corrected gently. "A fusion of steel and sorcery. That is your path."

"Steel and sorcery," she repeated, opening her eyes. Shadow nuzzled her hand, drawing her to her companion's quiet strength. She stroked his fur, grounding herself in the warmth of their bond.

"Tomorrow's training..." she began, but Elarion raised a hand.

"Tonight, reflect. Understand what you've accomplished," he urged. "Harnessing the natural energies is no small feat."

"Reflection," Lysandra mused, her thoughts drifting to Feyla, her distant friend. If only she could share this moment. Yet, she knew some roads had to be walked alone.

"Exactly," Elarion encouraged. "Let the triumphs fuel your spirit."

"Triumphs... fuel..." she trailed off, her eyes narrowing in thought. With each word, something within her ignited—a flame of determination that warmed her from within.

"Take this time," Elarion said, his presence a solid comfort beside her. "Forge your will."

"Will forged," she declared, the words slicing through any lingering doubt. Her fingers wrapped around the sword's grip, feeling the pulse of its ancient runes.

"Good." Elarion's gaze was unwavering. "When dawn breaks, we delve deeper into the arcane mysteries."

"Deeper," she agreed, her stance firm and her muscles ready for tomorrow's trials. I'll meet them head-on."

"Of that, I have no doubt," Elarion affirmed.

"Head-on," she whispered to herself, the promise of discovery—and danger—sparking a fierce joy within her heart.

"Rest now," he advised, though his eyes betrayed a glimmer of pride.

"Rest," Lysandra echoed, though her spirit felt anything but tired. It surged with newfound power, a tumultuous sea calmed by the certainty of her destiny—the last Mage of Erenor, embracing the shadows and the light alike.

"Tomorrow," she vowed, her voice steady as the earth itself, "I climb higher."

Chapter 9

EMBRACING DESTINY

Lysandra sat cross-legged on the cold stone floor, her fingers tracing the ancient runes etched into the hilt of her sword. The metal hummed with a faint vibration, a whisper of the power coursing through her veins—a legacy from the First Mage herself.

"Focus," Master Elarion said sternly, his silhouette outlined against the flickering torchlight. Remember the essence of the ether, how it flows like the sea currents."

Her eyes, as stormy as the tumultuous oceans, snapped shut, and she inhaled deeply. The smell of burning sage mingled with the mustiness of the hidden sanctum, grounding her to the present. She released a fragment of doubt with every exhale, weaving threads of arcane energy between her fingertips.

"Again, Lysandra," Elarion urged, his words slicing through her concentration. "Harness the tempest within you."

"By the ancients, I will not fail," she muttered, her voice

steel-wrapped in velvet. She thrust her palm outward, and sparks danced upon her skin, casting ghostly shadows across the chamber walls.

"Good," Elarion conceded with a nod. As your control grows stronger, do not become complacent. Power is a treacherous ally."

"Complacency is a luxury I can't afford," she retorted, standing up in one fluid motion.

"Indeed," he replied. "The weight of Erenor rests upon your shoulders."

Lysandra paced the room's perimeter, the soft clink of her armor punctuating each step. "I am ready. I feel it in my bones and the air I breathe."

"Remember, the greatest warriors are not those who fight without fear," Elarion said, his gaze piercing. "But those who face their fear and conquer it."

She nodded, squaring her jaw. "I will face whatever darkness awaits. My resolve is iron-clad."

"Then proceed, Last Mage of Erenor," he proclaimed, echoing off the chamber walls. "Embrace your destiny."

With a last glance at the man who had shaped her fate, Lysandra strode toward the sanctum's exit, the cool night air caressing her face like a lover's touch. The stars above beckoned, and the rhythm of her heart matched the pulsating energy of the world around her. She was the storm incarnate, and they would not deny her.

⋈

The scent of cold iron and embers filled the air as Lysandra emerged into the courtyard where Feyla awaited, her ingenious mind already churning out wonders. Shadow, with his fur-like midnight and eyes reflecting the moon's glow, paced at Lysandra's side, a silent guardian in the encroaching dusk.

"Finally," Feyla exclaimed, her voice ringing with relief and excitement. An array of gadgets seemed to defy the laws of nature surrounding her. "I thought you'd never get here," she said.

"Master Elarion believes in thorough goodbyes," Lysandra replied, her gaze drifting over Feyla's inventions. Her curiosity guided her hand toward the nearest device.

"Careful!" Feyla warned, a grin tugging at her lips. "That's my latest—Spectral Chains. They hold more than just metal; they bind magic itself."

"Useful," Lysandra murmured, impressed despite herself. Her eyes reflected the glinting metal. With each invention, Feyla blurred the line between arcane and artisan.

"Here," Feyla said, passing her a sleek band of silver. "A Wraith Band. It'll prevent you from being seen by prying magical eyes."

Lysandra slid the band onto her arm, feeling the tingle of concealed power against her skin. "Ingenious."

"Isn't it? But wait until you see this." Feyla revealed a compact crossbow, its limbs folded intricately. "The Boltwing. Silent and deadly, like the strike of a shadow."

"Perfect for a wolf at my side," Lysandra quipped, nodding at Shadow, who rumbled in agreement. Their bond ran deeper than blood or battle; he was shielded and sentinel, forged in darkness and loyalty.

"Speaking of which," Feyla continued, kneeling to adjust a set of leather straps around Shadow's torso, attaching various pouches and vials. "He can carry our essentials—and then some."

"Let's hope we won't need all of them," Lysandra said, though the edge in her voice betrayed her anticipation for the opposite.

"Hope is a luxury on the road ahead," Feyla replied, standing up and dusting off her hands. "Preparation will keep us alive."

"Agreed." Lysandra clenched her fists, feeling the call of destiny stir within her. The journey loomed large, fraught with unknown peril, but her resolve was steadfast. She would not, could not, must not falter.

"Ready, Shadow?" she asked, meeting the wolf's amber gaze. He responded with a low growl, the sound vibrating through the ground and into her bones—a fierce affirmation.

"Then we move at dawn," she declared, her voice resolute as steel.

Feyla nodded, her determination mirroring Lysandra's. "To reignite the ethereal wells...and heal what's been broken."

"Or die trying." The words hung heavy in the air, a solemn oath to the world of Erenor and each other.

"Death isn't in my plans," Feyla countered, her eyes sparkling with mischief and something wild. "Not when there's so much yet to invent."

"Nor mine," Lysandra said, a smirk playing on her lips. "Not when there's so much yet to conquer."

As night settled around them, cloaking their preparations in shadows, the two women and the wolf stood united—a trinity of purpose against the encroaching darkness. The path forward was shrouded in mystery and danger, but Lysandra knew one thing: they would face it together. With Feyla's brilliance and Shadow's might, she would embrace her destiny, one spell, one stroke, one step at a time.

Dawn broke over the jagged horizon of Erenor, painting the sky in hues of blood and gold.

Lysandra stood with Shadow at her side, the wolf's fur visible in the newborn light. The weight of her sword, etched with runes of ancient power, was comforting on her hip.

"Today, we step beyond the known," she murmured to Feyla, her eyes reflecting the enthusiasm of the morning sun.

"Into legend and danger," Feyla replied, securing a curious device onto her leather belt—a compass infused with glowing crystals that pulsed rhythmically. "My creations will guide us through the unseen."

"Let them guide us." Lysandra's voice conveyed the seriousness of their mission—to reignite ethereal wells long dormant and mend the world's fractured soul.

With a nod, they set forth, leaving the safety of their encampment behind. The air tasted of adventure, tinged with the metallic tang of uncertainty. Lysandra savored this taste.

"Watch for the signs," Feyla said, pointing to tracks invisible to untrained eyes. Shadow's kin are not the only beasts that stalk these lands."

"Then we need to tread carefully." Lysandra's hand drifted to her sword, and she felt the thrum of its latent enchantments.

The land unfurled before them, a tapestry of emerald forests and azure rivers, veined with the scars of past cataclysms. They ventured through valleys where the wind whispered secrets and climbed over craggy outcrops that tested their resolve.

"By the Ancients, would you look at that?" Feyla exclaimed as they crested a hill, revealing a valley where the trees seemed wrought from living crystal, sunlight refracting into a kaleidoscope of colors.

"Beautiful...and deadly," Lysandra noted, the splendor not blinding her to the peril. "The crystal bark is sharper than any blade."

"Indeed," Feyla agreed, extracting a pair of gloves from her pack. The fibers shone with a spider's silken sheen, But they were not impervious to her touch."

They wove between the crystalline sentinels, the air resonating with a haunting melody as the branches clinked like delicate chimes.

"Magic thrives here," Lysandra said, closing her eyes to feel the earth's pulse beneath her feet.

"Thrive it might, but so do the shadows," Feyla warned, her inventions humming with energy as if in agreement.

"Shadows we can handle, I'm sure of it," Lysandra replied, her confidence bolstered by the presence of her loyal wolf companion.

"Confidence or arrogance?" Feyla teased, though her gaze never stopped scanning the horizon. "Survival," Lysandra answered.

As they journeyed more profoundly into the realm of Erenor, the vistas transformed once more. Now, they ventured into a grove shrouded in twilight regardless of the sky above, where luminescent flowers bloomed with an inner light, casting an eerie glow upon their path.

"Like walking through a dream," Feyla breathed, her hand caressing one of her gadgets, ready to defend against the unseen.

"Or a nightmare," Lysandra added, her instincts on edge as Shadow growled low. His senses were attuned to dangers that lurked out of sight.

"Keep your blade ready," Feyla said, her voice a whisper in the hushed grove. "Always," came Lysandra's reply, her grip tightening around the hilt of her sword.

They pressed on, every step charged with the essence of Erenor's untamed magic, every breath filled with the scent of moss and mystery. Their quest lay ahead, fraught with the unknown, but

Lysandra felt the power of what she learned through Master Elarion's lessons flowing through her veins. She embraced her destiny with each stride, determined to heal the Celestial Fracture or perish in the attempt. And at this moment, between the beauty and the darkness, she knew they would face it as one no matter what lay ahead.

The ground trembled beneath their feet, a subtle yet insistent warning. Lysandra's eyes narrowed as she scanned the fog surrounding them.

"Earthquake," Feyla murmured, her voice steady despite the tremor. She withdrew a slender tube from her belt—her latest invention, a seismic resonator designed to counter the disruptive forces of Erenor's volatile landscape.

"Stand ready," Lysandra said, her words clipped with urgency. "Always," Feyla echoed, mirroring Lysandra's resolve.

A sudden fissure split the earth, a gaping maw hungry for prey. Shadow yelped, his lupine instincts recoiling from the chasm's edge. Lysandra reached out, her fingers grazing the wolf's fur, grounding him.

"Jump!" Lysandra commanded. Together, they leaped, barely clearing the widening gap. Landing hard, Lysandra rolled to her feet, sword drawn.

"Your turn!" she called back to Feyla.

With a running start, Feyla hurled herself across the abyss, clutching her resonator. The device hummed to life, emitting a counter-vibration that momentarily stilled the ground's upheaval.

"Quick thinking," Lysandra praised, her breath misting in the cold air.

"Your faith gives me strength," Feyla admitted, tucking away her invention.

"Trust is our ally here," Lysandra replied, her eyes softening before the next threat emerged.

Shadow hounds, remnants of darker times, materialized

from the mist with bared fangs and silent snarls. Shadow growled, hackles raised, as Lysandra squared her shoulders.

"Steel or magic?" Feyla asked, reaching for another one of her devices. "Both." Lysandra's voice was a blade itself, cutting through the tension.

Feyla nodded, tossing a shimmering powder into the air. It sparkled, illuminating their foes. Lysandra lunged forward, her sword's runes glowing with arcane light. Each stroke was precise, a dance of silver and shadow.

"Behind you!" Feyla shouted, launching a small, explosive orb at an approaching hound. The blast sent it reeling, allowing Lysandra to dispatch it with a swift, merciful thrust.

"Your aim improves," Lysandra quipped, parrying another beast.

"Your praise, rarer than diamonds," Feyla retorted, her brief smile hidden within the danger.

Back-to-back, they fought until the last shadow hound dissipated into the mist, leaving only panting breaths and the scent of charred earth.

"Will this be our lives now? An endless trial?" Feyla wondered aloud, her features etched with weariness.

"Trials forge strength," Lysandra replied, cleaning her blade. "And we are like iron in the fire, unyielding."

"Spoken like a true mage-warrior," Feyla said, her gaze holding admiration and something more profound—a trust forged in battle and shared hardship.

"Come," Lysandra gestured, sheathing her sword. "We must

move. The ethereal wells wait for no one."

"Lead on, Lysandra. I follow where you go," Feyla declared, their journey resuming with renewed determination.

Together, they continued their journey, venturing deeper into the folds of Erenor's dangerous beauty. Their bond was unbreakable, and their quest was unending.

Lysandra's eyes scanned the horizon, her gaze piercing through the twilight that shrouded the Forest of Whispers. The air was cool against her skin, carrying the smell of moss and ancient earth. She could feel the pulse of Erenor's magic throbbing beneath her feet, resonating with the beat of her heart.

"Another barrier," she murmured, pointing at the thicket of brambles that writhed like serpents before them.

"Your magic?" Feyla asked, her hand already reaching for one of her mechanical contraptions.

"Let me try." Lysandra stepped forward, recalling Master Elarion's words: "Magic is intention given form. Command it with purpose."

She extended her hand, focusing on the intertwining vines—a warmth spread through her veins, an energy-seeking release.

"*Verdantis!*" she commanded, and the brambles recoiled as if struck by an unseen force, parting to create a path.

"Remarkable," Feyla breathed, eyeing the clearing way with awe.

"More than spells and incantations," Lysandra said, stepping through. "It's about understanding the essence, the very soul of magic."

They ventured deeper into the forest, Shadow padding silently beside them. The wolf's ears twitched at distant howls, a reminder of the dangers lurking in the dark.

"Are you afraid?" Feyla's voice cut through the silence. "I know I am."

"Every day," Lysandra admitted, her voice softer than the whispering leaves around them. "Fear is a constant companion on this journey."

"Yet here you are, always unwavering."

"Because I must." Lysandra stopped, her gaze lost in the night. "If we fail, darkness will consume everything. Our world, our hopes... all will be lost."

"You won't let that happen," Feyla stated, conviction hardening her voice.

"Master Elarion believed, so I also cling to that belief." Lysandra traced the sword's runes with her fingers, feeling their ancient power hum in response.

"Your strength gives us hope," Feyla said, reassuringly touching Lysandra's shoulder.

"Hope can be a dangerous thing," Lysandra replied, a haunted look in her eyes. "It demands so much yet offers no guarantees."

"Better to fight with hope than surrender to despair," Feyla countered, her inventions clinking softly at her belt.

"True enough." Lysandra gave a tight smile and resumed walking, her resolve hardening with each step.

As they moved through the forest, an ethereal light flickered in the distance—a beacon or a trap? Lysandra reached within herself, seeking the tendrils of her burgeoning power. This quest, her destiny, weighed heavily upon her shoulders, and so did the lives of those who believed in her.

"Whatever awaits us," she whispered, drawing her sword, "we face it together." "Always," Feyla affirmed, keeping her weapon ready to strike.

The light grew brighter, the suspense building with each stride. Lysandra knew the genuine test of her abilities—and her bond with Feyla—lay just beyond the veil of shadows. With determination etched upon her features, she prepared to confront whatever challenge awaited, knowing the fate of Erenor rested in their hands.

The scent of charred earth stung Lysandra's nostrils as she and Feyla hastened through the scorched remnants of what had once been the Whispering Wood. Shadow prowled close; hackles raised, a low growl rumbling in his throat. The forest was silent now, aside from the crunch of their boots over the blackened underbrush.

"Something's wrong," Lysandra muttered, sea-green eyes scanning the devastation. "This destruction... it's not natural."

"An echo of dark magic," Feyla agreed, fingers twitching towards the gadgets that adorned her belt—a blend of iron and arcane crystals. "We need to be vigilant."

"Agreed." Lysandra's hand tightened around the hilt of her sword. Her senses, sharpened by Elarion's training, searched for the unseen threat, reaching out with tendrils of power that she understood.

They pressed on, quickening their pace. Feyla occasionally cast a wary glance behind them, her inventions rattling softly—a symphony of readiness. They could hardly afford delays; the ethereal wells wouldn't reignite themselves, and the Celestial Fracture in the sky above seemed to yawn wider with each passing moment.

"Look!" Feyla pointed ahead, where the ground trembled.

A fissure split the ashen soil, a gaping maw opening before them. A pack of shadow hounds erupted from its depths, their eyes glowing with malevolence.

"By the First Mage," Lysandra breathed, unsheathing her sword. Its runes glowed with an inner light, casting eerie shadows across her face.

"Stand back," Feyla commanded, unhooking a device. It whirred to life, spitting sparks.

Lysandra nodded, stepping forward, sword at the ready. The hounds surged forward, a tidal wave of darkness and fangs.

"Come, Shadow!" she called, and together with her wolf, they met the onslaught head-on. Steel sang against spectral hide, the crackle of Feyla's devices punctuating each blow.

"Watch your flank!" Feyla shouted, launching a barrage of explosive charges into the fray. "Got it!" Lysandra spun her blade a silver arc of death. She moved with a dancer's grace, each step precise, lethal. Her thoughts were a whirlwind, Master Elarion's lessons guiding her strikes: anticipate, react, strike accurately.

"More coming!" Feyla warned, reloading her contraption with swift, practiced movements.

"Can't keep this up forever!" Lysandra grunted, sweat mingling with the ash on her brow.

"Then let's end this!" Feyla's invention emitted a high-pitched whine, culminating in a blast of light that tore through the ranks of shadow hounds, dissipating them like mist before the sun.

Breathless, Lysandra scanned the battlefield. Their victory, though hard-won, was clear. Yet her sense of urgency only intensified.

"We can't linger," she said, wiping her blade clean. "The wells are waiting."

"Agreed," Feyla replied, checking her inventions for damage. "We'll need every advantage we can get."

"Whatever lies ahead," Lysandra murmured, gazing at the fractured sky, "we'll face it. Together." "Always," Feyla echoed, her eyes mirroring the resolve in Lysandra's own.

Together, they set off again, their path illuminated by the flickering runes of Lysandra's sword and the steady glow of Feyla's creations. Each step carried a promise—to reignite hope in a world teetering on the brink of darkness.

The dusk settled over Erenor like a shroud, the last vestiges of sunlight slipping through the fingers of the horizon. Feyla fixed her eyes on the path ahead, her mechanical contraptions emitting a soft hum, their inner workings a secret only she understood. Lysandra trudged beside her, each step heavy with purpose and fatigue.

"Nightfall comes," Lysandra said briefly, her voice barely more than a whisper against the encroaching darkness. "We should make camp."

"Here?" Feyla's voice was tinged with disbelief. "This close to the Whispering Woods?"

"Unless you fancy another run-in with those hounds," Lysandra said.

"Fine," Feyla conceded, setting down her pack. "But let's keep the fire small. We don't need any more attention."

As they worked in silence, the eerie chorus of the woods grew louder, a symphony of unknown terrors that set Lysandra's nerves on edge. She could sense Shadow's restlessness, the wolf pacing like a sentinel at the perimeter of their makeshift camp.

"Something's out there," Lysandra murmured, eyes scanning the treeline. It's watching us."

"Or waiting for us," Feyla added, her hands assembling a device from her pack. "Either way, we're not alone."

A sudden rustling in the underbrush sent them both to their feet, weapons drawn. The tension hung thick in the air, a palpable force that seemed to push down on their shoulders with the weight of the sky.

"Show yourself!" Lysandra demanded, her voice steady despite the fear clawing at her insides.

Silence answered, followed by a low growl that echoed through the woods. Shadow bared his teeth, fur bristling as he stood before Lysandra.

"Damn it," Feyla cursed under her breath. "I knew this place was bad news."

"Stay close," Lysandra instructed, her gaze unwavering. "Whatever it is, we'll face it together." "Like always," Feyla replied, though her hand trembled as she gripped her weapon tighter.

A figure emerged from the shadows, cloaked in darkness, its features obscured. Lysandra's heart pounded in her chest, and a drumbeat of war filled her ears.

"Who are you?" she called out, her blade reflecting the dim light of their dying fire.

No answer came, but the figure advanced slowly, deliberately. Lysandra felt a surge of power within her, Master Elarion's teachings coiling like a spring ready to release.

"Stay back!" Feyla warned, her invention buzzing with energy.

Lysandra stepped forward, her resolve hardening. "We won't let you stop us!"

The figure halted, and momentarily, the forest held its breath. Then, without warning, the ground beneath them shuddered, throwing them off balance.

"Earthquake!" Feyla shouted, struggling to maintain her footing.

"Or something worse," Lysandra thought, her mind racing. The earth continued to tremble, fissures snaking across the landscape, reaching towards them like the claws of some magnificent beast.

"Run!" Lysandra yelled, grabbing Feyla's arm.

They sprinted through the woods, the ground splintering

behind them, a chasm of darkness opening up to swallow the land. Shadow howled a desperate sound that pierced the chaos.

"Jump!" Feyla cried as they reached the ravine's edge, the other side visible through the gloom.

Without hesitation, Lysandra leaped, magic sparking at her fingertips, propelling them across the void. They landed hard on the other side, gasping for air and pounding their hearts.

"Are you—" Feyla began, but her words were cut short.

A roar filled the air, and a monstrous form rose from the depths of the chasm, its eyes glowing with malevolent fire.

"By the gods," Lysandra whispered, staring into the face of their greatest challenge yet. "Cliffhanger," Feyla muttered, half in awe, half in fear.

The dark ravine stretched out before them, its depths shrouded in shadow. On the other side, Lysandra and Feyla stood brave and determined, their faces etched with determination and fear. Rising from the darkness, a colossal figure emerged, its monstrous form silhouetted against the fiery glow of its eyes.

The ground shook as a dark chasm split open, its edges jagged and ominous. Across the void, the other side was barely visible through the mist and shadows.

It shrouded the chasm in darkness, with only the faint outline of the other side visible through the gloom. As they stood on the edge, the ground cracked beneath them, revealing the ominous form of a monstrous creature rising from the darkness.

"Quite," Lysandra responded, her grip tightening around her

sword. And with that, the beast surged forward, and the world went black.

Chapter 10

AN UNFORESEEN REUNION

Lysandra's heart pounded as the ground trembled beneath her boots, and an unnatural darkness engulfed the world around her. She turned to Feyla, who was frantically checking her mechanical tools.

"What's happening?" Feyla asked, her voice shaking.

"I don't know," Lysandra replied, unsheathing her sword. "But we need to be ready for anything."

As Lysandra scanned the darkness, she felt a sudden surge of power. The air pulsated with an ancient force, and a deep rumbling filled her ears. Suddenly, a colossal beast erupted from the abyss, its scales shimmering like obsidian in the stormy sky.

"By the gods," Feyla whispered, her eyes widening in terror.

"Stay behind me," Lysandra commanded, her voice steady despite the fear within her. She took a step forward, her sword drawn and ready. The beast roared, and Lysandra's instincts took over. She dove, rolling away from the snapping jaws, and rose fluidly, slashing at the creature's underbelly. Her blade met resistance, barely piercing the hide but enough to draw first blood.

"Hit it with everything!" she shouted to Feyla, who scrambled to assemble a contraption that hurled explosive charges. Lysandra knew brute strength alone couldn't destroy this enemy. Her raw and untamed magic surged within her, a fierce storm seeking release. With a cry, she unleashed a barrage of arcane energy that pierced the darkness, striking the beast and illuminating its vulnerabilities.

"Again!" Feyla cried out, setting off another round of explosives.

The creature reeled, its cries echoing into the void as it retreated into the depths. The encounter ended as suddenly as it began, leaving only the echoes of battle and their heavy breaths to fill the silence.

"Are you hurt?" Feyla asked, her voice tinged with awe and concern.

"Nothing I can't handle," Lysandra replied, though her hands trembled—not from weakness, but from the force she had struggled to contain. She was powerful, but each use of her magic reminded her of the fine line between control and chaos.

⸻ ⊠ ⸻

Lysandra and Feyla navigate the rugged terrain leading to the Guardians' sanctuary. Lysandra misses Shadow, her wolf companion, whom they left behind to distract King Draven's forces.

"Will Aerin be there?" Feyla asks.

"Perhaps," Lysandra replies. "Something profound happened, making him abandon his pursuit of me."

"Can we trust him?" Feyla inquires.

"Trust is earned," Lysandra says. "But he has reasons now to fight alongside us."

They arrive at the cave entrance, hidden by cascading vines and the remnants of old magic. They descend into the labyrinthine corridors until they reach the library.

"Remember, we face it together," Lysandra says.

"Always," Feyla affirms.

The cavernous library looms before them, with walls lined with towering shelves. They navigate through the dimly lit maze of ancient knowledge.

"It feels like we're walking into the heart of Erenor's past," Lysandra says.

"Or perhaps its future," comes a deep and resonant voice, interrupting the silence. Arannis, the leader of the Guardians, emerges from the labyrinthine stacks.

"Welcome," Arannis says, motioning for them to follow him deeper into the repository of lost wisdom.

"The journey here was not without its challenges," Lysandra says.

"Indeed, the path of destiny is seldom smooth," Arannis replies.

"Your wolf will return to you when the time is right," Arannis says, referring to Shadow.

"Of that, I have no doubt," Lysandra responded, her thoughts wandering to the loyal beast that had become more than a companion.

"I have a question," Feyla interrupted, looking around the room. "Will Aerin be joining us?"

"Ah, the hunter," Arannis replied thoughtfully. "Yes, he's found a new target - his darkness. He's on a different path, which may lead us to cross again."

"His presence adds an element of unpredictability," Lysandra said.

"Life is like a tapestry woven of many threads," Arannis said, stopping in front of a large table with scrolls and artifacts. "Each thread is important, even if its purpose is unclear."

"Interesting," Feyla said skeptically.

"But let's talk about why you're here," Arannis said, gesturing to the chairs before him. "The ethereal wells are waiting, and the fate of magic in Erenor hangs in the balance."

Lysandra sat down, focused on the task ahead. She and Feyla had been through a lot together and were ready to face anything. As Lysandra thought about her mission, the candles flickered, casting light on the maps and artifacts.

"The ethereal wells are the fountains of pure magic and the heartbeat of Erenor," Arannis said. "As they diminish, so does the life of this world."

"Without them, magic fades, and with it, hope?" Lysandra said, leaning forward.

"Exactly," Arannis nodded. "And you, Lysandra, are the key to their resurgence."

"We've fought beasts that would freeze your blood," Feyla said. "We've bled for this mission."

"And I've used my sword more times than I've summoned magic," Lysandra added. "Each encounter is a test, and each victory is a testament to our resolve."

The Guardians surrounding them exchanged glances of respect, acknowledging the warriors' trials.

"Your journey has made you stronger," Arannis said. "But the path ahead will demand even more."

"Bring it on," Lysandra said with determination.

"Magic must be restored," Feyla said. "For Erenor. For all."

"Your bravery is commendable," Arannis said, standing up. "But it won't be enough. You must outsmart the darkness that seeks to claim the wells."

"That's why we train and fight," Lysandra said, standing up to the mage's challenge. "We want to reclaim what's been lost."

"Indeed," Arannis said, looking at Lysandra before turning to the Guardians. "Then we will not falter."

"We won't," Lysandra said, with Feyla by her side.

"Go now," Arannis instructed. "Prepare, for the dawn comes, and with it, your next battle."

As they left the room, the magnitude of their quest was evident. They knew they were one step closer to the unknown perils, magic restoration, and fates intertwining.

Arannis unfurled a parchment on the table, its edges worn by age. The candlelight flickered, casting shadows on the map's creased surface. Lysandra leaned closer, tracing the intricate lines and symbols that formed the pathways to the ethereal wells.

"Here," Arannis began, his finger hovering above a mountain etched with runes, "lies the first well, guarded by the Galespine Wyrm—a creature of wind and fury." His voice carried the weight of many years, yet it did not tremble at the horrors he described.

"Wind and fury we can handle," Feyla interjected, her tone

defiant, but Lysandra could feel the tension in her friend's stance.

"Perhaps," Arannis conceded, "but the wyrm is no mere beast. It is born from the very essence of Erenor's storms." Lysandra held her sword, feeling the etchings as if they might reveal secrets. She knew their journey would be dangerous, but facing such a powerful foe stirred both fear and excitement within her.

"Do you have any weaknesses?" she asked Arannis. "Lightning," he replied. "It doesn't like what it can't control."

Their path led them to a dark forest on the map. Arannis's expression grew serious. "The Netherwood. Its Guardian, a specter, the Gloomstalker, wrapped in shadow, will test your resolve in ways steel and sorcery may not suffice."

"We're familiar with shadows," Lysandra said, thinking of her wolf companion, Shadow, lurking in the caves. "We'll find a way through."

"Confidence is key, but overconfidence..." Arannis trailed off, letting the warning hang between them.

"Understood," Feyla nodded, though her eyes showed unease.

"Good," Arannis said, revealing objects glinting with latent power. "You will need these." He gestured towards the array.

"Amulets to ward off dark energies, vials of lightning to ensnare the wyrm, and here—" he handed Lysandra a book, "a grimoire containing spells lost to time."

"Thank you," Lysandra said, feeling the power beneath her touch. She knew what they fought for.

"Study them well," Arannis advised. "Knowledge will be your ally when strength falters."

"Strength won't falter," Feyla declared, but her gaze lingered on the amulets with reverence.

"Let's hope not," Arannis murmured.

Lysandra sensed the enormity of their task. Each artifact and spell was a puzzle piece that could mean the difference between salvation and ruin for Erenor.

"Remember," Arannis said, "the path to the wells is fraught with more than physical dangers. Trust each other, and don't let the darkness consume your hearts."

"We understand," Lysandra assured him, thinking of Aerin, the tenuous thread of trust that connected them all.

"Then go," Arannis commanded, "with the blessings of the

ancients upon you."

Lysandra's grip tightened around her sword. The road ahead was uncertain, but the fire of purpose burned fiercely within her. With Feyla at her side and the Guardians' wisdom guiding them, they would face whatever obstacles awaited, their resolve unbroken, their spirits unyielding.

Lysandra traced the ancient symbols on her sword, each one an oath to the destiny she had embraced. The cavern air hung thick with the scent of must and old leather, a testament to the wisdom contained within these stone walls.

"Arannis," Lysandra began, "your guidance is the beacon in our darkest night. We won't falter. We'll return magic to Erenor or perish in the attempt."

Feyla, standing beside her, couldn't help but let out a soft gasp as she gazed at the relics on the table before them. "The power here... it's more than I ever dreamed," she whispered.

"Such dreams can turn to nightmares," Arannis intoned, his eyes narrowing. "The path you choose is lined with shadows that hunger for the unwary."

"Let them come," Lysandra retorted, her sea-green eyes catching the flicker of candlelight, stormy and unafraid. "I have walked through the darkness before."

"Bravery alone won't save you," the mage replied. He stepped closer, the lines on his face deepening. "Remember, the wells are ancient, guarded by creatures as old as the land. They'll sense your intentions and test your resolve."

"We've battled beasts before," Feyla said, clasping her weapon for comfort.

"Those were physical creatures," Arannis corrected. "But what we're up against now are magical beings, spiritual beasts. They prey on doubt and feed on fear."

"Then we'll deprive them," Lysandra said firmly, her suitcase heavy against her side, the grimoire tucked safely inside.

"Trust your instincts, Lysandra," Arannis advised, his gaze fixed on her. "And trust Feyla. The bond you form will protect you from the corruption that seeks to undermine your bravery."

Lysandra nodded, feeling Feyla's presence like a steady flame next to her. "We're ready," she declared, although a flicker of anxiety coiled inside her. The memory of Aerin's traumatic past lingered in her thoughts, reminding her that even the strongest could falter.

"Go forth with the watchful eyes of the ancient mages upon you," Arannis said. "May the light of Erenor guide your blades."

"Thank you, Arannis," Lysandra replied, grateful and determined. "For Erenor," she added, a vow bound her to the task ahead.

"Let's go, Feyla," Lysandra said, turning away from the Guardian. They strode into the corridor, their footsteps resolute against the cold stone.

"Are we prepared?" Feyla asked, her voice barely audible in the winding passage.

Lysandra placed a reassuring hand on Feyla's shoulder. "Together, we're more than prepared. We're destined."

Feyla nodded, drawing strength from Lysandra's touch. They moved forward, the maze-like cave swallowing their silhouettes. The journey ahead promised untold dangers, but they carried the hopes of a world awaiting its rebirth with every step.

The torchlight flickered against the cave's damp walls as Lysandra and Feyla exchanged a final, silent nod with the Guardians. They lingered outside the underground library, the weight of their mission pressing down on them like the earth above.

"May you have a swift journey." Arannis's voice echoed in the cavernous expanse, the air thick with the scent of must and ancient parchment.

"May our blades stay sharp," Lysandra replied, her eyes reflecting the determination that fortified her spirit. She turned on her heel. The map unfurled across a flat stone. The parchment crackled, the lines and symbols sprawling before them—a riddle woven in ink and intent.

"Here," Feyla pointed to a marking on the map, tracing the path to the first ethereal well. "The Guardians spoke of a guardian beast, the Gloom Stalker."

Lysandra leaned in closer, her breath stirring the dust motes caught in the torchlight. "We'll need to stay alert then. These caves are dangerous enough without adding hungry beasts."

"True," Feyla agreed, her gaze lingering on the map. "But we've faced worse and have what the Guardians gave us." She held up an amulet, its gem pulsating with a soft glow. "Enchanted to ward off lesser evils."

"Lesser evils," Lysandra echoed, a smirk tugging at her lips. "Because facing greater evils is what we do best."

"Always the optimist," Feyla said with a dry chuckle.

"Someone has to be," Lysandra retorted, but her fun faded as she studied the map. Her thoughts wandered to Aerin, the magic he denied, and the fate bound him to them. He was out there, his path murky and fraught with inner turmoil.

Feyla's intuition was sharp as she asked, "Are you thinking about him?"

Lysandra replied, "Who?"

"Aerin."

"Let him follow his path," Lysandra replied, a hint of frustration and unease in her voice. She felt his presence lurking just beyond her sight.

Feyla pondered, "But his magic could be useful."

Lysandra reminded her, "It was magic that killed his parents. He despises magic. We must rely on ourselves."

Feyla conceded, "Fine," but her doubt clung like a stubborn fog. "Sometimes our greatest enemy can become our strongest ally. Keep an open heart."

Lysandra countered, "An open heart can be a fatal weakness." Yet, deep down, she wondered if Feyla's words held some truth.

Feyla insisted, "Let it be our strength. Now, let's plan our approach to the Gloom stalker. We won't be caught off guard."

Lysandra agreed, her focus narrowing as they plotted their course through the winding tunnels, anticipating each potential ambush.

After a while, Feyla suggested, "Let's rest while we can. We'll need our energy for the challenges ahead."

Lysandra agreed though sleep seemed a distant luxury. Her thoughts churned with the unknown variables of their quest.

Feyla whispered, "Tomorrow, we face the darkness," her words tinged with foreboding.

"Then let's meet it with swords drawn and hearts fierce," Lysandra vowed, the fire in her veins burning away the shadows of doubt.

Together, they settled against the cold stone with maps and artifacts of their silent guardians. The flickering candlelight cast dancing shadows upon the cave walls, a prelude to the challenge awaiting them at dawn.

Lysandra and Feyla shared a silent understanding in the cave's hushed gloom, the weight of their quest forging an unspoken bond. The artifacts lay between them, talismans of hope amidst the encroaching darkness.

Feyla murmured, "Remember, the Guardians said the wells' magic is unpredictable. We must be vigilant."

Lysandra nodded in agreement, silently promising to protect and serve. They were more than companions. They were sisters-in-arms.

Lysandra said, "Unpredictable or not, we'll master the wells' power."

"Or die trying," Feyla replied wryly, the shadows playing across her features.

"Then we live," Lysandra declared, as if challenging fate itself. She rose, sheathing her sword with a resonant click that echoed through the cavern.

Feyla stood beside her, her resolve mirrored in her stance. "Let's ensure we're not easy prey for the Gloom Stalker."

"Agreed." Lysandra's hand lingered on her sword's hilt, feeling the thrum of latent power. "We face what comes together."

They gathered their gear, folded the maps, and tucked them securely away. Each step toward the mouth of the cave was measured and purposeful. The chill air clung to them, reminding them of the perils ahead.

"Stay close," Lysandra said, her voice just above a whisper. "The path to the wells is treacherous, and we've no room for missteps."

"Lead on," Feyla replied, touching the small dagger at her belt—a readiness gesture.

Together, they emerged from the cave sanctuary into the dim light of pre-dawn. The world around them was still as if holding its breath. Ahead, the land stretched out, shrouded in mist, hiding danger and destiny.

"We walk the edge of a knife," Feyla observed, her gaze scanning the horizon.

"Then let us not fall," Lysandra answered, her heart a steady drumbeat against the rising tide of adrenaline. "For Erenor."

"For Erenor," Feyla echoed.

Lysandra and Feyla were on a mission to reclaim the magic that was their birthright. They walked together towards the ethereal wells that sounded like a siren's song. Their path was dangerous, but they were an unbreakable force, ready to face anything ahead.

Lysandra stopped to take in the view as they approached the cave's threshold. The wind blew her hair back, but she didn't give up. She looked into the shadows and whispered, "It's hard to believe that such power lies with those who prefer candlelight to sunlight."

Feyla replied, "Books are their swords, and knowledge their armor. They've just knighted us."

Lysandra laughed, "If only words could shield us from what's out there." She held onto her sword, which was covered in ancient inscriptions.

Memories of her mother's demise, the beast from below, and

the darkening world flashed through her mind—a montage of dread and determination.

Feyla stepped beside her and reminded her that they were both Guardians. "Your gadgets, your wit... I owe you my life, Feyla."

"Enough debts tallied. We share a fate, you and I. And Aerin, too, wherever his path has led him since..."

"Since what?" Lysandra asked, knowing the unspoken history that bound the hunter to them both.

"Since magic revealed its dual edge to him," Feyla answered soberly. "He'll find us when the time is right. Or we'll stumble upon him, likely mid-battle."

"Let's hope it's on our side of the fight," Lysandra said. She missed her wolf, Shadow, who was also out there.

"Always prepare for the worst," Feyla chided.

"Expect the worst; hope for the best," Lysandra countered, hardening her features. "The Guardians have given us much, but it's up to us to see this through—for Erenor, for magic, for all those we lost—and for those we've yet to save."

"Then let's not keep destiny waiting," Feyla urged, extending her hand towards the undulating landscape before them.

Lysandra took a deep breath, filling her lungs with the crisp air of dawn. "Look!" Feyla pointed to the horizon, where the first rays of sunlight pierced the mist. "Dawn heralds our departure. It is a new beginning."

"Or an end," Lysandra added somberly, her gaze locked on the brightening sky. "Whatever awaits us, the Guardians' wisdom and artifacts will guide our hands."

"Your magic will, too," Feyla assured her. "You're stronger than any force we'll face."

"Strength means little without purpose," Lysandra reflected, feeling the weight of her destiny. "I won't fail them—the Guardians, Erenor, or you."

"Nor I, you," Feyla replied, clasping Lysandra's shoulder.

With their pact reaffirmed, they stepped forward, leaving the safety of the cave behind. Their journey was fraught with unknown dangers but buoyed by the trust and camaraderie between them. As they ventured toward the location of the first ethereal well, anticipation thrummed through their veins, igniting a fire that no darkness could extinguish.

"Magic awaits, and we are its vessel," Lysandra declared, her eyes alight with fierce determination.

"Let's bring it home," Feyla concurred, her excitement palpable.

Together, they ventured into the unknown, their steps echoing off the cavern's walls. Lysandra took the lead, scanning the darkness for any signs of danger.

Feyla followed closely behind, her senses on high alert. Suddenly, Lysandra stopped in her tracks, her hand resting on the hilt of her sword.

"What is it?" Feyla whispered, her eyes darting around the cave.

"I sense someone else is here," Lysandra replied, her voice barely above a whisper. "But I don't think they're a threat."

Feyla nodded, her eyes narrowing as she scanned the darkness for movement. "I can feel it, too," she said softly.

Lysandra took a deep breath and stepped forward. "Whoever you are, show yourself," she called into the darkness.

For a moment, there was silence. Then, a figure emerged from the shadows, his eyes flickering with an inner light.

"Who are you?" Lysandra demanded her hand still on the hilt of her sword.

The figure didn't answer. Instead, he stood there, his eyes fixed on them.

Feyla stepped forward, her hands held out in a gesture of peace. "We mean you no harm," she said softly. "We're just passing through."

The figure's eyes flickered for a moment, and then he spoke. "I know who you are," he said, his voice low and gravelly. "And why you're here."

Lysandra and Feyla exchanged glances. "Then you know we mean no harm," Lysandra said calmly and steadily.

The figure nodded slowly. "I do," he said. "But you must be careful. There are many dangers in these caves."

Lysandra and Feyla nodded in agreement. "We'll be careful," Lysandra said. "Thank you for the warning."

The figure nodded and disappeared into the shadows, leaving Lysandra and Feyla alone in the darkness again.

The cave walls echoed with his breath—erratic and strained as if carrying the weight of his internal turmoil. The cold, damp touch of the limestone underfoot brought him back to grim reality from his spiraling thoughts.

The air bore a distinct metallic scent found only in deep

caves, a reminder of his solitude. Each breath tasted like fear salted with determination—an odd blend that kept him pushing forward no matter what stared back at him from the abyss.

"Be careful, Aerin," Feyla called back, her distrust veiled. This place can be treacherous."

He nodded curtly, but his gaze lingered on Lysandra, standing close to her friend—watchful, assessing.

Lysandra regarded him coolly. "You've been quiet. What shadows haunt you?"

Aerin's face tensed as he spoke. "The shadows that have haunted me for years are the same. Magic took everything from me. My parents died because of it, leaving nothing but scorched earth and a son who wished he'd died with them."

Lysandra said, "But you're still carrying the curse you hate."

"Curse or blessing, it's a part of me," he admitted, looking down at his hands as if they held a secret. "I feel it stirring in my veins when danger is near. It even saved your life," he looked up at Lysandra with mixed emotions.

Lysandra replied, "Saved or damned?"

"Maybe both," he conceded. "But if it means protecting you, I'll use it again, even if it makes things worse between us."

"Enough talking," Feyla interrupted. "We must find the wells, not dwell on our problems."

They moved forward with an uneasy truce. The silence was only broken by their footsteps and the sound of water in the distance. Lysandra held her sword tightly, feeling the weight of their mission and the doubt of her companions.

Lysandra reminded herself, "Trust is earned."

Aerin said, "Trust is a luxury above ground, but down here, it's necessary. Without it, we're as good as dead."

"Then let's not die today," Feyla declared, holding her bow tightly.

"Agreed," Lysandra said, feeling the magic in the cave. It was both inviting and repelling.

"Look," Aerin whispered, pointing to a faint light in the distance. "Could it be the well?"

"An ethereal well?" Feyla wondered aloud, her voice tinged with hope. "Or a trap," Lysandra added, her senses on high alert.

"There is only one way to find out," Aerin said, stepping forward.

"Stay close," Lysandra instructed, leading them toward the glow. Her sword's runes flared brighter, a silent sentinel guiding their path.

They moved closer to the source of the light, feeling an electric energy in the air. It was a mix of power and danger intertwined inextricably. They were on the verge of a discovery, brought together by necessity but still keeping secrets from each other. The journey ahead would test their resolve, create new alliances, and reveal the cost of restoring magic to Erenor.

"We'll face whatever lies ahead together," Lysandra vowed. Her voice echoed in the chamber.

"Until the end," Feyla affirmed.

"Until the end," Aerin repeated, his features showing a newfound determination.

Together, they stepped into the light, ready to face any challenge. They were bound by a shared destiny and the unspoken fears of what might exist beyond the veil of shadows.

Chapter 11

GIFTS AND BLESSINGS

Lysandra was astounded by the riot of colors that surrounded them as they entered the Silfren Deor Forest. Unlike the gloomy woods of Darken Hollow, this place was filled with emerald leaves and sapphire blossoms that dazzled her senses.

"Wow," Feyla gasped. "It's like stepping into a dream."

Aerin's eyes gleamed as he looked around. "Or a painting," he said. "But be careful. Beauty often hides the deadliest of traps."

Lysandra nodded, feeling a powerful, otherworldly energy pulsing through the air. She sensed no malice but knew they needed to be cautious.

"Let's keep moving," she said, leading the way. Ancient trees with massive trunks covered in moss and lichen surrounded the path as it wound more profoundly into the forest. Sunlight filtered through the dense canopy, casting dappled shadows on the forest floor.

As they walked, Lysandra felt the forest's magic washing over her. It was as if the very soul of Erenor had taken root here, cradling the last vestiges of pure magic within its soil.

"This place is incredible," she said, feeling a sense of wonder and awe.

Feyla nodded. "I've never seen anything like it."

Aerin remained cautious. "Don't let your guard down," he warned. "I have a feeling there's more to this place than meets the eye."

Lysandra nodded in agreement. "We'll stay alert," she said, her hand hovering near the hilt of her sword.

"Remember the tales," Feyla said, her inventive mind already cataloging the flora and fauna around them. "Silfren Deor Forest is said to be the cradle of our world's enchantments. If there's any truth, we'll find it here."

Aerin, Lysandra, and Feyla ventured deep into Silfren Deor, a mystical forest, their guard up, prepared for anything that might emerge from the lush underbrush.

"Truth and danger both," said Aerin, his bow at the ready.

"Then it's a good thing we're not without our magic," Lysandra countered, feeling the energy stir in her fingertips. "And my wolf will alert us long before anything strikes."

"Magic and muscle," Feyla quipped, her pack full of her latest inventions. "We're quite the trio, aren't we?"

"An unlikely one, perhaps," Aerin conceded, "but I wouldn't have it any other way."

The forest was full of the scent of earth and blooms, and Lysandra felt the weight of her destiny urging her on, guiding her towards a goal written in the stars and rooted in the ground beneath her feet.

"Forward then," Lysandra declared. "Let the forest bear witness to the return of the First Mage's blood."

"Forward," Feyla echoed.

"Forward," Aerin affirmed, his warrior's heart finding solace in the journey and the companions at his side.

A melodic hum weaved through the forest, growing louder as

they drew closer. Lysandra paused, her ears perking up.

"Can you hear it?" she asked.

"It sounds like...singing," Aerin said.

"Or a greeting," Feyla added.

They heard a sound and went to a clearing where they saw huge Treants with bark-like skin covered in markings. The Treants' eyes glowed green, and a voice rumbled from the earth below them.

"Why do you walk this hallowed ground?" the voice asked.

"We seek knowledge and aid," Lysandra answered, confident in her skills as a warrior and sorcerer.

"Your presence is known to us," the Treants replied. "The forest whispers of your quest."

Lysandra felt the weight of her destiny as the Treants recognized her. She stepped forward, her sword glimmering in response.

"Guardians," Aerin spoke up. "We mean no harm. We come for guidance."

Together, they ventured further into Silfren Deor, excited for the magic that awaited them.

"Guidance," the second Treant mused, its voice the crack of breaking branches. "This forest has seen much, yet you bring a storm none can foresee."

"Storms can be weathered," Feyla chimed in, her mind racing with plans and possibilities. "Tell us how we may harness the tempest."

"First," the initial Treant intoned, "one must understand the calm."

"Understand... calm..." the echo followed, fading into the symphony of the woods.

"Will you grant us this understanding?" Lysandra pressed, her heart thundering against the stillness of the grove.

"Time will tell, Child of the First Mage," came the voice, deep and resounding, filling the clearing with a promise as old as the SilfrenDeor Forest itself.

Certainly! Here's the revised version without any references to sea-green eyes, runes, runic, rune-etched sword, and silver-blond hair:

Lysandra's heart skipped a beat as the tallest Treant leaned closer. Its bark was rough and gnarled like ancient wisdom. Its eyes flickered with green light, fixed on her with a deep intensity.

The Treant spoke in a deep voice that sounded like roots entwining within the earth. "We've been waiting for you for a long time," it said. "You are descended from the First Mage and carry the legacy of Erenor's arcane birthright."

Standing beside Lysandra, Aerin watched closely with his hand on his blade's hilt. His presence reassured Lysandra as she absorbed the significance of the Treant's words.

"Me?" she asked, her heart pounding with shock and wonder. The wolf at her side tensed, its ears pricked, sensing the moment's gravity.

"Indeed," another Treant affirmed, its voice echoing through the forest. "Your bloodline is key to the resurgence of magic's full might."

Feyla, ever curious and inventive, leaned in closer. "Tell us more about this First Mage," she urged. "How did they bind the balance?"

The first Treant gestured towards the horizon, where the sky met the trees in a blur of green and blue. "Through the ethereal wells," it explained. "They are the heart of power, the source from which all magic flows and ebbs."

Lysandra's mind raced as she imagined the dormant power within her veins. "Balance, power..." she murmured, trying to understand everything.

The Treant continued, "Darkness has corrupted the wells, and they now lie silent." "Awaiting one who can ignite their luminance."

"Darkness..." Feyla repeated, her eyes glinting with fierce determination. "We'll find a way to bring back the light."

As Lysandra and her companions approached the ancient Treants, they could feel the weight of Time and wisdom surrounding them. The Treants warned Lysandra that the challenges would require courage, sacrifice, and determination.

"Courage and sacrifice," the second Treant warned, its voice a rustle of dead leaves. "Then I shall face it," Lysandra vowed, gripping her sword tighter, resolve steeling within her. "For Erenor. For magic's rightful place."

"Many before you have faltered," the Treant cautioned. "Will you stand where others fell?"

"Others were not me," Lysandra shot back, defiance sparking in her stormy gaze.

"True," the tallest Treant conceded, a hint of approval in its ancient eyes. "The First Mage's spirit endures in you."

"Endures..." Lysandra repeated softly, the word resonating with a truth she felt but could not fully grasp.

The Treants instructed them to listen well and heed the whispers of the wells, for therein lay the path to restoration.

"Puzzle to solve. A challenge to meet," Feyla pondered aloud.

"And we will not turn back until the balance is restored," Lysandra added, determination surging like a tidal wave.

"Bold claims," the Treant murmured. "Let us hope they forge bold deeds."

The ancient Treants bestowed upon them the essence of their life's vigor, a golden pollen that enveloped them in a luminescent aura. As the energy embraced them, Lysandra and her companions felt a surge of power coursing through them. They sensed the pulsating rhythms of the forest within their chests.

"Embrace the knowledge," Aerin murmured, his voice just above a whisper.

"Let it guide you," Feyla added, her eyes wide with wonder.

"Let it strengthen you," the Treant intoned.

Lysandra felt the surge of power coursing through her. "Ancestors," she breathed, eyes ablaze with newfound purpose. "I feel them."

"Your bloodline awakens," another Treant confirmed, its voice a gentle echo.

The ancient Treants extended a gnarled limb toward Lysandra and her companions, and the air around them shivered with anticipation as leaves whispered secrets older than the stars.

"Step forth, children of destiny," the Treant rumbled like roots breaking through the earth.

Aerin moved first, his gaze firm, the muscles in his jaw tightening. Feyla followed, her curious eyes reflecting the dappling light, while Lysandra took a measured step forward, her hand resting on the hilt of her sword.

"By the ancients' breath that stirs the SilfrenDeor Forest," the Treant began, its leaves trembling. "We give you the essence of our life's vigor."

Something akin to golden pollen drifted from the Treant's palm, swirling in a dance choreographed by unseen forces. The light particles spiraled toward the trio, enveloping them in an aura of verdant luminescence.

Lysandra and her companions felt a tangible surge of power coursing through them. "This is amazing," Feyla whispered.

Aerin's eyes sparkled with wonder. "I can feel the knowledge flowing through me."

Lysandra felt a deep sense of connection. "I can feel the heartbeat of the forest."

"We bless this gift," the Treant said, its voice descending like dusk. "Carry it with you on your journey."

"We will not forget this moment," Lysandra declared.

"As long as we live, we will remember this gift," Aerin added.

The Treant nodded, the leaves rustling like a soft breeze. "Then go forth, and may the forest spirits guide you on your quest."

"Use this gift," the first Treant instructed, "but remember, power is but a tool. It is your will that must shape it."

Lysandra whispered to herself, wondering if she was strong enough for the task ahead. "Will I be enough?" Her grip tightened on the sword, which seemed to pulse with a mysterious energy. As if sensing her doubt, the Treant spoke, "You are the descendant of the First Mage, the one who turned the tide of ages past."

Feeling emboldened, Lysandra thanked the Treant and turned to her friends. "We have a quest to complete," she said, her voice filled with determination.

Aerin and Feyla nodded in agreement. "Let's make these blessings count," Feyla added excitedly.

As they walked away, the magic of the Treants filled their bodies, and Lysandra could feel her strength growing. The forest seemed to acknowledge them, with leaves rustling in a silent salute.

Feyla looked up at the towering Treants and asked for their guidance. "Your wisdom is as vast as the SilfrenDeor itself," she said. "I craft machines; how might they serve us in our quest?"

The air crackled with magic, and Feyla could feel the power of the forest pulsing within her. She couldn't wait to begin creating something that would help them on their journey.

As they walked deeper into the forest, the path ahead seemed to glow with promise. They had a long journey ahead of them, but with their newfound strength and the blessings of the Treants, they were ready for whatever lay ahead.

A gentle rumble echoed around them, carrying the weight of centuries. "Ingenious child," one Treant intoned, its voice like wind through leaves, "your creations are threads in the tapestry of fate. Weave them well, support the lineage bearer."

"Craft with purpose," another added, the glow of its eyes softening. "Your tools shall reveal paths hidden and doors long closed."

"Paths... doors..." Feyla repeated under her breath, ideas sparking like flint against steel. "I will forge it again to open the way for magic's return."

Aerin stepped forward, his dark eyes reflecting the muted light that filtered through the canopy. He asked the Treants, "What can you tell me?"

The Treants began to sway their branches in a silent dance that preluded their response. "Aerin of the lion gaze," one spoke, its voice a deep thrum that resonated within their chests. "Your strength lies not only in sinew and blade. Within you, there is a spark that waits to be ignited."

"A spark?" Aerin asked, his voice betraying a hint of uncertainty beneath his sturdy exterior.

"Yes," another Treant said. "A flame kindled by your need—a protector's fire."

"A protector?" Aerin repeated, his fists clenching with determination.

The first Treant continued, "Time will unveil your power. Remember that you are the shield it breaks upon when the darkness descends."

"I will be ready," Aerin said, glancing at Lysandra, his companion. She nodded in agreement, her eyes reflecting the same determination.

"We each have our roles," Lysandra said. "Together, we'll walk the path unseen and restore what was lost."

"Lost and found again," the Treants affirmed. Go forth, children of Erenor, with heart, blade, gear, and craft."

"Let's move," Lysandra declared, turning from the clearing with her companions flanking her. Their steps were sure, their resolve unyielding. They knew they carried the future of magic with them, each bearing the weight of destiny in their unique way, bound by a common purpose more significant than any of them had on their own.

Lysandra's fingers brushed the coarse bark of the Treant before her, an ultimate gesture of respect and farewell. "We will honor your wisdom," she said, voice steady despite the emotion that swelled in her chest.

"Be brave, children of Erenor," the Treant rumbled, its deep voice vibrating through SilfrenDeor Forest's rootsrest.

"Thank you for your blessings," Aerin added, his usual stoicism softened by the encounter.

"Your path is true," another Treant intoned, its eyes glowing like embers in the clearing's twilight.

Feyla clutched an intricate device to her chest, ticking and whirring with the promise of undiscovered addition. "With these hands, I'll build our victory."

A silence followed, filled only by the whisper of leaves and the distant call of forest creatures. Then, as one, they turned away from the Treants, their figures diminishing under the grandeur of the ancient trees.

Lysandra felt the shift—a thrumming beneath her feet, a symphony of life that resonated with the pulse of the forest. She paused, closing her eyes to let the sensation wash over her.

"Something's different," Feyla murmured, her gaze darting around the now luminous underbrush.

"Harmony," Lysandra breathed, sea-green eyes snapping open, capturing the subtle dance of light and shadow. "The Treants blessed more than just us."

"Let's not waste it," Aerin said, his hand resting on the hilt of his sword, a silent vow to protect whatever lay ahead.

"Agreed." Lysandra's hand went to the runes on her blade, feeling their power echo with the forest's newfound vitality. Sensing the change, the wolf let out a soft yip, circling her once before settling at her side.

"Every step we take," she declared, "is a step toward reclaiming what's ours."

"Through blood, sweat, and gears," Feyla added, her mechanical contraption now humming in tune with the Silfren-

Deor's energy.

Their determination was a tangible force, melding with the forest's essence. As they left the clearing, the air seemed to shimmer with potential, with the sacred charge of their quest.

"Remember," Lysandra said, glancing back at the now-distant Treants, "we carry the legacy of the First Mage."

"And we won't let it die," Aerin vowed, the weight of his future role as protector grounding him.

"Nor will the darkness consume us," Feyla asserted, her inventive mind racing with possibilities.

Pressing forward, each step was a testament to their unyielding resolve. The SilfrenDeor Forest stood witness to the beginning of a legend, its secrets entwined with the fates of those destined to bring about the rebirth of magic in Erenor.

Lysandra's boots crunched on the forest floor, every step infused with purpose. The SilfrenDeor Forest, once a whispering enigma, now sang to her very bones – a symphony of ancient magic and promises yet to be fulfilled.

"Can you feel it?" Aerin's voice cut through the verdant hush, his gaze set on the path ahead. "The forest breathes with us."

"More than that," Lysandra says, eyes scanning the foliage. "It's guiding us, strengthening our resolve with each breath."

Feyla hefted her pack, the gears within ticking. "We've been granted more than blessings. We've been given a task. The weight of history rests on our shoulders."

"History," Aerin echoed, his hand brushing his sword's

pommel. "And our futures."

They continued in rhythmic silence, their footfalls a cadence of unity. Shadows danced around them, but none reached for their flan unseen force kept the darkness at balance.

"Treants spoke of balance," Lysandra mused out loud, feeling the energy coursing through her veins. "Restoring magic isn't just about power; it's about restoring life to Erenor."

"Life... and hope," Feyla added. Her inventions rattled as if in agreement with the forest's very soul.

"Hope," Aerin said, a smirk tugging at his lips. "That might be the most potent magic of all."

Shadow trotted alongside Lysandra, his presence a warm comfort against the chill of uncertainty.

"Magic runs through us," she whispered, half to herself and her companions. It runs through me. It feels... right."

"Destined, one might say." Feyla's retort was lighthearted but laden with truth. Aerin nodded. "Let's not squander what we've been gifted."

"Okay, guys," Lysandra said, gripping her sword tightly, "we can't give up now."

The forest seemed to be listening, with the leaves rustling in a way that could be interpreted as either a soft applause or a warning. Their journey was dangerous, but the Treants' words had given them hope.

"The Guardian Treants have entrusted us with a lot," Aerin said as they reached a bend in the path. The sound of the SilfrenDeor's heartbeat echoed beneath their feet.

"We need to trust them," Lysandra said firmly.

"And we can't betray our hearts," Feyla added, fiddling with a small gadget and adjusting a dial, her eyes filled with determination.

"Betrayal is not an option," Aerin said, his past a shadow he was trying to leave behind.

They continued their journey with a renewed sense of urgency, the forest's embrace protecting them and reminding them of the challenging quest ahead. Every leaf that brushed Lysandra's skin, every birdcall that pierced the canopy above, reminded them of the importance of their mission.

"Remember this moment," Lysandra urged, as the sky darkens, "when the path gets tough and we start to lose hope."

"Remember and keep moving forward," Aerin said, his eyes reflecting the last rays of the setting sun.

"Forward," Feyla said, securing her pack. "Towards light, balance, and a future we create with our hands."

As night descended upon the SilfrenDeor forest, a cloak of stars unfurled above them, watching and waiting. The trio pressed on, the wisdom of the Treants etched into their souls, their fate linked to the essence of Erenor. Their determination was unbreakable, their purpose clear - they would either restore magic to the world or die trying.

Lysandra shivered as a chill ran down her spine. The night's breath was cold, whispering of challenges yet to come. The path ahead was narrow, winding like a serpent, its back glistening with dew and enchantments laid by Time itself.

"Are we sure this is the way?" Feyla asked, slicing through the darkness that had descended upon the SilfrenDeor forest.

"Trust in the forest," Lysandra replied, her gaze locked on the path ahead, every sense attuned to the hum of magic that guided their steps.

"Trust is earned," grumbled Aerin, his hand resting on the hilt of his sword, a silent companion in the quiet of the woods.

"Yet freely given by the Treants, remember?" Lysandra countered, feeling the pulse of power bestowed by the ancient guard within herians.

"Power doesn't ensure loyalty," Aerin said, a note of distrust lingering beneath his words.

"Nor does doubt foster strength," Lysandra shot back, the memory of the Treants' faith in her fueling a fire within.

"Enough." Feyla's words were commanding and sharp as

flint. "We've battles ahead that need us whole."

"True," Lysandra admitted, loosening her cloak and allowing the cool air to wash over her. The future loomed, vast and uncertain, but she felt rooted, like the Treants themselves.

"Watch your step," Aerin warned as the ground sloped sharply, his voice betraying concern.

"Always do," Feyla murmured, navigating the descent elegantly, her gadgets clinking softly.

Lysandra stopped. "Something's here," she breathed, the forest's whispers intensifying, hinting at unseen presences.

"Friend or enemy?" Aerin's question hung heavy like a blade poised to strike.

"Unknown," Lysandra confessed, using her heightened senses to find the source of the disturbance.

"Stay close," she instructed, feeling the weight of her role, the mantle of the First Mage heavy upon her shoulders.

"Lead on, Lysandra," Feyla said, her tone resolute despite the unknown dangers.

"Be ready for anything," Aerin added, drawing his sword with a rasp that cut the silence.

Together, they edged forward, the path revealing less with each step, yet their determination did not wane. They were bound by pure prophecy, by the magic that flowed in their veins, and by the destiny that called to them from beyond the veil of shadows.

"Whatever comes," Lysandra vowed, her voice steady, "we face it as one." "Until the end," Feyla and Aerin affirmed in unison.

Chapter 12

THE GUARDIANS

Lysandra and her companions walked through the forest, the morning sun shining through the trees and casting long shadows on the ground. They were heading towards the Iron Mountains, which loomed large in the distance. Shadow was walking by Lysandra's side.

"These mountains are making me feel uneasy," Aerin said, eyes scanning the horizon.

"Maybe they are watching us," Feyla said, adjusting her satchel. "I've heard that mountains have eyes and ears."

"Legends!" Aerin scoffed, but he was still uneasy. "We've seen enough on this journey to know that there are things out there that we can't explain."

Feyla nodded. "We need to keep our eyes open. It's not just the mountains that we have to worry about."

Lysandra felt the magic within her stirring. She sensed that dark forces lurked beneath the terrain's beauty. She held her breath, sensing the mountains' brooding presence. It was as if they were testing their resolve with invisible tendrils.

They kept their guard as they walked, watching for any signs of danger. The forest was quiet except for the occasional rustling of leaves. The only sound was the crunching of their footsteps on the path.

After a while, they reached a clearing, and the mountains loomed more prominent than ever in the distance. "We're getting closer," Lysandra said, her voice filled with determination.

Aerin nodded. "Let's keep moving."

"There's something off," Lysandra whispered, and Shadow growled softly, sensing the danger.

Her hand went to the hilt of her blade. "What is it, boy?"

"I feel it too," Feyla said, her devices buzzing with energy.

"We're not alone. Get ready," Aerin commanded, drawing his weapon.

"Can you sense it, Lysandra?" Feyla asked.

Lysandra closed her eyes and extended her senses outward. "It's twisted magic—malignant and faint."

"It could be anything this close to the mountains," Aerin said.

"Stay sharp."

The air grew denser and colder, and Shadow's muscles coiled in anticipation. "We'll be ready for anything," Feyla said, holding a curious contraption that hummed with potential.

"Ready for what?" Aerin asked.

"The thrill of the journey," Lysandra replied, feeling her heart race with adrenaline. "We'll face the unknown head-on."

"Exciting or foolish?" Aerin murmured.

"We'll face it together," Lysandra said, looking at her companions. "We'll find the ethereal wells. We must."

"We're going forward," Aerin said. They moved closer to the Iron Mountains, feeling a sense of foreboding grow with every step. As they approached, the path became narrower, and their footsteps muted against the hard stone that had been crushed into gravel for ages.

Lysandra looked around, taking in the strange changes in the flora and fauna. The trees were twisted into gnarled shapes, with leaves shining with metallic hues. The bark was as hard as iron. "Nature looks like it's armored," Feyla said, touching a silver-leafed branch that recoiled at her touch.

"And armed." Aerin pointed to a thicket where thorns bristled like the quills of an agitated porcupine. "But look," Lysandra said, "life still thrives even in adversity." She pointed to a cluster of vibrant blue mushrooms glowing against the grey stone. Shadow sniffed at a patch of luminescent lichen.

"This place is infused with magic," Lysandra said, feeling it resonate within her bones. "Can you feel it, Feyla?"

"I can taste it in the air," Feyla replied, her contraption pulsing more vigorously.

"Let's hope it doesn't eat us," Aerin said, scanning the horizon.

Lysandra and her companions were hiking through the mountains when they suddenly heard metal hitting stone.

Turning a corner, they saw a dwarf named Burlok chiseling away at a glowing boulder. "Friend or enemy?" he asked, without looking up from his work.

"We're friends," Lysandra replied, holding her hands up to show they weren't a threat.

Burlok was surprised. "It's rare to come across friendly travelers here. I'm Burlok, an artisan of the Ironpeak clan."

Lysandra admired the glowing boulder. "Your craft is unique," she said.

Burlok beamed with pride. "We coax the essence of the mountains into our work. It's no ordinary metalwork."

Feyla was intrigued. "Is it like the wells we're seeking?"

Burlock laughed. "You're on a bold and dangerous quest if you're seeking the ethereal wells."

Lysandra asked if Burlok's creations were protective. She noticed an intricate armor that seemed to hum with power.

Burlok nodded. "My creations are protective and potent, but nothing guarantees safety in these parts."

Feyla was interested in learning more, but Lysandra sensed a shift in the air and urged them to stay vigilant.

Burlok offered some advice before they parted ways. "Trust not only in strength but also in the whispers of the stone. It speaks the truth."

As they continued their journey, the terrain grew steeper, and the sense of something ancient and powerful grew stronger with every step. The Iron Mountains loomed ahead, shrouded in Shadow and mystery. They saw Dwarven runes etched into the stone, glowing with a mysterious luminescence.

Feyla observed that the symbols represented chapters of Dwarven history, including battles won and lost.

Aerin added that the Dwarven figures carved from the living

rock stood guard over ancient halls, reminding them of the legacy of a people who had become one with their domain.

Lysandra felt the weight of countless generations in the stones around them, bound to the earth. As they pressed forward, the secrets of the Iron Mountains awaited them.

"Traditions run deep here." Aerin's voice held a note of admiration. "Their magic is born of discipline and respect."

"Respect we must earn," Lysandra replied, her mind turning to the path ahead. "We'll need more than swords against what lies in wait."

"Then let us prepare," Feyla said, her determination mirrored in her companions' eyes.

They found a sheltered nook where they could take a break from the chilly winds and prepare for the challenges ahead. Lysandra unsheathed her sword and moved precisely; each exhaled move was a deadly dance honed through constant practice.

Feyla readied her bow and shot an arrow at a makeshift target while Aerin conjured a controlled inferno that danced around his body, illuminating the alcove.

"Controlled," Lysandra reminded him, watching the flames keenly.

Shadow paced restlessly, his senses alert to any threats beyond their sanctuary. His fur bristled, and he let out a low growl, his eyes fixed on the darkness outside.

"Even Shadow feels it," Lysandra noted. "The mountains are holding their breath."

"Let's not keep them waiting any longer," Feyla said, tension coiled in her stance.

"Agreed," Lysandra replied, sheathing her sword. "We move under the cover of night. Feyla, you take point with Shadow. Aerin, keep our path clear."

"Clear and guarded," Aerin agreed, his magical flames dimming to conserve his energy.

"Stay alert," Lysandra instructed, scanning the horizon where the peaks clawed at the sky. "The mountains are watching, judging if we're worthy."

"Then let's not disappoint," Feyla said with a determined smile.

"Neither," Lysandra said, locking eyes with her companions. "We face what comes together. And we survive."

"Survive and conquer," Aerin echoed, clenching his fists, sparks flickering between his fingers.

"Conquer and discover," Feyla added, testing the string of her bow with a confident pluck.

"Discover and protect," Lysandra concluded, her resolve unyielding as the stone beneath their feet.

As night fell, the trio stepped forward into the embrace of the Iron Mountains, their hearts steeling against the unknown horrors that awaited.

The chill of the mountains cut through their cloaks as they wound their way through the jagged pass. Before her, Lysandra's breath became hazy; each exhalation left a ghostly wisp that the night swallowed.

"Keep your eyes sharp," Feyla whispered, her voice carrying over the wind's whistle. Shadow's hackles rose in agreement, his amber eyes piercing the gloom.

Aerin's hands glowed with a faint blue light, ready to unleash his powers. "Something's coming," he murmured.

A low rumble echoed through the chasm like the mountains groaning under an unseen weight. Suddenly, a vast silhouette materialized from the shadows. Two molten eyes gleamed beneath a stone crown, and the earth trembled with its awakening.

"What is it?" Lysandra hissed, drawing her sword.

"It's a guardian," Feyla replied, readying her bow.

The creature roared, a sound that shook the ground and charged.

"Split up!" Lysandra commanded, dodging to the side as the beast crushed the ground where she stood.

"Draw its attention!" Aerin shouted, hurling a bolt of magic. It struck the beast, eliciting another roar.

"Got it!" Feyla released her arrow, finding a weak spot. The guardian stumbled, hindering its movements.

"Focus on the legs," Feyla called out. "Slow it down!"

"Creating an opening!" Aerin formed chains of light that snared the guardian's limbs. "Strike now!" he cried.

Lysandra leaped, driving her sword deep into the creature's exposed underbelly. Shadow lunged, biting the stone, his form melding with the darkness.

"Trust!" Lysandra thought, feeling the unity of their assault. "We can do this!"

"Brace!" Aerin warned as the guardian reared, breaking free of the magical bonds. "It's not over!"

"Never is," Feyla muttered, finding her mark again. "Blind it!" Lysandra seized on Feyla's success. "Aerin, now!"

"Understood!" a bright flash engulfed the guardian's head. "Finish this!" Lysandra roared, enthusiastically rallying her companions.

"Finishing," Feyla confirmed, her next arrow aimed with lethal precision.

"Ended!" Aerin exclaimed as his spell work amplified their efforts, sealing their victory. The guardian shuddered and succumbed to the quake, collapsing with a thunderous finality that echoed across the Iron Mountains. Silence fell thick upon them as if the air awaited their next breath.

"Is it?" Aerin gasped, his glow fading.

"Dead," Lysandra confirmed, her sword dripping with a sludge that smoked against the snow. "But there will be more."

Feyla, Aerin, Lysandra, and Shadow were on a mission to uncover the secrets hidden in the heart of the mountains. They knew there would be challenges and guardians, but they were determined to move forward together.

As they walked through a narrow valley, the mountains seemed to inhale their silence and exhale a chilling wind laden with whispers. The ancient dust stirred beneath their feet, and shadows surrounded them.

"Look here," Aerin called out, pointing to an etching in the stone. "These are the runes of binding."

"Binding what?" Feyla asked, her eyes scanning the shadows.

"Power," Lysandra replied, touching the cold rune. "Magic was tethered to the bones of the earth."

"Then this is the path," Aerin concluded, surveying the landscape ahead.

"Obvious paths lead to obvious traps," Shadow growled.

"We'll be cautious," Lysandra said with a warrior's grace.

"Wait!" Feyla interrupted, pointing towards a cluster of stones where glints of metal lay half-buried in the snow. "Artifacts."

"Careful, they could be cursed," Aerin warned, but curiosity gleamed in his eyes.

"Or they could help us," Lysandra said, picking up a gauntlet with intricate filigree. She felt its latent power, a piece of history yearning to be wielded again.

"Keep moving," Shadow urged, sniffing the air. "Danger still prowls these peaks."

"Always," Lysandra replied, setting her jaw and leading the way.

The terrain grew steeper, and the sky darkened. The air crackled, thick with magic and malice.

"Stop!" Aerin shouted, halting Lysandra mere inches from a glowing sigil that had appeared underfoot.

"Another guardian," Feyla muttered, eyeing the sigil.

"Or something worse," Lysandra said, stepping back as the sigil flared, casting an eerie light over the group.

"Brace yourselves," Aerin instructed, preparing to counter whatever came forth.

"Ready," Feyla affirmed, her bowstring taut with anticipation.

"Here it comes," Lysandra tensed, drawing her sword. The gauntlet's power surged as if answering the call to battle.

A roar shattered the tense calm, and a creature of smoke and iron emerged from the sigil. It towered above them, a behemoth wrought from the mountain's wrath.

Lysandra charged forward, commanding her companions to strike true, divide the creature's focus, and draw its attention. Aerin unleashed his magical bolts while Feyla's arrows found their mark on the beast's smoky hide.

The trio circled the creature, forcing it back with spells and arrows. Their loyal companion, Shadow, joined the fray, his sharp fangs baring against the night. They fought relentlessly, their bond unbreakable in the face of danger.

As they approached the heart of the cavern, Lysandra felt an ancient rhythm pulsing through her bones. Shadows flickered at the edges of her vision, and a chasm yawned wide before them. The artifacts they sought pointed in this direction.

"We need to cross," Lysandra said, her voice steady despite trembling hands. Feyla nodded and prepared her crossbow while Aerin watched for any threats.

Lysandra summoned her power, and a bridge of shimmering light formed across the chasm. Feyla carefully made her way across, supported by Aerin's steady hand.

As they reached the other side, something stirred. "Be ready for it," Lysandra said, feeling the raw energy of the surroundings feeding into her spells. Suddenly, a gale-force wind whipped through the cavern, threatening to sweep them into the abyss.

"Take cover!" Aerin shouted, anchoring himself as Feyla clung to his lifeline. Lysandra's focus was unyielding, her mastery over the ethereal wells apparent in the solidity of her conjuration.

Together, they stood firm, undaunted, facing the darkness. Their bond was the brightest light in the Iron Mountains' deepening gloom.

Lysandra, Feyla, and Aerin navigated through the Iron Mountains, their goal to reach the pulsing core. Along the way, they encountered a stone sentinel, a construct of old magic that came to life and attacked them. The trio fought back and ultimately defeated the guardian, demonstrating their growth and unity.

As they continued their journey, the air became charged with potential and the essence of the Iron Mountains. The trio moved forward, undeterred by the weight of the ancient presence that awaited them in the depths of the Iron Mountains.

"The heartbeat of the mountain," Lysandra whispered as they approached the cavernous maw of the Iron Mountains. The air was thick, and the dust of time made every breath heavy. With each step, the trio felt the echo of their footsteps in the silence of the underground expanse.

As they walked, Lysandra called out, "Windward glyphs!" to

create a bubble of calm around them. Feyla set up a defensive perimeter with traps, and Aerin watched for any signs of danger.

Suddenly, Aerin hissed, "Wait!" and pointed to a shifting shadow. Lysandra banished the darkness with a light globe, revealing a stone sentinel emerging from the gloom.

"Stone sentinel!" Aerin recognized the construct of old magic and instructed the trio to take defensive positions. Lysandra channeled her energies into offensive spells while Feyla aimed her crossbow at the sentinel.

"Strike now!" Aerin commanded, leading Shadow into a charge. The trio fought together, their attacks a blur of motion—Feyla's bolt lodged in the sentinel's joint, hindering its movements. Lysandra cast a binding hex that constricted the sentinel, and Aerin's blades found weak spots in the sentinel's armor. Shadow's fangs sank into exposed gears, and the guardian crumbled before them.

"Deeper in," Feyla said, reloading her crossbow. The trio felt the power emanating from the core, and they were too close to turn back now.

"Forward," Lysandra decided, leading towards the pulsing core. The essence of the Iron Mountains whispered secrets to Lysandra, and the trio moved forward undeterred by the ancient presence awaiting them.

As they approached the core, Lysandra asked, "Can you feel it?" The energy was palpable, and the trio knew they were close. They echoed, "Forever," and continued on their journey. Said light released. "That growling sound seems more like a slumbering beast," Feyla whispered, her crossbow at the ready, her eyes scanning the shadows. Aerin nodded, and Shadow released a low, rumbling growl, making their bones vibrate.

"Older than magic itself," Lysandra murmured, closing her eyes to feel the Power pulse resonating within the rock. "Get ready," Aerin said, tensing his muscles as they prepared for whatever lay ahead. "We're facing more than just stone and darkness."

"Whatever secrets this place holds," Feyla added, "we're going to have to fight for them."

"Easy victories teach us nothing," Lysandra said, determination shining in her eyes.

They moved forward in unison, their synchronized steps echoing through the cavern. Shadows slithered along the walls as if the mountain's essence acknowledged their presence.

"Be careful," Aerin whispered, halting their march. "The path ahead is not what it seems."

"An illusion?" Lysandra asked, holding her hand to sense the truth beneath the surface.

"Or a trap," Feyla suggested, eyeing the corridor.

"Let me try," Lysandra said, unfurling her spell. The silver glow revealed an illusion - a bridge where there was none, a chasm hidden beneath.

"Good call," Aerin grunted, his gaze fixed on the other side of the treacherous gap.

"Guide us, Lysandra," Feyla said, trusting the elf's magical prowess.

Lysandra focused, weaving ethereal strands into a light path across the abyss. "Quickly," she commanded, maintaining the construct.

They crossed the illuminated span one by one, Shadow's claws clicking against the luminescent threads. When they reached solid ground again, Feyla said, "We're almost there."

Aerin warned, "Stay sharp. It's too quiet."

"Quiet before the storm," Lysandra agreed, feeling the electric charge of imminent danger prickle her skin.

The air grew warmer as they descended, and the scent of molten earth filled their nostrils. A faint light emanated from ahead, casting long, dancing shadows against the jagged walls.

"Is that...?" Feyla began, but Lysandra silenced her with a gesture.

"Look," she whispered, pointing to the source of the light.

There, nestled within the heart of the mountain, stood an ancient forge - its fires burning without fuel, waiting for the hands of a master. Scattered around it were artifacts of unimaginable power, glowing with an inner light that pulsed in time with the mountain's beating heart.

climaxedAerin and Lysandra were exploring a chamber filled with raw magic when, suddenly, they were interrupted by a thunderous roar that shook the cavern. A living rock and flame creature emerged from the wall behind the forge.

"Prepare for battle!" Aerin cried, unsheathing his swords. "Stand together!" Lysandra shouted, conjuring shields of force around them. "Let's show it the strength of Erenor," Feyla declared, firing her bolt at the creature's hide.

The creature charged towards them, the ground trembling

beneath its weight. "Fight with everything you have!" Aerin roared, leaping forward to meet the onslaught. Lysandra cast spells, Feyla fired bolts, and Aerin's swords clashed with the creature's stony hide.

As the battle climaxed, the ground shook ominously, hinting at something more. "Brace yourselves!" Feyla yelled as the tremors grew more assertive. The mountain was awakening, and it was alive.

Chunks of rocks fell from the ceiling and walls, forcing the group to dodge debris as they approached a golden light from within a fissure in the wall. "We need to get to that light," Lysandra said, her eyes fixed on the goal.

They fought through the debris, defending themselves against falling rocks and the creature's attacks. "We can do this!" Aerin shouted, rallying the group.

Finally, they reached the fissure and stepped inside. The golden light illuminated the room, revealing a hidden chamber full of ancient artifacts. "This must be what we've been searching for," Lysandra said, her eyes excitedly shining.

Exploring the chamber, they discovered ancient texts and runes etched into the walls. "These runes are powerful," Feyla said, tracing her fingers over the ancient text. "I wonder what they mean."

Aerin picked up a rune-etched sword from the pile of artifacts. "This sword has magic in it," he said, feeling the power emanating from the weapon.

Excited by their discovery, the group exited the hidden chamber, ready to continue their quest with newfound strength and determination.

"Over there!" Lysandra shouted, pointing towards the light. "We have to get inside!" Aerin yelled back.

With renewed determination, they fought through the chaos and reached the fissure just as it closed again. With all their might, they pushed through and found themselves inside an enormous chamber filled with an otherworldly glow.

"This must be it," Feyla breathed in awe as she looked around at their surroundings.

The chamber was filled with intricate designs etched into every surface, glowing with energy. In the center of it all stood a towering figure made from gold.

"This is it," Aerin said as he looked upon the golden golem before them.

"But before we can claim it, we must defeat any guardians that may stand in our way," Lysandra added, holding her sword at the ready.

"Let's make it quick," Feyla said, loading a bolt into her crossbow.

Shadow growled low, sensing the danger that lay ahead.

The heroes approached the golem with their weapons drawn. As they drew near, they could feel its power emanating from every inch of its golden form.

"It's awake!" Aerin shouted over the noise.

The golem lifted its massive fists and slammed them down towards the heroes with incredible force. Aerin rolled to the side while Lysandra dodged. Feyla fired a bolt, which bounced harmlessly off the golem's armor. Shadow leaped onto its back and tried to claw its armor, but it seemed unaffected.

"We need to find its weakness!" Feyla yelled as she loaded another bolt and fired again. "I'll try to distract it!" Lysandra called out as she moved swiftly around the golem's legs.

Aerin searched the golem's body for any signs of vulnerability. He noticed that some of the golden runes were glowing brighter than others and seemed connected to different parts of its body.

"Feyla, aim for those glowing runes!" he shouted, pointing towards them.

They realized that these glowing runes powered the golem, and damaging it would weaken it. Lysandra continued to distract the golem while Feyla and Aerin worked together to target the glowing runes on its body. Shadow barked and snarled, trying to distract the golem as well.

The golem stumbled and fell to the ground, defeated. The heroes cheered in triumph.

With each successful hit, the golem's movements became slower and sluggish. But it was still a formidable opponent, swinging its massive fists and unleashing powerful energy blasts from its eyes.

"Stay focused!" Lysandra yelled as she dodged an energy blast. Feyla had run out of bolts, so she grabbed her sword and joined Lysandra in the fight. Together, they dodged the golem's attacks and landed blows on its glowing body.

Aerin used his magic to shield them from the golem's energy blasts and looked for other weak points. "I think it's vulnerable on its head," he called out.

The trio worked together, hitting the golem's head with all their might. The golem let out a roar and fell to the ground, inert.

"We did it!" Feyla exclaimed, relieved. Lysandra laughed triumphantly, and Aerin smiled at their victory. Shadow barked before collapsing, exhausted from the intense battle.

As they caught their breath, Feyla noticed something shining in the rubble where the golem had fallen. She walked over and picked up a tiny golden key with strange markings. "This must be the key we've been looking for," Feyla said, holding up the key.

Aerin nodded in agreement. "This key unlocks the hidden chamber in King Roderick's castle."

Lysandra chuckled. "Looks like our adventure isn't over yet."

With the key in hand, the group exited the underground chamber, ready for their next challenge.

Chapter 13

ANCIENT MEMORIES

Lysandra stood panting, her hair matted with sweat and dirt. The Golden Golem lay in pieces at their feet. Its once-majestic form is now nothing but scraps of metal scattered about.

Aerin leaned on his sword, scanning their surroundings as though expecting more trouble. "That should be the last of them, right?" he asked.

"I think so, for now," Lysandra replied, still catching her breath.

Feyla was already thinking, "What can we do with all this?" she said, gesturing towards the metal scraps.

Aerin turned to the two of them, "You both did great back there," he said, pride and concern in his voice. "Are you okay?"

Lysandra nodded, glancing around the cave. It was dark and damp, filled with shadows and secrets. "I'm okay, thanks," she said, feeling uneasy.

Aerin looked around the cave. "Let's stay alert," he said. This place is old and full of memories, not all good."

Lysandra couldn't shake the feeling that they were being watched. "I don't like this," she said, her voice low.

"Me neither," Feyla agreed, eyeing the shadows warily.

Claws scraping against stone followed a low growl that echoed throughout the cave. The three adventurers tensed, ready for whatever danger was ahead.

"Memories can't hurt us," Feyla muttered, adjusting her tool belt. But her eyes betrayed her fear of the mountain's gaze upon them.

"Can't they?" Aerin mused, his stride purposeful. "Sometimes memories are the most potent magic of all."

Lysandra felt an icy shiver down her spine but kept her face impassive. She had grown beyond fear, but the mountain reminded her that the world of Erenor was entirely of wondrous and terrible forces.

"Let's keep moving," she urged. "The sooner we leave this place, the better."

"Agreed," Aerin said. "I don't want to become part of the scenery."

"Nor do I," added Feyla. "Though the architecture is quite fascinating."

Lysandra admonished them, "Focus, we have a quest to complete." Together, they moved, bound by a quest larger than any of them—larger even than the dark, breathing cavern surrounding them.

Lysandra spotted the golden key, its form lying in stark contrast against the dark stone. She reached out, her fingers closing around it. The key was heavy. Its surface was warm as if thrummed with life.

"Is that...?" Aerin began, moving closer to examine the object.

"The key," Lysandra confirmed, revealing the intricate engravings that danced across its metal skin. "It bears the Elder Script," she murmured to herself.

"Be careful," Feyla warned. "Such things are often cursed."

"Or protected," Aerin added, studying the key's design. "The ancients did not leave their treasures unguarded."

"We'll be vigilant," Lysandra replied, securing the key in her pouch. "But this is what we came for."

"Let's not waste any more time," Aerin said, wiping grime from his brow. "These mountains have already taken enough from us."

"Agreed," Lysandra said, taking a deep breath. "The way out will be as dangerous as the way in."

With a collective nod, they began trekking out of the cavern. Each step was slow and deliberate, and they carefully placed their feet on the slick, uneven ground.

"Watch that loose stone," Aerin cautioned, pointing to a treacherous patch ahead.

"I got it," Feyla replied, reaching for the hilt of her weapon.

"Silence can be our ally," Lysandra whispered as they edged past a narrow rock column. Her wolf, silent as a shadow, followed close behind, its amber eyes alert.

"It feels like we're being watched," Aerin muttered, his hand resting on the pommel of his sword.

"Because we are," Lysandra replied, "by the mountain itself."

"That's superstitious nonsense," Feyla said, though she lacked conviction.

"Perhaps," Lysandra conceded, "but respect for the powers that dwell here has kept us alive."

"True enough," Aerin agreed. "And we'll need more than respect to face what lies beyond these peaks."

Aerin, Lysandra, and Feyla were on a mission to save Erenor, a country where darkness reigned. They had to leave the cave they were in and complete their task. As they neared the exit, Lysandra reminded them to stay vigilant.

As they stepped out into the bright sunlight, they saw a group of Dwarven artisans emerge from the shadows. The Dwarves were skilled craftsmen, with faces etched with the tales of a thousand hammer strikes and hands rough from a lifetime of perfecting their craft.

"Welcome, travelers," said the eldest Dwarven artisan. "You've fought hard to reach this hallowed forge."

"Thanks for welcoming us," said Lysandra. She saw a table with artifacts glinting with an otherworldly sheen and hummed with energy.

"These artifacts look amazing," said Feyla, admiring them.

"Can you tell us more about them?" asked Aerin.

"These artifacts are imbued with ancient magic that has been passed down through generations of Dwarven artisans," replied Balur, one of the Dwarves. "They can do many things and help you on your journey."

"We'll take them," said Feyla, determined.

The Dwarves handed over the artifacts, and the trio thanked them before continuing on their journey, feeling empowered by the magic of the artifacts.

Lysandra stepped forward, her fingers brushing over the artifacts, feeling the pulsing enchantments woven into their essence.

"Such power," she murmured, more to herself than to the Dwarves.

"Take them," urged Balur. "They are yours by right of conquest and destiny."

"Destiny is a fickle ally," Lysandra replied, locking eyes with the elder craftsman. "But I will wield these gifts with honor."

"May they serve you well against the darkness that festers," said another Dwarf, his tone grave. "For if it spreads, not even our forges will withstand its corruption."

"Then let us hope the Celestial Fracture yields to our efforts," Lysandra said, a resolve hardening her voice. She turned to her companions. "We have much to do."

"Go with the strength of the mountains at your back," Balur added.

"Thank you," Feyla interjected. "For your trust and your steel."

"Trust must be earned," the elder Dwarf reminded them. "And steel, tempered. Go now. Forge your path as we forge our creations."

With a last nod, Lysandra shouldered the burden of their hopes, the enchanted artifacts promising battles to come.

"Come," she commanded. "Let's bring light to the shadows."

As they turned away from the Dwarven enclave, each step took them further from the Iron Mountains and closer to the heart of Erenor's wounds. But with the might of Dwarven magic at their side, the shadows that loomed ahead seemed less daunting and the path less treacherous.

"Hope is a weapon, too," Aerin mused, his eyes on the horizon.

Lysandra felt the weight of the golden key in her pocket. It was a reminder of the golem's defeat and the challenges ahead. She admired the intricate patterns and the sapphire center-piece of the silver amulet. The Dwarven artisans who crafted it promised to channel her inner strength and storms.

Lysandra slid her hands into the gauntlets: a warmth spread up her arms, lending strength and precision to her spellcasting. The cloak woven from shadow silk offered protection spelled with whispers of ancient magic. Lysandra knew that these artifacts symbolized the unity between their races and the shared pur-pose of restoring what was shattered.

The Dwarven artisans formed a semi-circle around her. Lysan-dra implored them to tell her about the celestial structure and how it came to pass. The older Dwarf explained that it was a reckoning, a convergence of unchecked pride and power that tore through the veil, splintering the world's essence.

"I vow to wield these gifts with honor and to restore what was shattered," Lysandra said, her voice carrying the weight of her resolve. Thank you for trusting me with your craft and with the fate of Erenor."

"May they serve you well, Mage of Erenor," the lead artisan said. "In your hands, they're not just metal and magic. They're hope."

As Lysandra adjusted the cloak's clasp, the cool metal of the golden key pressed against her thigh. She was the last mage, the critical bearer, and the fractured world's final hope. She vowed to wield these gifts honorably, remembering that they symbolized hope.

Lysandra's companions shuffled closer, armor clinking, as the wolves growled low, sensing the gravity of the tale.

"Conduits... the ethereal wells," another dwarf chimed in, his hammer dangling at his side. "They're scattered and hidden, holding the remnants of what once was. To heal is to bind them, to weave magic anew."

"Binding..." The word hung heavy in Lysandra's mind as she wrestled with the enormity. Shadow nudged against her leg, his presence a silent vow to stand by her through the shadowed paths ahead.

"We need to be swift," Lysandra said, clutching the golden key tightly. "The last well is waiting for us, and it's our chance to restore balance to the land after the Fracture."

"You must hurry," a young artisan said, his voice filled with urgency. "Time is running out."

Lysandra nodded, feeling the weight of responsibility on her shoulders. "We must work together to forge a new dawn," she said, looking at her companions.

"May the mountains guide you," the dwarves said in unison, their voices echoing through the cavern.

Lysandra took a deep breath and secured the artifacts to her person. "Let's go," she said, leading the way with her companions following closely behind.

As they walked through the tunnel, Lysandra's hand traced the intricate carvings of the silver amulet. "This is our last chance," she whispered.

"We've come too far to give up now," Aerin said, determination etched on his face.

"You hold the power that we can only forge," a stout dwarf said, looking at Lysandra respectfully.

Lysandra nodded, feeling the weight of their trust. "We'll do this together," she said, looking at her companions.

"The road ahead won't be easy," a burly man said, his arms covered in scars. "But we'll face it together."

"We sharpen each other," a woman with raven hair added, her hand resting on the pommel of her dagger.

Lysandra smiled, feeling the warmth of her wolf pup against her leg. "We won't let the heartbeat of our world stop," she said, determined.

"You carry the might of the mountains with you," the lead artisan said, his hands smudged with soot.

A young dwarf stepped forward, holding out a stone flecked with veins of luminous ore. "Take this for light in darkness," he said. "May it guide you."

Lysandra took the stone, feeling its pulsating glow in her hand. "Thank you," she said, feeling grateful.

"Time is running out," the eldest Dwarf said, his voice rumbling like the earth. "Go now."

Lysandra nodded, turning to leave. "May your hammers never fall silent," she said, feeling the artifacts resonating with the promise of magic reborn.

"Nor your magic fades," the dwarves replied, their voices echoing as Lysandra and her companions disappeared into the shadows of the tunnel.

As they emerged into the daylight, the clatter of their boots against the stone faded away. Lysandra felt her sword at her side, ready to face the uncertainty ahead.

"Almost there," she murmured, her voice steady despite the weariness that clung to her bones like the dampness of the cave.

Aerin squinted at the bright light ahead. He turned to Lysandra, "Can you feel it?"

Lysandra shielded her eyes from the blinding sunlight and replied, "I can. The fracture awaits."

Feyla, the cynic, muttered, "Or walking into the afterlife."

Aerin gasped, "By the gods, it's like being reborn."

Lysandra reminded him, "Every step is a victory." She was anxious about the task ahead - healing what had been shattered with the help of the ethereal wells.

Aerin said, "Then we push on," scanning the horizon.

But Feyla had a valid point, "We need a plan. The legends didn't speak of what guards the last well."

Lysandra brushed her silver amulet, enhancing her focus, "Legends don't have all the answers. We adapt. We overcome."

Aerin added, "Like with the Golem. Never thought I'd see gold bleed."

Lysandra smiled briefly, "Let's not underestimate what lies ahead."

Feyla said, "I plan to be pleasantly surprised when some ancient horror does not ambush us."

Aerin chuckled, "Optimism, Feyla? You'll spoil your reputation."

Lysandra cut in, "We're close. I can feel the fractures in the air. The last well will test everything we are."

Aerin affirmed, "Then we stand ready."

Feyla flexed her fingers in anticipation, "Ready as we'll ever be."

Lysandra reminded them, "We fight for ourselves and Erenor. For every soul that dreams of peace."

Feyla confirmed her resolve, "Lead on, Lysandra."

Lysandra swore, "We all will move ahead," facing the path away from the mountain's shadow. Shadow let out a low growl and led the way. They were ready for whatever darkness awaited.

Chapter 14

THE HARROW

The ground shook beneath Lysandra's feet as the Harrow emerged from the smoldering ruins of the sacred grove. Once a majestic creature with beautiful earthy scales, it now looked corrupted and sickly due to the Celestial Fracture's vile signature. Its eyes locked onto Lysandra's, reflecting a soul under attack by the shadows.

Lysandra commanded, "Stay calm." She scanned the dragon, looking for any signs of its former nobility.

"It's huge," breathed Aerin, his hand on his sword's hilt, his eyes never leaving the dragon.

"We need to focus and end this torment," Lysandra replied.

The Harrow reared, wings unfurling like tattered war banners, casting a threatening shadow over them. It charged towards them, revealing its jagged teeth.

"Get out of the way!" Lysandra yelled, leaping aside as a jet of corrupted flame burst forth, scorching the ground where they had just stood.

She drew her sword and charged towards the dragon. The forest around them was ablaze with the dragon's fury, and the heat sang the air. Aerin followed her, his sword at the ready.

Lysandra shouted, "Aim for the eyes!"

They dodged the dragon's attacks and managed to land a few blows. The dragon roared in pain, its eyes flashing with anger.

"We're making progress!" Aerin shouted.

Lysandra nodded, "Keep going!"

Finally, they landed the fatal blow, and the dragon collapsed. The shadows attacking the Harrow dissipated, and Lysandra breathed a sigh of relief.

"We did it," she said, looking at Aerin with a smile. "We ended its torment."

Aerin and Lysandra faced off against The Harrow, a dragon threatening their lives. Aerin asked, "Can we even kill this thing?"

Lysandra replied, "Killing may not be our only option. We need to be smart." She watched the dragon's movements and realized they had to devise a new plan.

"Look at it. It's suffering," Lysandra said, dodging a lashing claw.

Aerin responded, "Then we give it peace—one way or another."

Lysandra knew that killing the dragon wouldn't solve the problem. "Trust me," she told Aerin before confronting The Harrow.
She had an idea that could end the battle and save the dragon's life.

Lysandra's sword swung through the air, dodging the Harrow's tail.

"Left flank, Aerin! Feyla, high!" Lysandra shouted. They fought the beast together, working as a team.

"Use your magic, Lysandra," Feyla said.

Lysandra unleashed her power, wrapping chains of light around The Harrow. The dragon roared, fighting against the spell.

"Keep pressing!" Aerin yelled, slashing at The Harrow's underbelly. Lysandra's sword glowed as she whispered an incantation, and vines erupted from the ground, entangling The Harrow's claws.

"Good, Lysandra! That's it!" Feyla cheered.

Lysandra dodged a burst of dragon fire. "I know what I'm doing," she said confidently.

Aerin insisted, "Let me take the next hit."

"No, we do this together," Lysandra responded fiercely. Their unity was a weapon as potent as any steel or spell.

"Let's do this, Lysandra. We've got your back," Aerin said, his voice low yet firm over the dragon's roar.

"Strike to heal," Lysandra corrected. She didn't want to destroy The Harrow but to redeem it. Together, they stood to face the consequences of their compassionate decision and maybe even find a way to heal the fractured skies.

The Harrow's scales shimmered with a sickly glow as it advanced, leaving deep scars on the ground with every step. Its claws tore into the soil like the talons of fate.

"Be careful!" Feyla warned. Her arrows hit their mark but did not affect the dragon's advance.

Lysandra dodged a tail lash, rolling to her feet as Aerin parried a claw swipe. The air was thick with the stench of corruption and magic energy.

"We can't keep this up much longer," Aerin grunted as his blade clashed against The Harrow's hardened scales.

"Then we change tactics," Lysandra suggested, her mind racing. Beneath the layers of dark magic binding The Harrow, she felt a glimmer of the creature it used to be - noble, powerful, pure.

"Can't you see he's too far gone, Lysandra?" Aerin argued, not understanding her hesitation.

But she shook her head, her eyes locked on The Harrow. "I believe there's still a chance to save him. We don't have to end this in blood," she said.

"But saving him could mean our deaths!" Aerin replied, casting a protective glance at her.

"Or it could mean life for all," Lysandra countered, weighing each word. She couldn't help but recall the wolf pup she once saved, now her loyal companion. She couldn't deny The Harrow the same chance.

"Decide, Lysandra!" Feyla called, stringing another arrow with unwavering focus.

"Trust me," Lysandra whispered as she raised her sword. She didn't want to challenge the dragon but to plead with it. Magic surged around her, a storm of her own making.

"Don't do anything foolish, Lysandra," Aerin warned, fear

creeping into his voice.

"Sometimes foolishness is just hope in disguise," Lysandra replied, her resolve hardening.

The Harrow loomed before them, malice in its eyes, yet Lysandra saw a flicker of Something pure within the darkness.

"Get ready!" she commanded, stepping forward with her hand outstretched, ready for whatever fate had in store for her.

The dragon's ear-piercing scream shook the ground, resonating with the pain of the Celestial Fracture. Lysandra stood her ground, her sword shimmering with iridescent light, her gaze fixed on The Harrow's tortured eyes.

Aerin was ready to fight, his hand on his blade. "Lyss, what are you waiting for?" he asked, his voice cutting through the chaos.

Lysandra whispered back, "Watch and learn."

Feyla looked confused, notching another arrow.

"Trust me," Lysandra said, trying to quell her rising fear. "I can save him."

Aerin retorted, "Save us all first," his voice trembling as the earth shook beneath their feet.

"I need stillness," Lysandra said, her words commanding yet delicate.

She advanced towards The Harrow, her heart drumming a

rhythm of ancient spells and unspoken promises. The dragon's dark scales seemed to absorb the light around it, a void where hope should be.

She whispered, "There is life within you still," her voice spreading like ripples across a still lake. The Harrow's snarl faltered, a glint of clarity sparking in its abyssal depths.

"Be ready to fight or flee," Lyss warned her companions.

"Always," Aerin replied tersely.

"Fix this, Lysandra," Feyla added, her aim unwavering despite her uncertainty.

Lysandra whispered an incantation, and her sword began to glow with a pure essence. She thrust her hand forward, not to pierce flesh but to channel the healing power that thrummed through her veins.

The Harrow's roar softened into a pained whimper, its form shuddering like battling an internal foe. Lyss's magic enveloped the dragon, weaving a tapestry of restoration where ruin once reigned.

"Is it working?" Aerin asked, his awe warring with skepticism. "See for yourself," Lyss answered without looking away from her task.

The dragon's transformation was a wonder to behold. Dark scales gave way to a lustrous sheen, the smog of malice clearing from its eyes to reveal orbs as deep and endless as the night sky unfettered by shadow.

The massive creature had been restless since its essence was fractured, but it had finally settled down peacefully. The Harrow exhaled the word "Free" in a language that was not human but was understood by all present. It then spoke again, expressing its gratitude to Lysandra.

She felt the weight of her decision, its risk, and its rightness. She commanded the Harrow to go and be what it was meant to be. The dragon bowed its head, acknowledging respect and vowing peace. It then took to the skies with a beat of mighty wings, its silhouette against the backdrop of a world on the brink of darkness and light. Lysandra called out after the departing dragon, wishing it a safe flight.

As Harrow ascended towards freedom, Aerin and Lysandra exchanged glances. They had fought a formidable beast together, turning its ferocity into a dance of death and salvation.

"Did you see that?" Aerin exclaimed, awe in his voice.

"Of course I did! Thanks to you," Lysandra replied, breathless.

A sudden gust from the dragon's departure sent them stumbling into each other. Their bodies pressed close for a fleeting moment before they regained balance. Aerin's cheeks flushed, not all of it from exertion.

"Careful there," Lysandra teased, hinting at Something more than camaraderie in her eyes.

"I wouldn't want to be anywhere else," Aerin replied, the words slipping out before he could corral them. Lysandra's genuine laugh was a sound. He'd fight a thousand dragons to keep safe.

"Focus," she said, the laughter still tinting her voice. "We're not done yet."

"Right," he nodded with newfound resolve, feeling the weight of his sword as if for the first time.

They surveyed the battlefield together, where smoldering craters and scorched earth bore testament to the dragon's wrath and their determination.

"Your sword work is impressive," Aerin remarked.

"Thank you. Yours aren't so bad either," Lysandra countered with a grin.

"Maybe you can teach me a few tricks sometimes," he offered.

"Sure, only if you promise to show me some of your hunting skills," she replied.

"Deal," he agreed, the word binding more than just an exchange of skills.

Their gazes locked, a silent understanding passing between

them. It was a pact forged in the heat of battle and the shared recognition of each other's strengths and weaknesses.

"Look out!" Lysandra warned as a shadow loomed overhead. Aerin stepped in front of her, raising his sword against falling debris.

"Thanks," she breathed, peering around him. Her expression was a mix of gratitude and Something deeper, Something he had dared not yet name.

"Don't mention it," he said, his heart hammering in his chest for reasons beyond the adrenaline of combat.

Lysandra and Aerin cleared the area before any more surprises found them. As they walked side by side with weapons ready, they became more connected with every glance and exchanged words.

After they finished, Aerin said he had Something to say. "About us," he added.

"Us?" Lysandra echoed, feeling hopeful.

"Yeah. After we finish what we started," Aerin promised, feeling more confident in her presence.

"Then let's make sure we do," Lysandra smiled.

"I didn't know you had that in you," Aerin murmured, admiring her.

"There are many things you don't know about me," Lysandra replied, concentrating on the task.

"Care to enlighten me - after?" Aerin asked.

"Perhaps," Lysandra replied, sensing a connection forming between them.

"Promise I'll listen," Aerin vowed.

"Let's survive first," Lysandra reminded him, feeling her heart pounding with more than just the exertion of the fight.

"Deal," he agreed, standing guard as she knelt before the mighty Harrow, her hands glowing with healing light.

As the dragon's rage ebbed away under her touch, Lysandra realized that perhaps there was strength in the protective circle of someone who cared, even if she was still learning to accept it.

The Harrow's massive form lay subdued before them, the once-crimson scales now a lustrous gold.

"Is it...?" Feyla began, her bowstring still taut, her gaze never leaving the transformed beast.

"Alive, yes," Lysandra confirmed, sheathing her sword. "And free from corruption."

"By the gods, you've done it," Aerin said, his voice reverent.

"I did what needed to be done," Lysandra corrected. "But this is just a single thread mended in a torn world."

"Then we mend more," Aerin said, taking her hand in a pledge.

"Indeed," Lysandra murmured, turning to survey the charred battlefield, the cost of their victory etched into every blackened tree and scorched stone.

"Perhaps our scaled friend can aid us now," Feyla suggested, catching the lingering touch between Aerin and Lysandra. "What say you, Harrow?"

The dragon inclined its massive head, understanding or grateful.

Lysandra thought out loud, "An ally from an enemy," weighing her decision. She felt a shift within herself, a glimmer of hope that they could heal more than just the dragons.

Aerin said, "Let's not get ahead of ourselves. We have a long way to go, and the Celestial Fracture won't wait for us."

Feyla added, "Neither will shadow hounds. We should move. Our path won't get any easier with a dragon in tow."

Lysandra decided, "Then we'll travel by night. We have a fracture to mend, and time is not on our side."

Aerin agreed, "Understood." He glanced at Harrow, and they gathered their few things and set out into the dark.

Lysandra led the way, urging them to stay alert. Aerin quipped, "Unless you're staring at our fearless leader," earning a sharp look from Lysandra and an embarrassed cough from himself.

Feyla teased, "Focus, children," as they vanished into the night, the ember of unity burning between them.

A rustle shook the underbrush, and tension snapped taut. Lysandra drew her sword, ready for anything.

Feyla whispered, "Something approaches. Friend or enemy?" Aerin scanned the shadows with his hand on his blade.

Lysandra replied, "Unknown," sensing the disturbance. She summoned a whisper of light to reveal the gleaming eyes of woodland creatures.

She murmured, "False alarm. Stay sharp." They continued, but

Something wasn't right, and they were all on high alert.

Lysandra said, "Magic stirs," feeling the energy coiling within her. They prepared themselves for what was coming.

Feyla commanded, "Show yourself!" The forest growled in response, and shadows shifted to form creatures wrought with nightmare and malice, eyes

glinting with evil intent. Shadow Hounds.

"Defend!" Lysandra cried out, power flaring from her fingertips, illuminating their assailants.

"Protect her!" Aerin barked, stepping closer to Lysandra, his blade singing as it cut through the air.

"Back to back!" Feyla shouted, shooting arrows with precision.

"Stay out of my way," Lysandra warned Aerin, frustration evident in her tone.

"Wouldn't dream of it," Aerin replied as he dodged a clawed swipe.

"Focus on your targets!" Lysandra reminded as she combined magic and steel in a deadly dance.

"I can't help it," Aerin grunted as he dispatched another beast. "You're magnetic."

"Shut up and fight," Lysandra snapped, her heart racing for more reasons than one.

"Always," Aerin promised, matching her blow for blow.

"Watch out!" Feyla warned as an arrow barely missed Lysandra and a creature lunged toward her blind spot.

"Thanks," Lysandra gasped, grateful despite herself.

"Anytime," Feyla replied with a wink.

"Enough!" Lysandra roared, unleashing a torrent of magic that swept through their enemies like a storm, leaving destruction in its wake.

"Is everyone—" Aerin began, but Lysandra silenced him with a raised hand.

"Listen," she instructed, breathless from the exertion.

Silence. Then, a low rumble grew steadily.

"Dragon," Lysandra confirmed, her companions' eyes meeting hers.

"Friend or foe?" Feyla questioned, her tension returning.

"Let's find out," Lysandra said, striding forward to meet the unknown, her companions at her heels. She was bound by purpose, magic, and Something close to affection.

Chapter 15

DRAGONBOND

The Iron Mountains towered above them, their jagged peaks piercing the sky like ancient guardians. Lysandra led her companions through the rugged terrain, her breath misting in the chilly air.

"Be on your guard," she cautioned, unsheathing her sword. "The Harrow should be close."

Aerin, dressed in dark leather armor, nodded with a furrowed brow. "If the tales are true, this dragon could change the tide for us," he said, his eyes scanning the surroundings.

"Or roast us where we stand," Feyla added, her violet eyes severe beneath her hood.

Shadow padded silently beside Lysandra, ready to protect her from any threat.

As they rounded a bend, they saw the Harrow, its scales shimmering like black diamonds in the weak sun. The massive creature lay curled up, a silent sentinel amid the desolate landscape.

"Stay back," Lysandra whispered, holding an arm to halt her companions. She took a step forward, her heart racing.

"Are you sure about this?" Aerin's voice was low, laced with concern.

"Trust me." Her words were more confident than she felt. She took another step, then another, until she stood before the dragon.

"Hello, Harrow," she whispered, extending her hand in a gesture of connection.

"Careful, Lysandra," Feyla warned from behind. But her voice was amazed - a recognition of the moment's gravity.

Shadow growled a rumble that vibrated through the silence.

"Shh, it's alright," Lysandra murmured. "I won't let anything happen."

"Nor I," Aerin added, his voice barely audible. He sounded softer than his usual warrior self.

"Easy, Harrow," Lysandra continued, inching closer. Her hand hovered just above the dragon's snout, its breath warming her chilled skin.

"Let her do this," Feyla said, sensing Aerin's urge to protect.

"Come on," Lysandra coaxed. "We're not your enemies."

As her fingers brushed the scales, a hush fell over the world, the wind dying to whisper. All eyes were on them—human, wolf, and dragon—as fates converged in the heart of the Iron Mountains.

The Harrow's golden eyes flickered open, cutting through the dimness with an ethereal glow. Lysandra held her breath, and the air between them was charged with unspoken words. Their gazes locked, each searching and finding an echo of their solitude in the other.

"See me," she whispered. "Not as a mage, not as a threat—just... Lysandra."

The dragon's pupils dilated, and a bridge between species was built on the fragile pillars of hope and shared silence.

"Are you sure about this?" Aerin's voice cracked through the quiet, laced with an undercurrent of concern he couldn't mask.

"Absolutely," Lysandra replied, her gaze never wavering from the Harrow.

Her fingertips grazed the dragon's scales, and a jolt of energy surged up her arm, igniting every nerve with a tingling promise of power and kinship. Magic hummed between them, an ancient call resonating deep within her bones.

"By the gods," she gasped, the connection rooting her to the spot as if the mountain claimed her as its own.

"Is it... happening?" Feyla's voice cut through Lysandra's reverie.

"More than that," Lysandra replied, her body thrumming with newfound strength. "It's like coming home."

Lysandra stood before the Harrow, a magnificent dragon. She ran her fingers along its snout, feeling its warmth.

"Can you feel it, Harrow?" she asked. "This is what we've been waiting for."

The dragon let out a warm breath, affirming its bond with

Lysandra. Feyla and Aerin stood by, watching in awe.

"This is remarkable," Feyla said.

"Indeed," Aerin agreed, his voice trembling with emotion.

Lysandra felt a fierce determination inside her. She knew they were allying to stand against the darkness.

"Let's hope it's enough," Aerin said, looking at Lysandra.

"It will be," Lysandra replied confidently. "With The Harrow by our side, we are more than enough."

The dragon's golden eye dilated, revealing its understanding.

"See the storm within me?" Lysandra whispered. "It rages for you, for us."

The dragon lowered its head in a rare gesture of equality. It was evident that they shared a purpose.

The bond between Lysandra and The Harrow was tangible. It pulsed through her veins, igniting every fiber of her being. It was more than a bond. It was a living force.

Together, they were ready to face whatever lay ahead.

"United," she whispered, feeling the word echo through her body. She could feel her heart pounding, full of the excitement of the battles they were about to face together.

"Bound by blood and storm," The Harrow responded with a deep rumble that shook the ground beneath them. Its wings spread wide, casting a protective shadow over them.

"Your courage is an honor to me," the dragon said, its voice low and powerful. It looked at her with recognition as if it had found a kinship with her.

"Thanks, Harrow," Lysandra said, looking at the dragon with gratitude. "You don't owe me anything."

"But I offer you everything," the dragon replied, its tail sweeping slowly across the rocky terrain. As it did, Lysandra's sword glowed mystically, a testament to their growing bond.

"Everything," Lysandra echoed, feeling the weight of the promise. She could feel the dragon's loyalty, as strong as the wind whipped around them.

"Then let us rise, my friend," Lysandra said, gripping her sword. "Erenor calls and we must answer."

The Harrow lifted its head, and the mountains seemed to bow

respectfully. "To the end," it swore, sealing their pact with words as much as with the mystical bond that now linked them.

"Let's forge our path," Aerin said, his voice cutting through the charged air. He looked at Lysandra and the dragon with awe and apprehension, knowing they were about to embark on a dangerous journey together.

Feyla, Lysandra, and Aerin stood together, ready for the trials ahead. "We make our stand with fire and steel," Feyla said.

Lysandra repeated the words, "Fire and steel." She glanced at Aerin and noticed the conflict in his gaze. They were more than comrades now; they were a team, each member contributing their unique strength and skill.

"Dawn approaches, and with it, our destiny," Lysandra said, looking at both Feyla and Aerin.

The three of them were united in their quest to harness the power of magic and the beating heart of a dragon. They were an unspoken alliance, their bond as vital as the cool mountain air around them.

Suddenly, Shadow growled, his hackles rising. He was staring at Harrow, a giant creature that loomed over them.

"Shadow, stand down," Lysandra commanded, her voice cutting through the tension. She touched the wolf's fur, trying to soothe him. "The Harrow is with us now."

Shadow continued to growl, clearly distrustful of Harrow. Lysandra spoke softly, trying to calm him. "He won't harm me. Trust me, as I trust him."

Shadow looked at Lysandra, his amber eyes searching for deceit or danger. He was unsure about Harrow, a legendary and feared creature.

Lysandra continued to speak softly to Shadow, "We've faced darker fates than this. Our bond is our hope, our weapon. He's part of the path we walk now and our destiny."

Gradually, Shadow's tension eased, and he became silent. He remained close to Lysandra, guarding her and watching The Harrow with a wary eye.

"Thank you," Lysandra breathed a sigh of relief. She was grateful that Shadow had accepted The Harrow's presence. Her fingers traced the hilt of her sword, a promise to protect both the wolf and the man who stood by her side.

The three of them settled in, each with their brand of magic and strength. They were ready to face whatever lay ahead in the veiled mists of dawn.

Aerin gazed at Lysandra, admiring her strength and determination. Together, they would overcome any obstacle that lay ahead.

The group stood before a massive dragon, shrouded in shadows, a creature that seemed to be made of flesh and bone.

The dragon was mighty and untamed, but Lysandra appeared to control the situation.

Aerin whispered to himself, "Shadow trusts her. And that beast… it might just follow."

Lysandra's eyes met the dragon's, and there was a sense of recognition. The dragon's scales sparkled in the twilight, and its eyes glowed like ancient fire.

Aerin was skeptical and asked, "Is this wise?"

Lysandra replied, "Trust is our only currency here."

Aerin was hesitant about their alliance with the dragon but trusted Lysandra's judgment.

Their wolf companion, Shadow, growled at the dragon, but Lysandra's touch calmed him down.

Aerin asked, "Does it understand us?"

Lysandra replied, "Better than we understand ourselves."

Aerin admired Lysandra's courage and determination. He said, "The Harrow could turn the tides for us."

Lysandra replied, "With or without our understanding," and Aerin knew they would stand together against whatever lay ahead.

The dragon rumbled, and Aerin felt the electric charge of potential. He said, "Fire and steel," echoing Lysandra's earlier whisper. The magic that flowed through their veins bound them together more than loyalty.

Lysandra declared, "Let the night come. We are ready." Aerin agreed, and the stars blinked awake overhead as their journey changed. The alliance with the dragon was a testament to their strength and the bond weaving itself between him and Lysandra.

Feyla watched as the last light of day disappeared behind the Iron Mountains. She regarded the dragon with a mixture of awe and pragmatic calculation.

"We need that dragon," she said, looking up at The Harrow. "It changes the game."

Lysandra nodded in agreement. "Having an ally in the skies is worth more than having ten on the ground."

"Especially when it breathes fire," Aerin said, tossing another log onto the campfire.

"Fire can either forge our path or incinerate it," Feyla said, reminding them of the risks.

"But I'd rather have the beast with us than against us," she added.

"Agreed," Lysandra said, looking at Aerin.

The night fell around them, and Shadow paced at Lysandra's feet, still eyeing The Harrow. Aerin watched the wolf, sensing his unease mirrored in the animal's behavior. But they needed the dragon's help. There was no room for doubt.

"Let's rest now," Lysandra commanded, resting her hand on Shadow's head. "We rise with the first light of dawn."

"Rest with one eye open," Feyla muttered, checking her daggers.

Aerin smiled at Feyla's vigilance. He joined Lysandra on the ground and talked about the challenges ahead. Sleep would be difficult, but they hoped their dreams would show them the way forward.

"Let's dream of victory," Lysandra whispered.

"Victory and survival," Aerin added, looking at the stars above.

"Survival," Feyla agreed, scanning their surroundings.

As they settled for the night, the Harrow stood guard over them, a silent vow of protection. Their alliance with the dragon was more than a tactical advantage; it symbolized their resolve to fight against the darkness.

They packed their camp the next day and prepared for the journey ahead. They discussed their plan of attack, knowing that their enemies would not go down without a fight.

"We need to use the dragon's fire to our advantage," Lysandra said.

"And be prepared for any counterattacks," Aerin added.

Shadow growled, sensing the tension in the air. Feyla reassured him before joining the discussion.

As they strategized, Lysandra felt grateful for their team. They were each skilled in their own way and made a formidable force together.

Their quest had become more than a mission. It was a testament to the power of unity against the darkness.

"Tomorrow, we face our fate," Lysandra said.

"Whatever it brings, we'll face it together," Aerin vowed.

Lysandra reached out to Aerin, brushing his hand with hers. They sat silently, lost in their thoughts and fears but ready to face the trials ahead.

Chapter 16

LUMINAR

Luminar was a city sprawled beneath a sky blushing with the last embers of twilight. Its streets were lit with lanterns that swung from the eaves of high-roofed shops, casting a warm glow over throngs of cloaked figures that moved like a river through the cobbled arteries. The air hummed with the chatter of merchants, the clink of coins, and the tantalizing scents of sizzling meats and sweetmeats vying for attention.

Aerin muttered, "Wow, I've never seen anything like this before," as he gazed at the grand spires that crowned the city's skyline. Lysandra whispered, "Me neither. But we can't let it distract us. We must be vigilant."

Feyla agreed, and they set off to find a place to rest.

Harrow, the great-scaled beast that had carried them across the skies, looked tired. His wings drooped with an exhaustion that only the ancients could comprehend.

Aerin suggested, "Let's find a place where Harrow can recover." Feyla nodded and said, "He knows these lands better than us. He'll lead us to safety."

"Follow me," Harrow rumbled, leading them through the lesser-known paths of Luminar, away from prying eyes and curious crowds.

After some time, Harrow declared, "Here," coming to a halt in a secluded grove. The hidden grove lay nestled in the city's embrace, guarded by ancient magic and rustling leaves. "I will rest here, shielded from those who might wish harm."

"Thanks, Harrow. Rest up, we'll keep watch," Lysandra said, reaching out to touch the dragon's snout.

As the dragon settled amidst the foliage, his massive form blended with the evening shadows, a testament to his kind's mastery over concealment.

Aerin noticed Lysandra's subtle tremor and asked, "Are you okay?"

"Sure," she said, but her eyes betrayed a hint of fear or admiration as she looked at him.

"Then let's keep going," said Aerin, thoughts of their mission consuming his mind. The weight of their purpose was always with him.

"Lead the way," Feyla said, her determination unyielding like the steel she carried. Together, the trio turned their backs to the resting Harrow and stepped back into the vibrant chaos of Luminar. Their bond had been forged in the fires of shared trials, a unity that would be their greatest strength against the darkness ahead.

"Do you think they'll help us?" Aerin's voice murmured as they navigated the intricate alleyways of Luminar, revealing more of the city's erratic nature at every turn.

"I'm more than certain," said Feyla, her strides confident. "The Gnomish Tinkers are legends." She stopped mid-sentence as they rounded a corner and came upon a storefront that seemed to buzz with otherworldly energy.

The sign above read 'Gizmos & Grimoires,' and beneath it, the Tinkers' workshop sprawled like a spider's web of ingenuity made manifest. Cogs spun in mesmerizing patterns, intertwining with glowing runes and shimmering baubles that hovered without strings.

"Welcome, travelers!" A gnome with thick spectacles magnifying his eyes greeted them. His beard was a patchwork of singed hair and braids adorned with miniature tools.

"Good evening," Lysandra responded. "We're looking for information on the final ethereal well."

"Ah! The seekers of secrets!" Another gnome chimed in,

emerging from behind a stack of books that defied gravity. "I see determination in your eyes."

"Time isn't on our side," Aerin interjected. "We must find the well before the dark tide rises."

"There are risks untold for those who tread that path," the first gnome said, scratching his head. "But for a price, we'll share what we know."

"Name it," Lysandra said, her voice steady despite the flutter in her chest.

"An exchange," the second gnome replied, his eyes glinting. "A story for a story. Tell us your journey's tale, and we'll share the well's secrets."

"Deal," Lysandra asserted, her hand already resting on the pommel of her sword, silently promising to protect the narrative of their quest.

"Then speak while fate is in your favor," the gnomes said in unison, gesturing towards a table cluttered with artifacts that seemed to hum with anticipation.

'From the Ashen Plains to the Veiled Peaks, we've fought shadows and flames, ' Aerin began, memories igniting a fire within him. We fight to redeem ourselves, to find hope, and to rekindle the magic of Erenor before it is consumed by darkness.'

"I will reward bravery," the first gnome acknowledged, nodding. The final well is located deep within the Caverns of Sorrow, and the phantoms of despair guard it."

"Many have tried to find it," the second gnome added, his tone somber. "None have returned to share its wonders or its dangers."

"But we must try," Lysandra said, looking at Aerin for an instant longer than necessary. "For Erenor."

"Indeed, for Erenor," echoed the gnomes, their quirky demeanor replaced by solemn understanding. "We give you our blessings, and this—" One of them produced a crystalline shard, pulsing with a light that mirrored the stars outside. "It will guide you through the darkness of the cavern."

"Thank you," Feyla said, taking the shard, her eyes reflecting its glow. Her mind raced with thoughts of the inventions around her, each one a key to unlocking further power.

"The darkness is approaching," Aerin noted, the urgency of their mission returning like an icy wind.

"Then don't be unprepared," the first gnome warned. "Beware of the whispers of sorrow; they ensnare the unwary."

"Stay close and trust each other," the second added.

"Always," Lysandra affirmed, though her heart stirred with a tumultuous mix of fear and something else—an unspoken bond with Aerin growing more assertive in the face of impending doom.

"Let's go," Aerin said, his resolve hardening like forged steel. "We have a well to find."

"Stay alert," Feyla added, eager to confront the unknown

challenge against the brewing storm.

The trio returned to the labyrinth of Luminar with nods of gratitude to the Gnomish Tinkers, the weight of their destiny pressing upon them but bolstered by newfound knowledge and the ethereal light of the guiding shard.

The narrow alleyways of Luminar twisted like serpentine veins, pulsating with the city's heartbeat. Aerin led the way, his senses alert, as they navigated through the evening's shadowy embrace.

"Keep your blade ready," he said over his shoulder, his voice a low rumble.

Lysandra nodded, her hand on the hilt of her runic sword, the metal whispering promises of battles to come. Shadow, a fierce presence, trotted beside her, ears pricked and eyes watchful.

"Always," she replied, her eyes catching the last flickers of daylight.

As they moved through the dense crowd of people, a strange tingling sensation crept along Aerin's spine. It was unfamiliar, yet it resonated within him like a call to awakening.

"Wait," he halted, causing Lysandra to stumble into him.

"Is something wrong?" Her concern cut through the din around them.

"I don't know," Aerin admitted, clenching and unclenching his fists. The tingling grew, concentrated in his palms, a searing heat that demanded release.

"Show me your hands," Lysandra instructed, stepping closer. Her proximity sent a jolt through him unrelated to the burgeoning magic.

Their eyes met, and a glow emanated from Aerin's skin. Lysandra was amazed and whispered, "Is this magic?"

Aerin nodded, "It seems so. But it's a power I never expected to bear."

Lysandra said, "You must control it. Now more than ever."

"I know," Aerin replied. "I'll do my best."

As the light receded, Aerin felt a new strength fuse in the core of his being, a force to be honed. He urged Lysandra, "Let's keep moving."

They arrived at a bustling square. Aerin reminded Lysandra to stay focused, "We can't afford to lose sight of our mission."

Lysandra agreed, "Focus has kept me alive."

He felt her hand brush against his, and his heart skipped a beat. They silently vowed to protect each other with swords, magic, and the fierce bond that was shaping itself around their hearts.

Time to find the well, "Before darkness finds us first."

Lysandra nodded, "Let's go. We'll face whatever comes our way together."

Aerin, Lysandra, and Feyla left the safety of the city of Luminar to search for the ethereal well. They walked down unfamiliar paths, determined to fight the looming threat. As they marched towards the outskirts, they left the bustling streets and towering spires behind, and the city faded into the distance.

Lysandra fixed her gaze on the horizon, urging her companions to move quickly. "The longer we wait, the more the darkness festers," she said, her voice tinged with urgency.

Aerin nodded, feeling the weight of his sword at his side. He reassured Lysandra that they would find the well, even though they were unsure of what lay ahead.

As they approached a clearing with gadgets and widgets, Feyla's eyes sparkled with wonder as she approached the Gnomish Tinkers' workshop. "Look at these marvels!" she exclaimed, picking up a brass device that whirred and clicked in her hands.

Aerin reminded Feyla to stay focused, but he couldn't help but smile at her joy. Her curiosity had saved them in the past.

Lysandra watched Feyla's excitement before reminding her they couldn't afford any distractions. "We must stay focused, even with these impressive devices," she said.

Feyla countered, asking if these gadgets could be the key to their victory. Aerin was also curious, but their mission was urgent. They gathered what could aid them and moved on.

As they searched the workshop's cluttered surfaces, they heard a distant howl carried by the wind—a reminder of the danger that awaited them.

"Time is slipping through our fingers," Lysandra said.

"Then we'll grasp it tighter," Aerin declared with newfound power pulsing beneath his skin.

"Let's not keep destiny waiting," Lysandra urged them forward.

The Gnomish Tinker unfurled a map and explained that the final ethereal well was in the Cavern of Sorrows. However, the cavern was ensnared with curses and guarded by the Wraiths of Despair.

Aerin was puzzled. "How do we fight what's already dead?" he asked.

"Your sword is useless against such enemies," the Tinker warned. "It will take more than steel to navigate the darkness there."

"Magic," Lysandra murmured.

"Magic… and cunning," Feyla added.

"Then it's settled," Lysandra decided. "We approach with stealth and sorcery."

With each step away from the haven of the Gnomish Tinkers' workshop, the air grew heavier. The scent of an impending storm hung in the air. They marched onward, bound by duty and the unspoken vows that tethered their fates together.

"I object," Aerin said, his brow furrowed. "Shouldn't we seek out allies first? There are old bonds we could call upon, warriors who owe us their blades."

"We don't have the luxury of time," Lysandra replied sharply. "Every moment we delay, Erenor suffers."

"But rushing in risks everything!" Aerin countered, stepping closer. "I won't let you—"

"This isn't about protecting me, Aerin," Lysandra interrupted, her voice rising. "It's about saving our world."

Their faces were inches apart, a tempest brewing between them. Silence hung heavy, charged with unspoken words and emotional desires.

"We need both caution and haste," Feyla said, cutting through the tension. "Call upon those who can reach us and march on the morrow."

Aerin exhaled, the storm in his chest relenting. "Agreed," he conceded, his voice edged with something fierce.

"Good," Lysandra nodded, though her eyes held a glimmer of regret, a whisper of what might have been.

"Remember," the Tinker interjected, "the journey is treacherous. Trust in your strengths and each other."

"Thank you," Feyla said, offering the Tinkers a grateful smile before turning to her companions. "Let's prepare. We have much to do before dawn."

As they gathered their gear and stepped beyond the sanctuary of knowledge and invention, the trio felt the weight of destiny pressing on their shoulders.

Aerin's hand felt the reassuring heft of his sword as they left the Gnomish Tinkers' enclave.

Lysandra and Aerin walked together while Feyla, with newfound knowledge in her eyes, led the way, tapping her staff on the cobblestones.

Aerin scanned the shadowed alleys of Luminar, warning the group to keep their wits sharp as the Cavern of Sorrows would be unforgiving. The creatures lurking within would pose a significant threat, but Feyla reminded them that knowledge was their torch in the darkness, and they had just been enlightened.

"We can't let our guard down," Lysandra said. "We have to be ready for whatever lies ahead."

Aerin nodded. "She's right. We can't afford any mistakes."

Feyla smiled, twirling her staff. "But with our newfound knowledge, we're better equipped to face the dangers ahead."

Aerin looked at her with a hint of admiration in his eyes. "You're right. Knowledge is power. We'll use it to our advantage."

Lysandra tightened her grip on her weapon. "We'll ensure we come out of this alive and victorious."

As they walked, the trio discussed their plan of attack, each contributing their ideas and strategies. They knew the journey ahead would be challenging but determined to see it through.

As they made camp for the night, the trio sat around the fire, taking turns keeping watch. They shared little conversation, conserving their strength, but their silence was filled with understanding and an unspoken oath to see their journey through to its end.

Aerin lay back, staring at the tapestry of stars above. "We have to be prepared for anything," he said. "Whatever lies ahead, we'll face it together."

Lysandra leaned back against a tree, her eyes closed. "We're not just fighting for ourselves, but for everyone who's counting on us."

Feyla nodded. "We are responsible for protecting the world from the darkness that threatens to consume it."

The darkness enveloped them, but they found a fragile peace in its embrace. With each heartbeat, they edged closer to the Cavern of Sorrows, the final ethereal well, and revelations that could shatter worlds or rebuild them. They were ready, armed with knowledge, determination, and a fierce desire to succeed.

Chapter 17

THE ETHEREAL WELLS

Lysandra and her companions emerged from the trees into a clearing. Before them lay the first ethereal well, whose waters shimmered with an inner light that outshone the rising sun. The landscape was alive, with vivid colors pulsating with raw magic.

"Wow," Feyla breathed, her voice echoing in the vastness of the vale.

Standing next to Lysandra, Aerin fixed his gaze on the spectacle before them. "I've heard tales, but this is incredible. I can feel the power radiating from it."

"I can feel it, too," Lysandra said as she stepped closer to the well. She could sense the magic as if it were alive. A wolf pup at her side nuzzled her hand, its instincts attuned to the energy in the air.

"Nature is healing," Feyla observed, stepping forward to touch a flower that bloomed with unnatural vibrancy. "This is what we're fighting for."

Lysandra nodded, feeling the weight of their quest settle on her shoulders. "There must be more wells like this," she said. "More lands to awaken."

"More places to explore," Aerin agreed, his hand drifting to the hilt of his sword.

"Let's not get too comfortable," Feyla cautioned, scanning the perimeter. "The shadow hounds could be lurking nearby."

Aerin met Lysandra's eyes; a silent pact was forged between them. "We'll stand guard," he promised. "You do what you must, Lysandra. Reignite the well."

"Stay vigilant," Lysandra replied, returning to the well, ready to embrace the destiny that beckoned.

As Lysandra prepared herself for the task, a sense of unity flowed through the group. Each member braced for the unknown yet was sure of their shared purpose. Together, they would face whatever dangers awaited them, their path illuminated by the resurgent magic of Erenor.

Lysandra exhaled a mist of resolve in the cool air. Every muscle tensed as she approached the well's edge.

"Are you ready?" Aerin's question anchored her thoughts.

"Always," Lysandra replied, her eyes fixed on the shimmering waters before her. She could feel the magic coursing through her veins. Her vigilant Shadow sensed the shift, a low growl rumbling in its throat.

"Concentrate, Lysandra," Feyla urged as the magical hum filled the air. Lysandra began the ritual with a soft but clear chant, resonating with the pulse of the land. She drew a circle in the air, her movements fluid, and practiced. Symbols of power glowed at her fingertips, casting a luminous dance upon the water's surface.

"Feel the energy; use it," Feyla whispered. "Magic is your ally, not your master," Aerin added, his voice steady despite the rising tension that quivered like a bowstring around them.

As the ritual unfolded, Lysandra's confidence surged. Each step stoked the dormant power within the well, and the air crackled with potential as if nature held its breath.

"Almost there," Aerin said, his gaze darting between Lysandra and the shadows that threatened to creep. "Stay strong."

With a last word and a last movement, the world seemed to pause. Then, with a gasp from the well, the ritual reached its crescendo.

"Stand firm," Aerin's voice cut through the charged air. His muscular frame was a pillar of strength beside Lysandra, sword unsheathed, its edge hungry for a fight.

"Your magic is a beacon," Feyla added. She clutched a device of her own making, its gears whirring in anticipation.

Lysandra felt the power coursing through her, invigorating her very soul. A burst of light exploded from the depths of the well. It surged upward, a pillar of radiance splintered into a thousand threads of energy weaving through the air.

"Look at it, Lysandra!" Aerin's shout was half-cheer, half-challenge. "You've done it!"

The raw power of the well coursed through Lysandra, connecting with the wolf at her side, a silent guardian whose fierce loyalty matched her newfound courage. The creature howled, a sound of victory and freedom that mingled with the renewed magic.

"More than done," Lysandra breathed, reveling in the triumph. "Magic reborn," Aerin said, his tone a mix of reverence and something more profound that stirred when he looked at her.

"Through us," Lysandra corrected, her gaze sweeping over her companions. "We reignited this well together."

"Indeed," Aerin agreed. "And we'll see this quest through, side by side."

"Come," Lysandra said, her voice a call to action. "More wells are waiting. More darkness to banish."

"Lead on, Lysandra," Aerin's affirmation was a vow, his sword raised in salute.

"Feyla, what do you think?" Lysandra asked, gesturing to the well. Feyla's mind was already buzzing with new ideas inspired by the magic they had just witnessed.

Together, they turned away from the well and looked around. The once-dormant land was now alive with possibility. The air hummed with vitality as the magic from the well spread like wildfire. Trees burst into bloom, their branches unfurling with leaves of emerald and gold. Flowers sprang from the earth in a riot of color, each petal a testament to the well's rebirth.

"It's... it's miraculous," Feyla gasped, eyeing the spectacle with wonder.

"Look at the sky!" Aerin exclaimed, pointing upward. The once-ashen clouds now danced away, revealing a canvas of azure. The sun's golden fingers stretched across the land, caressing the newly awakened life.

Lysandra watched in awe as a nearby brook bubbled to life. Its waters were clear and singing over smooth stones. The air tasted sweeter, laden with the scent of jasmine and fresh pine. She could feel the magic coursing through her veins—a symphony of power resonating with her core.

"Is this your doing?" a voice quivered from the gathering crowd of villagers who had come to witness the wonder.

"Our doing," Lysandra replied. "The well's magic belongs to all of Erenor."

"Truly?" a woman asked, her face lighting up with hope.

"Truly," Lysandra affirmed.

"You've given us back our lives!" a man shouted, his voice cracking with emotion. Laughter and cheers erupted from the crowd as they embraced one another.

"Did we...did we do this?" Feyla asked, her voice laced with disbelief.

"Yes, we did," Aerin replied. "But let's not forget, others need us."

Lysandra nodded in agreement. "We still have much to do."

"Then let's not waste time," Feyla declared, her tools clinking with her relentless movement.

"Let's move forward together," Lysandra said, turning to Aerin with determination etched on her face.

"Always," he replied.

"We did it," Lysandra murmured, looking around. The land was now pulsating with life.

"Because it is," Lysandra replied, reflecting on the vibrancy around her. For a moment, she stood still, letting the significance of her actions wash over her. She had changed the course of history today and rekindled hope in a once-starved place.

"Hey!" Aerin's voice broke through her reverie. "You did it, Lyss."

"Did what?" She asked, feeling a wave of emotions.

"You brought life back to the land," Aerin replied, smiling.

"Saved us all," he said, a smile on his lips.

"Us?" Feyla interjected, arching an eyebrow. "I believe it was a team effort."

"Indeed," Lysandra agreed, Shadow nuzzling against her leg, sensing her stormy emotions. "But without the well…"

"Without you," Aerin corrected, stepping closer. "None of this would have happened."

"That's enough," she said, feeling a warmth spread through her as she heard his words. Let's not dwell on the past. Tonight, we celebrate, for tomorrow, our journey continues."

"Agreed," Feyla said, lifting her flask in a toast. "To Lysandra, the Last Mage of Erenor, and to the many adventures yet to come!"

They clinked their cups together, the sound ringing in the evening air. Lysandra took a deep drink from her cup, feeling the cool liquid soothe her. She exhaled, feeling a weight she didn't know she was carrying lift off her shoulders.

"Come on," Aerin said, his hand lingering on hers for a moment longer than necessary. "The people want to thank their savior."

"Is that so?" Lysandra met his gaze, feeling something unspoken pass between them. "Undoubtedly."

"Then let's not keep them waiting," she said, her voice steady despite the flutter in her stomach. They walked together, her wolf bounding ahead, as laughter and music filled the air.

As heroes, they were united in victory and magic, ready to face whatever darkness awaited them tomorrow with an unshakable resolve.

Lysandra stood on a verdant hill, the healed land stretching before her like a tapestry reborn. Her wolf sniffed the air, wagging its tail with energy that echoed her uplifted spirit.

"Thank you," she said, turning to Feyla and Aerin. "Thank you for standing by me, even when the shadows threatened our hope."

"We believe in you, Lysandra. We believe in your cause," Feyla replied, her armor glinting in the fading light.

"I'd follow you into the abyss and back," Aerin declared, his solemn vow carried on a gentle breeze.

"Let's hope it doesn't come to that," she replied with a slight smile, her fingers tightening on her leather rucksack.

"Hope is what you've given this land," Aerin said, stepping closer. "What you give us every day."

"Hope is our blade against despair," she murmured, her thoughts a whirling gust of possibility and peril.

"Then we'll wield it together," Feyla said, clasping Lysandra's shoulder with a gauntleted hand. Her touch was both comforting and a call to arms.

"United," Lysandra confirmed, her resolve steeling. They looked out at the thriving wilderness, the emerald leaves whispering secrets of resilience and renewal.

"Until the end," Aerin promised, his voice low.

"Until the end," she repeated, her heart surging with determination. They were the ones to save the world; their fates intertwined like the roots of the ancient trees surrounding them.

The last embers of daylight clung to the horizon, casting long shadows across the grove as Lysandra and her companions packed their sparse belongings—the light from the reignited ethereal well pulsed, a heartbeat in the darkening world.

"Every step we take is a step towards victory," Lysandra said, tightening a strap on her leather rucksack. Her wolf nuzzled her hand, his amber eyes reflecting the fading light.

Aerin quipped, "Or towards our doom," but his grin didn't quite reach his eyes. Feyla shouldered her pack and nodded towards the path that wound into the thickening forest, "Let's just keep looking forward. That's where our fate lies."

Lysandra spoke with the resolution, "The next well waits. We can't let the darkness win."

Aerin stepped up beside her, "Nor shall we."

"The shadow hounds won't be the last threat we face," Lysandra cautioned.

Feyla drew her broadsword, "Whatever comes, we face it together. We are united as one."

"Until the end," Aerin affirmed.

"Until the end," Lysandra repeated. She felt the tapestry of their fates weaving tighter, the threads of destiny pulling them onward. "Ready?" she asked.

"Always," Aerin replied.

"Then let's move out," Lysandra commanded. They moved as one entity—three warriors bound by magic, oath, and something deeper still.

As their footsteps echoed with the nocturnal symphony of the forest, Lysandra knew that this victory was only the beginning. The night held secrets yet to be uncovered, and the path forward would test the limits of their courage and hearts.

The sky bled into twilight, and the air hummed with renewed vitality. They stood shoulder to shoulder, the afterglow of magic from the well casting their shadows long across the landscape.

"It's like the land's taken a deep breath," Feyla whispered.

"We've given it life again," Lysandra replied.

"We'll do it again as ordered often as we must," Aerin said.

"Until Erenor is free," Feyla added.

"Until the shadow is no more," Lysandra finished.

"Remember this moment," Aerin said. "When darkness comes, remember the light we've seen here."

"Always," Lysandra replied, feeling their unspoken connection stronger.

"Let's not get too cozy," Feyla joked. "Night's falling, and who knows what lurks in the shadows?"

"We have the light on our side now," Aerin said.

"Then let the shadows beware," Lysandra replied, grinning fiercely.

"Shall we?" Feyla gestured towards the path leading into the thickening darkness.

"Let's." Lysandra took point, Aerin flanking her left and Feyla to the right. Together, they stepped into the embrace of night, the wolf at their heels, its yellow eyes gleaming with an otherworldly intelligence.

"Tomorrow, we reach the Shrouded Vale," Lysandra declared.

"I'm eager to see what secrets it holds," Aerin said.

"Secrets have teeth in the Vale," Feyla warned.

"Then we'll be the ones to bite back," Lysandra replied.

The three companions took a moment to catch their breath and share a laugh. They had been on a perilous journey, but the twinkling stars above them gave them hope and courage to move forward.

As they made their way through the rough terrain, Aerin brushed his arm against Lysandra's. "No matter what happens next, we'll face it together," he said softly.

Lysandra felt her heart skip a beat at the contact. "We're a united team," she said, sounding confident.

Feyla's voice was steady. "Always," she affirmed.

They marched forward, their determination shining as brightly as the stars above. They were ready to overcome any obstacles that lay ahead.

As they walked, they felt the weight of their mission on their shoulders. But they knew that they had each other to lean on. They had already faced significant danger and were prepared to face whatever lay ahead.

Their laughter had been a brief respite from the seriousness of their quest, but it had also given them the strength and courage to move forward. As long as they were together, they were ready to conquer any darkness ahead.

Chapter 18

CHALLENGING KING DRAVEN

Lysandra and her allies trekked through the narrow pass, with the Ironspire Mountains' jagged peaks looming over them. Their path was precarious, with an abyss below and the oppressive weight of the stone above. Each step was a testament to their urgency, as King Draven's scouts were never far behind and occasionally visible against the twilight sky.

"Keep moving," Lysandra whispered, scanning the horizon. The wolf at her heels let out a low growl, sensing the tension in the air.

Feyla asked through labored breaths, "Are we sure this is the fastest way?"

"Unless you want to walk through Draven's encampments,"

Lysandra replied, her voice firm. "We must press on."

The group fell into a rhythm, their footsteps a hushed cadence against the gravel. They slipped through the terrain like ghosts, and shadows clung to the crevices and ravines like cobwebs. The occasional cry of a predator in the distance pierced the dense scent of pine and damp earth.

Lysandra felt the weight of her lineage, the legacy of the last mage of Erenor, pressing upon her shoulders. It was not just the throne that called her back to Tyrannis, but the fate of magic itself. She knew that if they failed, darkness would swallow their world whole.

As they walked, they felt the urgency of their quest. King Draven's scouts were always close behind, and each step they took was closer to the confrontation that awaited them in Tyrannis. Lysandra knew that she had to stay strong and lead her allies to victory, even if it meant putting her life on the line.

The group moved forward, their eyes scanning the horizon for any sign of danger. They knew that the fate of their world was in their hands, and they were determined to succeed.

Elian, a rogue and one of Lysandra's confidants spoke in a low voice, "Draven has made allies with sorcerers. How do we know he won't detect us?"

Lysandra looked unfazed and replied confidently, "We have something he doesn't. The element of surprise. And we have each other."

Elian smirked and retorted, "Cheerful sentiments for a march towards death."

Lysandra remained stoic and replied, "Death doesn't scare me. Living under Draven's tyranny chills me to the bone."

The group continued their climb up the mountain. The city of Tyrannis was now a dark smudge against the night sky. Draven's rule had reduced its once magnificent towers to cruel spikes. The oppressive atmosphere of the city reached out to them even from that distance, yearning for liberation.

Feyla whispered, "Look!" and pointed ahead. The flickering torches marked the palace's outer defenses. "We're close now."

Lysandra unsheathed her sword and declared, "It's time—for Erenor, for magic, for freedom."

Her allies echoed, "Until the end," and drew their weapons in solidarity. They were ready to breach the palace and confront Draven, the dark usurper of the throne.

With their hearts pounding and the adrenaline surging, Lysandra led the charge down the mountain's slope. King Draven's reign of terror would end tonight, or they would die trying. The urgency of their mission was a fire in their veins, and their looming confrontation with Draven was a promise carved in stone.

Lysandra traced her fingers along her sword's hilt, feeling its weight, burden, and honor. Her allies huddled in the shadows of gnarled trees, their breaths visible in the cold air.

"Every step we take is a step towards our destiny," Lysandra murmured. Her wolf nuzzled her hand, offering warmth and comfort.

Feyla sharpened her blade with quick, precise strokes and grumbled, "Or our doom."

Lysandra replied, "Then let it be a glorious one. We've fought for this cause. We won't falter now."

"Words are easy to say before blood spills," countered Feyla, her brow furrowed under a mane of curls. "But what if—"

"No 'what ifs,'" Lysandra said, standing tall. Doubt is a luxury we can't afford."

"Listen to her," Aerin called out, his dark eyes scanning the horizon. She knows the cost of hesitation."

"Cost, I've seen too often," Lysandra thought, clenching her jaw.

Aerin interrupted, "Magic runs thin. We must trust steel and heart."

Lysandra nodded in agreement, "Steel has never failed me."

"Nor has the heart," Aerin added.

"Let's move," Lysandra ordered, silencing the doubts that clawed at her resolve.

Her allies rose and moved through the dark, bound by fate and forged in the fires of rebellion.

"Keep close," Lysandra whispered, leading them through a labyrinth of alleys.

"Always," Aerin murmured back, his presence a steady beat beside her.

"Look sharp," Feyla hissed, pointing to a shadowy figure shifting against the walls. "Shadow hounds," she spat, readying her bow. "Draven's pets."

"Stay together," Lysandra ordered, tightening her grip on her sword.

"Side by side," Feyla promised, her eyes reflecting the torchlight like a predator's.

"Through darkness," said Aerin, drawing closer to Lysandra.

"Into the light," Lysandra finished, her heart a drumbeat of war and hope beyond tonight's shadows.

"Forward!" she cried, and they surged ahead, a tide of defiance ready to break upon Tyrannis's walls.

As they descended into the gloom, despair hung over the cobbled streets. Citizens peered out from behind shuttered windows, their eyes hollow with fear and resignation. Yet, as word spread of Lysandra's return, a flicker of hope began to light their gaze.

"Let them see we're not afraid," Lysandra said, her voice cutting through the dense air.

"Nor should you be," a woman called out from a balcony. "The Last Mage has come."

"Tonight, shadows will flee before dawn," Feyla instructed.

"Draven will fall," Lysandra declared, her sword resonating with her conviction.

"Tonight, we fight," Feyla added. "Not just for Erenor, but for ourselves."

"Freedom is worth every blade was drawn and every spell cast," Lysandra continued, the magic within her stirring like a storm about to break.

"Like a storm," Aerin echoed, the touch of his hand sending a jolt through her.

"May the gods be with us," someone whispered from the crowd.

"Tonight, we reclaim our city," Lysandra vowed. "For Erenor, for freedom!"

The group charged forward with a battle cry of "FOR ERENOR!" Lysandra led them towards the heart of Tyrannis, where their destiny awaited them. The gates of Tyrannis were dark and foreboding, their ancient stones corrupted by King Draven's rule. Arrow slits stared like empty eyes, and the silhouettes of soldiers atop the battlements merged with the darkness of the night.

Lysandra whispered, "Look at it," as they approached the gates.

"It's a fortress of nightmares," Feyla grunted, her hand resting on her sword's hilt.

"Or dreams," Aerin countered, standing close to Lysandra. "If we make it so."

Lysandra's wolf companion tensed by her side, and she found comfort in petting it as they surveyed the defenses ahead.

"What do you see?" she asked one of her allies, a mage whose eyes glowed with premonition.

"Enchanted barriers, archers, and something else... something dark," he murmured.

Lysandra's mind raced through incantations as she instructed, "Break the barrier; I'll handle the archers."

Feyla asked, "What's the signal?"

"Wait for my light," Lysandra replied.

They entered the shadows, feeling the palace's oppressive might. A shimmering field crackled before the main entrance, Draven's magic designed to repel intruders.

"Time to dance," she muttered, drawing her blade. The runes ignited, casting an eerie glow. "Make it sing," Aerin encouraged, his eyes locked on hers.

With a mighty swing of her sword, the magical barrier shuddered and shattered into wisps of spent magic. She yelled at her companions to charge forward towards the throne room. They fought back-to-back with a seamless dance of death. Combined, they finally made it through the massive iron door, which burst open with a resounding boom. The throne room lay steeped in ominous silence, its air thick with the stench of dark sorcery.

As she strode towards the dais where King Draven sat cloaked in shadows, his eyes fixed on her with ruthless calculation. "Ah, the prodigal usurper returns. How quaint that you believe lineage grants you power," he sneered.

"Lineage doesn't," she retorted, tightening her grip on her sword. "Courage does. Something you wouldn't understand." She charged towards him, ready to face him in battle.

Draven stood up from his throne, looking down on Lysandra. "Courage?" He scoffed. "I see desperation. And it reeks."

Lysandra circled him, feeling the weight of her ancestors' whispers within her. "You're wrong. It's resolved. The kind that ends tyrants."

Draven gestured to the empty hall, mocking her. "Ends me? With what army? Your allies are preoccupied."

Lysandra responded, "An army isn't always soldiers. It's the will of the oppressed who clamor for justice."

Draven sneered, "Poetic nonsense. You think yourself a hero."

Lysandra retorted, "Actions, not thoughts, make heroes."
   Shadow growled at her side, sensing the tension.

Draven drew his blackened sword, which seemed to swallow light. "Let's see your actions."

Their swords met with a loud clang, sparks dancing between them. Draven was strong, but Lysandra's resolve lent her blows a weight that took him by surprise.

"You lack control," Draven taunted, his strikes methodical and probing.

"No. I've learned control," Lysandra said, ducking a vicious slash.

"Learned from whom?" Draven taunted, still thrusting his sword towards her. "That boy who follows you like a lost pup or that puny girl, Feyla?"

Lysandra warned, "Be careful. Love is a strength, not a weakness."

Draven laughed cruelly. "In war, love is a liability."

"Then you've already lost," Lysandra pushed him off balance, her heart pounding with the thrill of the fight.

Draven regained his footing, his eyes glinting with malice. "We shall see who stands when the dust settles."

Lysandra urged him to look around. "Your kingdom crumbles. Your magic fades."

Draven spat, "Magic is a tool, girl. One I wield without mercy."

"Then you will fall for it," she declared, sensing an opening.

Their dance of death quickened each strike of a note in a deadly symphony. Lysandra's muscles screamed, but she pushed through, fueled by the chorus of those who had suffered under Draven's rule.

"Enough!" Draven bellowed, the force of his magic shuddering through the room. "You think you can unseat me? I am King!"

"Titles don't grant righteousness," she grunted, feeling his power onslaught like a storm against her will.

"Nor do they guarantee victory!" Draven roared, advancing.

"True," Lysandra breathed, sidestepping and thrusting. Her blade found its mark, piercing his armor.

Draven staggered. Disbelief, etching his features. "How?"

"By knowing what's worth fighting for," she replied, her breath heavy. "For Erenor, for freedom."

"Curse you," Draven growled, his form beginning to wane.

"Curse me all you want," Lysandra said, standing tall amidst the ruin of his ambition. "But Erenor will remember me as its liberator."

"Remember this," Draven gasped, "there's always another."

"Another tyrant?" she finished. "We'll be ready."

As he fell, the oppressive atmosphere lifted, giving way to a brief hope that fluttered through the air like the first breath of dawn. Lysandra stood, her sword dripping with the end of tyranny, her spirit alight with the fire of a new era.

Blood sprayed the cold stones of Tyrannis's throne room as King Draven's form crumpled to the ground, his final breath escaping in ragged whispers. Lysandra stood over him, her sword still quivering from the impact. Sweat and grime matted her hair, but her eyes burned with a triumphant fire.

"Your reign ends here," she panted, echoing off the high, vaulted ceilings.

"Long live the queen," Aerin murmured from behind her. His tone was proud, but something more profound, unspoken, thrummed between them like a charged current.

Lysandra turned to him, her gaze locking onto his for a fleeting moment before she tore it away, refocusing on the task. "To the Wells!" she commanded, her voice slicing through the tension.

The group surged forward, their footsteps ringing as they descended into the bowels of the palace, where the Heart of Erenor lay dormant. The air grew thick with magic, each breath laced with the latent power that awaited them.

"Guard my back," she instructed Aerin, who nodded and drew his blade—a weapon less ornate than hers but no less deadly.

Together, they entered the sanctum, the chamber pulsing with an ancient rhythm. In its center stood the heart, a crystalline structure that throbbed with a dying light.

"Begin the ritual," Lysandra ordered, her voice steady despite the storm of emotions within her.

Aerin took his position, his stance protective as he watched her back. She could feel his presence like a shield, his resolve fortifying her own.

"*Sanctus cor Erenor, exaudi nos,*" she chanted, the words old as time itself, handed down through generations of mages now lost. As she spoke, the runes on her blade flared brighter, casting eerie shadows across the walls.

"Rise anew, the essence of life," Aerin joined in, his low rumble complementing her clear tones.

"*Animam Liberatus,*" they intoned together, their voices weaving a spell that bound them to the fate of their world.

The heart pulsed with a slow beat that quickened with every word they uttered. Its light spread, tendrils of energy reaching out to caress the ethereal wells scattered across Erenor.

"Feel that?" Aerin said, his voice was taut with anticipation. The world's waking up."

"Let's hope it's not too late," Lysandra replied, her focus unyielding even as she allowed herself to lean into his strength for support.

The chamber shook, stones grinding against each other as the ritual reached its zenith. The heart's light exploded into brilliance, bathing them in its radiance.

"*Vincula frangimus*!" they cried in unison, their command echoing as chains of darkness that had choked the wells shattered into nothingness.

"Is it done?" Aerin asked, his gaze meeting hers again, searching for confirmation in her stormy eyes.

"It's done," she confirmed, though her tone carried the weight of uncertainty. The battle for Tyrannis may have ended, but the war for Erenor's soul was beginning.

"Then let's return to the light," he said, offering her his hand.

She took it, feeling the calluses of countless battles and the warmth of unspoken promises. Together, they stepped out of the sanctum into the dawning hope of a new era.

The air crackled with magic, a tangible force that thrummed through the streets of Tyrannis. It was as if the very stones beneath their feet pulsed with life, and above them, the sky shimmered with newfound vibrancy.

The people of the city, once oppressed under King Draven's rule, now spilled into the squares and alleys, their faces tilted upwards, drinking in the light that cascaded from the heavens.

"By the gods," one man murmured, his voice laced with disbelief. "The wells... they sing again."

"Look at them, Lysandra," Aerin said, a shocked grin splitting his face as he watched a mother lift her child high, both laughing amidst tears. "The chains are broken. You did this."

Lysandra stood, the runes on her sword catching the ethereal glow. Shadow nuzzled against her, his eyes reflecting the reborn brilliance of Erenor. "We did this," she corrected softly, her gaze meeting those of her allies.

They were weary, their armor dented, and their swords nicked, but a fire in their eyes mirrored the renewed spirit of the world around them.

"Feels like breathing after an age underwater," Lysandra breathed out, the weight of the world settling on her shoulders even as it lifted.

"Or waking from a nightmare," another ally added, his voice a hoarse whisper.

"Except this is no dream." Lysandra's hand found the pommel of her sword, fingers tracing the runes. "This reality we fought for, we bled for."

"Lost for," someone else chimed in, a sad note threading through the jubilation.

"Yes," Lysandra agreed, her eyes darkening with memory. "But look at what we've gained." "Hope," Aerin declared, stepping beside her. "A future."

"Freedom." Another voice joined the word, spreading like wildfire.

"Exactly," Lysandra said, her voice rising over the city. "Tyrannis breathes free once more. And with each breath, we honor those who are not here to witness it."

"May their spirits find peace in this new Erenor," an ally intoned, head bowed in reverence. "Peace," the crowd echoed, a solemn promise.

"Let us remember then," Lysandra continued, "that our fight was not for power or glory but for the very essence of our world. For every life touched by darkness, for every hope smothered."

"Here's to the fallen," Aerin said, lifting an imaginary glass, his eyes locking onto Lysandra's. "And to the living—may we never forget."

"Never," they vowed together, a chorus of conviction amidst the celebration.

"Come," Lysandra urged, turning to her companions with a determined glint in her eye. "Our journey doesn't end with victory. We rebuild, heal, and guard what we've won."

"Side by side," Aerin affirmed, their unspoken bond more potent than any spell.

"Always," Lysandra whispered, her heart swelling with pride. As she looked upon the faces of her allies, she saw reflections of herself—scarred yet unbroken, tested yet triumphant. Together, they had faced the abyss and returned to forge a path forward, illuminated by the restored magic of Erenor and the enduring flame of their united wills.

The city of Tyrannis lay before them, a mosaic of light and shadow under the budding stars. Lysandra's eyes reflected the flicker of torches that now burned where darkness had once reigned. The wolf at her side, a silent sentinel, bristled with anticipation.

"Tomorrow, we march," she declared, her voice slicing through the cool air. "Draven's stronghold will be ours to reclaim."

"Reclaim and rebuild," Aerin added, stepping closer, his gaze never leaving hers. "But there's more. Whispers of unrest stir beyond the northern border."

"Unrest?" Lysandra's hand found the hilt of her rune-etched sword, a spontaneous gesture. "Speak plainly."

"Scouts report movements—unnatural, shadowy. Perhaps remnants of Draven's influence, or something older, waking with the return of magic," he said, the weight of concern in his tone.

"Then let it wake," she retorted, her resolve as unyielding as tempered steel. "We'll be ready. We've faced darkness before."

"True." Aerin's lips twitched into a half-smile, hinting at the spice of shared battles past. "But this feels different. As if the land itself is shifting."

"Change is our ally," Lysandra replied, staring into the distance. Her mind raced, plotting strategies and anticipating the trials ahead. "But first, we fortify. Strengthen the defenses, secure the Heart of Erenor."

"Agreed." He stepped beside her, shoulder to shoulder, their presence a united front against the uncertainty of the future. "There's talk among the people—they're calling you 'Lysandra the Dawn bringer.'"

Lysandra raised an eyebrow at the moniker, a mix of amusement and wariness flickering in her eyes. "And what do you make of it?"

"It's fitting," he said, his gaze steady and sure. "You brought light back to this land, after all."

"I didn't do it alone," she reminded him, her voice softening as she looked upon his face—the familiar angles and lines that had become so dear to her over the years.

"But you led us," Aerin pointed out, his hand finding hers in a silent gesture of support. "And now we follow where you lead."

Lysandra squeezed his hand in gratitude before releasing it with a sigh. As much as she relished these moments alone with Aerin, work was to be done. The city needed rebuilding, supplies had to be gathered, and defenses had to be strengthened in preparation for whatever threat lay beyond their borders.

Together, they set about their tasks—meeting with leaders from various factions, discussing plans for trade and defense alliances, and organizing teams to gather resources and rebuild structures damaged by Draven's forces.

Days turned into weeks as they worked towards their goal. With each passing day, Lysandra could feel the weight on her shoulders becoming heavier as she realized that not only did she have the responsibility of rebuilding Tyrannis on her shoulders but also protecting it from any potential threats.

However, amidst the chaos and hard work, there were moments of respite—moments where Lysandra would steal away with Aerin to watch the sunset or take long walks through the city streets.

And even though others surrounded them, these moments felt like stolen time, just the two of them against the world.

Shadow found companionship with Feyla and stayed close to her. There was now a new and unspoken bond between them. "Well, it seems I have a brand new friend," said Feyla, pleased with Shadow's sudden friendly attitude.

"He has seen for himself that you can be trusted." Lysandra stroked his fur and patted his head in approval.

"Well, Lysandra Dawnbringer," said Feyla, tapping her leg to invite Shadow to her side. "Shadow and I are going to have some food and drink and a dry bed to sleep in, though I'm sure he will leave my side for yours quite soon."

"You two, enjoy your well-earned rest as well," she said, smiling at a red-faced Lysandra and Aerin, who needed to fidget with his sword.

A low laugh escaped Lysandra, tinged with irony and desperate to ease the heat she felt creeping up her neck and washing over her face.

"Dawnbringer, huh? I bring the light, yet darkness seems to follow."

"Light casts shadows," Aerin mused, finishing with his sword, satisfied that it was harnessed tightly in its sheath. "It's the nature of things."

"Let's shape that nature," she proposed, a sudden determination etched in every line of her face. They stood together, three allies in arms, and Shadow was at their side, gazing upon the city that was both home and battlefield.

"Feyla, you and Shadow go and have your rest," she said, patting Shadow on the head and squeezing Feyla's shoulder.

"Come dawn, we move," Lysandra stated, turning to address the gathering crowd. They responded with affirming nods and murmured assents.

Her companions nodded and smiled at the apparent warmth the people around them displayed. "Rest well," Lysandra repeated. We leave early tomorrow morning.

As night deepened, the air thrummed with power—magic restored, possibilities unfolding. Lysandra felt it in her bones—a call to the journey ahead. She looked at Aerin; her thoughts lingered on the sparks flying between them, embers threatening to ignite with the slightest breath.

"Whatever comes," Aerin vowed, his eyes holding a promise that stirred more than just the warrior within her.

"Whatever comes," she echoed, feeling the pull of destiny tugging at her soul.

Chapter 19

MESSAGE FROM THE HIGH SEER

The sound of clanging steel and cheers filled the air as twilight descended upon the liberated city of Erenor.

"Look at it, Aerin!" she exclaimed, her eyes sparkling excitedly. "Erenor is finally free!"

Aerin stood tall next to her, sharing her exuberance. "We took down the tyrants before nightfall," he said, his voice deep and resonant. "This is something worth celebrating."

"Hey, don't forget about me!" Feyla jumped in, her excitement tangible as she joined them. Shadow playfully weaved between her legs with a low growl. The wolf's coat shimmered in the firelight, a creature of darkness and light.

"Never!" Aerin laughed, reaching out to ruffle Shadow's fur. "How could we ever forget our bravest warrior?"

Feyla playfully nudged him. "That's right! Don't you forget it!"

Lysandra sheathed her sword as she watched the people of Erenor. They were finally free, and their faces were alight with hope and joy. Her heart swelled at the sight; this is what they fought for.

Lysandra smiled as she added another log to the fire. "I can already hear the bards singing our tale," she said, settling back into her seat.

Aerin laughed. "I'm not sure I'm ready for all that attention."

Lysandra smiled, feeling grateful for Aerin's presence.

A sharp whistle that pierced the night stopped their laughter. Suddenly, a raven landed nearby with an envelope carrying the seal of the High Seer. Feyla, who had intercepted the bird, opened the envelope and read the message.

"It's not over. Darkness... it lingers," Feyla announced, her voice serious. "It's spreading in the North, corrupting everything it touches."

Aerin tensed, ready for any threat that might emerge from the shadows. "What do we do?" he asked.

"We need to go and investigate," Feyla replied, her eyes scanning the letter. "The High Seer has requested our assistance."

Lysandra and Aerin nodded, knowing they couldn't ignore the call to action. They gathered their belongings and prepared to face the darkness that lay ahead.

Lysandra cursed under her breath while Aerin gazed at the stars, unaware of their danger. Draven had been defeated, but his Shadow Councilors were still a threat. Feyla handed Lysandra a letter from the Seer with vague, riddling messages about a lurking "dark seed" that couldn't be killed.

"We need to find it," Lysandra declared with determination. As she thought through their strategies, she knew their only hope was to uncover the secrets hidden in ancient lore. Aerin added, "We can't let this fester. We need to move fast and strike hard."

Feyla suggested they prepare, and Lysandra agreed. They were more than just warriors. They were friends with a shared determination to protect their land and people. As they prepared, their spirits remained unbroken, and they knew they would fight until the end.

The trio remained unified and ready for the looming danger as the sounds of worry and clanging steel filled the air. Their victory began a much larger battle, but they were prepared and determined to face it together.

Lysandra gripped her sword as the torches crackled around them. She turned to face her companions. "We need Master Elarion's wisdom. Let's journey to his sanctum," she said, cutting through the tension.

Aerin unfurled a map. "The quickest route is through the Darkwood. It's treacherous this time of year, but we can avoid known shadow beast dens."

Feyla gathered supplies, including healing herbs, food, and firestones. Aerin brought dried meat and bread.

Lysandra whispered to her sword. "Watch over us," she said. The magic within stirred in response.

"Even the shadows fear your blade," Aerin remarked.

Lysandra sheathed her sword. "Let's hope they do," she replied. "It may be all that stands between us and what lies ahead."

They dispersed to gather their gear, each movement promising the struggle. "Rest while you can," Lysandra instructed, "Darkness won't wait, and neither shall we."

The next day, they set out through the Darkwood, traveling

with a sense of urgency. The chill of the woods threatened them, but their supplies gave them hope.

As the night grew darker, three figures moved purposefully towards the unknown. They were ready to face Erenor's lingering darkness.

In the dusky twilight of Erenor's forest, Lysandra and Aerin found a secluded glade where the first stars peeked through the canopy. Lysandra's dog, Shadow, lay nearby, his ears twitching in his sleep.

"I can't shake the feeling that darkness still clings to us, like burrs on cloth," Aerin said, his golden eyes reflecting the flicker of their campfire.

"We've torn much of it away, but some roots run deeper than others," Lysandra replied, picking at the hem of her cloak.

"Like this... tension between us?" Aerin asked.

"Perhaps," Lysandra said, looking up at him.

"But it's not all shadows and dread, is it?" Aerin said, smiling.

"Never," Lysandra agreed, smiling back. "There's light too. Like the sparks we strike together."

"Sparks can ignite flames," Lysandra said.

"Flames can forge fresh paths... or consume," Aerin said, inching his hand closer to hers.

"Consume," Lysandra said, closing the distance and clasping his hand. His touch was familiar and electric, sending ripples of anticipation through her veins.

"Are we ready for that fire?" he asked.

"Fire cleanses," she replied, her voice firm. "And from ash, we rise anew."

"Then together, we face whatever comes," Aerin whispered.

"Together," she agreed, squeezing his hand.

From the other side of the camp, Feyla's voice broke the hush. "Imagine learning from Master Elarion himself! The lore he possesses and our enemies' secrets—he'll have answers!"

"Enthusiasm suits you, Feyla," Lysandra called over, smiling.

"Answers are only the beginning," Feyla declared, her gaze sweeping over the darkened forest. "Master Elarion will guide us to wield light against the encroaching gloom."

"Let's hope his guidance is enough," Aerin said, standing beside Feyla.

"Whatever knowledge he imparts, we'll use it to banish the darkness for good," Lysandra said, rising to join them.

"Or die trying," Feyla said solemnly yet fiercely.

"Tonight, we rest," said Aerin. "Tomorrow, we seek wisdom - or it seeks us," agreed Lysandra. "Rest well, for tomorrow brings its challenges," added Feyla.

The trio settled under the starry sky, each with a glimmer of hope. They knew that death was always a possibility on their dangerous journey.

As dawn broke, they set off on their journey, cloaked in specter-like garments to ward off the morning chill. They silently vowed to face whatever destiny had in store for them.

Lysandra led the way with her wolf companion, Shadow, keeping pace. Aerin and Feyla flanked her sides, their eyes scanning the surroundings for any signs of danger.

"The path is treacherous, and King Draven's corruption still lingers," warned Lysandra as they navigated through a grove of skeletal trees. "Stay vigilant."

Aerin's hand rested on the hilt of his sword, ready to draw it at a moment's notice. "It feels like we're being watched," he muttered.

"That's because we are," replied Feyla. "But don't worry, Shadow senses danger before it strikes."

As they continued on their journey, they encountered sinkholes and chasms that required careful navigation. Finally, they settled by a brook for a brief rest.

"How should we approach Master Elarion?" asked Aerin.

"We should be honest and disclose our victories and uncertainties," replied Lysandra. He values honesty above all."

"But what if our victory feels incomplete?" questioned Aerin.

Lysandra met his intense gaze with a determined one of her own. "We will face it together," she said. "As one."

"Especially then." She straightened, sealing the waterskin. "Our honesty may be the key to unlocking his wisdom."

"Then let's hope he can provide the clarity we need," Aerin said, standing shoulder to shoulder with her, their proximity a silent echo of their conversation last night.

"Clarity and more," Lysandra added, her sea-green eyes

searching his. "We need to understand the depth of this darkness to stand a chance."

"Agreed," Aerin nodded, his gaze lingering a moment longer than necessary before turning to survey their surroundings. "The journey ahead won't be easy."

"Nothing worthwhile ever is," she replied, her voice steady yet soft, imbued with a strength forged from battles fought and yet to come.

"Indeed." Aerin cracked a half-smile that didn't reach his eyes. "Shall we continue?" "Let's," Lysandra said, stepping forward.

As they resumed their trek, the land grew more forbidding, and the air tinged with a magic that was both exhilarating and ominous. Their path narrowed, forcing them to proceed in single file. Shadow now took the lead, his nostrils flaring as he sniffed out safe passage.

"Careful," Lysanra warned, her hand on the pommel of her sword, runes humming. "These cliffs have claimed many a traveler."

"I wouldn't want to add our names to that list," Aerin quipped, though the fun was strained. "Indeed," Lysandra agreed, her focus unyielding as they traversed the rugged terrain.

When they finally emerged from the treacherous pass, the sun hung low, casting long shadows that seemed to whisper lurking threats. Ahead lay a stretch of open land dotted with the ruins of once-mighty towers, their stones entwined with the relentless embrace of ivy.

"Master Elarion's abode is beyond these ruins," Lysandra announced, gauging the distance. "One final push."

"Lead on," Aerin said, offering a supportive nod. "We follow your sword."

"May it guide us true," she murmured, her grip tightening around the hilt as they moved towards the remnants of a fallen empire, their hearts set on piercing the veiled mysteries that awaited them with Master Elarion.

The ruins gave way to an ancient forest, where gnarled trees whispered secrets of the old world. The air grew thick with power, the scent of earth and magic intertwining like lovers' tendrils.

Lysandra led them through the underbrush, her senses sharp as blades. "Nearly there," she breathed, her voice barely above the rustling leaves.

"Does he expect us?" Aerin asked, ducking a low-hanging branch. His hand never strayed far from the hilt of his sword.

"Elarion knows more than we can fathom," Feyla chimed in, her gaze darting around with a tinkerer's curiosity.

"Expected or not, we need answers," Lysandra said, her resolve a silent vow.

They reached a clearing where it stood – Master Elarion's home. A tower spiraled towards the heavens, its stones imbued with runes puling faintly in the dying light. The door loomed before them, oak and iron melding into a sentinel of ancient times.

"Here we are," Aerin declared, his pulse quickening. "The

threshold of knowledge." "Or a precipice," Lysandra mused, her mind racing with possibilities and peril. "Shall I knock?" Feyla offered, stepping forward with an eager sparkle in her eyes.

"Wait," Lysandra hesitated, her fingers tracing the sigils on her sword. She turned to Aerin, seeking the steadiness in his gaze. "Together?"

"Always," he affirmed, their bond unspoken yet felt, a current between their clasped hands.

"Ready?" Lysandra asked, meeting the eyes of her companions. They nodded, a trinity of determination forged in fire and Shadow.

"Ready," they echoed.

Lysandra stood before the door, her hand raised in a fist, the weight of their fate heavy on her shoulders. The carvings on the door seemed alive, as if they held secrets waiting to be unveiled.

She knocked three times, and the sounds echoed like a call to arms. The silence that followed was thick enough to slice through, laden with expectation and dread.

"We seek your wisdom, Master Elarion," Aerin called out, his voice steady.

No answer came, but the door creaked open an inch as if by unseen hands. Darkness peered out from the gap.

"Enter," a voice rumbled from within, ancient as the stones

themselves.

They exchanged glances, steeling themselves for the unknown. Lysandra pushed the door more expansive, and their silhouettes crossed the threshold. The mysteries of Master Elarion and the darkness they faced lay just beyond.

Chapter 20

THE FIRST MAGE

Just before dawn, Lysandra and Master Elarion stood in an old grove's hollow amid the rustling of leaves and the hum of antiquated magic. The power that lay dormant for centuries thrummed beneath their feet, making the air electric.

"Close your eyes," Master Elarion instructed, his voice echoing softly among the towering oaks. "Breathe in the energy from the soil and feel the pulse of Erenor in your veins."

Lysandra's heart raced. She took a deep breath, her senses sharpening. There was a moment of charged silence before she exhaled, her eyes fluttering shut.

"Am I doing this right?" she asked, feeling the cool night air brush against her skin like ethereal fingers.

"Be patient, child," Master Elarion replied, his eyes closed and his hands raised, palms facing the sky. Reach out beyond the veil."

Trying to focus, Lysandra felt a sense of excitement bubbling within her. A shiver danced as she imagined meeting her great ancestor—the legendary First Mage.

"First Mage," she whispered, the runes on her sword pulsing lightly against her thigh. "I seek your wisdom."

"Envision the lineage that binds you," Elarion murmured, guiding her through the rite. "See the thread of magic that weaves through your bloodline."

A wind stirred, rustling the leaves around them, carrying a familiar and alien resonance. Lysandra's breathing hitched. Was it happening? Could she—

"Shh," Elarion cautioned. "Let go of doubt. Embrace what comes."

The world fell silent, and an ethereal glow appeared before her closed eyelids. Fear and wonder warred within her as she dared to peek through her lashes.

"Ancestor?" Her voice faltered, not daring to hope.

The voice spoke with a timbre of ages past and was tethered to Lysandra's soul. "Great-granddaughter," it said, and Lysandra gasped, staring at the wraith-like figure before her. Its inner light painted the shadows away. This was Lysandra's heritage, and her destiny was made manifest.

"Your journey is fraught with danger," the First Mage said, her form flickering like a flame caught in a draft. "But your spirit blazes bright."

Lysandra trembled, "Will I be strong enough?"

"Strength comes in many forms," the First Mage intoned. "And courage is already yours."

The spectral mage continued, fading into the dawn, "Remember, you are never alone."

The remnants of the First Mage's essence dissipated, leaving an invisible chill in the secluded glen where Lysandra and Master Elarion stood. Dawn's light cast a haunting glow over the towering oaks that encircled them.

"Something stirs beyond the veil of the seen world," Master Elarion murmured, "A darkness unfurls its grasp."

Lysandra scanned the creeping shadows, half-expecting them to solidify into foes, "An enemy?"

Master Elarion's eyes were steel, reflecting the troubled skies, "Indeed. A malignancy that seeps into Erenor, poisoning our lands."

Lysandra clenched her fists, "Then we must act."

Master Elarion nodded, "The path to destiny awaits."

Lysandra's resolve hardened, "Let's begin." She drew her sword, a reminder of who she was and what she must do.

With a silent accord sealed, Lysandra knew the looming trials ahead would be difficult.

She would need Shadow and the Harrow; they were critical to this.

"Are you certain?" Doubt laced Elarion's tone, though his gaze never wavered from hers.

"Absolutely," she said, the certainty in her voice belying the tumult within. "Shadow knows these woods and the Harrow..." She trailed off, the image of the wounded warrior flashing across her mind – fierce, loyal, indomitable.

"Each has a role to play," Elarion relented, beginning to pace, his cloak sweeping behind him like a raven's wing. "But they are scattered, hidden. It won't be easy to bring them together."

"Then we start now." Purpose propelled her forward, her feet moving across the damp earth as she headed toward where she knew Shadow would be waiting. "Time is against us."

"Agreed." Master Elarion fell into step beside her. "We move at once." "Shadow!" she called, her voice slicing through the quiet of the glen.

A hulking form emerged from the underbrush, sinewy muscle rippling beneath glistening black fur. Yellow eyes pierced the dimness, locking onto Lysandra. A low growl rumbled from Shadow's throat—a greeting, an acknowledgment of their bond.

"Good boy," she said, her hand finding the warmth of his neck and feeling the thrum of his mighty heart. We have work to do."

"More than work," Elarion added gravely. "A quest that might very well shape the fate of Erenor."

"Then let us shape it well." Lysandra's gaze returned to the horizon, where the sun crested, casting long shadows that seemed to reach for them with dark intent. "We will find the Harrow and face this threat together."

"May the light guide us," Elarion intoned, a silent prayer for the journey ahead.

Lysandra echoed, "May it indeed," with her thoughts whirling in a mix of strategy and concern, fuelled by the fire of determination ignited within her soul.

Together, with Shadow at their side, they set forth, the weight of destiny heavy upon their shoulders, yet with the promise of hope glimmering just beyond the darkness.

"Elarion," Lysandra began, her voice steady as the thrum of Shadow's heart beneath her palm, "the Harrow has stood by me through flame and darkness. His flame is an extension of his will, just as my magic is of mine."

"His loyalty is not in question, Lysandra. It is his strength that concerns me." Elarion's eyes, dark like the churning sea before a storm, held hers.

"Strength or not, he would follow me into the Abyss itself if I asked," she said, tightening her grip on the hilt of her sword.

"Would you ask it of him?" The mage's challenge was evident, cutting through the air sharper than any sword.

"Only if there were no other way." Her gaze drifted over to

where the Harrow lay, his chest rising and falling with the slow rhythm of recovery. "But I fear this new darkness might demand it."

"Then we shall stand together," Elarion affirmed, "as we have always done."

"Always," she echoed, the word resonating with the weight of shared battles and victories hard-won.

"Let us hope the Harrow can endure what lies ahead." Concern etched Elarion's features, and he seemed composed amidst the turmoil.

"Endure? He will conquer," Lysandra replied, the fierceness in her tone matching the resolve in her eyes. "He has never known defeat, only the pain from the celestial fracture."

"Nor you," Elarion mused, a faint smile tugging at the corner of his mouth. "Perhaps that is why Erenor chose you, Last Mage."

"Chose us," she corrected. "I am nothing without those who fight at my side."

"Indeed." Elarion's agreement was solemn, yet beneath it lay a thread of pride.

"Come, let us speak with him," Lysandra decided, striding purposefully toward Harrow. "If our fates are to be entwined with the shadows, then we face them as one."

"We need to be cautious, Lysandra," Elarion replied, stroking his beard. "We cannot risk exposing our plans to the darkness."

Lysandra nodded in agreement. "You're right. We must be careful not to reveal anything that could compromise our efforts."

"Exactly," Elarion said with a nod. We must send messages through trusted channels and keep our movements hidden from prying eyes."

Lysandra sighed. "This is going to be more difficult than I thought."

Elarion put a hand on her shoulder. "We'll get through this, Lysandra. We've faced great challenges before and always come out victorious."

Lysandra smiled weakly. "I hope you're right."

"I am," Elarion said firmly. "Now, let's get to work. We have allies to gather and darkness to conquer."

"Each ally we find brings hope." The corners of her lips twitched upward, a fleeting smile. "Hope is a weapon, too."

"Indeed." Elarion's voice softened. "And perhaps, within that hope, you'll find more than allies." "Perhaps," she allowed Aerin's unspoken thoughts to stir like embers in her heart. "Prepare yourself. We embark at dawn," he declared, turning toward the shelter of old oaks.

"Ready I am, and ready I'll stay," she vowed, her thoughts weaving spells of protection and unity that would shield them when morning came.

———◦◦———

As night descended, Lysandra wrote a call to arms filled with urgency and power. By dawn, a group of determined individuals would face the approaching darkness.

Under the cover of night, Lysandra gazed at her wolf's silhouette against the flickering campfire. Shadow's vigilant stare pierced the darkness that threatened to consume their camp.

"You're steadfast, aren't you?" she whispered, running her hand over his coarse fur. The wolf leaned into her touch, a silent guardian bound to her by fate and loyalty.

"Every step we take is a risk," she said, more to herself than to the wolf.

"Yet you would follow me to the abyss without hesitation." Her voice quivered, admitting the weight of responsibility she bore.

Shadow's rumbling growl filled the space between them, his presence both comforting and intimidating.

"Your spirit is indomitable," she continued, "But what if this battle demands too high a price? What if--"

———◦◦———

"Are you talking to shadows again, Lysandra?" Aerin's voice interrupted her thoughts, filled with the warmth of shared secrets and unspoken desires.

"I'm considering the cost of loyalty," she said, her determination growing stronger.

"Shadow will follow wherever you lead," Aerin stated, stepping closer, the crackling fire casting his features in sharp relief. "His strength is yours."

"Is it fair to him?" Her question hung heavily in the air, filled with concern.

"The Harrow chose this path as much as you did. He trusts you, as do I," Aerin reassured her.

Lysandra looked down at their entwined fingers, the heat from his touch igniting a flame within her chest. "I can't falter. Not when so much depends on us."

"Then let's not shy away from what's ahead," he urged. "Together, with Feyla, Shadow, and the Harrow, we'll turn the tide."

Their eyes locked, and a silent vow passed between them in that moment—a promise to stand united against the encroaching darkness.

"Very well," she declared, releasing Aerin's hand to place her own atop Shadow's head. "We journey forth at dawn. All of us."

"Then rest now, warrior mage," Aerin advised, a hint of tenderness creeping into his tone. "Dawn comes, and with it, our fate."

"Rest is a luxury," she countered, though her body ached for it.

"Even the mightiest mage needs her strength." His smile was fleeting but genuine.

"True." She conceded, allowing herself a moment's respite in his company. "But only for a moment. Then we prepare."

"Agreed," Aerin said as he left Lysandra to her thoughts.

Lysandra sat beside her wolf, and closed her eyes, focusing on spells of protection, unity, and victory. She was preparing for the challenges ahead.

"Are the swords sharp?" Lysandra asked Aerin, who stood behind her.

"They're as sharp as the night's edge," he replied confidently. "And your sword hums with power."

"Good," Lysandra said, feeling her resolve strengthen. She was the Last Mage, responsible for Erenor's fate, and felt the weight of that responsibility. But within her, a fire kindled - defiance against the darkness threatening her world.

"The horses are restless," Aerin said. "They sense the change coming."

"Let them be," Lysandra said. "It suits the hour."

"You have no fear," Aerin observed.

"Only resolve," Lysandra replied, gripping her sword. "Fear is a luxury we can no longer afford."

"Lead us," Aerin urged, taking her hand briefly.

"By sunset, we'll have breached the Wailing Pass," Lysandra declared, mounting her horse. She looked at Shadow, who growled in readiness to follow her into battle if needed.

"Forward!" she commanded, her voice clear and strong. Shadow bounded ahead, leading the way.

"Stay close," Aerin called to the others as they formed a line behind Lysandra.

"We tread upon a knife's edge," Lysandra warned, scanning the horizon. "Stay alert."

"Always," Aerin replied, their armor and weapons filling the air.

Lysandra's mind swirled with spells, each adding to the protection she wove around them. This journey would define her destiny, and she would not falter.

The sky bled from indigo to gold as they rode towards the horizon. The vast and vulnerable land of Erenor lay before them. They rode for the future and hope.

"Stay vigilant," Lysandra reminded her allies. "Trust in your strength and trust in our cause."

"Until the very end," Aerin vowed.

Lysandra echoed his words, and with the rising sun at their backs, they surged forward - a band of warriors bound by magic and grit into the unknown.

Chapter 21

A NEW THREAT

The forest clearing was still as five figures gathered. They moved in a silent accord, like the ancient trees that surrounded them.

Lysandra stood in the center, her sharp eyes scanning the area. Her companion, Shadow, stood beside her, his eyes alert and watchful.

"We need to time this perfectly," Lysandra said in a low voice, her words carrying the weight of command.

Aerin stepped forward, his arms tense as he surveyed their surroundings. "We're all here. What's the plan?"

Lysandra's eyes flicked to him, the unspoken challenge in her gaze. "The Harrow will take to the skies," she said finally. "He'll scout from above and spot their movements before they sense him."

The Harrow stepped forward, his voice rumbling deep and resonant. "I'll move unseen and bring back the information we need."

Shadow growled softly as if sensing the tension in the air.

"Be careful," Lysandra said, her voice low and urgent. "We need you back in one piece."

The Harrow nodded, his eyes meeting Lysandra's momentarily before he turned and disappeared into the trees.

Feyla leaned against a tree, twirling a dagger in her fingers. "And I'm supposed to charm information from stones and streams, am I?"

Aerin half-smiled. "Your wit might be better served elsewhere, Feyla. But your instincts have never led us astray."

Feyla smirked. "Keep smirking, hunter. It'll be your face I'll look for when the world turns dark."

Lysandra interrupted, "We'll meet at the cave once our tasks are done—not a moment later."

Aerin frowned. "Is it wise to split up? Our strength lies in unity."

Lysandra replied, "We'll reunite stronger with the knowledge we gather. Trust in that, Aerin."

"Trust is a luxury in times like these," Aerin muttered.

"Then consider it an investment," Lysandra said. "One I am willing to make in you."

Their gazes locked, and the world seemed to slow down. After a moment, Aerin said, "Be safe."

"Safe is a shadow's promise," Lysandra replied. "But I'll keep my end of the bargain."

With that, the group dispersed, each to their task, leaving only the whispering trees as witnesses to their resolve.

Lysandra paused momentarily, still thinking about the man who had just left. She looked at Shadow, said, "Let's go, boy," and disappeared into the foliage.

As they walked, Lysandra told Aerin and Feyla about the First Mage's warning of a new threat in the north. "He said there's a fortress shrouded in a maelstrom, and something dangerous is inside."

Aerin looked worried. "Are we strong enough to face it?" he asked.

Lysandra put a hand on his shoulder. "We've faced tough battles before, and we've won. Together, we can do anything."

Aerin looked doubtful. "But what if I fail? What if my sword arm isn't strong enough?"

Lysandra smiled. "Then I'll stand by your side and fight with you. We're in this together."

Feyla nodded in agreement. "We've got this. We'll fight until the end."

And with that, they continued their journey, ready to face whatever lay ahead.

"Your confidence—" He began, but she interrupted him.

"Is not misplaced." She reached out, her fingertips grazing the stubble along his jaw. "Have faith, as I do."

"Faith is a tricky beast," Aerin murmured, though he did not pull away from her touch.

"Then let us tame it together," she whispered, her proximity closing the space for doubt.

Feyla cleared her throat pointedly, and they both started, stepping apart as if burned. "We'll need more than faith and whispered promises," she reminded them, her voice laced with impatience.

"Agreed," Lysandra conceded, turning to face the gathering darkness. "We strike with blade, claw, and the very elements at our command."

"Until then, we prepare," Aerin added, straightening his shoulders as resolve seemed to flow back into his veins.

"Preparation is key," Lysandra said, nodding. "But remember, the heart is also a weapon that can drive us beyond our fears and limits."

"Let's hope it's sharp enough," Aerin said, a wry smile touching his lips for the first time since the grim reunion.

"Sharper than any blade we carry," she assured him, her lips curving.

The moon rose higher, casting eerie shadows across the clearing. Lysandra turned her back on the others, followed by Shadow. They were warriors, bound by fate, magic, and something more profound. They were ready to face the new threat together.

Aerin stared at the ground, lost in thought. Feyla walked up to him, her silhouette outlined by moonlight. "Do you remember the Siege of Hollow Fort?" she asked, her voice sharp.

Aerin clenched his fists. "Those were different times," he muttered.

"Times change, but we endure," Feyla said firmly, reassuringly touching his shoulder. "We've overcome darkness before."

"By relying on chance," Aerin argued.

"Skill," Feyla corrected him. "Unity."

"Perhaps," Aerin agreed, looking away.

"More than perhaps," Feyla insisted. "We are like steel that sharpens with each strike."

Aerin thought for a moment. Suddenly, they heard a rustling noise in the bushes. Master Elarion emerged from the shadows, his cloak sweeping like a ghost's shroud. The air shifted, and a feeling of anticipation ran through the clearing like a whispered spell.

Lysandra greeted Master Elarion respectfully, ready to hear his advice. "Time is running out," he said, his voice full of knowledge and weariness. "We must take action, not just react."

"Agreed," Aerin said, standing up straight as if the sage's words had strengthened him. "But we need a plan."

"Then let's find a plan together," Master Elarion said, looking at everyone's faces. "We have strength here. Do not doubt it."

"We have strength and determination," Feyla added, lifting her chin.

"Determination will guide us through the darkness," Master Elarion confirmed. "Hold strong to it."

Everyone stood in silence, feeling the weight of his presence. It was more than just reassurance - a call to arms, a reminder of what they were fighting for, and the unity that had become their anchor in the storm.

Master Elarion's gaze rested on the group's faces, each etched with their brand of resilience. "The threat we face," he began, his voice as steady as the ancient trees surrounding them, "comes from a darkness that predates the oldest grimoires in existence."

"How do we fight something that old?" Lysandra murmured.

"By understanding its nature," Elarion replied. He tapped his staff on the ground, sending a pulse through the earth that hummed with hidden power. "It feeds on magic, twisting and distorting it into something unnatural."

"An abomination," Feyla spat, reaching for her sword.

"Indeed," Elarion confirmed. "If left unchecked, this entity will not only consume all magic but corrupt the essence of life itself."

"Then we must stop it," Aerin said, trying to sound brave, but his voice was a little too high.

"We need a solid plan," Lysandra cut in, narrowing her eyes in thought.

"Yes," Aerin agreed, nodding. "We need to play to our strengths."

"Let's map out the terrain of our confrontation," Master Elarion suggested, painting an invisible battlefield before them. "Consider every angle, every possibility."

"Lysandra and Shadow can navigate the unseen paths," Lysandra offered, stroking her companion.

"Good," Elarion nodded. "And Feyla, your intuition and swordsmanship are essential."

Aerin ran a hand through his hair, exhaling a shaky breath. "I'm no strategist or mage."

"That's okay," Master Elarion said. "We'll work together to find a way to stop this darkness."

The group huddled together, brainstorming ideas and mapping out a plan of attack. They knew what was at stake and were committed to stopping the darkness that threatened their world.

"Your heart," Lysandra said, touching his arm. Her fingers brushed against the worn leather of his bracers. "That's where your power lies."

He met her gaze, seeing the belief in her eyes he struggled to find within himself. "My heart," he echoed, the words like a promise.

"Unity is our tactic," Elarion declared. "Together, we shall turn the tide." "United," Feyla affirmed, her smile fierce.

"Until the end," Lysandra vowed, a glint of steel in her tone that matched the edge of her resolve. "Until the end," Aerin echoed, his doubts eclipsed by the collective conviction of his allies.

"Prepare yourselves," Elarion warned, his eyes reflecting the somber hues of the dawning challenge. "Our path is dangerous, our enemy relentless. But our will is ironclad."

"Then let's forge ahead," Feyla said, her hand falling from her sword. Ready.

"Ready," they all whispered, a chorus of determination that resonated through the clearing and beyond into the heart of the dark forest that held their fate.

The clearing hummed with an uneasy silence, a prelude to the storm that was to come. Lysandra's silver hair shimmered like moonlight against the dark canvas of the woods, her stormy eyes reflecting the gravity of their situation. Shadow, her loyal wolf companion, lay at her feet, ears perked, and senses alert.

"Divide and conquer," Lysandra declared, her voice slicing through the tension. "Feyla, your devices could uncover secrets we might otherwise miss in their encampment."

"Understood." Feyla nodded, her fingers twitching as if already manipulating the gears of her inventions. "I'll decipher whatever they're hiding."

"Aerin," she continued, turning to face him, "you know the wilds better than any of us. Scout their location. Find us a way in—or out."

"Consider it done." Aerin's words were a low growl. His golden eyes were scanning the perimeter, already mapping this route into enemy territory.

Lysandra's gaze shifted upwards, where The Harrow's massive silhouette cut across the sky, blotting out stars with its leathery wings. "And you, Harrow. We need eyes above. Can you sweep the skies without drawing their attention?"

The dragon circled once before landing with a ground-shaking thud, great plumes of dust rising around him. His golden scales were black as a starless night and seemed to absorb little moonlight. As he spoke, his voice rumbled like distant thunder, "I can dance with the clouds unseen. But more—I know their kind, their weaknesses."

"Speak," Lysandra urged, her hand resting on the hilt of her rune-etched sword, ready for the knowledge that may tip the scales in their favor.

"Fire," The Harrow began, his golden eyes narrowing and his voice a low rumble. "It is both a weapon and a bane. They shield themselves against it, but underneath, they are vulnerable. Strike there."

"Fire," Aerin mused aloud, his thoughts firing, considering every tactical advantage. "We can use that. Feyla—"

"Already plotting," Feyla interjected, her mind whirring as fast as the gears in her gadgets.

"Explosives, distractions. I have a few ideas to make them wish they'd never slithered out of their holes."

"Then we move at dawn," Lysandra decided, her tone leaving no room for debate. "Each task brings us closer to victory or defeat. We cannot fail."

"Fail?" Aerin scoffed, his chest swelling with newfound purpose. "Not in our stars, not today."

"Today, we soar on the wings of fate," The Harrow intoned, his voice carrying the weight of centuries.

"Let fate follow our lead," Lysandra replied, her conviction unyielding.

As the others dispersed, each to their given tasks, Lysandra remained, her breath misting in the cool night air. A shadow rose, pressing close to her side, a silent sentinel. Together, they would walk this path wherever it led. She looked at the sky, where The Harrow had once again taken flight, a specter in the night, and whispered, "For Erenor, for us all."

The clearing was veiled in shadows, and an eerie silence permeated the air as the group convened around the remnants of a cold campfire. Lysandra's silver hair shimmered under the moon's touch, and her eyes reflected a storm of worry and resolve.

"Midnight at the Moon's Crest Cave," she said, the runes on her sword glowing faintly as if in agreement. "It's hidden, defensible. We'll make our stand there."

Aerin stepped forward, his lion eyes scanning their faces and lingering on Lysandra's. "Agreed," he grunted, his voice low and steady. The cave will shield us until we strike."

Their gazes locked, an unspoken language flowing between them. Shadow, silent since their arrival, padded to Lysandra's side, his hackles raised. The wolf sensed the undercurrent of danger, the bond forming amidst the chaos.

"Stay sharp out there," Lysandra told Aerin, her hand reaching out to clasp his arm. "I can't afford to lose you."

"Nor I, you." His grip tightened for a moment, conveying more than words could. He glanced down at her sword, then back into her stormy eyes. "You saved the Harrow with that blade. Now, it must save us."

"Magic is unpredictable," she admitted, releasing his arm. "But my swordplay is not. If magic fails, steel will prevail."

"Your courage gives me strength," Aerin confessed, his fears abating. "But this enemy... we've never faced anything like it."

"We face it together," she assured him, her voice unwavering. "That makes us stronger than any dark sorcery."

"Then let's ensure we reunite." Aerin stepped back, the golden hue of his gaze almost flickering with an inner fire. "Moon's Crest Cave, at the stroke of midnight."

"Until then, may fortune favor your path," Lysandra said, watching Aerin turn and disappear between the trees, the darkness swallowing his form.

She remained motionless, the weight of leadership heavy upon her shoulders. The rustle of leaves whispered secrets only the night knew, and Lysandra closed her eyes, letting the cool forest air fill her lungs. She would need every ounce of her resolve when the time came to confront what lay ahead.

"Come, Shadow," she murmured, turning toward the cave. "We have much to prepare, and daylight will not wait for the weary."

With a last glance at the stars above, Lysandra strode through the forest, her thoughts a swirling vortex of strategy and the simmering heat of something new—something akin to hope or perhaps even the beginnings of love.

The silence in the clearing was like a tangible shroud, each breath drawn by the companions laden with the gravity of their task. Lysandra's gaze swept across the faces of her comrades, finding in each the resolve that had become the sinew binding their fates together.

"Right," Feyla broke in, her tone slicing through the heaviness. "While you're all busy brooding like statues, remember, it's not just doom and gloom. We've got a Harrow on our side, and I'd wager he's worth at least a hundred of whatever horrors we're about to face."

"Only a hundred?" The Harrow rumbled his voice, a low thunder that stirred the leaves around them.

"Fine, a thousand," Feyla amended with an exaggerated roll of her eyes, drawing a collective, if faint, smile from the group. "But let's not inflate his ego too much; he'll start demanding tribute in cattle."

Lysandra couldn't help but chuckle as her mind raced with strategies. "We count on you, Feyla, not just for fun but for the intelligence you'll gather. You have a knack for uncovering what's hidden and keeping spirits high when shadows loom."

"Someone's got to be the light in the darkness," Feyla winked. "Besides, who else will keep you all from getting too gloomy? No, off you go. Scout the enemy, Aerin. Remember, stealth over strength."

Aerin nodded, his usual reluctance giving way to a brisk nod. He shot Lysandra a look filled with unspoken words and needs before disappearing into the underbrush, silent as the night itself.

"Be safe," Lysandra murmured, though he was already gone. Her heart hitched with worry, not just for Aerin but for them all.

"Safe as a fox in its den," Feyla assured, though her gaze followed Aerin's path with equal concern. She then turned to the mighty Harrow. "You, keep your eyes sharp and your wings steady."

"Of course," the Harrow replied, his majestic golden wings unfurling like sails catching the wind. With a mighty leap, he ascended, leaving a whirlwind of fallen leaves dancing in his wake.

"Remember the plan," Lysandra called out, her voice firm. "Moon's Crest Cave, midnight. Not a moment later."

"Got it, boss," Feyla responded, saluting before turning on her heel and vanishing with a grace that belied her jesting nature.

Lysandra stood alone now, the forest's quiet surrounding her like a cloak. In the stillness, doubts whispered to her, but she pushed them aside. They were more than this fear and the sum of their might. Together, they were a force woven out of trust and shared purpose.

She took a deep breath, feeling the magic within her. It was a silent vow to protect, lead, and unite. With Shadow at her side, she stepped forward, her stride resolute as she began the journey toward their rendezvous point. Each step was a silent promise to her friends, Aerin, and the world they were fighting to save.

The forest was alive with the murmurs of nocturnal creatures and the rustle of leaves underfoot. Lysandra's boots pressed into the damp earth, each step deliberate, carving a path through the underbrush. Shadow padded beside her, his keen eyes scanning the darkening woods, vigilant against unseen threats.

"Easy, boy," she whispered, her voice just audible above the whisper of the wind. "We're not alone out here."

Shadow's ears twitched at her words, his muzzle lifting to scent the air. He growled lowly, a rumble that resonated in his chest, mirroring the unease that knotted Lysandra's stomach.

"Shadows within shadows," she muttered, the runes on her

sword glowing faintly as if in response to her growing apprehension. The light flickered across her eyes, casting them in a stormy hue. She tightened her grip on the hilt, prepared for whatever might spring from the darkness.

Ahead, the cave loomed like a gaping maw, its entrance shrouded by moss and creeping vines. Lysandra paused at the threshold, her breath forming clouds in the cool night air. Shadow whined, pressing close to her leg.

"We'll make it quick," she reassured him, though the promise was also for herself. "In and out before anything knows, we're there."

Her heart pounded a fierce rhythm as she stepped into the cave, the darkness enveloping her like an icy embrace. A water drip echoed, amplifying the heavy silence around them.

"Keep your senses sharp, Shadow," she instructed, her hand never leaving her sword. "We can't afford any surprises."

Master Elarion stood on the edge of the clearing, watching the last of his charges disappear into the tree line. His robes, once vibrant, were now dulled with the dust of travel and the weight of years. His eyes, reflecting the wisdom of ages, held a deep sadness that few could understand.

"Old friend," he murmured to the night, "what have we become?"

He traced the lines of an ancient rune in the air, a spell of protection for those who ventured forth in the name of all that was good and true. Its glow faded, absorbed by the encroaching darkness.

"Power wanes, darkness grows," he continued, his voice a solemn chant. "But we must stand, for if we fall, all falls with us."

A flicker of movement caught his eye—a shadow within the shadows—and he steeled himself. He was the last sage of the old guilds, the last bastion against the encroaching void. His knowledge was a beacon, and his power was a shield. Yet doubt gnawed at him, a relentless beast.

"Will it be enough?" he whispered to the unseen forces lurking beyond perception. Have I taught them enough to survive what is to come?"

His gaze followed Lysandra and Shadow's paths, a silent prayer woven into every glance.

"Be swift, young warriors," he intoned, the words laced with magic and hope. "Your fates are intertwined with the very threads of Erenor."

With that, Master Elarion turned back towards the forest, his cloak billowing behind him as he melded with the night. His thoughts were as much a weapon as any blade or spell.

Chapter 22

AN ANCIENT EVIL

The winds in Erenor's northern expanse were fierce and unrelenting, whipping through the craggy terrain, seeking to tear flesh from bone. Aerin led the way, and Shadow trotted close behind, ears flattened to its skull.

"Storm's getting worse," Aerin shouted over the wind's roar, his voice barely audible.

"Let me try something," Lysandra said, tracing symbols in the air. A barrier appeared, and the wind battered against it like waves upon a rocky shore.

"Nice trick!" Aerin smirked, impressed.

"Keep moving!" Lysandra urged, ignoring the flutter in her chest. The path held dangers beyond the weather.

They shuffled forward, each step a battle against the frozen earth. An ice bridge spanned a chasm up ahead, groaning ominously as they approached.

"It looks about as stable as our chances against the Dark Mage," Feyla muttered from behind, her breath forming icicles.

"Quiet, Feyla," Lysandra whispered. "We can do this."

"By 'we,' you mean you and your magic," Feyla retorted, though her gaze held respect.

Lysandra concentrated, extending her palms outward. She focused her mind on the ice, and warmth twisted around it, solidifying it further. They crossed cautiously, the bridge holding firm under Lysandra's enchantment.

Once they were safely across, Aerin said, "Remind me never to doubt you again," his voice filled with admiration.

"Don't make promises you can't keep," Lysandra teased back, feeling the tension between them shift into something lighter despite the oppressive environment.

"Is this what it's going to be like? With you two flirting while the world freezes over?" Feyla interjected, half-serious.

Lysandra rolled her eyes, "We're trying to survive here, Feyla."

"Jealous?" Aerin said with a grin, but his smile faded as he looked at Lysandra. "How are you doing? This is taking a lot out of you."

"I'm doing better than letting the cold take us," she replied, but the strain was evident beneath the surface. Even though she had strong powers, Lysandra had her limits.

"Then we need to keep moving—and quickly," Feyla added, looking at the darkening sky. Those clouds don't look good."

"I agree," Lysandra said, her worry etched in her face as she looked at the gathering storm clouds. As they continued on their journey through Erenor, the challenges mounted.

However, as Lysandra's magic overcame each obstacle and navigated each icy precipice, their bonds grew tighter, and their resolve became more muscular. But they also felt that something was watching them, waiting for a chance to attack when weak.

"Stay alert," Lysandra murmured. "We're not alone in this wilderness."

"I never thought we were," Aerin said, drawing his sword, ready for anything that came their way.

"Neither did I," Feyla added, looking over her gadgets. She was always one step ahead of despair.

That night, they camped under Lysandra's magic dome. They shared a meal in silence, the fire casting long shadows that danced like ghosts around them.

Aerin caught Lysandra's gaze across the flames, and they exchanged a silent promise of battles to come and unexplored feelings.

"Rest up," Lysandra said softly. "Tomorrow, we face our fears."

"Or they face us," Feyla added.

———◇———

In the stillness of the night, Lysandra thought about the ancient evil that hunted them, feeling a growing chill in her bones. As her companions slept, she remained awake, guarding against the darkness with a weary but unwavering eye.

The wind's rasping breath gave way to a low growl, echoing through Erenor's stark landscape. Aerin's eyes narrowed, his hand tightening around his sword. "We've got company," he said, tense and ready for anything.

"More than one?" Feyla asked, her fingers dancing over her gadgets.

"A pack of ice wraiths," Aerin replied, never taking his gaze off the swirling snow ahead.

"Perfect," Lysandra said, her voice a mix of sarcasm and determination. She raised her hands, readying a spell.

"Wait for my signal," Aerin said, stepping forward as shapes emerged from the blizzard.

"Like we have a choice," Feyla muttered, pulling out a cylindrical device that clicked into a crossbow. "Let's do this."

Aerin lunged, his sword gleaming in the dim light.

He met the first ice wraith with a fierce strike that sent it stumbling back. His movements were precise, each attack a dance of death for the creatures that dared to challenge them.

"Behind you!" shouted Lysandra, throwing up a magical shield as another wraith attacked.

"Thanks!" grunted Aerin, dodging the attack and defeating another wraith.

"Use this!" Feyla tossed Aerin a tiny orb, which he smashed on the ground. It exploded, scorching the nearby wraiths and sending them howling into the darkness.

"Nice one," said Aerin, pleased with the result.

"Don't let your guard down," warned Lysandra, casting another spell to protect them.

"I won't," replied Aerin, focused on the battle.

"Looks like we're clear," said Lysandra, scanning the area.

"Let's move on," Feyla said, putting away her crossbow. Hopefully, we'll find something less undead."

"Agreed," said Aerin, cleaning his sword. "You good, Lysandra?"

"Better now," said Lysandra, smiling at him.

"Great," said Aerin, relieved. "What's next, Feyla?"

"Looks like a puzzle," said Lysandra, examining some carved pillars.

"Leave it to me," Feyla said, studying the carvings. These symbols look like instructions."

"Can you figure it out?" asked Aerin.

"Easy," replied Feyla, quickly manipulating the pillars until they all clicked into place.

"Nice one," said Aerin, impressed with Feyla's skills.

"Let's see where this path leads," said Lysandra as they entered the hidden passage.

"Watch out for dangers," reminded Feyla.

"Always," said Aerin, ready for whatever lay ahead.

They made their way through a passage that opened into a clearing where the bones of ancient history lay exposed under a gray sky. Pillars like sentinels stood around what was once a grand citadel, now just a memory cradled by the earth.

Aerin gasped in awe, "By the ancients, this is it! The lost city of Veridian."

Feyla remarked, "Looks more like Veridian's graveyard," as she touched a frost-covered relic.

Lysandra studied the runes etched into the monoliths and said, "There are secrets here." She stepped forward, and Aerin joined her side.

"Can you make anything out?" Aerin asked.

Lysandra studied the ancient script for a moment. "The Celestial Fracture. It wasn't just an event...it was a weapon."

Aerin rested his hand on his blade's hilt, ready for unseen threats, "Used by whom?"

Lysandra replied, "It doesn't say, but there's mention of a 'Harbinger,' one who would unite the fracture."

"To what end?" Aerin asked.

"Power," Lysandra whispered. "Control."

"Then we must be the ones to find it first," Aerin said, determination hardening his voice.

Lysandra nodded in agreement, though unease coiled within her. "Let's keep moving. Time isn't our ally."

Feyla added, "Neither is whatever left these clues."

Lysandra felt a connection to this place, a thrumming beneath her skin that resonated with the dark energy of the ruins. They delved deeper into the ruins, each step taking them closer to truths long buried and darkness eager to rise again.

The air in the ruins hummed with an ancient hunger, a craving for dominion that seemed to resonate from the very stones that lined the decrepit halls. Lysandra's fingers brushed against the cold, etched symbols, feeling the thrum of dark power beneath her touch.

As they progressed through the ruins, the tension rose. They had to stay vigilant, for they knew not what lay ahead.

"I can feel it," she whispered, barely audible over the howling wind outside. Aerin nodded, scanning the dim corridors. "It's like the ground is alive," he said. "Alive and evil," Lysandra confirmed, her voice trembling. They were playing a dangerous game, and something far more sinister than they'd imagined was controlling Erenor.

"We've been dancing to its tune," Feyla said, adjusting her mechanical contrivances. "It's time to change the melody," Aerin suggested, tightening his grip on his sword.

"Wait," Shadow growled, his ears flat against his head. Lysandra stretched out her senses, feeling the arcane energies around her. Suddenly, a wave of darkness hit them, and figures emerged from the shadows. They were minions of an ancient evil.

"Defensive positions!" Aerin shouted, unsheathing his sword. "Barrier up!" Lysandra commanded, weaving a shimmering wall of energy before them.

"Watch your left!" Feyla shouted, dispatching a bolt from her crossbow. "Thanks," Aerin grunted, spinning to cleave another attacker.

"Keep them off me!" Lysandra called, maintaining the barrier. "Got your back," Aerin replied, his movements deadly.

"Shadow, now!" Feyla commanded, and the wolf leaped forward, tearing into their assailants. "I can't hold this much longer," Lysandra gasped, sweat on her brow.

"Push through!" Aerin encouraged. "We're clearing a path!" "Almost... there..." Feyla reloaded, firing with desperation.

"Go!" Aerin pulled Lysandra away from the epicenter of her spell. "Shadow!" Feyla called urgently. Together, they sprinted through the narrow opening in the ranks of the minions.

"I can't believe we made it," Feyla panted, looking back at the chaos they'd left behind. Shadow growled in agreement, his flanks heaving.

Lysandra and Aerin stood together, facing the darkness with determination. Shadow, the wolf, followed them, sensing danger in the air. They were in the ruins of an ancient civilization, and Lysandra recognized some symbols etched on a crumbling wall. She traced them with her fingers, and memories flooded her mind.

"These symbols are familiar," she said. "I remember them from my dreams, dark dreams."

Feyla, the inventor, warned her about possible traps, but Lysandra was determined to unravel the mystery of the symbols. She felt a connection to the dark power that had created them.

"We need a plan," Lysandra said, shaking off the vestiges of her visions.

"We'll need distractions and defenses," Aerin said. "I'll lead the charge and draw their focus."

"I can fortify us against their attacks," Lysandra added, recalling the strength of her spells.

"I'll exploit their weaknesses," Feyla said, showing a small gadget that sparkled with potential.

"I'll guard our flank," Lysandra said, stroking Shadow's fur. The wolf responded with a soft nuzzle, reassuring his loyalty.

Lysandra felt a shiver down her spine. "This evil is old, part of my bloodline. I am connected to it."

"Then you're our best weapon," Aerin said. "You can unravel this."

"Or be unraveled," Lysandra countered, meeting his intense gaze. The unspoken fear lingered between them, the possibility that she might lose herself to the darkness.

"Then we anchor you," Feyla said. "We keep you grounded."

They nodded, and Lysandra focused on the symbols. She felt the power within her and knew she could unravel the mystery. The three companions moved forward with determination, ready to face whatever lay ahead.

"Then it's set," Aerin declared. "We confront this... together."

"Prepare yourselves," Lysandra warned. Her rune sword sang as she drew it, the metallic sound a simple note amid the oppressive silence. "This confrontation—it's bigger than any of us."

"It's a good thing we're not alone, then," Aerin replied, his eyes softening before hardening with resolve.

"Whatever happens," Feyla added, adjusting her pack with determination, "we're changing history today."

"History," Lysandra echoed, feeling the weight of the past on her shoulders. "Let's ensure it remembers us."

"Or in awe," Aerin said wryly, taking a protective stance before her. "Preferably both," Feyla quipped, readying her inventions.

As they positioned themselves, the air thrummed with power, and the ruins were a testament to the battle that would soon unfold. Each knew the risks, the very fabric of Erenor at stake. Yet within that

scary moment, amidst the rising tension and whispered chants of ancient magic, there was an undeniable unity—a fierce bond forged in the fires of adversity.

"Time to end this nightmare," Lysandra whispered, her stormy eyes reflecting the flickering light of her burgeoning power. And as the shadows danced around them, her heartbeat with equal parts dread and determination. For here, in the heart of darkness, they would either find victory or oblivion.

The ruins of Erenor quaked as Lysandra's voice wove through the crevices and over the crumbling stones. "By the wells of ethereal light," she incanted, her sea green eyes shimmering with an unnatural luster, "I invoke thee."

"Be careful, Lysandra," Aerin warned, looking towards the shadows where danger lurked. "If you draw too much power, it could be dangerous."

Feyla interrupted, "Shh, she knows what she's doing."

Lysandra felt the ancient wells calling to her, and power surged into her veins. It was exhilarating and terrifying at the same time. She thrust her sword forward and unleashed a wave of force that rippled through the battlefield.

"Here they come!" Aerin shouted, unsheathing his blade.

"Stand firm!" Lysandra commanded.

Shadow, her wolf, growled beside her, senses heightened, fur bristling with a static charge.

"Got your back!" Feyla exclaimed, releasing a swarm of mechanical buzzers that scanned the area for weaknesses in their foes.

The ancient evil appeared, its form shifting like smoke and ash, its eyes burning with malice and shock.

"You?" it hissed, its gaze fixed on Lysandra. "The last mage?"

Lysandra flung herself back at it, her heart pounding. She remembered the symbols she once feared and how they gave her strength.

"You should have stayed hidden!" the entity roared, launching a volley of dark magic at her.

The Creature emitted a low, menacing growl as it stalked toward the group, its voice a mix of eerie whispers and guttural roars.

Aerin leaped, intercepting the blast with a shield of golden energy that materialized from his outstretched hand. "Not today!"

"Nor any day after!" Feyla added, her devices whirring, creating a harmonic disruption that weakened their adversary.

"Look up!" The cry came from Aerin, his voice urgent with triumph.

The Harrow joined the fray, its scales reflecting the fractured light, its roar a symphony of defiance. It collided with the Ancient Evil, talons tearing and fire engulfing.

"Didn't expect that, did you?" Lysandra yelled over the din as the Creature recoiled, screeching in rage.

"Push forward!" Aerin urged, his blade cutting through the minions that emerged from the swirling darkness.

"Focus, Lysandra," Feyla's voice was steady amidst the chaos. "Use the connection."

"Using it!" Lysandra replied, sweat beading on her brow as she channeled the raw power of the wells, her mind crafting a counter-spell that shimmered with promise and peril.

"End this," Aerin said, glancing at her with an intensity that sent an unexpected shiver down her spine.

"Ending it," Lysandra affirmed, thrusting her sword into the earth. Magic surged outward, entwined with the dragon's flame, Shadow's ferocity, Aerin's courage, and Feyla's ingenuity.

"NOW!" she screamed, and the world exploded in light.

The group of survivors was panting in silence as their enemy surrounded them after the dust had settled. They looked at each other, and each face showed relief and exhaustion. However, the Ancient Evil still lingered, although it was now weakened.

"I can't believe it," Aerin said, leaning on his sword.

"Believe it," replied Lysandra, breathing heavily.

"Did we win?" Feyla asked, sounding overwhelmed by the enormity of their task.

"We were close," Lysandra answered, reaching for Aerin's hand.

Their fingers intertwined, and they drew strength from each other.

"Close isn't good enough," Aerin said, brushing his thumb across Lysandra's knuckles.

"Then let's finish this," Lysandra declared, her determination unwavering even as darkness once again descended upon them.

The ruins trembled, and a shadow stretched across the land, a harbinger of the final clash. The ground quaked beneath them as they braced themselves against the resurgence of the Ancient Evil.

Before them was an abyss of dark energy, crackling with malice and seeking to reclaim Erenor.

"Stand firm!" Lysandra shouted as she drew her sword.

Aerin nodded, positioning himself back-to-back with her, his blade ready.

"I never thought I'd die fighting alongside a mage," he grunted, scanning for any sign of movement.

"Nor am I with a hunter," Lysandra retorted, but there was no bite in her voice, only camaraderie.

Feyla tossed one of her devices into the chasm, and a brilliant flare erupted, pushing back the shadows.

"This won't hold it off for long!" she called out, reloading her crossbow.

"Every second counts," Lysandra replied, focusing on the darkness. Shadow growled beside her, hackles raised, while the Harrow circled above, a silent guardian.

"Something's different," Aerin breathed, his gaze locked on Lysandra.

The Creature's presence had shifted its attention to Lysandra.

Lysandra felt a pull in her chest, a connection she couldn't sever. Memories surged within her—flashes of a time before when power flowed unchecked, and ambition led to her downfall.

"Your lineage...you bear the mark," the Creature's voice slithered into her mind.

"Silence!" Lysandra spat, although her heart hammered with

the truth. She descended from those who had first torn the veil and ushered this darkness into Erenor.

"Tell me, Lysandra, does your wolf companion know of your ancestors' betrayal?" The voice taunted.

Aerin's hand tightened on hers, grounding her. "Ignore it. We're here now, together. That's all that matters."

The adventurers united to defeat the ancient evil that had plagued their land for centuries. A voice taunted them as they approached their foe, "Unity is fragile. Will it hold when the truths are laid bare?"

Lysandra had had enough, and with fierce determination, she channeled her magic into her sword to create a protective shield around them. Her companion, Aerin, reminded her that her past did not define her and that she had the power to choose her destiny.

Feyla, always ready for a fight, urged them to show their enemy actual Unity, and together, they charged forward. The Harrow swooped down, breathing fire, and Feyla's bolts hit their target with deadly accuracy.

Lysandra cast a spell that collided with the abyss. Aerin invoked the power of their ancestors, and the air vibrated with the strength of their Unity. The darkness writhed and dissipated, but not entirely. A fragment remained, connected to Lysandra.

Feyla reloaded her weapon, but the fragment was still clinging to something. Lysandra realized it was connected to her, and despite her friends' warnings, she stepped forward to face her destiny.

Aerin reminded her she was not alone, and Lysandra confronted the remaining darkness with his support. The fate of their land rested on this pivotal moment as they waited in silence.

"I see it, Lyss," whispered Lysandra's friend, Aerin, as they stared at the fragment of darkness that refused to yield. It pulsed with a heart of Shadow, reflecting the ghostly luminescence of the ethereal wells. Lysandra's hand trembled as she touched it, feeling its power hum against her skin like static before a storm.

Aerin tightened his grip on his sword, ready for anything. "You're the key. We always knew it."

Lysandra's mind raced as she flickered through spells and every shard of arcane knowledge she'd ever gleaned. "I'm not sure," she said hesitantly, her voice tinged with doubt.

"Can you sever it?" Feyla asked, stepping up beside them, her crossbow at the ready.

Shadow growled low in his throat, sensing the impending danger.

With a deep breath, Lysandra closed her eyes and invoked the deepest reserves of her power. The air crackled, and a tapestry of energy wove around them. She could feel the gnawing void clawing at the edges of her soul, a whisper from the past that promised both salvation and ruin.

A surge of malice erupted from the fragment, and a tendril of pure malevolence aimed straight for Lysandra's heart. Time slowed, and each heartbeat lasted an eternity.

Aerin lunged forward, sword cleaving through the dark tendril. His battle cry melded with the metallic ring of the blade, meeting baleful magic. Feyla fired, a bolt ensnared in light streaking past Lysandra's cheek, so close she felt its passing as a brush of death's passionless kiss.

"Back, Lyss!" Aerin shouted, parrying another lash of darkness with a grunt of effort. "You must break free!"

But Lysandra stood fast, her senses sharpening as the scent of burning flesh and hair filled her nostrils. It had struck Aerin. Pain and fear surged within her, a maelstrom threatening to drown her resolve.

"Stay with me, Lyss," Aerin gasped, blood trickling down his arm.

"Focus, Lysandra!" Feyla's voice cut through the chaos, grounding Lysandra. She knew the ancient evil was close. She murmured the words to the spell that only she could complete, feeling power coiling inside her.

"Now, Lysandra!" Aerin and Feyla urged her on.

Lysandra opened her eyes, the power of the spell ablaze in them. "Be unmade!" she screamed, unleashing the spell. Light and Shadow clashed in an explosion of ancient and arcane forces. A terrible howl pierced the night, and then silence descended.

Lysandra felt her vision blur as she staggered and saw her companions breathing raggedly. The scent of charred destiny hung in the air. Lysandra looked at the scorched earth where the fragment had been and knew something was wrong. The darkness hadn't disappeared. It had hidden itself away.

"Where is it?" Feyla asked, loading another bolt.

Lysandra scanned the ruins, feeling like they were being watched. Suddenly, the ground shook, and the stones of Erenor cried out in anguish.

"Prepare yourselves," Lysandra warned. "It's coming back."

"We'll face it together," Aerin vowed, gripping his sword.

"Until the end," Feyla affirmed, standing shoulder to shoulder with them.

They waited, poised on the brink of revelation and ruin. Then, a roar shattered the night, a sound of fury and ancient hatred reborn. The ground split open, and a form too terrible to behold emerged. Its eyes burned with a hatred older than the stars.

"Stand firm," Aerin commanded. Feyla's finger trembled on the trigger, her breath held tight in her chest. Lysandra froze, but she knew she had to act. She whispered the spell once more, the power coursing through her veins.

The Ancient Evil charged towards them, but Lysandra stood her ground. She released the spell; the darkness was defeated this time, and the world was safe again.

The Creature issued a bone-rattling roar and stepped into the wells' ghostly radiance. Its hulking frame was wreathed in tendrils of Shadow that lashed about like serpents. Eyes like smoldering embers fixed the trio with an evil glare as it advanced, and massive claws left gouges in the ancient stone floor.

They had never faced a demon like this before, and Lysandra feared that not all of them would live to see the dawn.

Chapter 23

VICTORY OVER EVIL

The group stood before the mouth of the lair, which looked like an ominous, twisted root. Aerin gripped his sword as he surveyed their destination while Lysandra stood calmly by his side. Feyla felt uneasy and fidgeted with her inventions, sensing something ominous.

Aerin reassured the group that they were doing this together. Lysandra nodded, and her wolf pup growled, anticipating the coming danger. She closed her eyes and drew upon the power of Erenor, the land they were sworn to protect. A surge of magic flowed through her, empowering her for the fight ahead.

As they entered the cave, Feyla was eager to begin, while Aerin remained protective of Lysandra. The wind howled around them as they prepared for the fight ahead.

"Remember, Lys," Aerin shouted, "your magic is our edge!"

Lysandra nodded, her eyes blazing with magic. She felt a newfound strength within her, knowing it would be crucial in defeating the hostility that had befallen their land.

"Let's do this," Feyla said with determination, and the group charged forward into the darkness.

She smiled tightly, taking courage from the presence of her companions. "Your blade is ours, Aerin."

"Let's end this nightmare," Lysandra said, her voice clear and commanding.

"Let's make it afraid of us," Aerin replied fiercely.

They stepped forward, crossing the threshold of the lair. Shadows clung to them, but Lysandra's light pushed them back.

Their fate was intertwined as they marched into the heart of evil, where the actual test of their bond awaited.

"Positions!" Lysandra commanded, her voice sharp.

Aerin moved to shield her flank. "Stay alert for signs of magic suppression," he warned.

"Watch out for traps," Feyla added, fiddling with one of her gadgets.

The Harrow grunted, ready to unleash fire and fury.

"Let's make it count," Lysandra said, feeling the magic at her fingertips.

"Move out!" Aerin led the charge, his blade gleaming.

They surged forward, stepping in unison. The first wave of minions emerged from the shadows.

"Engage!" Lysandra thrust her hand forward, releasing a pulse of energy.

Aerin's sword cut down the minions with precision. "For Erenor!"

Feyla's gadgets sprang to life, darts and nets flying through the air.

The Harrow roared, unleashing fire on their enemies.

"Push!" Lysandra urged a barrier shimmering with energy.

Together, they fought through the minions, their bond growing stronger with each victory.

"Stay close!" Aerin's voice was a lifeline amidst the chaos.

"Got your back!" Feyla called out, even as she launched another device into the fray—a tangle of wires that ensnared a cluster of minions.

"More incoming!" Harrow's warning came just as a new tide of darkness surged toward them.

"Ready, Lys?" Aerin's question was laced with concern and something else—an ember of something more profound.

"Always," she shot back, feeling a peculiar mix of adrenaline and something akin to exhilaration. This was their moment—their destiny unfurled with every spell cast, and the enemy fell.

"Focus," she whispered, her magic a blazing torrent within. Her companions fought with unparalleled enthusiasm, a symphony of destruction that carved a path through the horde.

"Press on!" Lysandra's shout rallied them; her will was indomitable. Their onslaught was relentless, and for a fleeting moment, victory seemed more than just a distant dream—it felt inevitable.

The cave was filled with the stench of burning flesh and ozone. Lysandra's fingers moved quickly, casting spells that created a whirlwind of light and shadow around her. She thrust her hand forward, and radiant barriers emerged from the ground, blocking the dark attacks.

"Protect me!" she shouted, her voice rising above the noise of the battle.

"I've got you!" Aerin replied, stepping in front of her with his sword raised. His blade sliced through the enemies with lethal precision.

"Behind you!" Feyla warned as the sound of gears and a spring-loaded net entangling an attacker could be heard.

"Thanks!" Aerin grunted, turning around to defeat another foe.

"Topside!" Harrow yelled. He swooped down from the cavern's heights, breathing dragon fire that destroyed the minions.

"Keep pushing!" Lysandra commanded, her magic lashing out like lightning. A surge of energy blasted a swath of enemies aside, clearing the path ahead.

"Watch your left!" Aerin parried a blow meant for Lysandra.

"Do you have a trick for this?" Lysandra asked, nodding towards a cluster of minions gathering at their side.

"I do," Feyla smirked, throwing a handful of metallic spheres into the fray. They exploded in a cacophony of light, disorienting the horde.

"Good work, Feyla!" Lysandra praised, feeling a rush of warmth for her friend's ingenuity. "Aerin, now!"

"Clearing the way!" Aerin shouted, leaping into the crowd of dazed minions with lethal strikes.

"Do you need a break?" The Harrow landed with a thud, his fiery breath scorching a protective ring around them.

"I can't stop," Lysandra panted, her determination unwavering. "Not when we're this close."

"Then let's finish this!" Aerin called, his sword arm unwavering despite the fatigue.

"Finishing touches!" Feyla moved quickly, setting up tripwires connected to explosive charges.

"Are you ready for the grand finale?" Lysandra asked her companions with a fierce grin.

"Let's light it up!" The Harrow roared in approval.

"See you on the other side," Aerin said, his gaze holding hers for a moment.

"Count on it," Lysandra whispered back. Together, they

plunged deeper into the abyss, their unity and determination shining brighter than any spell she could muster.

The group stood at the entrance of a cavernous lair, facing a looming figure that radiated dark energy. The air was thick with tension and fear.

"Steady," said Lysandra, her eyes fixed on the looming entity. Aerin tightened his grip on his sword, ready for battle.

"Death will learn to fall today," added The Harrow, his massive form coiled, ready to unleash hellfire.

Feyla murmured, "It looks like death learned to walk." Her fingers danced over the gadgets strapped to her belt.

Lysandra closed her eyes and drew upon her power. She envisioned the wolf waiting for her beyond this darkness—the innocence she fought to protect. Her magic responded, surging through her veins with the promise of victory or oblivion.

"Is it enough?" whispered Aerin.

"Has to be," Lysandra said, her words a silent vow to herself as much as an answer to him.

"Give us an opening, Lyss," pleaded Feyla, her gaze flickering with hope.

"Watch closely," Lysandra replied, lifting her arms as if to embrace the sky. Her magic was a crescendo of raw energy, etching runes of light into the darkness.

"Blind it!" she cried out, releasing the pent-up force. A brilliant light erupted from her hands, illuminating the lair and scattering the shadows.

The creature faltered beneath the assault of light. "Now! Strike hard!" commanded Lysandra.

"Let's make this count!" shouted Aerin, charging forward with his blade.

Feyla sent a volley of traps toward the enemy, exploding upon impact and sending tendrils of lightning snaking across the ground. The Harrow swooped down from above, unleashing a torrent of flame and tearing into the fabric of the evil force's existence.

Their combined efforts proved successful as the darkness dissipated. Lysandra knew their path was difficult, but they were the precursors of dawn against the longest night.

"Ha! Burn, creature, burn!" The Harrow's triumphant shout bolstered their spirits, the group's morale soaring high like the flames themselves.

"Let's not celebrate just yet!" Aerin cautioned, parrying a shadow tendril that sought to strike while they were distracted. "Stay focused."

"Right behind you," Lysandra said, her tone a mixture of fierce determination and something softer, something that made Aerin's heartbeat just a fraction faster.

"Finish it," she whispered, her words meant only for him.

"Count on it." His reply was a promise, a pledge to see this through—not just for Erenor, but for her, for what simmered between them, unspoken but real.

"Always," Lysandra breathed, and Aerin felt the weight of those words, heavy with future battles and shared glances beneath starlit skies.

"Cover me, Harrow!" Aerin called out, ready to push forward once more. The Harrow responded with a roar, the heat of his flames lighting a path for victory.

Their combined might was a symphony of destruction, an ode to the unwavering resolve of heroes bound by fate and forged in the fires of adversity. Each blow took them closer to triumph, each moment etched into the annals of time.

"Steady," Lysandra murmured, her voice a calm counterpoint to the chaos around them. Her fingers traced the runes on her sword, each symbol pulsing with light as if alive. She sheathed the blade—this was no time for steel.

"Magic?" Aerin glanced back at her, his eyes questioning as he fended off another wave of shadows.

"More than that." Lysandra closed her eyes, taking a deep

breath that drew in the very essence of the lair, its dark whispers, and the cries of their enemies.

"Make it count!" Feyla shouted, throwing a satchel that exploded into a shimmering net, ensnaring a cluster of minions.

Lysandra's eyes snapped open, now stormy with power. She extended her arms, her palms outstretched toward the towering malevolence before them. "Aerin, shield!"

His response was immediate: as he stepped closer to her, his body formed a protective arc, and his sword became an extension of his will.

"By Erenor's light!" Lysandra invoked the words, igniting the air itself. A torrent of energy gathered, crackling and hissing as it spiraled between her hands.

"Unleash hell, Lysandra," Harrow growled, sweeping his wings to buffet away the encroaching darkness.

With a cry that merged fury and hope, she unleashed the spell. A beam of pure, blinding energy rocketed forth, striking the heart of the ancient evil. It howled, a sound that scraped against their souls.

"Is it working?" Aerin yelled over the din, his voice laced with concern and awe.

"Feel that?" She didn't have to look at him to know he did—the quivering air and the faltering of the dark force's aura.

"Keep pushing!" Feyla urged her gadgets to whirl and buzz, lending their strength to the fray.

The ancient evil staggered, its form flickering like a dying flame. Lysandra felt the shift—the ebb of its vile presence. This was it—their chance.

"Everyone, together!" Aerin's command was clear and decisive.

"Let's strike now!" Lysandra exclaimed with renewed energy, stepping forward to take on the enemy. The Harrow roared, adding force to their battle cry, while his flames consumed the last remnants of the enemy.

"End this nightmare!" he bellowed.

"Go down!" Lysandra hissed, channeling all her magic into the fight.

"Die!" Aerin lunged forward with his sword, aimed at the heart of darkness.

Feyla's devices detonated in a symphony of sparks and shrapnel, tearing at the weakened foe. The Harrow's talons ripped through shadow and sinew while they all delivered a final blow, united in a common purpose.

As the enemy crumbled, a weight that had persisted for centuries lifted from Lysandra's chest, leaving her feeling victorious and alive.

"Is it over?" Aerin asked, his sword still ready.

"We did it!" Feyla exclaimed with excitement.

The Harrow landed beside them with a thud, his scales shimmering with residual heat. "Our enemies are vanquished," he said with a nod.

Lysandra looked at her allies, their faces etched with fatigue and triumph. Her heart swelled with the sense of shared purpose that had brought them thus far.

She stepped closer to Aerin, and as their arms brushed, she felt a dangerous spark igniting within her.

"Thank you," she whispered, allowing herself a moment of vulnerability.

"We have each other's backs," Aerin replied with a squeeze of her shoulder.

"Let's stay alert," Feyla interjected teasingly. "There might be traps."

"True," Lysandra agreed, regaining her composure. "We stay vigilant until we're clear of this place."

"Let's move out," Aerin announced, taking the lead with a protective glance back at Lysandra. His steps were sure, each one a testament to their shared purpose.

"Does anyone else need a long bath after this?" Feyla grumbled, gathering her scattered inventions.

"First, let us ensure Erenor is safe," Lysandra said, her voice full of determination.

"Then baths and feasts," the Harrow said, his fiery breath warming the chill that clung to the cavern walls.

"Sounds like a plan," Aerin chuckled, his camaraderie a balm to Lysandra's soul.

"Victory first. Celebrations later," Lysandra affirmed, leading them away from the scene of their greatest trial and toward the future they were destined to forge together.

The dust settled like a shroud over the remnants of what had been an ancient nexus of malevolence.

Lysandra's chest heaved, her breaths coming in sharp, crystalline gasps that cut through the silence of the now-still lair. She scanned the debris. Each shattered stone and scorching mark is a testament to their ferocious struggle.

"Is it done?" Feyla asked, her eyes wide with amazement as she pushed her soot-smeared goggles onto her forehead.

"Done enough," Lysandra replied, her voice steady despite her fatigue. "For now."

Aerin knelt to examine a pulsating fragment of dark crystal, his sword still smeared with the enemy's black blood. "This might have been the source of its power," he said, pointing to the crystal.

"Let me see," Lysandra commanded, her fingertips sparking with latent magic as she reached for the shard.

"Careful," Aerin warned as she took the crystal, studying the shadows that seemed to shift and whisper within it.

Her brow furrowed as she felt the icy touch of darkness caressing her thoughts. She quickly crushed the crystal, releasing energy that dissipated into the air.

"Good riddance," the Harrow growled, his scales still glowing from the fire he had unleashed upon their enemy.

"Yet, for every shadow we dispel, another lurks," Lysandra pondered aloud, her mind racing ahead to the challenges that awaited them beyond the lair's walls.

"Then we face them together," Aerin said, rising to his feet. His eyes locked with Lysandra's, and the unspoken promise sent a thrill through her.

"United," Feyla added, already fidgeting with a new gadget she had created during the fight.

"Always," the Harrow affirmed, his fiery eyes reflecting their shared conviction.

"Let's make sure there are no more threats here," Lysandra said, her determination fueling her next steps. The group fanned out, examining every corner and shadowy recess for danger.

"Seems all clear," Feyla called out after a while, her voice echoing off the walls.

"Then we leave no trace behind," Aerin declared, shattering the remaining crystals with a few swift swings of his sword.

"It's time to return to Erenor," Lysandra said, leading them towards the exit. "Our victory today changes everything. Power abhors a vacuum, so we must be ready for whatever seeks to fill the void we've created."

"Sounds ominous," Feyla quipped, though her eyes reflected the gravity of their situation.

"Ominous but necessary," Lysandra countered, stepping into the fading light of day that greeted them at the lair's entrance. The sun hung low on the horizon, casting a golden hue that belied the darkness they had just defeated.

"Tonight, we rest. Tomorrow, we plan," Aerin said, symbolizing the end of one chapter and the readiness to begin another.

"Rest sounds good," Feyla said, showing her exhaustion.

"Indeed," Lysandra agreed, thinking about taking a break. "But keep your wits about you. This is just the calm before the storm."

"Then let's enjoy the peace while we can," Aerin suggested, offering his arm to Feyla with a half-smile.

"Indeed," Lysandra echoed, accepting Aerin's arm and feeling the warmth of his skin through his tunic. It was a quiet acknowledgment of the bond that had formed between them.

Their footsteps echoed in unison, united in purpose and strengthened by the challenges they had faced. Behind them, the lair stood silent, a hollow monument to their triumph, while ahead lay the vast and uncertain future of Erenor.

Chapter 24

A NEW BEGINNING

The gates of Tyrannis opened slowly, welcoming the travelers home. The air was filled with the scent of roasting meats, baked bread, and the sounds of a waking city. People were relieved to see them and shouted joyfully as they entered the streets. They had not come to fight but to celebrate.

"Have you mended the sky?" a woman asked, her voice shaking with hope.

"Word spreads fast," Lysandra replied. "The Celestial Fracture is healed."

Cheers erupted around them, and Aerin stepped forward with pride in his eyes. He whispered to Lysandra, "Your mother would be proud."

"Thank you," Lysandra said, feeling the warmth of his arm brushing hers.

"Hero of Erenor!" someone shouted, "Lysandra, our savior!"

"Looks like they won't let you disappear into the shadows this time," Aerin teased softly.

"Nor you," she replied with a smile.

"Come, let's give them what they want." Aerin offered her his arm, which she took with feigned reluctance. Together, they walked towards the heart of the celebration, the wolf at her heels.

"Tell us, mage-born!" an old man exclaimed. "How did you close the wound in the heavens?"

"Magic," Lysandra replied, "and steel. And the courage of those who stood beside me."

"Here's to courage!" a burly blacksmith bellowed, raising his tankard.

"Here's to Lysandra!" echoed the crowd, their voices ringing like a song.

"Here's to all of us," Lysandra corrected them. "For it is together that we are mighty."

"Spoken like a true leader," Aerin whispered.

"Let's not forget the stubborn swordsman who refuses to leave my side," Lysandra replied, glancing at Aerin.

"Wouldn't dream of it," he said, his eyes alight with something more.

As the city of Tyrannis embraced its champions, Lysandra stood tall amidst the people who called her hero, her spirit intertwined with Aerin's. A new beginning was marked at the grand plaza of Tyrannis. Every race and creed of Erenor had gathered, and a council was formed not of one but of all.

"Today marks a new beginning," Master Elarion declared. "We forge a council not of one but of all."

As representatives approached the dais, Lysandra watched from just offstage, Aerin at her side. A Draconian, an Elvarin, and a dwarf, each a testament to the diversity that had once teetered on the brink of destruction.

"Your oaths," prompted Elarion, his gaze sweeping the council members.

The council of Tyrannis had gathered to take vows to uphold peace and honor the sacrifices made by their people. The Draconian unfurled a scroll, her nails clicking against the parchment. "I vow, by flame and scale, to uphold the peace of Erenor, to honor the sacrifices made and the blood spilled."

"By forest's whisper, I pledge to bridge the divides, to heal the wounds of our lands," the Elvarin intoned, bowing his head.

"By the forge's fire and mountain's might, I swear to stand firm beside my kin and kind," the dwarf rumbled, striking his chest with a fist.

Lysandra listened to the council members speak, and their words were powerful. She knew that words were where it began, but their actions would seal them. As the council finished their vows, Master Elarion raised his staff high, and lightning crackled around the crystal atop it. The crowd chanted back, "United, we rise," as if the air they breathed was now laced with the power of a collective will.

Lysandra stood before the Council Hall, and the crowd gasped and applauded as she was introduced as the First Mage's last descendant. Aerin stood beside her, his hand resting on his sword hilt. She sensed his unspoken pride and warmth, and it beckoned her to trust the unfamiliar terrain of emotion.

The council's words were powerful, but Lysandra knew their actions would seal them. She shared a look with Aerin, and they both knew that trials were yet to come. The scene was a testament to the fragile edge of their hope—a reminder that peace was as much a journey as a destination. But through unity, they would rise, and through unity, they would live in peace.

As the jubilant crowd of Tyrannis celebrated, Lysandra felt the moment's gravity settle in her bones. She knew that she would stand alone without the strength of Tyrannis and its people's courage. She lifted her gaze to meet the sea of faces and saw in their eyes the power of a collective will.

Lysandra and Aerin found a moment of peace away from the noisy celebrations. They sat on a bench in a secluded alleyway. Lysandra was staring at the ground, deep in thought.

"Is something bothering you?" Aerin asked, concerned.

Lysandra looked up at him with a furrowed brow. "I don't know. That fight with the demon...He said...she swallowed. He said that his blood is as much in my veins as that of the First Mage. I'm afraid that I might have demon blood inside me, too."

Aerin reached out and took her hand. "You're not your fore-bearers, Lysandra. You're your person."

"I know, but what if I have some demon inside me that I can't control?" Lysandra's voice trembled.

Aerin placed a hand on her cheek and turned her face towards him. "Whatever you have inside you, we'll face it together. We've faced demons before, remember?"

Lysandra nodded, feeling comforted by his words. "Thank you, Aerin. You always know what to say."

Aerin smiled. "That's what I'm here for."

They sat silently for a few moments, enjoying the peace.

"I'm glad I have you by my side," Lysandra said, breaking the silence.

"I'm glad I have you, too," Aerin replied, squeezing her hand.

Lysandra leaned her head on his shoulder, feeling safe enough to bury her concern about her lineage deep inside her. She knew that whatever the future held, they would face it together.

They didn't need words; their shared silence spoke volumes more than any mage's incantation could. As the fire crackled, casting long shadows into the night, Lysandra knew that whatever magic or menace they faced next, they would not face it alone. With Aerin and her companions by her side, the darkness would always yield to dawn.

<hr/>

The fire had dwindled to a few embers, casting a faint glow on the assembly of warriors and mages. Lysandra sat cross-legged. Her eyes scanned the faces of the people she now considered family. Master Elarion approached, casting a long shadow on the ground.

"Your courage has altered the tapestry of fate itself, Lysandra," Elarion began, his voice barely above the crackle of the fire. "You wield not just the sword and the arcane arts but the will to mend a fractured world."

Lysandra inclined her head, acknowledging the gravity in his tone. "I was the instrument, Master Elarion. It was our unity that wielded the power."

Elarion smiled at Lysandra, "Modesty becomes you, but you should not undervalue your role. Remember, darkness never sleeps. It's always watchful for moments of complacency."

Lysandra gripped her sword's hilt, "Then we shall face it head-on. What should I be on the lookout for?"

Elarion looked at the wolf by her side, "For now, enjoy the peace you've fought for, but be vigilant. Power stirs not only within you but also around you. Allies and enemies alike will seek the Last Mage of Erenor."

Aerin, standing nearby, asked, "So, what's next, Mage? What are we conquering?"

Lysandra corrected him, "We're not here to conquer but to explore, discover, and protect. There are many mysteries in Erenor, and we aim to uncover them."

Feyla appeared, grinning, "And where you go, trouble tends to follow. Count me in."

They laughed, and Lysandra stood up, "It's settled then. Tomorrow, we chart our course. Erenor's heart beats strongly, singing a song only we can hear. To the Chronicles of Erenor!"

They echoed, "To the Chronicles of Erenor!" and went to rest.

Lysandra felt anticipation curl in her stomach like a serpent coiled tight. The unknown lay beyond, but with her companions by her side, every step was a step towards destiny. And in the silence that followed, her heart whispered an oath — for Erenor, the magic woven into its very essence, and the uncharted tales that awaited their swords and sorcery.

Chapter 25

A FIRM BOND AND UNITY

The fire crackled, sending orange and yellow tendrils into the night sky as if trying to grab stars. Lysandra's eyes mirrored the flames' dance. Shadow lay with its head on its paws, his dark form well-muscled.

"Remember when we thought crossing the Gormyre Swamps was our biggest challenge?" Lysandra's voice cut through the fire's crackling, laced with a hard-earned weariness that did not hide the pride underneath.

Aerin, his dark hair falling over his forehead, turned his dark eyes toward her, and the fire's light played across his unscarred cheeks. "Every step seemed like it could be our last," he agreed, stretching his calloused hands toward the warmth.

"Yet here we are," Lysandra said.

"Your guidance never faltered," Aerin said, his gaze lingering on her with such intensity that it spoke of unsaid things and emotions held back like the darkness surrounding their little oasis of light.

"Nor your blade," Feyla added, her eyes gleaming with the spark of her ever-present curiosity. She fiddled with a strange contraption of gears and springs, another invention born of necessity and ingenuity.

"Without all of you…" Lysandra paused, her throat tightening. "I would have been lost. Your strength and loyalty mean more than I can say."

"Then don't say it," Aerin suggested, a grin tugging at the corner of his mouth. Now, more than just words bind us.

"True," Lysandra agreed, feeling the warmth in her chest that had nothing to do with the fire's heat. "We forged our bond in battle, sealed in blood and shadow."

"Blood, shadow, and something more, I think," Feyla mused, a mischievous twinkle in her eye as she glanced between Lysandra and Aerin.

"What's next for us then?" Aerin asked, leaning forward, his countenance shifting to one of resolve. "Beyond this fire's light?"

"Tomorrow, we face what comes," Lysandra declared, standing and drawing her sword. "Tonight, we rest with grateful hearts and undaunted spirits."

Aerin rose to stand beside her and said, "Undaunted... I like that." Their silhouettes merged with the shadows cast by the fire.

"Undaunted," Feyla echoed, snapping her contraption closed with a decisive click, sealing their pact for the future.

The three stood there, united before the roaring fire, ready to carve their path through Erenor's mysteries with sword, strength, and sorcery.

As Aerin threw another log into the heart of the flames, the fire crackled and popped, sending a shower of sparks skyward. He watched them rise, brief stars in the night's canvas, before turning to his companions with a steadiness that belied the turmoil within.

"Before all this," Aerin began, his voice a low rumble against the backdrop of the night, "I was just a fighter, a hunter alone. But this journey has shown me the strength we have together."

"Unity?" Feyla quipped, arching an eyebrow as she tinkered with a small metal device.

"Exactly," he replied, nodding at her contraption. Like your inventions, they're more than just cogs and springs. They're symbols of what we can accomplish. I was a skeptic, you know? But now, I see that magic and nature are like two sides of the same coin."

"Nature has its magic," Lysandra added, gazing into the flames. The light danced across her face, casting shadows that whispered ancient secrets and untold power.

Aerin looked down at his hands, remembering how they had thrummed with energy as he stood between Lysandra and Harrow, wielding a force he'd never known he possessed. "I've always trusted my sword, arm, and instincts. But when I felt that surge of raw magic, I realized there's so much more out there. And within me."

"Your instincts were right, though," Feyla said, fastening a wire with deft fingers. "You didn't kill the dragon. You agreed with Lysandra and chose to protect him."

"Sometimes, the hardest battles are the ones we fight against ourselves," he admitted, his dark eyes reflecting the firelight as they met Lysandra's. There was a spark there, something unspoken but understood.

"Speaking of fighting battles," Feyla continued, holding up her gadget, "I've fought my fair share against doubt." She flicked a switch, and the device hummed to life, glowing with an inner light. "I used to think my place was behind the scenes, but I've learned to trust these hands," she said, raising her palms, streaked with oil and soot, "and the ideas that spring from my mind."

"Your 'behind the scenes' work saved us more times than I can count," Lysandra said with a smile and warmth in her tone. "Without your resourcefulness, we wouldn't have made it this far."

Feyla's lips curled into a grin as she stowed away her invention, the satisfaction of creation evident in her posture. "And we'll go," she declared. "There's no limit to what we can achieve."

"True," Aerin agreed, his gaze lingering on Lysandra before returning to the fire. "With every battle, every choice, we grow stronger. Not just as warriors or mages, but as..."

Feyla broke the silence, "Friends?" she asked, looking at her companions. They smiled at each other, feeling the bond that had grown stronger with every challenge they faced.

"A lot more than that," Aerin said with a grin. "We're comrades, bonded by our shared willpower and magic."

"Destiny brought us together," Lysandra said, gazing at the fire wonderfully. And we've promised to protect Erenor from the dark forces threatening it."

Feyla nodded, "There are still pockets of darkness all over Erenor that we need to destroy. But we've come a long way since we first set out on this mission."

Aerin agreed: "We've faced countless challenges, but we've always emerged stronger and more determined."

Lysandra looked at her companions, feeling a sense of warmth and safety in their company. "We've been through so much together, and I'm grateful for each of you. But we can't rest yet. There's still work to be done."

Feyla smiled, "And we'll do it together, just like we always have."

Aerin nodded, "We'll hunt down every last bit of darkness in Erenor and make it a safe place for everyone."

Lysandra reached out to clasp their hands, feeling their bond grow more robust. "We've come so far, and we'll keep going until Erenor is finally at peace. I miss Elarion and The Harrow, but they needed the healing and the rest. They'll always be a part of any new mission."

The fire crackled, casting a warm glow on their faces. Above them, the stars shone brightly, a silent witness to their resolve and determination.

A small smile grazed Lysandra's lips. Her gaze met Aerin's momentarily, and they held a silent conversation before she turned to look at both her companions and Shadow.

"Thank you," she whispered, clasping her hands over her heart and feeling Erenor's pulse resonate through her veins. Together, we will face whatever comes—with swords, sorcery, and the bonds that unite us."

"United," they affirmed once more, the word a vow cast into the night.

Aerin's dark gaze met Lysandra's, a silent promise etched within. "I've seen what lies in the depths of your spirit," he said, his voice low and resolute. "Faced with the demon, with darkness incarnate, you've never flinched. I stand with you, Lysandra. Wherever this path leads, through whatever trials await, I am yours to command."

"Your courage is the steel we need," Feyla chimed in, her eyes sparkling with the ingenuity that had saved them countless times. She reached out, her hand fiddling with a curious contraption at her belt. "My inventions have been forged in the fire of our journey, honed by necessity. But it is your leadership that has sharpened our resolve. My loyalty doesn't waver."

"Thank you," Lysandra breathed out, feeling the weight of

their words settle like armor over her shoulders. In the fire's crackle, she saw not just flames but the fiery spirit of her companions.

"Then let us prepare," Aerin said, standing. His movements were swift and decisive as he shouldered his pack. Dawn will find us on new ground, facing what remains hidden in Erenor's shadows."

"Ready for enchantments and gears to blend," Feyla added, her fingers dancing over metallic cogs. Her latest creation, a crossbow with gleaming silver, caught the light of the fire, hinting at magic yet unleashed.

"Let it come," Lysandra declared, her grip tightening around her sword hilt. Her heart hammered with anticipation, the thrill of the unknown paths ahead. In her wolf's eyes is the reflection of an unyielding bond, and in her veins is the pulse of ancient power.

"United," they repeated, their voices interweaving with the night's whispers.

The fire crackled its approval, sparks ascending toward the dark canvas of the night. The trio sat in silence, each lost in thoughts of what lay ahead, the ember of camaraderie glowing brighter than the flames before them.

"Rest now," Aerin finally said, breaking the quiet. "We'll need our strength."

"Agreed." Feyla nodded, curling up beneath her cloak, her inventive mind never quite still.

"Goodnight," Lysandra whispered before settling beside the

loyal wolf. They closed their eyes, not in surrender to sleep but as a brief respite before the dawn of their next great adventure.

"Goodnight" echoed through the camp, and as sleep claimed them, their dreams were filled with visions of Erenor—vast, untamed, and waiting for the touch of heroes.

THIS IS NOT THE END OF LYSANDRA AND HER COMPANIONS' ADVENTURES. JOIN THEM ON THEIR NEXT ADVENTURE IN THE CHRONI-CLES OF ERENOR:
BOOK 2, ERENOR'S DAWN

About the author Kim Bock

KIM BOCK BOOKS

Kim Bock is a successful bilingual Indie author and co-owner of a thriving website design business based in South Africa, which she runs with her husband, Eitel. She has already published a historical romance novel in South Africa and released the final book in her trilogy, "The Chronicles of Erenor," on Amazon—Kim's writing benefits from her varied viewpoints and love of storytelling, which she draws on. While working on a website design with her husband, she dedicates her free time to crafting captivating fiction that draws readers into new realms of imagination. Join Kim Bock on her literary adventure, where her novels reflect her diverse experiences and offer readers a glimpse into her imaginative world.

You can find out more on her website at www.kimbock-books.com

past, stirs, threatening to unravel the fabric of magic. Lysandra travels beyond the known boundaries of magic with steadfast allies like Aerin, Feyla, the wise Elarion, and Harrow, the fearless dragon.

This thrilling sequel tests alliances, and passionate love blossoms amidst the chaos. Feyla finds unexpected love with Eolande, an enigmatic elf, while Lysandra and Aerin's bond deepens, and they fall deeply in love amidst the trials.

Lysandra faces her most formidable challenge yet: will her powers be enough to preserve Erenor's delicate balance?

"The Last Mage" is the first book in the Chronicles of

Erenor series, following Lysandra, a hidden mage and skilled swordswoman, on her quest to restore balance to her world. She battles King Draven's oppressive rule and evil forces with the help of her loyal black wolf, Shadow, the hunter Aerin, and the inventor, Feyla. Along the way, Lysandra confronts ancient secrets and combats evil creatures like the Shadow Hounds and the corrupted dragon, The Harrow. In the process, she unexpectedly finds love and embraces her destiny as the last descendant of the First Mage.

After defeating King Draven and restoring Erenor's magic, Lysandra and her allies discover an even greater danger looming—a mysterious evil wielding black magic and the power to summon ancient creatures. In an explosive battle, Lysandra faces the shocking truth about her connection to this demon and the struggle between her light and dark sides. With the help of her companions, she emerges victorious, but the triumph is bittersweet as new threats arise from the celestial fracture.

"The Last Mage" is an enthralling fantasy adventure that intertwines themes of magic, bravery, love, and the eternal battle between light and darkness. This book is ideal for fans of stories featuring mythical creatures, loyal companionship, and the quest for balance in a fractured world. Join Lysandra on her epic journey in The Chronicles of Erenor and discover a realm where the fate of all hangs in the balance.

To leave your review, visit the book's page on Amazon.Or at your preferred online bookstore! Here's the revised text:

Again, thank you for your support and participation in this epic adventure!